THE PRINCES OF SHELBY COUNTY

#2 Murder in the Mississippi Delta series

MARNIE GELLHORN
Copyright 2024

Princes of Shelby County

For

Corporal Leroy Johnston (369th Infantry regimen), and his brothers; Gibson Allen Johnston, Dr. David Augustine Elihue Johnston, Dr. Lewis Harris Johnston and their families. This book is also dedicated to all the other soldiers who served our nation honorably overseas only to return home to face racism, hatred, threats and violence. Your sacrifice has not been forgotten.

And to

Ahmad Adnan Khairallah (Al-Tikriti)

Princes of Shelby County

In memory of

Robert "Bob" Haley Jr.

October 9th, 1961 – December 8th, 2023

Bob Haley was so much more than a wise-cracking character in my books. The real Bob Haley was a dedicated health professional, a surgical assistant in operating room at Methodist Hospital in Memphis, TN. Second only to the cardiothoracic surgeon, Bob helped to save lives every day, week in and week out, on weekends, on holidays, on Christmas. It was his job to harvest the vein used to create coronary artery bypasses, and he was highly skilled at it. He was also the right hand of various Memphis cardiac surgeons in a variety of other life-saving operations. But Bob was more than his job; he was a dedicated family man. He and his wife Julie were the proud parents of two beautiful daughters, Shari and Sean. He was a doting grandfather to his young grandchildren, though he sadly missed the opportunity to meet the newest member of the Haley family, who was born into this world just as Bob was leaving.

I like to think that he enjoyed being a character in these books, he certainly found it amusing.

Robert was a wonderful friend, a generous and kind co-worker and neighbor. He was also a knowledgeable and patient mentor to many. This is his legacy, and he is dearly missed.

Contents

Authors Note: 8

Meet The Prince Family 11

The Prince Family Tree 16

Prologue : Ember, 2021-2, Six months before 23

Book One : Langston R. & Catherine 1856 28

   Langston, Florida and Josephine 52

      Death takes the city, 1878 57

   Book Two: Lysander 67

   Mary and Arthur, 1888 76

      Langston and the Law, 1890's 78

      Lysander, 1910 84

      Harriet, 1917 97

      March 1919 108

Book Three: Lysander, Desdemona and the spectre of death 1930 - 1932 112

Langston Henry & Bernice, 1934 - 1940 119

   Harriet, 1928 - 1944 122

   Mercy Hospital, 1929 126

   Makeshift operating theater, Rowen, 1944 156

Book Four: Bernice & Barbara 160

   Bernice 1954 -1956 160

   Barbara, 1954 165

Book Five: Bobby, Jack & Desdemona, 1968- 1975 192
   Memphis, Tennessee – The Prince home, 1968 193
   Port Authority Bus Terminal, June 1968 196
      Desdemona 1969 - 1975 215
Book Six: Jonah, Ember, and Robert Jr. the 1990's 218
   LINKS 1990 218
   Memphis State University, 1993 219
   Jonah, Georgetown, 1993 229
   Ember, Los Angeles 1995 232
Book Seven: Rebuilding the Legacy 2005 - 241
   Jack, Robert and Desdemona 241
   Ember: New Year's Day, 2022 246
   Veronica, March 17th, 2022 247
   Ember, March 2022 252
   Marnie, Sonoma, March 2022 260
   Veronica, March 2022 288
   The Triana Family, Venezuela 1920's – 1990's 289
   Shelby County District Attorney's Office, April 2022
   298
      Judge's outer office 300
   Ember, Family Compound, a few hours later 302
   Sandra and Rex Lester, Olive Branch, 2022 307
   Marnie, Silky O' Sullivans 312

- The Lesters' residence, Olive Branch, Mississippi, 10 days later 314
- Prosecutor's' Office 315
  - Meanwhile 322
- Book Eight – The People vs. Ember Prince 326
  - First day of trial, defense cross-examination begins 356
    - Trial, Day Two 381
    - The Defense presents their case 407
    - Closing Arguments 450
    - The Verdict 457
- Epilogue 460
  - East Memphis apartment during initial arguments 460
  - Midtown Memphis, following the verdict 461
  - Just a few streets away, at the same time 463
  - Olive Branch, Mississippi – 2 days later 463
  - Dykstra Hall, UCLA – Los Angeles 465
- The End.. 465

Authors Note:

This book, The Princes of Shelby County touches on some very dark and disturbing periods of American and Memphis history. It is inevitable, in any story set in anything but the most modern of times, or the most superficial of circumstances to be forced to confront widespread injustices and systematic cruelties.

For something like this novel, which chronicles the trials, tears, tribulations and triumphs of one family spanning 150 years and many generations, it would be impossible to ignore. It would also be disingenuous to pretend that many of the racist and white supremacist attitudes that underlined slavery, and systematic and institutional oppression don't continue to exist.

I am a storyteller, I am not a historian, but the history of the Prince family is essential for the story. This story was painful and difficult to write at times, even as an outsider, looking in. I cannot imagine how it must feel, to the people who have lived these stories. But I want to. I want to be part of the solution, not the problem.

There is no separating the (fictional) Prince family history from the history of Memphis, slavery and racism. In this historical context, terms that are considered offensive are used within the story, such as colored, or negro. Additionally, racist attitudes and sentiments are expressed by many of the characters. To do anything else, would be to sanitize and suppress accurate depictions of people (and characters derived thereof) in this timeframe. I sincerely apologize for any hurt or offense this language may cause. But to change it, would rob these characters of their veracity, and in the case of the Prince family and families like the Princes, to rob them of their strength, determination and fortitude to advance and succeed despite these immense barriers.

The Prince family of Shelby County is entirely fictious but there have been many families like the Princes, who had triumphed despite incredible odds. I write this story not to tear down or disparage these families, but to express my admiration for what they have accomplished. If I add in gratuitous scandals, lies, rumors and murder, well – that's just good, juicy fiction. As with my first novel, the names of real people have been used for entirely imaginary characters. There is no rhyme or reason with the naming of characters, except that I do it to honor friends, and family. Yet again, I am grateful for these many friends and family who were willing to lend their name to this project, without knowing if their character would be friend, foe, hero or villain.

I also incorporate the names of real historical figures into this story in entirely fictional circumstances. This is particularly true for historical figures from Memphis, such as the Church family. Entire storylines involving this family and other notable Memphians are creative fictions designed to give flavor to the story herein.

Josephine Baker and Ada Bricktop Smith most certainly did live in Paris, but Harriet and her interactions with them are entirely based in my imagination. The same goes for the wonderfully real and brave Jackson family, Szlama Grzywacz and many of the other characters in this story. Many of their real stories ended in tragedy, and by mentioning them, I wish to honor their sacrifice.

As for Coco Chanel, probably not enough terrible, but true things have been written about this Nazi collaborator, rabid antisemite and homophobe. Somehow when hundreds of thousands of French woman's heads were forcibly shaved, and marched thru jeering crowds; she, Arletty and other high-profile and known collaborators managed to escape any real scrutiny or consequences.

I also want to thank everyone who supported me after the publication of my first book. It was a huge endeavor for me, in many ways, that goes far deeper than writing a novel. It was a re-awakening after personal tragedy and loss. For that reason, I am more heavily invested in these characters, these books and the forthcoming novels in the series. I dream about these characters, I dissect them, I live with them, and I breathe in their personalities, their flaws and their strengths. I am grateful for them. I don't expect readers to feel the same way, but I do hope that readers are able to identify with and engage with some of the characters in these books. I hope you can empathize with Ember Prince and show compassion for her struggles despite her flaws. I hope you can relish the triumph of this family as they push forward. I also hope, on a lighter note, that you can enjoy the scoundrels in all their glory and that you can hate the villains with equal passion.

Thank you and enjoy the story!

Love,

Marnie G.

Meet The Prince Family
Frederick, the patriarch

He is the first of the family to be free of bondage, and he is determined to build a life for himself and his family. He is a strong, stoic and logical man. He is unable to forgive or forget any of the horrors inflicted on his family as he watches his young wife, Catherine grow bitter.

Catherine, his wife

From their initial flight to Virginia, through the birth of their children, Catherine has been friend, helpmate and lover to her husband, Frederick. But after betrayal, heartbreak, and tragedy, she has changed into the matriarch of the family, with a steel backbone and unforgiving nature.

The children and their spouses: (the second generation)

Langston, the oldest. He carries the weight of responsibility on his shoulders along with the expectations and ambitions of this family. He is the first to enter politics. With his ambitious second wife, **Dorothy** by his side, Langston will pull the Prince family up the rungs of Memphis society.

Florida – Langston's young and beautiful first wife

Arthur – a doomed romance with a local girl changes his life forever.

Josephine – too beautiful for her own good.

Their children: (third generation)

Florida and Langston's children:

George and Jack – their strong, and headstrong sons

Daphne their oldest daughter, so different from her shy, sweet mother. She and her second husband, **Marion Johnson** will lead their branch of the family in an entirely different direction.

Lucinda and Tamar – daughters

With second wife, Dorothy:

Lysander and his wife, **Desdemona** who are the first to establish the family's empire. Desdemona, daughter of a clergyman, is a woman who becomes hardened by grief.

Issac – as the youngest child of **Langston**, he is able to enjoy the family's new found wealth without memories of previous hardships

Teremity – **Arthur's** only child shouldn't exist but she does. She is lost to the Prince family.

And their children: (fourth generation)

of Lysander and Desdemona:

Harriet: Headstrong, stubborn and strong. Life will test her, but she remains unbroken.

Langston Henry: Unforgiving and unwavering. He marries **Bernice**, who is equally resolute that she will live up to the Prince name.

And their children: (fifth generation)

Langson – his mother never gets over his tragic loss at a young age

Barbara - a conservative exterior hides her heartfelt convictions as the oldest daughter

Marvin – the next eldest son, often intimidated by his older sister

Louis – lost within the large brood

Joyce – marked by a rebellious streak fed by anger and envy

Jack for which it all comes so easily

Byron – uninterested in the family business, he goes into medicine instead

Robert "Bobby" the prodigal son, who will do anything to win

Richard - who feels bound by family tradition to stay the course

Desdemona "Dessie" - the youngest daughter, named after her grandmother, but looking to make her own name in life

Joseph and Emmitt – the two youngest sons, who grow up in a different era than their oldest siblings, who can't always relate

Two other lost souls – who are forever mourned by their mother despite her large, busy family

And their children: (sixth generation)*

Ember – the daughter of the rakish Jack

Jonah - Bobby's other son, who, like Ember, he struggles to carry the legacy of the Prince family on his slim shoulders.

Robert Jr. following in the footsteps of his namesake

*partial listing of the many offspring of Langston & Bernice's children

The other Memphis Players

Robert Church – unorthodox and uncompromising, this shrewd businessman was the wealthiest man in the community. However, his unscrupulous ways earned him the enmity of the Prince family.

Julia Hooks – A musical prodigy, this angel of Beale Street is dealing with her own demons.

E. H. Crump – the unofficial emperor of Memphis, who rules with an iron fist. Defy him and you would pay the price.

Georgia Tann – ostensibly a kind and caring social worker, helping out women in unfortunate circumstances. But hidden behind her rounded face and form, is a woman willing to make a profit at any price. She has friends in high places.

The Spanish lady – the 1919 – 20 influenza pandemic

Martin Luther King, Jr. – while not a native Memphian, he changed the city (and the nation) forever

Hunter Lee Baron - the dissolute, alcoholic wastrel son of a former Memphis senator and member of the social scene

Rod Barron – the illegitimate son of the Hunter Baron, Sr. he must fight for his rightful inheritance

Lee Filderman - a silver-tongued lawyer whose clientele often challenged his love of the law

Carrie Bryant - A small-town Mississippi native, she is a new young prosecutor in the crime-heavy city of Memphis. She aims to become a worthy adversary of the cocksure defense attorney after overcoming a recent humiliating defeat

Sgt. Rex Lester and Renee Payne – two members of the famed and beleaguered homicide division of the Memphis Police Department

The French Connection

Josephine Baker – the legendary and risqué performer, the former Missouri native is now fiercely loyal to her adopted homeland.

Dr. Frank Stewart – the ship surgeon of the SS Leviathan

Joe Alex – bartender, performer and close confidante

Ada Beatrice Queen Victoria Louise Virginia Smith – her name was a mouthful and she had a personality to match

Dr. Sumner Jackson & Toquette Jackson – an American couple who made Paris and the American Hospital in Paris their home.

Szlama Grzywacz – brave member of the French Resistence

The Prince Family Tree

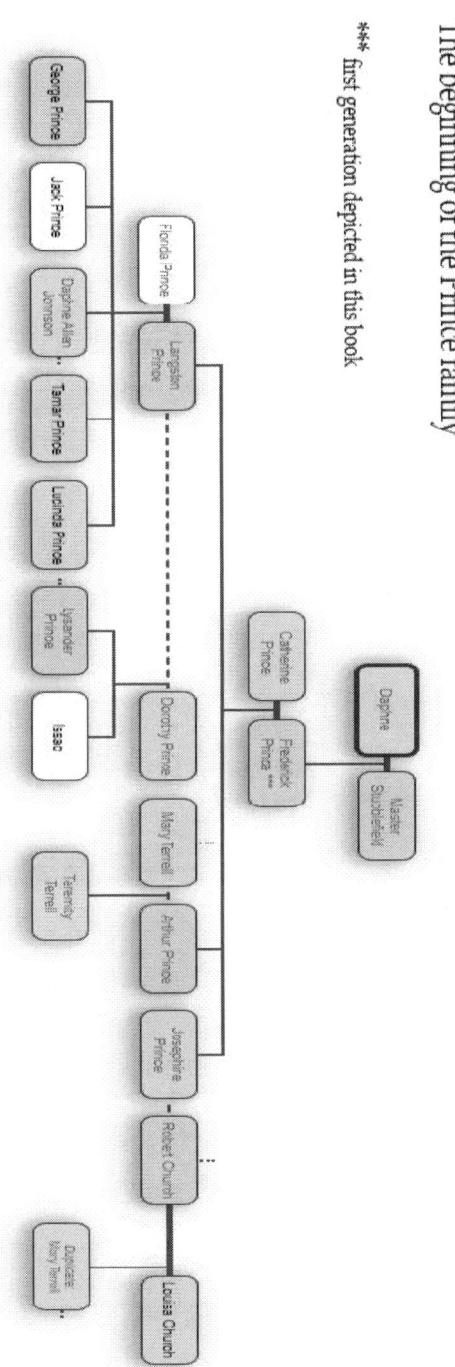

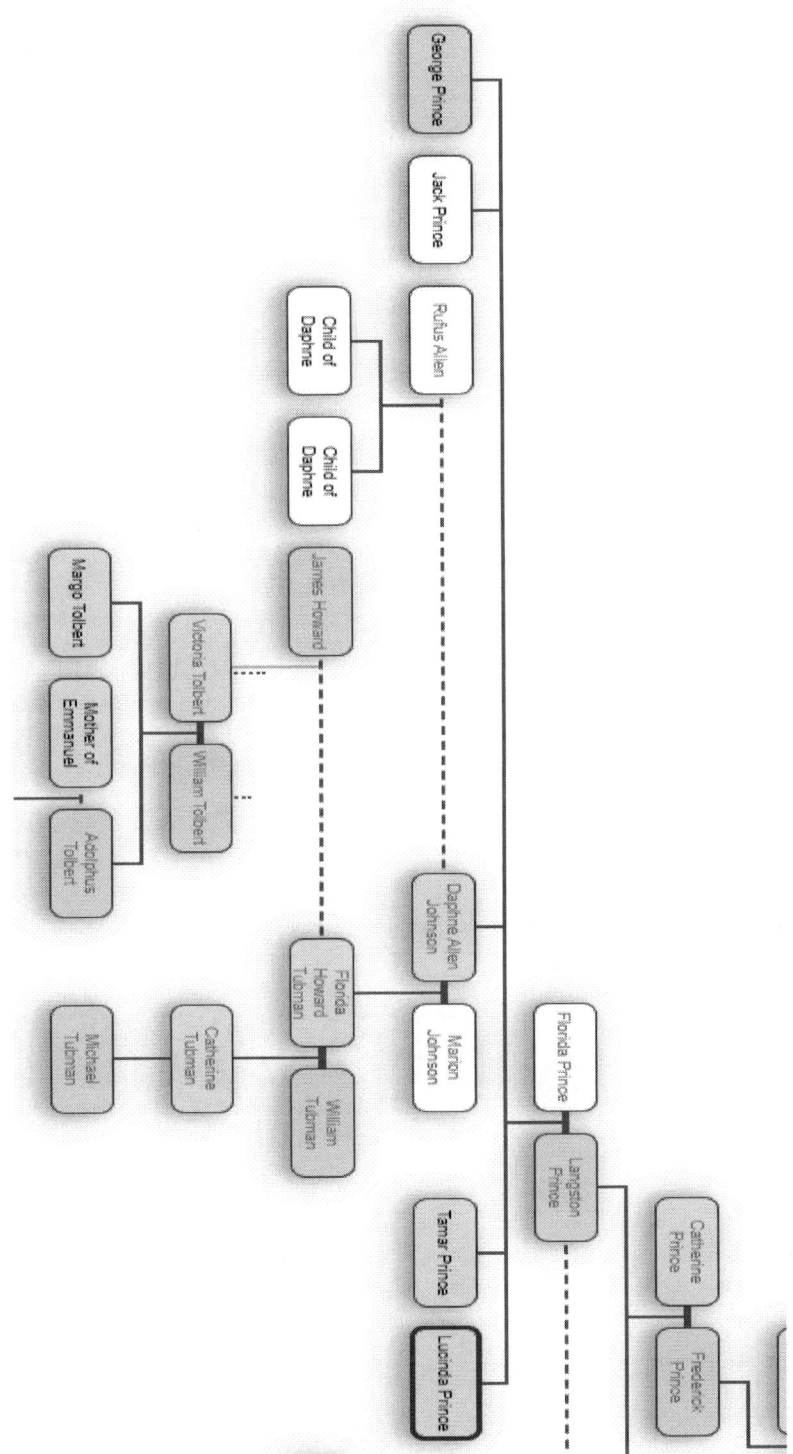

1 Family tree for Florida & Langston – not all descendants shown

Princes of Shelby County

Langston & Dorothy Prince and their descendants

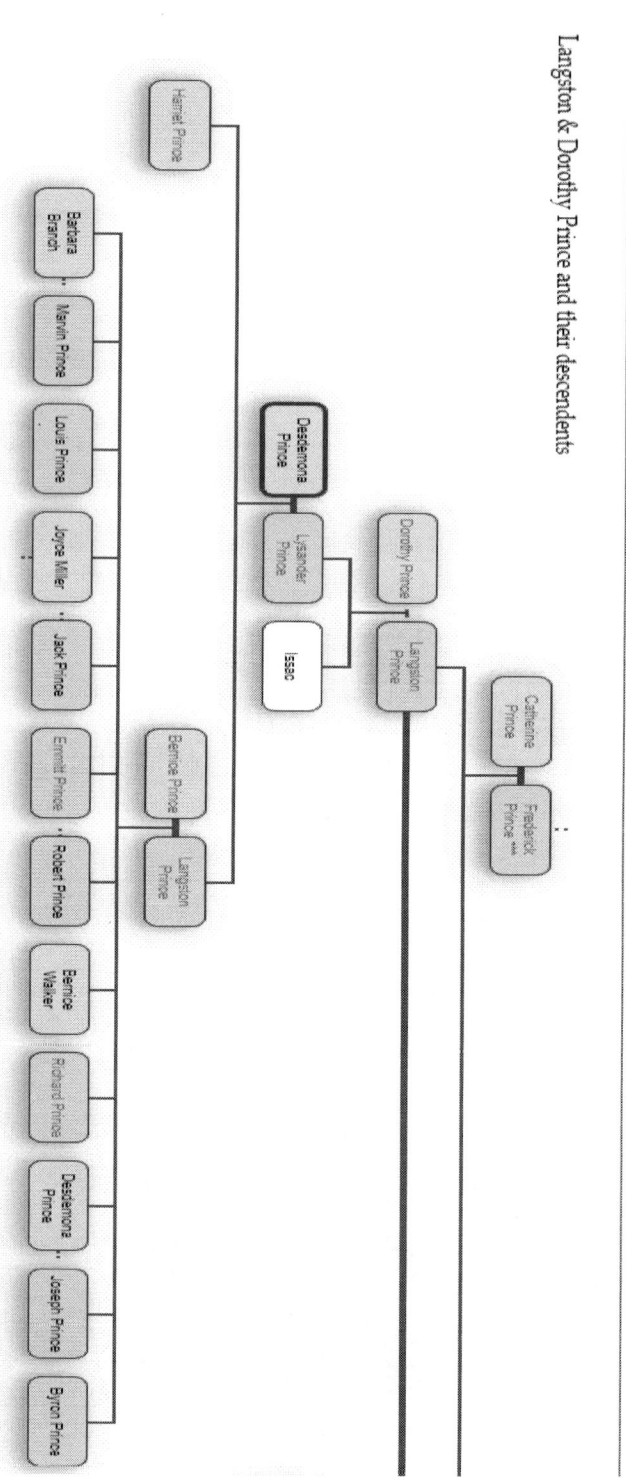

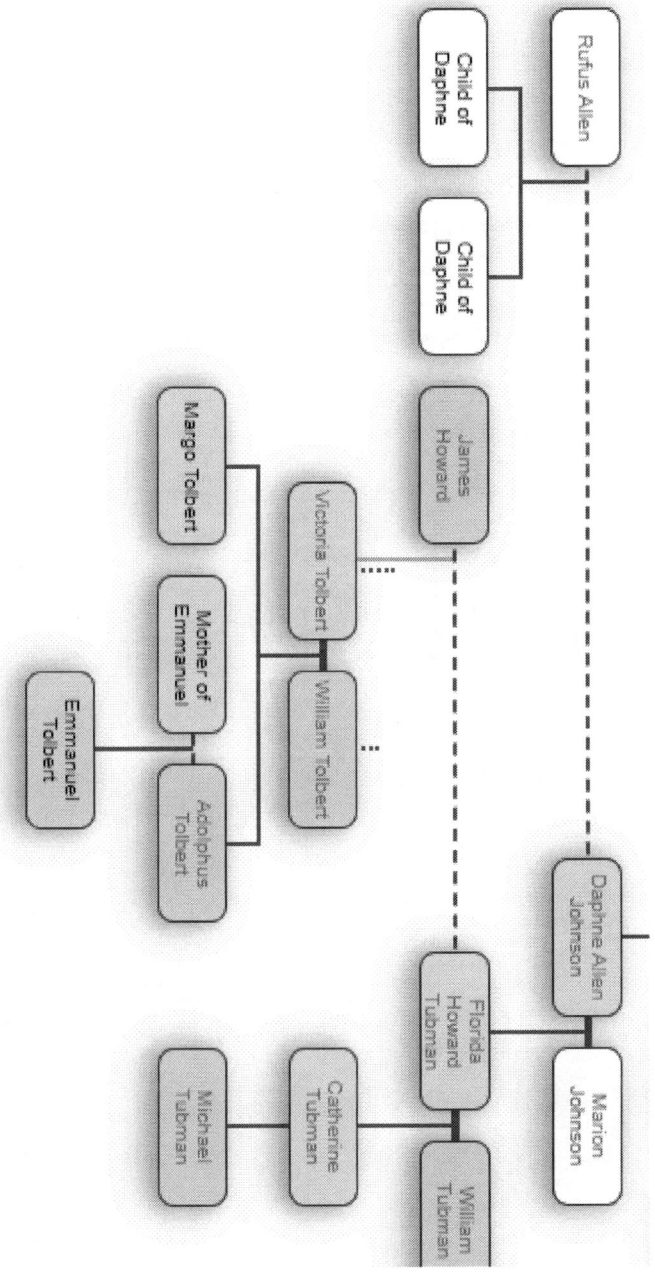

2 *The Liberian Connection - Daphne Prince*

Princes of Shelby County

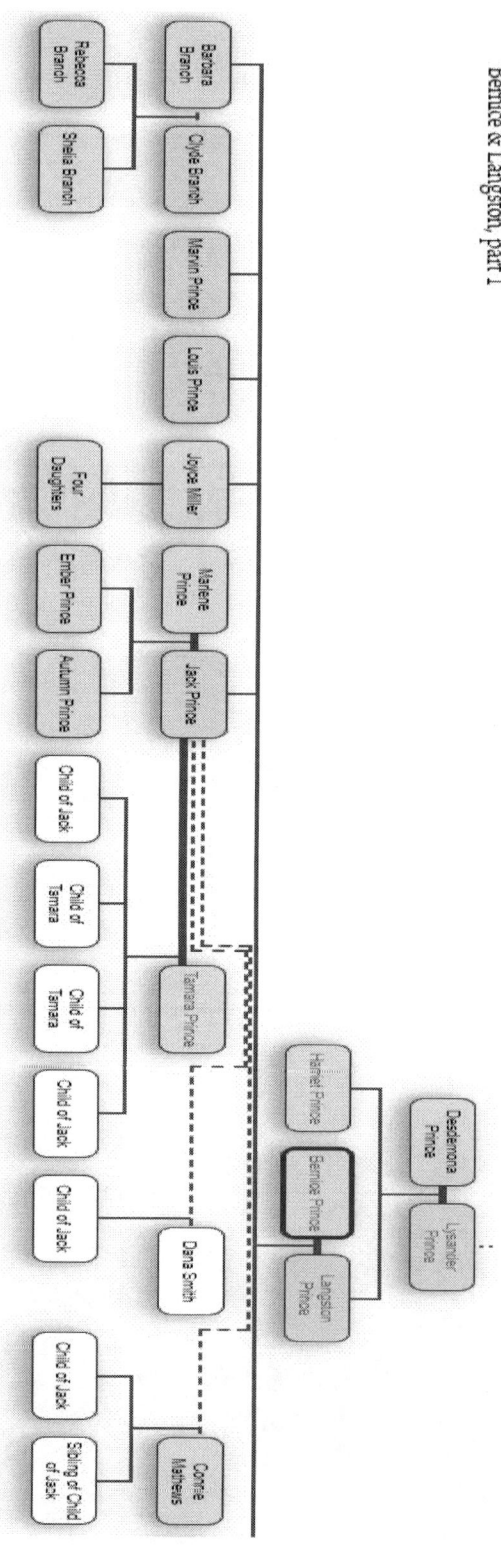

Bernice & Langston, part 1

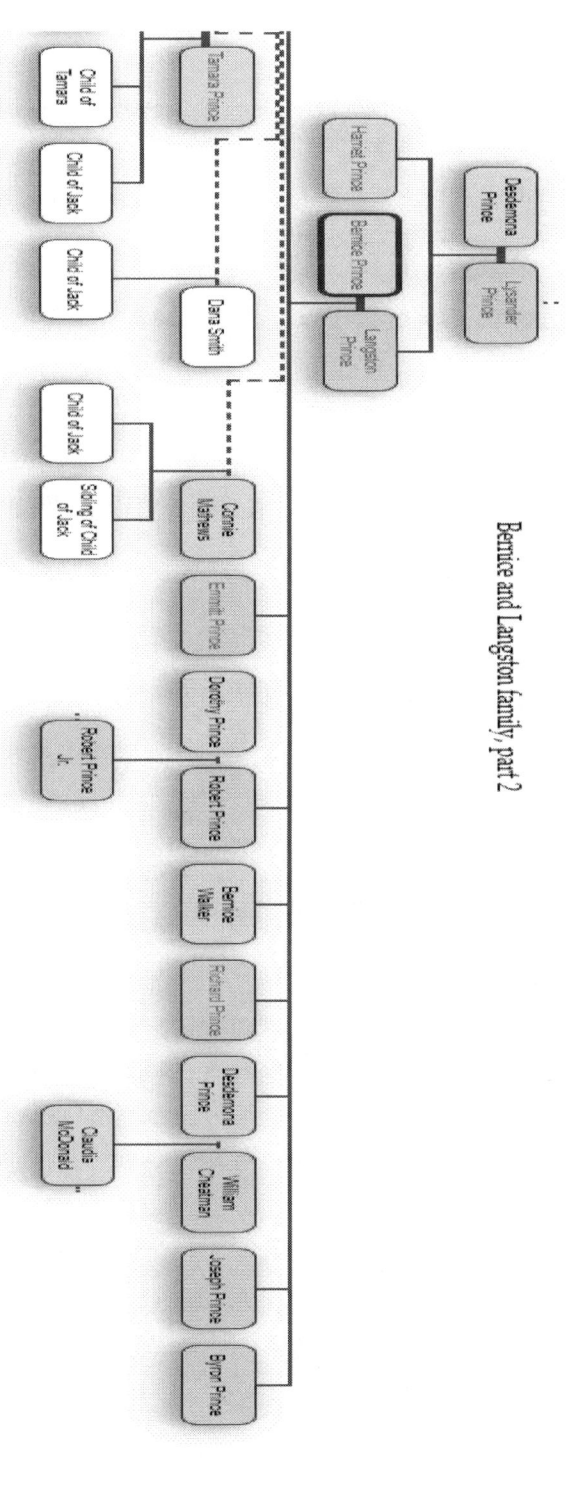

Bernice and Langston family, part 2

> "Surely the day will come when color means nothing more than skin tone, when religion is seen uniquely as a way to speak one's soul; when birth places have the weight of a throw of the dice and all men are born free, when understanding breeds love and brotherhood".
>
> Josephine Baker, 1977

Prologue: Ember, 2021-2, Six months before

Sunlight filtered through the bent slats of the cheap blinds to Ember's closed eyelids. She slowly stretched out on the bed before opening her eyes. Immediately, the bright sunlight blinded her, and caused her head to pound. She didn't recognize her surroundings or remember how she got there. She had the fuzzy confusion brought on by too little sleep and too many drugs. She was naked underneath a sheet that appeared dingy and stained. A familiar soreness between her legs gave her some indication of the previous night's activities.

She turned away from the light and discovered the source of the intermittent drone of noise. She found herself looking at the pasty, flabby, naked backside of what appeared to be a middle-aged man, who was snoring loudly. A wheelchair was sitting next to that side of the large, king-size bed. As she was contemplating how to make her escape, she heard the body behind her break wind. She felt slightly ill, dirty, and disgusted as she looked at him. Quietly, she turned back around and got out of the bed to gather her clothing that was strewn all over the floor.

As she leaned over to slip her underwear back on, whap! She felt a hand slapping her ass. She turned around quickly, to see that the snoring lump had awakened. Hunter Baron, looking worse for wear, was now leaning back against the headboard with a smug smile on his face. His grey-blond hair was sleep tousled and hanging in his face. "Ready for another go?" he asked, with a wolfish smile on his face.

"I gotta go. I gotta get home," Ember half mumbled as she pulled up her jeans. The semi-sheer sequined top was next. She felt almost frantic to leave, as she looked around the room for her shoes.

"Come on now, you sure you don't want a little pick-me-up before you go?" Hunter asked. He had already picked up the small mirror that had been laying on the bedside table. He started making small lines of cocaine. Just beyond Hunter, Ember could see the remains of a syringe, with a small rubber tourniquet on the nightstand. Hunter began making his efforts louder, as he used a credit card to scrap the mirror. He grabbed a twenty-dollar bill from the table, and carefully re-arranged himself so that the cocaine on the mirror precariously balanced on his lap. He watched Ember watching the mirror wobble slightly with his movements. "You sure?" he said, with a shit-eating grin on his face. He saw her briefly hesitate, before she abandoned all efforts to find her second shoe. With a sandal in one hand, she slammed open the bedroom door and stepped out. As she did, she saw her second sandal laying abandoned halfway down the hallway. She could hear Hunter's laughter as she left. As she hurried down the hallway past several closed doors, a door to another bedroom opened because the occupant had been aroused by the door slam. Her cousin, Jake, poked his head out. "You going, Ember?" he asked as she rushed past. "Give me a sec, and I'll go with you," he continued.

Ember continued down the hallway into the living room, where she paused to put on her sandals at the front door while she waited for her cousin. As she passed thru the living room, detritus from the preceding night's events were scattered throughout the large, overly decorated, and cluttered space. A man lay sleeping on the couch with two partially nude, young women sleeping on the floor nearby on discarded couch cushions. There was clothing scattered throughout the room, along with overflowing ashtrays, and a sea of empty beer cans. Several bottles of heftier spirits were also laying on the rug by the couch. An overwhelming smell of old smoke lingered, along with a slightly rancid odor of old food. Several pizza boxes lay open, with crumbs and crusts inside. Paper plates, and cups were placed on every available surface including end tables, bookcases and a coffee table that was overloaded with crushed cigarette butts, dirty drinking glasses, overflowing ashtrays, empty potato chip bags, a glass crack pipe, a couple of syringes with needles, and some empty, glassine envelopes. She opened the front door as Jake came running into the living room, buttoning his pants. As they were closing the door to the apartment, they heard another door down the hall quietly close. Ember pivoted in the hallway, but it was blessedly empty.

The ride down the elevator to the lobby of the Parkview Apartments, was silent as Ember contemplated her life, and this new low. Jake spent the short trip adjusting his clothing and smoothing his hair, staring at the mirror in the elevator for the entire time.

She handed Jake her keys and stayed silent the whole way home. Ember was a failed actress. She was pretty but not pretty enough for Hollywood and now, in her forties, not youthful or dewy enough for the good parts. She had come home to Memphis a decade ago after landing her one and only speaking part. The film was direct-to-video and forgotten shortly after that. Her role was equally forgettable, and barely worth the film credit. She had hoped that it would lead to something bigger, but it never had. Ever since she came home, she had wallowed on the fringes of Memphis society. Her birthright meant that she was always welcome, but her reputation was increasingly in tatters and her cache as a Hollywood insider had faded away years ago. She was now a has-been, who never was.

Last night was just the latest in a series of failures and fiascos, starting with dropping out of college in the early 1990's, a string of dead-end jobs, wasted dreams and spoiled romances. It was ending with a failed political campaign and waking up next to a known murderer.

Her family had once been Memphis royalty, but over the decades, and after a series of scandals, the Prince name was losing it's luster. Prior to the 21st century, this would have been unthinkable. In the world of political dynasties and American aristocracy, only the original Adams family, which had produced two American presidents, had more family members in elected and appointed positions. If nothing altered it's current trajectory, the once proud Prince dynasty was destined to end much like the Adams family, whose dominance of the political landscape dimmed well before the current century. Notably, Ember's Adams family counterpart lost his 2017 bid for attorney general of Virginia just as she'd faced her most recent unsuccessful bid for the Memphis city council. It was a sobering thought in the harsh morning light.

Once Hunter heard the door slam shut, he reached into a drawer, and with a smug and self-satisfied look on his face, clicked a remote. Then he rolled over and went back to sleep.

Princes of Shelby County

The beginning of the Prince family

*** first generation depicted in this book

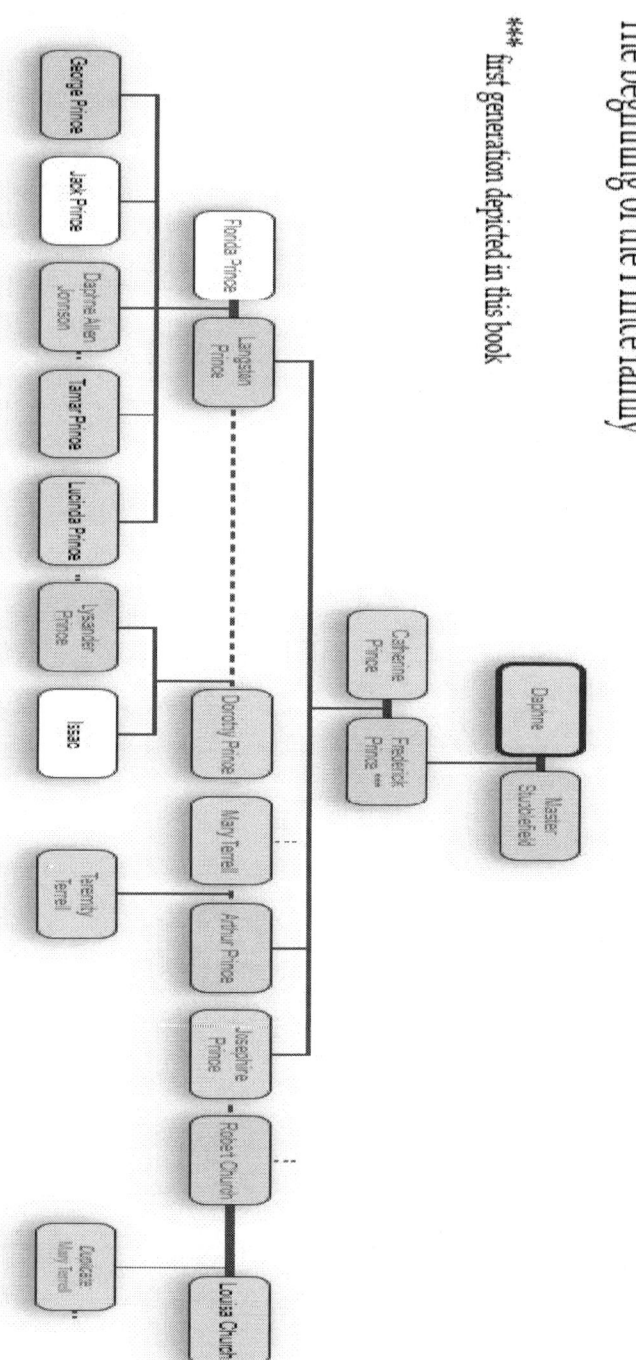

I do not ask you about the dead past. I bring you to the living present.

Frederick Douglass (1863)

Book One: Langston R. & Catherine 1856

Langston Roy Prince was born on a hot and sultry day in 1856. His father, Frederick Prince was a former slave. Frederick had attained his freedom from bondage on the death of his father, who was the master of Southall Manor in Virginia. Frederick, who had no desire to revisit those memories, thus had adopted the name of Prince during the long journey west to Shelby County, Tennessee. The only reminder of that life was his wife, Catherine. She had been 14 when he purchased her freedom at the same time that he received his own. His mother, Daphne had died more than a few years past after losing her place in the household and being sent to Richmond to be sold. He had heard of her fate from the servants of Berkeley farm.

His father, Master Stubblefield, in a contorted sense of paternal responsibility, had left him twenty-five dollars and his freedom as his birthright. The expression of complete hatred on his widow's face once the will was read had made Frederick more than eager to flee her reach.

In a cruel twist of the knife, a law passed twenty years prior made their move to Tennessee as freedmen illegal, but the law was poorly and infrequently enforced in this part of the state. A later city ordinance passed in 1849, restricted freedmen like himself from moving into Memphis city proper. He hadn't known about these restrictions when they had fled Virginia. He'd come west knowing only that the land he'd left offered him nothing by way of the future. He hadn't obtained his freedom to waste it fighting both the land and hostile neighbors to eke out a living.

He had been educated to read and write some, though he'd had to hide this knowledge. He'd heard talk amongst visitors to the plantation about Tennessee and the lands beyond. He knew there was a settlement of free blacks near Memphis, so he'd made his way here. It wasn't what he'd expected after hearing guests rant and yell over the 'way those negros think they are just about anybody' in Memphis. The truth wasn't that optimistic. Life as a freedman in Memphis was hard, and the community of his fellow, free blacks was very small. He wondered now if he had made a mistake coming west.

Frederick came back to the present as he waited outside the cabin, while a neighboring woman cared for his wife. Now 16, Catherine strained to birth their first child in the dark and still air of their tiny cabin on the outskirts of South Memphis. The morning passed, and the sun grew high in the sky, and still Catherine labored inside. The afternoon wore on, and Frederick continued to wait. Catherine was a religious sort, but Frederick was not. He could hear her inside praying for their babe. But he couldn't believe in a deity that would watch as men enslaved others like animals, without intervening. He was thankful that belief gave her comfort, but for him, it was an empty sentiment. His wished that he could find some ray of wishful thinking, or optimistic beliefs that made life seem like less of a struggle, but the pragmatist in him just couldn't bridge the gap between the kingdom of heaven and the bleak reality of life in South Memphis. He heard the neighbor make an incantation as she lit a candle as the dark began to fall, in an attempt to hasten the birth. Everyone had their beliefs, he thought, but him. After what seemed like an endless wait, he heard a loud wail of a babe, and he sighed with relief. The neighbor called out the gender, and Langston was born.

It was a hot, and humid June day in 1862, but at six, Langston was strong enough and old enough to help Frederick on the small farm and did so, pulling weeds under the close supervision of his parents. Catherine, his mother, made sure that his tiny nimble fingers stayed away from the precious strawberry plants that lined the garden, as she carefully collected the ripe fruit. His baby brother, Arthur, played near her side.

Langston was growing up as the happy and much beloved eldest child of his hard-working and enterprising parents. He was smart but obedient and helped his mother around the cabin. He also liked to emulate his tall, strong father as he worked the garden and worked to support the family. His mother, Catherine had been learning her sums from Frederick and had started her own small sideline making peach and strawberry compotes to sell at the Beale Street Market house. Catherine had her own secret blend of spices that she added to the popular mixture. She made a steady if modest income for her efforts. They often made a family event of it, bringing the kids to town, and wandering past the fancy Gayoso House and other downtown landmarks in the bustling city. The children were too young to dream, but Catherine wasn't.

Catherine wasn't daydreaming now; she had a worried look and a furrowed brow as she spoke in soft dulcet tones to Langston's father, as she kept one eye on the baby, and the other on Langston. She was talking to Frederick about the recent Union victory at Corinth. As a result, railroad travel had been cut off from the rest of the confederacy. The port, always important for Memphis, was now vital for economic survival, for the delivery of necessary goods. Since early that morning, ships had been arriving outside Memphis on the Mississippi river. Catherine had heard from a neighbor that more and more ships were arriving from New Orleans and were planning to challenge the Mississippi River Squadron, a poorly organized unit that served as the Union's navy that was poised just north of the city on the Mississippi river.

After speaking with Catherine for several minutes, Frederick called to his son, and took his hand. Together they walked toward the river, hitching a ride on a buckboard with a mule team driven by a local, Isaiah, who was intent on heading to Beale Street Market house. He passed a few words with Frederick while Langston swung his legs over the side of the cart. Abruptly, Isaiah decided to change course, saying, "Ships amassing in the river, you say?". He led the team up to the Bluffs above the city, where they joined a mixed crowd of Memphians who had gathered to watch. It was still early in the day, and the weather was relatively cool, with an uncommon breeze coming across the bluffs.

Langston, Frederick, Isaiah and the other negros stood to one side of the bluff, as several of the faster cottonclad ships advanced towards a Union flotilla. Suddenly, a Union gunship, the *Queen of the West* turned and rammed the *CSS Colonel Lovell*. Like its namesake, the confederate ship floundered quickly, especially after being rammed again, this time by the *USS Monarch*. The commander of the *USS Queen of the West,* Colonel Charles Ellet, Jr. fiercely defended his little steamboat when the *CSS Sumpter* and the *CSS Beauregard* came after his ship in retaliation. Even after the attack sheared off one of the *Queen of the West's* paddlewheels and pushed the boat to shore, Colonel Charles Ellet, Jr. continued the fight. He led a boarding party onto the decks of the *CSS General Sterling Price* despite being wounded in the fray as he took control of the vessel.

A fog of smoke, and gunpowder began to roll in, as in quick succession, the *CSS General Beauregard,* the *CSS General Bragg,* the *CSS General M. Jeff Thompson,* the *CSS General Sumpter,* and the *CSS Little Rebel,* were lost. Only the *CSS General Earl Van Dorn* was able to limp away. The entire battle took less than two hours from start to finish.

As the crowd on the bluff stood, stunned, Frederick looked at his son, and said solemnly and quietly, "Life in Memphis is about to change, son. We are about to be an occupied city." He took Langston's hand, and they wordlessly began to make their way back to the little cabin. Frederick was afraid the mood of the crowd would turn ugly, and he wanted to be well away from the scene before it did. Langston for his part, had many questions, but seeing his father's resolute posture, he knew better than to ask. When they arrived back at the cabin, Frederick filled in Catherine on the situation and they discussed it, even as they remained unsure of what, exactly it meant. "Frederick, do you think things will be better now? Now that everyone like us will be free?" Catherine asked.

Frederick looked at her sweet, lovely face, the face of the mother of his children, as he answered pragmatically, "Well, it's still the white folks in charge, so I don't guess things will change all that much. We will just keep doing what we are doing, and keep our heads down for now," he answered.

As a free black, Frederick had no illusion as to the reality of the Union army. While the abolition of slavery was a noble and worthwhile goal, the preservation of the United States was the first and foremost goal of the Union forces. Frederick knew that some Union sympathizers and troops alike blamed the war on blacks and abolitionists. Unlike popular cartoons of the northern papers, he wouldn't find the forces in blue to be friends, even if some of them shared his skin color. He knew he and his family would continue to walk a fine line of existing within a larger society that held regard for their lives and welfare, only if it proved convenient.

The Union occupation of the city began shortly after that. The soldiers from nearby Fort Pillow began to patrol the city. The white citizens of Memphis were dismayed to see that many of the armed soldiers patrolling the city were black. The local papers, including *The Appeal* were unabashedly pro-Confederacy. Frederick kept his growing family close in South Memphis, accompanying his wife, Catherine, and the growing family on their weekly excursion to the Beale Street Market House. Otherwise, the family, which now had new baby, Josephine, continued to thrive. Frederick had added several acres to his plot and was now able to grow more than subsistence crops. He had added additional crops of corn, tomatoes, okra and potatoes. He was able to sell the surplus to neighbors as well as at the local market. In the meantime, as he watched Memphis changing, under Union occupation and war-time hardship, he educated his children as to the ways of the world, and through stories and fables. His oldest, Langston, had also learned about the boogeymen of Byrd Hill and Nathan Bedford Forrest, the main slave traders of the city. His children were not born in bondage, but it was all around them, and he needed his children to understand the fragile and delicate balance they walked in southern society. He hoped that it would change, but he wasn't confident he'd see it in his lifetime.

For Langston, life wasn't all hard work in the fields with his dad. A new school had been set up and his mother made certain to enroll him. She also sent small baskets of comfits from the garden to his teachers to ensure that any of Langston's natural high spirits might be overlooked.

As Memphis and the surrounding area's population began to swell due to blacks fleeing slavery, war and the nearby plantations, the city of South Memphis grew as well. Refugees crowded into the surrounding neighborhoods, as 15,000 negros swarmed into the city. Crude huts were constructed on President's Island, and in an area of the city known as Chelsea. These refugee camps were filthy and unsanitary due to the haphazard expansion. Union forces offered food, clothing, and shelter in exchange for assistance in constructing Fort Pickering. They also provided additional supplies to other members of the burgeoning, bustling mass of blacks that sheltered in the camps. After the fort was completed, these families stayed in the nearby area as many black males answered Lincoln's call for more troops since it was a steady paycheck for their families and three hot meals for the newly enlisted black troops. The previously quiet, watchful neighborhood was lively and bustling with activity. Over the next year, Frederick sold more produce and expanded his farm. He added a small room to the cabin for the growing family and hoped that their luck held. At the same time, he encouraged Catherine to make and preserve a small amount of hardtack and extra foodstuffs that he put aside in a small hidden cellar he had built into the cabin's dirt floor.

He placed their thin mattress and bedding over the entrance to it, to disguise his activities. He slept better at night knowing he had made preparations for his family should the tide of the war turn back in favor of the Confederacy. He'd starve and allow his family to die before he'd allow his children to be taken into slavery. First, they'd run, if they had to.

He and Catherine had celebrated, quietly and at home, the victories of the Union armies over the Confederacy. They mourned the grievous and senseless losses of Fort Pillow, particularly as they had come to recognize and know many of their fellow freedmen in the troops that patrolled the city. Unfortunately, the outright murder of their black brethren was a surprise to only the Union forces. Any black man living in the confederacy could have attested to and predicted such an outcome, gentlemanly behavior be damned. They'd already seen enough of what this so-called southern hospitality really meant.

When finally, victory was declared for the Union and the end of the war, they again celebrated, quietly and privately. They knew too well that the city of Memphis and its white inhabitants didn't feel the same. The Prince family was sure to cloak their feelings whenever they left the confines of their small cabin. Frederick hated this, absolutely hated that they couldn't ever let their guard down, but he knew no other life. He again thought about California, but again put the dream aside. With three small children, the dream was even farther out of reach, but the hardtack remained ready and replenished in his small hiding place.

The Freedmen's Bureau and Mr. Waters along with the Western Sanitary Commission moved into the areas nearby to clean up the camps. Then General Davis Tillson attempted to establish military courts for the use of the black community. But others, like the superintendent of the Freedmen's Bureau, General

Dudley seemed more incline to force the newly freed members of the camps back into plantation servitude. Frederick carried on his life as before, keeping his head down and breaking his back to expand the small farm while trying to escape notice of the various authorities who seem to have little to no use for an independent black man like himself. He stayed away from the various meetings on Beale Street that spring, the black dances, and the Fort Pickering military parade. He didn't read the scathing reports in the Memphis Daily Avalanche or the Appeal condemning his fellow blacks as "the most drunken, blasphemous and licentious wretches that can be found among the negro race, in any city on this continent," but it wouldn't have surprised him. War wasn't going to change people's minds. If anything, it only made white Memphians cling tighter to their beliefs, now that they were under threat. Had he read that day's paper, the rest of the article would have confirmed his suspicions. The editor opined, "Such people deserved no mercy or consideration, especially since their refusal to accept plantation work threatened starvation on themselves, and financial ruin on the planters." He didn't need to be able to read the daily newspapers to feel the sentiment of gross resentment, particularly among the low whites in the city.

But many of Frederick's neighbors were jubilant at the end of the war, and South Memphis was a very different place. Now, ten-years-old, Langston often escaped the reigns of his parents to wander the busy streets. Sometimes, he let Arthur tag along, especially if he had been tasked with specific errands for his mother, or deliveries for his father. He became a frequent and familiar site in the neighborhood; a polite, light-skinned boy with his baby brother in tow. As local schools were being established to allow colored children, Catherine steered Langston and Arthur to class. After class, the boys would either help their father in the field or take on the task of watching Josephine while their mother stoked the fire in the cabin, and prepared food for the regular market. Still, the ugly resentment among the humiliated former confederates, and poor whites continued to grow. For the first time, Frederick also found himself at odds with Catherine. She had started attending church services at the African Methodist Church. It was only now that the confederacy was in ruins, that she and the children could even attend services led by another black person or learn to read the bible. Frederick was happy to have Catherine improve her letters; her reading skills were minimal in comparison to his. But, between the orations of H. N. Rankin and the impassioned, but areligious discussions led by Ed Shaw, Frederick felt like Catherine was turning away from him. One day she brought home a faded, slightly stained but legible pamphlet of a speech by Frederick Douglass. The original speech had been delivered several years earlier, but Frederick took the pamphlet from Catherine, and painstakingly read it by candlelight. While slavery may have been abolished, the many fierce statements of disenfranchisement from white society remained so very painfully, obviously true. He personally agreed with Mr. Douglass, but he was appalled that this speech was being circulated in Memphis, and very concerned that his wife would carry it openly. It was a call to action that would not be well-received by white residents. He tried to discuss this with Catherine, but he could see she was disappointed in his stance.

"Don't you see, Frederick? It's not just us anymore, it's everybody. Everybody is free now! It's our time, don't you see?" She said with a shimmer of excitement. She had a light sheen of perspiration on her still dewy and youthful face.

Frederick tried to explain to her, but he could see that she didn't understand. She had been so young when he'd bought her freedom. She didn't remember the absolute ease that which Master Stubblefield welded power over their very lives and deaths. She'd been isolated and sheltered as a young playmate to Stubblefield's legitimate children, so she'd never seen him order Rufus, his overseer, to whip someone to death. She never knew his mother, so she didn't know what would have been her possible future, had they stayed. His mother, Daphne, had been a lovely, gracious creature but she had been sold to another plantation for having the temerity to displease him by repeated pregnancies after he'd used her as his sexual plaything. Unlike many plantation owners, Master Stubblefield found her pregnancies inconvenient, even if her offspring added to his wealth. He had been repulsed by her physically when she was pregnant with Frederick. When he'd tired of her sexually, after forcing her to ingest multiple concoctions from the local abortionist, on several occasions, he'd allowed his angry wife, Anne to vent her jealousy on his young mother. She'd done so by selling Daphne to the neighboring plantation, where the main overseer, Angus was well-known for his sadistic proclivities. Anne, despite her devout Christian upbringing and frigid nature, took a secret delight in making sure Angus knew of Daphne's so-called "wanton and promiscuous nature", before settling on a good price for her. She and her close friends at church took pleasure in making money by selling "such a devilish creature." Of course, Anne never talked about her husband's repeated rapes of Daphne, but it was tactically understood among the wives on neighboring plantation that the purchase of attractive female slaves was to be avoided. After Daphne was sold, Anne made it a regular habit to attend slave auctions with her husband to oversee the purchase of any other slave women.

But Frederick's young wife, Catherine didn't seem to know or remember any of these realities. She didn't seem to appreciate how it related to post-confederacy life. She only looked at Frederick as if he was weak, and cowardly for his caution. It hurt him to see her look at him that way, even as he was envious of her spark and vigor. In the years since their flight from Virginia, Catherine had been his only confidant, helpmate and friend. It also bothered Frederick that Catherine was teaching their children about the "promised land" of an afterlife. He didn't know how she could embrace the idea of violent revolt while encouraging the white man's teachings of passivity and patience. Then too, he sometimes thought that the idea of an afterlife cheapened their actual life. It was easy to be calm about risking your life and that of your family's safety if you believed that paradise awaited, he thought angrily. But the rest of us know that only this 'earthy hell' existed, he muttered under his breath as he crumbled up another one of those damn pamphlets.

But Catherine wasn't as obtuse and ignorant as Frederick chose to believe. Just a few months after the birth of their daughter, Josephine, Catherine had been at home, doing the family's laundry when a trio of confederates had stumbled across their homestead. Frederick and the boys had been away, running errands and baby Josephine was sleeping in a nearby basket. The soundly sleeping innocent babe was the reason Catherine put up little resistance once she saw the look in their eyes, the leers on their faces and the telltale bulge in their poorly fitting and filthy butternut britches, and the blood-stained bayonets on their rifles. They looked as if they would almost rather kill her than rape her. It was this look of jaded, unbridled and cold brutality in their face that made her stay quiet. They wanted an excuse, any excuse to harm her and her family.

The oldest looked no more than twenty, despite rotting teeth and a sadistic grin. He'd had his two friends hold her down, as he took her first. Then they each had their turn, as tears rolled down her cheeks. She stayed silent and prayed for Josephine to stay asleep too. She was very afraid of what they would do to her babe if they noticed her. Out of the corner of her gaze, she saw the baby begin to yawn and fidget as the last soldier, who looked more like a dirty street urchin than a member of the losing confederacy's remaining fighting force, began to assault her. She began to panic, and as the other two soldiers laughed in her face, she began to move her hips in a gross attempt to get him to finish and leave before the baby could make a sound and betray its existence. At the same time, she heard the sound of a nearby wagon, and she again held her breath, not wanted to bring any further misfortune on her family or neighbors. Finally, after what seemed an eternity, the last man was finished and he pulled his pants closed, while chortling to his pals. "Sees how she wanted me, she was all kinds of eager for me. Just needed you two to warm that missy up," he laughed. The ringleader looked at Catherine thoughtfully, as if he'd like to go again, when the noise of nearby horses, and a cascade of voices jolted the three soldiers into action, as they hurried to rejoin their unit.

Catherine sat up, stunned and traumatized by the violent interlude. She wanted to lay there until it all went away, but the noise of the troops galvanized her into action. She had to protect her family. She quickly grabbed a wet rag that she had been preparing to hang on the line and cleaned herself. She wouldn't let her husband's anger serve as someone else's justification for murder. She forced back her tears and ignored the pain that spiked with every step as she gathered up the baby, and made her way back to the small cabin, where she barricaded them both inside until Frederick and the boys returned.

Several months later, she watched her husband mourn his lost son, after she expelled the tiny dead and twisted fetus, thanking God and the neighboring midwife for keeping her secret. Whenever Catherine's resolve would weaken, she would think back to that revolting laughter of the three soldiers as they abused her. It was Frederick Douglass, Sojourner Truth and the others who gave voice to her great pain and her anger. They gave voice to her impotence to fight these injustices, and she needed to hear that she wasn't alone in this.

But it was her faith that sustained her during the dark hours and the years that followed, after she drank the foul mixture that miscarried the reminder of her tormenters. It was her faith that restored her. Frederick didn't understand it all, but as far as Catherine was concerned, he didn't need to.

****

Just as Frederick began to consider relaxing his precautions, and his sense of impending calamity started to fade; in May of 1866, violence broke out. It was widely reported as a riot, but that was a misnomer. It was more of a murderous horde bent on genocide. Frederick had heard whisperings and rumblings of angry former confederates taking up arms against unarmed negros, so he stayed alert and watchful. This continuous vigilance was exhausting but necessary. There had been trouble at the Mary Grady's dance hall. Then the former hero of the confederacy, slave trader, and the man responsible for the savage slaughter of surrendering troops at Ford Pillow, Nathan Bedford Forest, brazenly murdered a negro worker, publicly with an axe. The south may be defeated but the southern white male was not. Each incident left Frederick more uneasy then the last. The sense of impending doom, which had finally faded a few months after the war ended, retuned to haunt him.

After the axe murder, Frederick was on edge. As soon as he heard rumors of angry white men organizing in the city, he packed up as much food as they could carry and gathered his family.

Frederick was able to get his family out of South Memphis just before the slaughter began. They watched from a nearby bluff as their friends and neighbors were terrorized, raped, beaten and murdered over several days. Catherine watched, trembling, with tears pouring down her cheeks as their home and farm was wantonly destroyed and burned by people from their own city. Frederick wanted to help his neighbors, and every fiber in his body urged him to go, even as his brain, and Catherine were determined to keep him safe on the hill overlooking the city. They watched, as no one came to the aid of the small negro community. They watched as the churches and schools burned.

From their distant location, they were unable to follow the news, but they could see the smoke, and hear the bullets as the events unfolded before their eyes. It wasn't until later that they would hear the excuses and know that truly nothing had changed. Mayor Park claimed to be too intoxicated to stop the destruction. The Daily Memphis Avalanche insisted on calling it a riot, but it was far too deliberate for that. Over a thousand armed men organized and systematically gang-raped, whipped, terrorized, and murdered members of the small black community. Once the terror started, the Irish police force joined in, with officer Roach leading the way, "It's a white man's day," he proclaimed, as he burned homes and businesses. Even after sobering up, the mayor refused to do anything about it, despite the repeated urging of local generals. Finally, late on the second day of the massacre, General Stoneman sent in his troops from Fort Pickering to restore order. He waited long enough that numerous men, women and children, like the entire Hatcher family, including young Harmony, were already dead. "The negros had learned their lesson", General Stoneman thought, "now Memphis and the rest of those traitorous confederates will learn theirs."

Frederick just nodded sadly as his wife, Catherine clung to him, with their children at their feet. He watched the flames consume everything he called his own, while thick black smoke drifted eastward on the river breeze. He thought he had been resigned to his station before this, but now he felt akin to the flames that were consuming his cabin, he felt a hot, blazing rage. He pushed it down deep, as he felt the blood race to his face and felt a throbbing at his temples. He listened to their young daughter wail and watched the tears flow down his wife's face. He forced his sons to watch, because he wanted them to remember and behold this heinous truth.

In the aftermath of the Memphis massacre, several things happened. Negro citizens fled Memphis in droves. The federal government was able to use this incident to pass the 14th and 15th amendments to the constitution, guaranteeing rights and freedoms to negro citizens. They were also able to push forward legislation to force former confederate cities and states into following military and federal guidelines as a price for re-admission into the Union. While these acts may not have been specifically designed to inflame white southerners hated for the negro, it was designed to punish them for their traitorous deeds. By passing the 14th amendment quickly, Memphis and Tennessee as a whole was able to avoid the majority of the constraints of Reconstruction, but they were still forced to allow negros to participate in local politics. So it was that in the subsequent decade, several black members were admitted into the Memphis Board of Common Councilmen, at least until Memphis lost its charter in the aftermath of another tragedy.

In the meantime, Frederick and his family had returned to their farm, which had burned to ashes. Even the tiny gravesite of their lost child had burned into oblivion. Surprisingly, some of the underground supplies survived despite the intense heat of the flames. Frederick and Catherine didn't know what to do besides re-build. They discussed travelling up north, or to Maryland, but ultimately, Frederick figured that it was unlikely that the north held any real opportunity for people like himself, and that the situation was probably only worsened by the recent arrival of large numbers of negros. He still thought that west Tennessee with its mild climate allowing two growing seasons, was his family's best chance for survival. He didn't dare hope for more than survival. For now, it was enough.

Langston didn't understand what had happened as he looked at the devastation all around their neighborhood. "Why do they hate us so much, papa?" he asked with tears in his voice. Frederick's heart ached to hear the pain and confusion in his son's voice. But he also wanted to make sure his son never forgot the legacy of pain inherited from bondage. Langston was too young to understand much about the difference between his family and so many others. He had been too young to understand the gruesome spectacle of the slave mart at 87 Adams Street. He didn't know the pain of manacles or the whip, and for this, Frederick was eternally grateful. But he also wanted his son, and his family to always remember and understand the great cruelties that the white man was capable of inflicting upon them. War or no war, Lincoln or no, the darkness that lurked in white men's hearts did not dissipate at the signing of a document. Langston would need to understand these lessons, to navigate the world as an adult someday far too soon, and while it pained Frederick to have to teach it, teach it he must. Already, upstart northern whites had come poking around again in south Memphis, attempting to agitate amongst the community.

Frederick knew it would take only a spark, to re-light the fires of hatred against the dry tinder of a newly formed peace. He'd already heard whispers and rumors of gangs of white men, terrorizing his brethren in the area of Memphis known as the Curve. It was only a matter of time until they ventured back here to finish what they had started.

If there was a god, why would he have forsaken them so? If there was a god, what kind of god would allow his children to suffer so? He bit his tongue but did not forbid Catherine and the children from attending church services in the old Union tent that had been erected down the street among the rubble. If he felt resentment watching the rush to re-build the church at the expense of the rest of the neighborhood, well, he kept it to himself. As he watched his wife and his neighbors working in the hot, humid summer to construct a modest church for services, he quietly began clearing his land to begin the process of re-planting. He'd had to trade some of his protected supplies for seed, but what other choice did he have? He kept Langston at his side, working the soil while Catherine and the younger children dedicated their efforts to the church.

Thankfully, Memphis was spared the tornados that damaged the surrounding areas later that month. Frederick didn't think his little community could survive much more. Already, the little community had shrunk considerably. Jonas Freedman and his family of eight had already left, along with Ezra Black and his family, Wiley Day and his family, Hercules and so many more. Frederick and his son continued working, and by summer's end an extra 5 acres had been added to the homestead. All of those who may have disputed this annexation had already fled the city. He had had to borrow money from the Sons of Ham, after the Freedmen's Bureau of Shelby County had denied him. He used the money to re-build his cabin and a cart to carry his harvest. None of the other money lenders in town, even the Jews, who often turned a blind eye to race, were willing to sell to a black man without collateral. A small one room home grew from the ashes of the old place, and Catherine and the family began working the garden once more. Frederick and Langston began to resume their visits to Beale Street and the bustling downtown. Workers had just recently completed laying the new wooden Mickelson pavement, and the strong smell of creosote mixed with the urine and feces of the mules and horses pulling the various carts created an almost unbearable but invisible cloud that wafted up the street in the hot, humid and still late September day. There was no river breeze that afternoon. Langston and his father trudged further into the stink, pulling the handcart with a small number of vegetables from their first harvest. As they pulled the cart onto Beale Street, a fine and fancy landau carriage pulled past them, the hooves of the horses kicking up dirt, grit, and small particles of waste in their wake. Quickly, Frederick and his son looked away, but not before Langston caught a glance of an elegantly dressed man with a heavy bandage around his head. A pretty redheaded woman in a violently colored purple dress was in the carriage with him. Her small flower adored hat was askew, and her hair flowed freely down in her shoulders. She had cherry-colored lips and flashing green eyes. She wore soft kidskin gloves, one of which lovingly caressed the man's face.

Frederick saw the question on Langston's face, and said, "That's Robert Church. They say he's one of us, even if it's just a couple drops. He's the wealthiest colored man in the city, maybe the state," he paused, "but even that didn't stop *them* from trying to kill him," he said, voice heavy with bitterness. He continued, "I heard that a couple of those Irish policemen came to his bar with a big group of folks and shot him. I am surprised to see he's still alive." Frederick hoped that his words would be a lesson to Langston, but looking at his son's face, he saw it had the opposite effect of what he'd hoped. His son's eyes had lit up when he discovered that the well-dressed man in the fancy carriage was black. He didn't seem daunted by the news of the assassination attempt. Frederick could almost see wheels turning in his son's mind. He barked sharply at his son, to get moving with the cart, to try and erase the admiration and awe in his eyes. They continued down the street towards the river to meet with the grocers.

As his daddy was negotiating with a clerk from Mr. Finnie's grocery for the sale of his crop of green beans, cucumbers, greens and squash, Langston took the opportunity to survey the busy street. There was a chaotic but intoxicating array of sights, sounds and smells. Horse-led carts and wagons clamored past, along with the new mule drawn streetcars with a cacophony of sounds; of hooves clattering, wheels creaking on the wooden street, the yells of passengers and pedestrians alike. A small group of black men stood outside a tavern having a lively discussion, before slapping each other on the back and entering the establishment. Young boys zig zagged through the traffic on the street, holding newspapers and bellowing the headlines for a three-cent copy of The Appeal or the newly minted Memphis Post. As Langston perused the street, he saw the well-dressed man again, entering a building near the corner, this time accompanied by a light-skinned well-dressed black woman, in subdued clothing. She had her hand lightly resting in the crook of his elbow as he escorted her in. Langston watched until they disappeared into the depths of the building before turning back to his father. Frederick completed the transaction, and he and Langston began the trip home with the now empty cart. That night after dinner, as Catherine and Frederick talked about the events of the day, Langston told Arthur about the man he had seen in short whispers. They made a pact then and there to find out more about Mr. Robert Church, the black man with the landeau carriage.

****

One day, in a wet and miserable January of 1868, while Langston and Arthur were playing their favorite game of 'Tail the rich man,' they unexpectedly encountered Robert Church walking with a small young girl in a white beribboned dress, as they came around the corner on Main Street. Arthur was at a loss for words, while a flustered Langston managed to stammer his apologies. Robert Church tipped his hat to them, handing Langston a small coin, while the tiny young girl curtsied prettily before they walked on down the street. The boys were too embarrassed at being caught out while stalking their quarry to follow after them.

At almost 12, Langston had grown into a lanky lad, who was almost as tall as his father. He had a deep baritone voice that was at odds with his thin, but well-muscled frame. He was dressed in clean but worn homespun clothing that his mother had sewn during the evenings before bed. In the last couple of years, their farm had continued to expand, and Frederick had been able to maintain a respectable earning to support the family. Langston and his siblings had been learning to read, to spell, and to do basic sums at the small schoolhouse in South Memphis. Classes at the church, and evening bible readings with their mother rounded out their studies. Langston had recently approached his dad about working with a neighbor at his shop to learn a trade. Initially his father wasn't happy about the idea, until Langston reminded him that it was a good way for him to practice his sums and other math skills, as well as earning some additional money for the family. With his father's reluctant approval, he went to work at a small dry goods store called Seessel's. He worked in the back, lifting boxes, and carting supplies and other general unskilled labor for 4 dollars a month. His only opportunity to use his math skills came with the extracurricular activities in the store. On nights, and weekends, a secret area in the back of the storeroom was converted into a low-rent gaming hell. Friday afternoons, Langston was tasked with cleaning and setting up a temporary bar just outside the hidden room. He was responsible for pouring drinks and maintaining the tabs of the customers until the end of each gaming session. Then, the manager, Roger Beasley and his nephew, a former Captain in the confederacy, J. Theodore Adams would review Langston's calculations and present the bills to customers. The nephew was also responsible for watering down the booze and providing the evening's entertainment, which was generally a couple of slatterns from a nearby brothel. Two small cots were placed in between rows containing sacks of flour and grain for a modicum of privacy. They rented these cots to randy gamblers while collecting a 20% cut of the women's fees. There was a lot of grumbling about this, but the women generally paid up promptly because on a successful evening, each of the two girls could service 5 to 8 men and make a tidy profit. Only a small portion of this had to returned to the madam. Beasley paid an additional small fee to the madam to cover her losses from having two of her girls off the house schedule for the evening. The store owner, Henry Seessel seemed oblivious to Mr. Beasley's schemes. Henry Seessel was occupied with acquiring, maintaining and selling the meat products that were Seessel's main claim to fame.

Langston didn't tell his dad about the weekend activities, and he made certain to steer clear of the prostitutes. He got an extra dollar if he worked the weekends, and he knew his folks could use it. He also knew that his dad wouldn't want him all tied up in "white man's folly" as he liked to refer to the more unsavory practices. His mom would have been even more upset, due to her religious beliefs.

One Saturday, when Langston was almost 14, Robert Church entered the backroom. Langston couldn't have been more disappointed to see his hero in such low rent surroundings. Mr. Church surveyed the scene with almost visible disgust. Finally, he said, in a deep dry voice, "well, the girls sure weren't lying." Mr. Church looked over at Mr. Beasley and then said, "I came to see why you are in arrears. Madam LaSalle tells me that she hasn't gotten her fees from you for an entire month".

One of the gamblers who had been sitting at the table, intently staring at his cards, while sipping a watered-down local whiskey said, "Roger, are you going to let a nigger talk to you like that?"

Before Roger or anyone else could respond, Mr. Church had turned around, and in a steady motion, brought out a small pistol, which he aimed at the gambler's head. "You got anything else to say, Mr. Bigmouth?" he asked. He snapped his fingers, and his assistant, who had been standing silently behind him, left the storeroom to return with six other men armed with army rifles. The gambler blanched and looked around to see that all of his fellow gamblers were looking steadfastly at the floor, the ceiling, their cards, anywhere but at him or Mr. Church.

Mr. Beasley hustled forward and said, "Now, Mr. Church, this must be a misunderstanding. I sent my little nigger here (pointing at Langston) to pay you earlier this evening. I guess you will have to take the matter up with him." His nephew, Mr. Adams, stood to the side, nodding silently, in agreement.

Langston was in shock. This was the first he'd heard of any of this, and he hadn't been sent on any errands to see Mr. Church. He'd certainly never been given any money to carry for Mr. Beasley, that's for sure. The only time he was able to handle money at the store was when they handed him his monthly salary. He opened his mouth to deny it, when Mr. Beasley said, "Now, none of your lying now, boy. Give Mr. Church his money before something bad happens to you. I won't be able to protect you – and I don't protect liars and thieves."

Langston looked up to see Mr. Church's hard eyes boring down on him. Langston started to panic, "Mr. Church, sir. I swear," he eeked out, "I never had any money to give to you. I swear. They never gave me anything to take to you or anybody else. I'm not lying sir, please believe me," he finished.

Mr. Church turned back to Mr. Beasley and then looked at his men and nodded. One of the men aimed his rifle and shot down at a 50-pound sack of flour.

"Mr. Beasley, I don't care for any excuses, and I am not going to chase down a child. You owe me fifteen dollars and you are going to pay me, or my men here are going to pay you, and your family with fifteen dollars' worth of lead," Mr. Church stated.

His men raised their rifles simultaneously and pointed them at Mr. Beasley and his nephew. Mr. Beasley briefly maintained his bravado while at the same time, his nephew's face drained of all color. But then, without meeting Mr. Church's eyes, Mr. Beasley pulled out a thick stack of bills and began to count off fifteen dollars. Instead of handing them to Mr. Church, he slammed them down on the nearby gaming table, as the gamblers watched in silence.

Mr. Church's eyes gleamed with amusement, as he scooped up the bills that Mr. Beasley had laid down on the gaming table. Then he turned on his heel and left, with his men trailing behind him. Mr. Beasley and his nephew looked sharply at the gamblers, as if daring them to say anything. Langston kept his head down and pretended he hadn't seen his employer's humiliation while he slowly backed out of the room, ostensibly to get a broom, but really to avoid antagonizing the room full of white men.

****

Langston continued to work for Mr. Beasley and assist with the backroom card games. The extra coin, along with the heavy manual labor in the store helped the young man to fill out and attract attention of young women around town. By the time he was fifteen, the formerly lanky boy had the strong physique of a man. He had recently caught the eye of a young woman named Florida. She had honey brown eyes, soft, clear skin and was quick to smile in his direction. She was the nursemaid of none other than the be-ribboned young girl that had so fascinated his younger brother, Arthur. She would often bring her young charge to Seessel's store and gaze at Langston under her lashes while keeping a demure poise while standing at the section of the store open to colored people like themselves. While Langston had been working at the store, attending school in the one-room schoolhouse and helping his father on the farm, his younger brother had been wooing the young Mary at every opportunity. The young boy brought her sweets from Catherine's kitchens along with small possets of flowers growing wild on the farm. As the two young children played under the watchful eye of Florida, Langston could only be amused. Had either of their fathers known about this childhood crush, they would not have been entertained. Soon however, the young Mary became bold in the knowledge of her social position. By the age of only eight, Florida could no longer control her, and her parents made the decision to send her north for schooling. Arthur was crushed to hear the news, and only Florida could console him.

It was watching his younger brother cry with his head in Florida's lap while she stroked Arthur's head and soothed him that convinced Langston that he needed to take her to wife. But before he did, he had a brief dalliance with Anna Wright, one of the bright skinned girls working for Mr. Church at one of his many brothels near main street. Since the encounter at Seessel's, Mr. Beasley had been sending Langston with regular payments for the use of "his girls." While Anna was Langston's age, she was already a house favorite. Much of her popularity was due to her appearance in several nude photographs depicting her in the most innocent of activities; bathing, housecleaning and leaning over to do wash. Each photograph was part of a pack of a dozen that cost about a 1.20 and were frequently traded amongst young men. She had taken a liking to the polite, shy seeming young man, with bulging muscles and a respectful attitude. One afternoon while the madame was out, Langston was shown to the parlor where Anna awaited to collect the weekly sum. Very quickly after, Langston made his own deposit, deep within the soft, creamy colored thighs of the house favorite. Thereafter, Anna and Langston had a standing engagement for the next several weeks. If Florida had noticed any inattention from Langston, during the summer of 1871, she never mentioned it. Very shortly after, his charge, the little miss Mary was dispatched to Ohio, and Langston became determined to marry Florida. Anna fell by the wayside with neither an apology nor any spoken gratitude for her erstwhile introduction to manhood.

His mother, Catherine was aghast at the idea of such a youthful marriage, but his father, Frederick supported him in his endeavor. It meant more help on the farm, and Florida was a year older than his own Catherine had been when they fled Virginia. Even after Mary went to Ohio, Florida continued to work for the Churches, bringing both additional income and stature to the Prince family. Florida now cared for baby Thomas, as his own mother spent much of her time away from the home managing a beauty salon catering to wealthy white women. These women were happy to come down to Court Street to be catered to, in a way that no longer existed in their own homes as it had pre-emancipation. Now they had to pay for the privilege but that somehow added to the cache. For the growing Prince family, this connection to the wealthy Church family would impact their lives for the years to come. For the young Arthur, it allowed him to maintain contact with Miss Mary. On brief visits home, she would often stop in on the excuse of seeing her old nursemaid.

Often while the carriage remained outside the modest Prince farm, Mary would sneak off to have time alone with Arthur beneath the full leaves of the great Poplar trees. Soon enough, Florida would signal to Mary that she must return to the carriage, and off she would go, journeying north once again. After these visits, Arthur would brood quietly and neither Florida, nor Josephine could cajole him into better spirits.

****

Langston, Florida and Josephine

"To those weary of life, but who do not have the courage to shoot or hang themselves, we recommend a trip to Memphis" – an editorial in a northern newspaper of the time

Very quickly despite their youth, Langston and Florida began their own family and Langston began to try and climb the economic ladder. As he watched Ed Shaw assume public office, he began to feel that like Mr. Church, his color was not an insurmountable barrier to wealth and success. He began meeting with the Mr. Shaw, to see what advice he could pass on about getting a toehold into Memphis politics. The fiery Mr. Shaw was happy to tutor the eager young man. While Langston pursed outside advancement, Florida worked at maintaining their family while caring for someone else's. Their son George arrived in 1874, just as their own cabin was completed and was followed by another son, Jack shortly after. Despite her apparent appreciation for Florida's services taking care of the growing Thomas, Miss Louisa did not extend that courtesy to allow Florida to include her own children while completing her duties. So, George and Jack's 12 year-old aunt, Josephine was reluctantly pressed into service.

The young Josephine was a beauty that easily surpassed that of her mother. Her fair complexion and ripe figure attracted the attention of men, regardless of their race or station. Catherine had hoped that caring for two small infants would keep Josephine too busy to receive the flatteries and ardor of the men around her but was dismayed to see that Josephine seemed to reveal in the attention. She kept a very close and watchful eye on Josephine, while expressing her concerns to Frederick. It was much to her surprise when Frederick arrived home to supper one night accompanied by the elegantly dressed Mr. Church. They were ostensibly talking about farm business with various sums passed back and forth in their discussion before they agreed upon a price of 100 dollars. It was a huge sum of money, and it would help secure the future of the rest of the family. Frederick didn't think Mr. Church would offer that much money for something he didn't value. Catherine was devastated to see that once business was concluded and Mr. Church arose from the table, that her husband called Josephine to attention. She fought briefly with her husband only to be rewarded with a slap, the first of their long marriage, as Josephine bundled a small bag of belongings. Her face stinging and eyes watering, Catherine watched as her beloved daughter left with Mr. Church's arm about her shoulders. She felt her heart harden against her husband.

For his part, Frederick felt relieved to know his daughter's future was secured as the mistress to one of the most powerful men in Memphis. While it wasn't an entirely respectable position in society, it did offer a measure of safety and security that Frederick was not sure that other men in the community would be able to offer his daughter, particularly if she was the one doing the choosing. It frankly didn't even occur to him to offer her that option.

After watching the sale of his mother when he was young and helpless, he was determined that his child not be the plaything of a white man. Of course, unbeknownst to Frederick, Mr. Church would soon tire of Josephine after enjoying her innocence and had no intention of honoring his promises to Frederick. He had wanted to be the first to enjoy such a ripe peach of a girl. But he had no intention of being the last. He knew that he could easily make his money back; looks such as hers for far too valuable for that kind of personal vanity. Mr. Church had brothels all over the city. If he put Josephine in one of the nicer ones, her life wouldn't be any poorer than it was now, or so he reasoned.

While Mr. Church had intended to keep Josephine as his own for a few more months, by 1876, his wife had discovered her presence and grown cold to him. Louisa had overlooked his dalliances before, but the existence of such a beautiful young girl as an exclusive mistress was not to be tolerated. Faced with

Louisa's great displeasure, and ever-growing anger, Mr. Church decided to divest himself of Josephine sooner than he had anticipated. He was able to arrange her trade to a wealthy white businessman during a subsequent poker game. He was able to secure an interest free loan, and extract promises of protection from the police and tax collectors in exchange for such a juicy young thing.

While slavery had ended, women remained chattel and at the mercy of their protectors. Without Mr. Church to protect her, Josephine had no choice but to become the mistress to the aging, potbellied Judge Flippin. After being rejected by Mr. Church, she didn't think her family would have her anymore, and she was too ashamed to return. She also harbored too much hate for her father to do so. Despite her fears, Judge Flippin treated her somewhat kindly, though she was under no illusions anymore. She had believed that Mr. Church loved her, but now she knew it was just easier to manage her that way. She stayed submissive and attentive to her new lover's needs and in return the Mayor of Memphis treated her respectfully and gently despite her lineage and history. He was at heart a lonely man, and while he didn't fool himself into thinking this way more than a business transaction, he enjoyed having such a young beauty all to his own. As long as she knew her place, and didn't embarrass him, he was inclined to dress her in costly fabrics in the latest styles and adorn her with jewelry. She was light-skinned enough that she could accompany him to all but the most official events to the envy of many of his peers. He even arranged for a tutor to supplement her meager schooling, mainly to correct her diction and to give her the sound of an educated northerner. This paid off during a visit to Boston that fall, where he paraded her as his paramour throughout town, with none the wiser as to her ancestry. Josephine, while not happy with this arrangement that was not of her choosing, could have been almost content with his on-going generosity, if not for a sequence of events that led to her abandonment as John Flippin had a change of heart. Once again, she was left adrift, but at least this time, she had a margin of wealth to insulate her. John had gifted her with her own house, not far from her erstwhile lover, Mr. Church's home on Lauderdale Street. John Flippin didn't do it entirely out of the goodness of his heart; it put her under his control but out of his way. He couldn't afford to have any lingering embarrassments now that he'd tidied up his life. But a house was a house, and Josephine quickly converted it into a parlor house, where she could earn a tidy sum with her newly taught skills. It satisfied her to have her place of business within sight of Louisa's home, and she dared her former lover, to try and impose a tax on her and her house. She openly recruited the most popular women and girls away from his houses, with a promise of dignity and fair wages. This was how she, Anna, Marie and Elsbeth found themselves under the same roof during the deadly summer of 1878. Josephine had recruited the light-skinned, and well-known Anna, and the darker but very popular Marie when she'd first moved into the house. Elsbeth, a solidly build daughter of German immigrants, had shown up on the doorstep some time later. She had arrived in Memphis by way of New Orleans on her own, so there was a story to be had, but Josephine didn't ask any questions. Right now, the house survived with just a small group of regulars, but Josephine knew that once word got around that she had a white woman working under her roof, that there would be trouble. If Elsbeth been an olive skinned Italian, Josephine could have probably just gotten away with a few bribes, but with a blonde, blue-eyed girl, she wasn't sure. In the meantime, she continued building her clientele and her reputation as a madame with two of the city's most popular girls. It put her in direct competition with Robert Church's many brothels and she liked that. She wasn't going to let him forget her that easily.

****

As for Langston and Florida, their little family, was no longer so little. After Jack, they had a couple of daughters, Daphne and Lucinda. Florida was newly pregnant with Lucinda when tragedy overcame the city. By this time, Florida no longer worked for the Church family, after having been fired for her familial association with the object of Louisa Church's humiliation. But Langston and Florida had annexed several parcels of land surrounding the family farm, and with the help and approval of Frederick, the Prince Family Farm extended farther into Shelby County. The matriarch of the family, Catherine had withdrawn into herself, so Florida had assumed this role, taking over the canning and preparation of goods for sale. In return, Catherine threw herself into the care of children and avoided any contact with her own husband. She also abandoned the faith that had once brought her much comfort. She began to seek out those with claims to the second sight, who stayed in the now rundown rooms of the Gayoso Hotel. She could barter some of her candied violets for a glimpse into the future and the hereafter. Also, in more direct defiance of her husband, she began to ally herself with Martha Ferguson and the other women of Beale Street who now pushed for more opportunities for black women.

When the fourth of July parade came rolling around, Catherine used the excuse to gather up the children, along with Florida and head towards main street. She joined thousands in the crowd to watch the proud McClelland Guards, Brown's Zouaves march past. They were joined by the exquisitely dressed Daughters of Zion, with their companions, then followed by the Sons of Ham. The Prince Hall Masonic Order was there with its mysterious imagery and reportedly ancient traditions, along with the Knights of Phythias. Ed Shaw and the Independent Pole-Bearers led the organization, followed by a group of the Sisters of Zion who sang sweetly. McClellan's guards performed a military exercise, that stirred the crowd with pride, while the St. John's Relief society collected coins. Each group came bearing its own standard, which flapped gently in the river breeze. Horatio Rankin brought up the tail of the parade, bearing the United States flag. The crowd rose and stood at attention as he passed. The parade ended in the park, where local musicians were setting up along with games, for children and adults alike. There were booths and tables set up in the park with the aroma of simmering greens, beans and smoked barbeque filling the air with a tantalizing scent. For this annual event, Catherine and her brethren could relax and enjoy. There was nary a white face in sight to destroy the festive atmosphere. Not even the Irish bullies posing as police were present in any quantity. She drew coins from her pocket and gave them to Florida to get them some ale while she and the children joined their friends and neighbors at the makeshift tables to picnic. She added a collection of the family preserves to the communal table and felt vindicated to see people immediately reach for her wares. It was hot and sticky out, but as the sun began to set, the heat of the day eased. As the children slowly drifted off to sleep at their feet, Florida rocked the baby gently. Members of the Daughters of Zion made their way thru the crowd, soliciting new members. Florida nodded affirmatively when they approached her, as Catherine looked on, approvingly. Shortly after, Langston and Frederick came to the park and joined them. Each carried a sleeping child for the wordless walk back to the cart. As Langston helped Florida up into the cart, their eyes met, and they smiled. Meanwhile, Catherine did her best to avoid Frederick's touch.

Death takes the city, 1878

So it was, and so it all started with the arrival of a cargo ship from that Queen city to the south of the Mississippi, New Orleans, much like it had in previous years. The heat had started early that year, and for weeks rumors about the fever had swirled ever closer. The ever-present fear of contagion was no match for this year's strain, but for families like the Princes, an inborn genetic immunity gave a measure of freedom not enjoyed by their Caucasian counterparts. A makeshift quarantine had been set in to place for all ships in the harbor after reports that the summer fever had reached New Orleans. It became more urgent as the fever reached Grenada, Mississippi and other parts south on the mighty river, but this quarantine was no match for the wily determination of one horny sailor, who was determined to get to shore and sow his oats in his favorite bawdy house. After escaping the quarantine encapsuling the Golden Crown steamship, William Warren snuck into town. But before William Warren checked in with his favorite bawd, he stopped in for a bite to eat at Kate Bionda's little lunch counter on Front Street. As he slurped warm beer, and chewed grits, he slapped lazily and ineffectively at a small cloud of mosquitos that were also determined to feast. This seemingly innocuous activity set into motion a series of events that would change the lives of everyone in the city. Shortly after his meal, he stopped in to see the ladies, who seemed outraged that he hadn't washed in quite some time. Finally, Mazie, who was the daughter of a shiftless Irishman who had encouraged her place in the brothel to help settle some debts, was willing to accommodate him, once he wiped himself with a dingy cloth. He finished quickly, as Mazie complained about the heat, sweat and odors emanating from his compact, and sinewy body. His skin was so hot, it felt like it was burning her. The buzz of mosquitos in the close, dark room was unmistakable as he labored over her in the still heat. As he left, he threw some bills at Mazie, while she scratched, and readied herself for the next client. By nightfall, William lay sweltering yet shivering under a sheet in quarantine on President's Island. Overnight, he began vomiting copious amounts of blood as his skin took on the telltale shade of yellow. By late the next day, he was dead. As Dr. John Erskine watched flies crawl in and out of the corpse's open mouth, word began to spread across the city that the dreaded Yellowjack was here. Looking at the gruesome and tortured expression on what had been William Warren, Dr. Erskine could only pray that they were wrong. Very quickly, as Kate Bionda, Mazie and several of their regular patrons became ill, then died, it became apparent that the rumors were true. Panic set in as anyone with the means, did their best to escape the city. Hordes of white families headed east, away from the plague that descended on the city of 50,000.

The Prince Family, while steadily increasing their acreage, did not have the means to flee. But they had the melanin to help protect them, while white residents all around them sickened and died. Florida was recalled by the Church family to nurse both Louisa and son, Thomas, who had taken ill. As she nursed them through their fevers, she remembered little Mary, up north and isolated from this hell that now consumed Memphis.

All across town, the streets emptied of the living as residents, fled, hid or died. The dead began to take over the streets and sidewalks of the city, as they were piled outside homes. The stench of death rose like a cloud to envelope the city, as corpses rotted in the sun faster than teams of black men could collect them. By default, the black community assumed power, as their white counterparts were stricken down. Whole congregations died after being overwhelmingly abandoned by their pastors for greener pasters outside the cursed city. While the black community was not completely immune, the fever overwhelmingly affected whites, with a 70% mortality. City services were wholly adopted and carried out by people who had been previously shut out and prevented from participating. Now they served as the saviors of the city. It would have been an ideal time for those seeking to avenge long held grudges for the daily injustices plaguing their existence. But it didn't happen that way despite the ongoing rhetoric of the Daily Avalanche, and the Appeal since the end days of the Confederacy. Instead, the Colored Central Committee was formed to prevent the city from descending into chaos. Blacks were recruited into the police force, the militia and multiple relief units. William Porter and Ed Shaw took control of the city, while everyday citizens like Josephine, Anna and Annie Cook converted their brothels into makeshift infirmaries for those stricken with disease.

Dr. R. H. Tate had come to the house to solicit her assistance in nursing the overflowing flood of patients. He was a fine-looking, attractive and fit, young physician from Ohio. In any other circumstances, Josephine would have attempted to entice him into becoming her protector. In a very short time, she'd gone from her father's house to being under the protection of two very powerful men. She knew she needed another such patron to ensure her safety, and the safety of her house. But for now, the flood of sick Memphians overwhelmed any thought of vice for the average resident. While many had previously thought that black people were completely immune to the disease, the flood of sick black people who were transported to Josephine's house by any sort of conveyance possible proved otherwise. While the majority of ill people stayed in their own homes, single men, sailors, dock workers and others sought the comfort of the familiar surroundings of the local brothels for care.

Just like Annie Cook on Gayoso Street, Josephine pitched in to try and ward off the death of their fellow citizens. She and the other women scrubbed the house endlessly with carbolic acid, giving it a pungent aroma of tar, which was not quite strong enough to overcome the rotting sweet smell of decomposing bodies that engulfed the house, the street and eventually, the entire city itself. She washed down patients aggressively to try and bring down the fevers, made a thin but savory gruel of grits and marrow broth, then she and her companions spent the afternoon trying to feed their fragile patients. Then there was laundry, the endless shrouds and more cleaning to be done.

It was backbreaking labor, which mostly went unrewarded, after patient after patient fevered, then expelled a river of black before dying. Some mornings, Josephine and the other women labored for hours trying to scrub the black harbinger of death and its stickiness out of the wooden floors. The ornate patterned carpets had long since been destroyed. Josephine herself briefly sickened with a blazing fever that was high enough to roast her unborn child. As the fetus was expelled, Anna feared that she'd begun the bleeding time, that heralded certain death. But once the little shriveled body was passed, her bleeding stopped. In a day, she was able to once again, care for the deluge of patients that seemed cursed by an uncaring and callous god. She became hollow eyed from seeing so much death. She never even acknowledged her own loss, and she bathed another patient, and then later, wrapped another corpse.

As the city became emptier and the streets more deserted; poor, and indigent whites began arriving on her doorstep. If they were embarrassed or ashamed to be cared for in a negro brothel, they were too sick to say so. Sometimes, the patients were so sick, the girls couldn't tell what color they were.

Josephine had long since run out of supplies at their own home and had taken to raiding the homes of the dead for all that was necessary. When he could, Dr. R. H. Tate or one of the Howard Association members would bring supplies as well as rations of flour, beans, bacon and coffee, and send someone to cart away the dead. Later, when the fever had claimed Dr. Tate, yet another came to take his place. Josephine was grateful for their dedication in making sure that the house had enough supplies to avoid the hunger that was affecting so many houses in the city. Josephine and the girls also kept a loaded rifle handy to ward off the roving bands of thieves that were looting the city.

Until the dead were moved, they were stacked outside on the street, like a pile of lumber to be used for paving. Late in the evening, a group of gravesmen came down the street, hauling as many bodies away to the Elmwood cemetery as their carts could hold. But the piles of the dead continued to stack in the street. Abandoned animals and strays had to be chased from sites as they began to feast of the hills of flesh before them.

One evening, an ill, elderly black man was brought to the house, dizzy, shivering and wrapped in a blanket. He was accompanied by his wife, and several children. His wife explained that their own home was serving as a home for orphaned children and that she didn't want any of the children to sicken. As Josephine and Amelia helped the elderly man to a cot, Josephine saw that she recognized the man as Father Africa. He was one of the ministers that her mother had taken her to see as a child. Josephine felt deeply ashamed to have them see her fall from grace. Josephine kept her eyes downcast in shame but Mother Emma, took her chin in hand, and said, "No, my child. Do not be shamed by the deeds than man has forced upon you. But instead take the opportunities giveth by the Lord to redeem yourself in his eyes and ours". Mother Emma, smoothed her hand down Josephine's cheek and Josephine felt it as a calming balm on her soul. After Mother Emma, and several of her children left, Josephine threw herself into the care of Father Africa, as if her own soul depended on it. She dipped cool cloths into a basin and did her best to ease his blazing fever. She wiped his sweaty body cool a thousand times. When he began to vomit the blackness, it threatened to engulf her very spirit, as she cleaned him over and over again. She tried to force him to take small sips of water, or even tiny drops dripped onto his parched lips, but he could not do so. She worked tirelessly for two days and two nights, without food, rest or relief. She waved away the efforts of Amelia, Anna or Marie. Finally in the darkness of the second night, after Father Africa had fallen into a deep coma, she got down on her knees, in a fashion unfamiliar to her, to pray for his immortal soul, and his survival. She woke in the cool pre-dawn light, and immediately checked her charge, only to feel his body to be cool to the touch. Devastated, she was almost catatonic, and survived herself only by the efforts of Marie, who fed small morsels and sips of cooled broth between her lips until Josephine was able to once again, arise, and function. She moved through the days mechanically, and methodically, with no sense of time passing. Only death and more death to mark her days.

It was a Tuesday when they had their first survivor. The fever had abated, and instead of returning with massive hemorrhage, it had stayed away. The fever glazed eyes returned to normal, and in a small voice the patient, a young man, asked for water. It was their first and only victory over the fever for some time. Another evening, as a middle-aged woman thrashed in the throes of the fever, Josephine and Amelia, another one of her girls, did their best to restrain her. But with a quick arch of her back and shoulder, the woman flailed her arm and raked her long nails deep into Josephine's cheek before the woman lapsed into a coma. Josephine examined the wounds in the mirror and wiped the furrows that burned deep into her face. She felt as if she'd been injured by 'Old Scratch' himself.

The next morning, the unnamed woman was dead, and Josephine's wounds continued to burn, almost down into the bones in her jaw. The wounds gaped open, and the area surrounding the furrows were a deep, deep purple. By the third day, as the wounds began to smell and leak a thick purulent fluid, one of her girls volunteered a family recipe for a moldy bread poultice. It immediately eased some of the pain, and over the next few days, the drainage stopped, the redness receded, but it was too late to prevent the destruction of her beauty. As August slipped into an equally sweltering and hellish September, Josephine was surprised one day to see her brother, Langston, in the doorway. He'd not sought her out since she had been led away from the farm, and she had no desire to see him now. His pleas for her to leave this place fell on deaf ears. She felt numb, almost dead inside. He finally left after pleading with her, only for her worn down mother to take his place the next day. She could only look at Catherine with glazed eyes and shake her head as she too tried to displace her from her home. She was scrubbing the floors with a brush, in vain, to erase the signs of scores of deaths when her last, and final visitor came to the door one late September day.

Her spirit briefly came alive as her one-time savior stepped upon her threshold with surprisingly shiny boots. She stared at the gleaming leather for a moment, as she tried to rise off of her knees, but the hours of scrubbing had taken their toll on her weary body, and her back rebelled. She looked up at him with hope in her eyes. This was quickly dashed as he called for Anna.

Anna appeared, somehow, fresh smelling in a clean and unwrinkled frock. Josephine was in an old, torn and stained gown that was almost crusty with blood. Her hair was tied back with an old rag, and her hands were dry, with chipped and broken nails from her efforts to clear the filth from her home as death maintained a grip on the patients that surrounded her. Anna carried a small valise and quickly hurried to Robert's side. She looked down at Josephine with pity in her eyes. With much effort, Josephine straightened and forced herself to stand on legs numb from kneeling most of the morning.

Robert looked at her with disgust and shrunk back lest she touch his attire with her filth. She felt her spirit sinking in a way that had been previously unaffected by the mountain of death around her. He looked at her ruined face, and laughed, coldly. "Not so much of a prize, are you now," he said before turning on his heel.

"Wait," she said with her voice cracking and betraying her. "Did you ever love me?" she asked with all the pain and suffering of the last months heavy in her voice.

He turned his head, to face her, but didn't move towards her.

"How could I?" he said. As her heart crumpled into a tiny ball of pain, he turned back towards Anna and threw over his shoulder, "You just aren't bright enough," as he left the house.

Josephine wanted to hurt him, she wanted to point out that Anna was no jewel to be sought after. She'd been passed around Memphis, in the most common of houses from before Josephine had ever left the farm. But she had seen in his eyes, that he didn't care, so she let him leave unmolested. Her heart hurt too much for her to do otherwise. She was gasping thru the tears that began coursing down her cheeks and falling to the ground.

Robert didn't care that Anna had been a prostitute for the last several years. It didn't bother him even that she had spent much of that time servicing the lowest of all the ranks of men; the sailors, the men working the docks, even sharecroppers with a bit of coin. He'd seen her and he knew he had to have her for his own. His own wife and child were now out of death's grip, and he would no longer be denied. What little regard he had held for Louisa and her happiness had died as he watched her and Thomas suffer with the fever. Their illness had forced him to confront his own mortality. Whereas he had once given up Josephine rather than endure his wife, Louisa's on-going displeasure, he now relished the thought of it. He knew he risked the enmity and alienation of his teenaged son, but he didn't care. His son, Thomas had proven to be a mama's boy and thus, no use to him. Besides, he now had a new filly to breed an army of sons and daughters on. He'd just had to urge Louisa to leave him so he could legitimize his newest offspring. He'd already left one family behind when he'd first come to Memphis. Discarding this one wouldn't prove to be much of a challenge.

While Robert and Anna were heading away in his fine carriage to one of his properties across town, Josephine had roused herself to check on the dozen or so unfortunate souls that still rested in her home. She was surprised to find that most of her patients were white. It was almost certain that the majority would die. Elsbeth and Marie could see to themselves, she thought, as she wearily climbed the stairs to her personal rooms. She used a damp cloth from the kitchen to clean herself the best she could. She felt too tired to do much more. She changed into a dressing gown and brushed her hair before drinking the entire bottle of laudanum the surgeon had entrusted to her at the beginning of this nightmare. It had been used only sparingly for the patients since they all seemed to vomit almost immediately after getting it. She climbed into bed and arranged herself prettily with the ruined side of her face turned away from the door. She drifted off to sleep, never to awaken, just one more casualty of the deadly summer of 1878. For all that she had lived, she was only 16 years old.

****

Finally, as the temperatures began to cool in mid-October, the fever seemed to loosen its grip on the city. But the death of Josephine along with so many others, wrought a change in Catherine. She became determined in a way she hadn't known before. She drew upon an inner strength that was stronger than steel and sharper than a diamond. She focused all of this energy on her two remaining sons, and she would preach to them day and night on the need to seek power, and control. She used her still attractive face and figure and considerable charm, along with her friendship with Martha and the other negro entrepreneurs to gain access to the local leaders. They were finally beginning to re-organize the negro community out of the ashes of the illness that had brought much of Memphis to its knees. She sought out Ed Shaw, Alexander Dickenson, and a small group of fellow negroes that were actively trying to advance black citizens. She became interested in making sure that negro voices, so long ignored, could no longer go unheard. She pushed her new daughter-in-law and Langston to do the same. She raised the coin necessary for Langston to vote in the upcoming elections. She did her best to ignite ambition within Langston and to extinguish the sense of futility that her estranged husband had embraced.

Book Two: Lysander

Memphis after the yellow fever epidemic of 1878 was a very different place. The formerly bustling city had lost half its population to relocation, and over 5000 people had perished of yellow fever. The city had sunk further and further into debt, resulting in bankruptcy. Even prior to the yellow fever epidemic, the city had been unable to meet its payroll and many police officers had gone unpaid for months. When yellow fever illness and the preceding white flight decimated the ranks of the police force, negros were recruited into the ranks in unprecedented numbers. As the city foundered, the colored citizenry stepped forward to save the struggling city and stepped into leadership. Men like Robert Church, Langston's childhood hero, came forward monetarily to support the city. That he did this as he was accumulating additional land and properties around Shelby County did not go unnoticed. As the yellow fever epidemic receded, the Memphis city scape was forever altered, as many of the affluent and prosperous white citizens never returned. Not only were negro citizens in the majority now, but many of these citizens were also finding their place in local governance, even as the city relinquished it's charter, and eliminated much of the city's bloated infrastructure. These residents, long denied their voice, began to make themselves heard. As Langston Prince pushed forward into his position as county squire and magistrate, he was part of a newly emerging upper class negro society. This did not go unnoticed by Memphis' remaining white residents, many of whom were immigrants and part of the impoverished classes themselves. These poorer white residents became increasingly embittered as they watched their colored counterparts pull themselves out of poverty.

As for the Prince family, they managed to survive the Yellowjack, but not everything that ensued. Josephine was gone, and others would soon follow.

****

Of all of Langston's children, his son, Lysander, by his second wife, Dorothy, was the only one who seemed interested in carrying on the family affairs.

Langston's first wife, Florida, had died from a canker in her breast the year after yellow fever spread thru Memphis. Langston was quick to seek another wife to assist him with his large family. His mother, Catherine, didn't approve, but her face had taken on a permanent scowl which had only deepened since the death of his sister, Josephine. Dorothy was no beauty, but she was light-skinned, had a strong back, and was willing to be a mother to his children. She also had thick strong thighs in which to engulf a man and make him feel needed. In the years that followed his remarriage, in 1884, his father, Frederick died, which only increased Langston's burden. He watched as his mother kept a bedside vigil in the hours before Frederick's death and waited to see if she would make amends with Frederick before he died. He'd suffered a fit a week before that had left one side of his body limp and useless. Instead, he heard his mother chastise his father and berate him for his weakness. He'd had to send her from his father's bedside and have Dorothy care for him, in his last days. Catherine was too consumed by bitterness and grief to do anything to mitigate his father's suffering. But Dorothy proved a more than adequate nurse, and mate.

She gave birth to his son, Lysander several years later, just after Langston celebrated his 32nd birthday. It was also the year Langston was elected County Squire for Shelby County. The initial push from his mother, Catherine had encouraged Langston to confront the racism that was so pervasive in the city, and to take on the city government. Along with Lymus Wallace, and emboldened by the enormously charismatic Ed Shaw, Langston ran for office and won.

His last child, Isaac, was born a year later. As Shelby County Squire, the family's fortunes improved considerably and rapidly. As county squire, Langston was a legally sworn magistrate, and justice of the court. He also declared himself responsible for tax collection and property valuation. While tax collection had traditionally been overlooked amongst families friendly to the city mayor, in the aftermath of Memphis's bankruptcy and restoration of the city charter, no family was exempt. However, the exact amount owed, and it's enforcement was determined by Langston and his fellow politicians. This put him in the unique position of being able to extort families and businesses as a representative of law and order. It also offered him an opportunity to settle the score with some of the people that had abused his family and his trust. He quickly learned that he could assess many of the properties at a lower tax value and pocket much of the difference in a one-time gratuity fee that made up much of the difference. Or, if he wanted, he could assess outrageous values, and force his enemies to pay exorbitant taxes. In cash-strapped Shelby County, no one in government blinked an eye when his vengeance helped replenish the county's coffers. Much of this ire was directed at his former hero for his role in the debasement of his sister. But Robert Church was not without resources and power of his own, so there was a limit to what he could do. Instead of being an avenging angel welding a golden hammer, Langston was more of a buzzing gnat, irritating his foes but never really doing any noticeable damage.

As Langston Prince exercised his duties as a local magistrate, his family's fortunes visibly improved. His wife, Dorothy, was now dressed in stiff polished cottons in brilliant colors, along with the occasional silk or velvet dress, or fine lawn, as they traveled through town to join their newly prominent neighbors and recent affluent transplants. They began attending social events and parties among the fashionable set of negro Memphians. Since the end of the confederacy, negros no longer had to have a permit to hold social events. As the constant degradations and humiliations of the confederacy faded into the past, and the strict period of mourning for fever victims ended, negro Memphians relished the chance to join together and socialize without fear or interruption. That evening, a ball was being held at an elegant home at 363 Lauderdale Street in honor of the Great Worshipful

Master, Mr. Evans, of the Prince Hall Masons Grand Lodge of Tennessee.

As the rented carriage pulled up to the massive 14 room, three-story Queen Anne style home, Langston Price, his wife and his mother couldn't help but be impressed. Dorothy knew it must be costing Catherine all of her pride to cross the threshold of Robert Church's new home. She knew that Catherine was responsible for the growing resentment that her husband had towards his erstwhile hero and role model. That, along with Catherine's continued indifference towards Dorothy enraged her. While Dorothy knew of Robert Church's immediate role in Josephine's suicide, Catherine didn't. Dorothy didn't care because the animosity between the two men was costing Langston additional business opportunities. She could hardly feel sorry for a woman who had debased herself the way Langston's sister had.

For Catherine, it was a different story. Langston had deliberately kept the more lurid details from his mother, to spare her additional pain, and to prevent a worsening rift between Catherine and his father. In the years since Frederick's death, Langston had done nothing to enlighten her. Catherine thought that Josephine had died of yellow fever, while being maintained as a kept woman by Robert Church; the truth would only devastate her. He needed his mother to maintain that thin veneer of civility towards the Churches even as he continued his machinations against them. The Churches were an integral and essential part of negro society. If that meant that Catherine busied herself with her other special causes, even if they annoyed his wife, so be it. It was the price Langston would gladly pay.

Dorothy plastered a fake smile on her face and held it there even as Catherine inserted herself between Dorothy and Langston. Langston said nothing as his mother pushed her way to his side, to clasp her gloved hand around Langston's forearm, displacing Dorothy, and forcing Dorothy to trail behind as their party made its way up the walkway to the door. Langston, as usual Dorothy thought, seemed oblivious to the maneuverings of his mother. Though her face felt like it would crack in half, Dorothy kept a smile firmly in place as they joined other guests in the Churches' massive salon.

As Langston rubbed elbows with a former transplant, Josiah Settle, who was now part of the Criminal Court, his wife was enchanted by the delicate elegance of the music prodigy whose piano playing graced many of the city's social gatherings. She stayed in the main ballroom while Langston, Lymus Wallance and several aldermen, gathered in the drawing room; smoking and playing cards at one of several tables set up for that purpose. The drawing room was crowded with men escaping the watchful eyes of their wives and mothers. As Lymus dealt cards, he turned to Langston and remarked, "Be careful now because soon they will come for you." He nodded toward a group of wives and widows visible through the open door to the adjacent ballroom that included Dorothy, Emma Cassels, Stella Norris, his mother and several other ladies. Each woman was an elegant example of the latest fashions. As Langston considered Lymus' words, he noticed his mother looking over her fan, with hard eyes at Anna Church, who was dancing in the center or the room with her husband, Robert. Her face flashed a look of intense hatred before she settled a smooth bland expression on her face. He forgot all about it a moment later, as Isaac Norris made a joke about wives and their spending.

Isaac was quickly and mildly rebuked by the more serious Settle, who said, "if you think that's the only problem we have, you are privily mistaken." He spoke with dulcet tones in a flawless and unaccented English that belied his origins in east Tennessee as the son of a slave and her master. His diction had been corrected and polished during his tenure back east, in the halls of academia. It set him apart from many of the Memphis natives, and his words carried weight. "Don't think that the white men haven't noticed when our ladies appear in their finery. Don't be fooled into thinking that they don't care that we've educated our children and moved into fine homes. Don't think that that stunt that Ms. Hooks did a few years ago is forgotten. We may have climbed up, my friends, but it's a treacherous and dangerous path, and they will trip us up at any opportunity," he finished. Many of the men nodded in agreement, and Langston thought back to his father, Frederick, who had spent Langston's childhood cautioning him against trusting the words of white men.

"It's not what they say to you, Langston. It's what they do!" Frederick had cautioned him so many times in the days and years after the war, as they worked in the hot sun to rebuild their home after the massacre. He repeated it as they watched the Freedmen's Bureau come to Memphis, and then folded. He had repeated it after each of the brutal murders of Jeremiah Hale, Frank Jones, Christopher Bender, Bud Whitfield, John Schofield, and John Brown. He repeated it every time a body too mutilated and decomposed to be identified as anything more than a negro male was found. It became his mantra every time they returned with an empty wagon from the marketplace but with not enough coins. He muttered it under his breath while he slowly worked his way through the words of Taylor Nightingale of the Memphis Free Speech newspaper. It was even on his lips shortly before his fatal stroke. Langston shook his head and came back to the present.

The conversation turned to the recent visit by President Cleveland, and Judge H. T. Elliot's sudden demise. William Field, who sat to Langston's left, grunted and laid down his cards with a flourish showing a full house, saying, "It couldn't happen to a more deserving guy."

Judge Elliot was a proud son of the now vanquished confederacy, and a senator from Mississippi, who was believed to be part of Nathan Bedford Forrest's cadre. This was a group of disgruntled whites that terrorized much of South Memphis while hiding their identities in bizarre, robed and hooded costumes. He, along with fellow Mississippian, Walter Sillers, helped recruit local whites in the Mississippi Delta and Memphis area to their cause. While Forrest had died before the yellow fever epidemic, his disciples were still roaming the streets of Shelby County, looking to punish colored folks for their existence. The men at the card table were united in their determination not to be terrorized into submission. While they guffawed and joked about it at the gaming table, it was a very serious endeavor. everal of the men banded together at night along with other members of the community to control South Memphis and Beale Street to try to prevent violence against their neighbors and property destruction, which were the hallmarks of the Klan activity in this area. Most recently, the Klan had targeted the First Baptist Church of Beale Street and Joseph Clouston, who was a former Memphis City Council member. They suspected that Judge Julius Dubose had organized it to intimidate the community out of voting in the upcoming election. Playing cards was just a front for the men gathered in the drawing room as they planned their defense.

While Langston was thus occupied in the drawing room, Dorothy and the other women were in deep conversation with Hattie Britton, Julia Hook's younger sister. The witty, charming, sweet-faced 20-year-old had recently moved from the family home in Kentucky to join her sister. She was regaling the ladies with stories about the private school she had graduated. While many of her siblings went on to Berea College, Hattie had come to Memphis to help her sister with a music club she had started. She stayed close to her sister at the Ball so she could avoid the disapproving glares of her brother-in-law, Charles. She didn't like her sister's second husband. He often looked at her in a way that made her feel cheap and dirty. She didn't want to go back to Kentucky, so she kept quiet about her distaste for the stern, unforgiving man. He was cheerless, acerbic man, dominated by his belief in a cruel and unpredictable god, that punished sinners without mercy. She spent most of her time trying to escape his notice as he ruled the family home with a strict and overbearing manner.

As Hattie spoke, Dorothy dreamed of giving her son the same types of opportunities. She wasn't content for her infant son to follow the path of his older siblings. She stroked her gown over her slightly curved belly. It had taken her several years to carry a babe to term, and now that she had Lysander and his tiny future sibling, she was determined to instill in her children a sense of ambition and pride.

"Did you hear that Alice Mitchell died? You know, the crazy white girl who slit her friend's throat down on Hernando Street because she wouldn't marry her," Emma said, eyes ablaze with naughty delight at having a scandalous tidbit to share with her friends. Catherine rolled her eyes and stepped away, unwilling to engage in such trivial and undignified discussion. As she stepped away, she saw her daughter-in-law lean in closer for more salacious details and rehash the old crime. This only confirmed her opinion that Dorothy was common, much more common than Langston's first wife. Dear Florida, God rest her soul. Her son had used up that poor child until she could do no more, dying while the cancer took over her body. Catherine sighed, then perked up when she saw her friend Martha across the room. Now, there's a good woman, Catherine thought as she walked toward her hard-working friend.

****

As time passed, Lysander watched as a small child as his father used his position as County Squire to improve life for the family. Langston had made agreements with shopkeepers, saloon owners and rooming houses all over the city. He was in quiet but open competition with Robert Church for pay-offs and property. Robert Church had become a prominent hero of the city after helping the city recover from bankruptcy in the aftermath of the plague that had killed so many, but he wasn't a hero to Langston. He still mourned his lovely younger sister, Josephine, and her fall from grace. As he formed uneasy alliances with P. Wee and other white saloon owners, he gained a reputation for his cold and calculating nature. He could just as easily collect his monthly tithe from barkeeps as he could light the match to destroy their businesses. His young son watched all of this without a word and noticed how his father earned the grudging respect of businesspeople all over the city, particularly those who already resented Church and his growing empire. As Josiah Settle took his place as Assistant Attorney of the General Criminal Court, Langston moved around town with apparent impunity, seemingly immune from prosecution even as he continued to extort, bribe and scheme his way to prosperity.

While Langston was amassing his power in the city, his younger brother, Arthur, continued to work the land and help support the family. He remained a bachelor and pined for the woman he couldn't have. She remained in Ohio until 1888 when she traveled in Memphis. Her parents had been long divorced by then. Her father had remarried quickly, to Anna Wright, the one-time prostitute. Mary was devastated by the divorce, and its impact on her mother, Louisa Ayers Church. She was a successful businesswoman in her own right. Louisa had fled to New York just after the epidemic when her husband had unabashedly replaced her in his affections with a much younger, brighter model while she was still recuperating from yellow fever. Mary had stayed in Ohio to continue her education, completing not just her high school education but a bachelor's and master's degree at Oberlin as something of an oddity. There weren't many women, much less black woman with advanced education degrees, even in the progressive state of Ohio. She then traveled to Washington to teach Latin. By the time she returned to Memphis, her father had already produced two more offspring, essentially replacing Mary and her brother, Thomas. His newest son was not only his new heir apparent but his namesake as well. Mary had heard the news in numerous letters from old friends but didn't believe that her father would replace her in his affections so easily. She had invented multiple reasons why her letters to her father remained unanswered. Principle among them was the thought that his new wife had ensured that he had never received them. But, this was not the case, and she crushed by seeing her father in person and having him dismiss her from his presence like a servant. She quickly sought out her oldest friend, and confidant, Arthur.

****

Mary and Arthur, 1888

"Do you love me, Mary?" Arthur asked as he stared at their entwined hands outstretched in the air. Mary lay in his arms, naked, in the aftermath of their lovemaking. He'd expected a ready reply after that afternoon's pleasures, only to hear his question go unanswered. Instead, Mary turned in his arms, to face him and began kissing him once more. They spent the summer thusly. Mary would recite poetry to Arthur, who was enraptured by her intellect. Mary was charmed by Arthur and profoundly affected by his steadfast loyalty, but she was no fool. She knew there was no place for an educated woman in Memphis, and she wasn't ready to give up her life to become a wife to anyone. She also wasn't ready to give Arthur up. She had waited a lifetime to experience love and was only just now exploring her sexuality, with him. But after a few months, as Arthur pressed her to marry him, she knew she had to leave, before she was forced into a position when she wasn't ready. She made another appointment to see her father, and then presented him with a proposal that she knew he would think better of rejecting.

That fall she headed for New York with a white female companion for an extended tour of Europe. In the spring of the following year her daughter, Temerity May, was born in a private hospital in Switzerland. The tiny baby was whisked away from Mary before she even had a chance to see or hold her. Even her name was provided by the sour-faced chaperone her father had insisted on accompanying her, as part of his condition in exchange for financial support. Mary was sure that the chaperone and erstwhile prison matron, was there to ensure that news of the existence of baby Temerity never made its way back across the Atlantic. Mary left Temerity and part of her heart at the hospital in Zurich, and then continued traveling for several more months before returning to teaching. When she returned to Washington D.C. it was with a dampened spirit. She no longer had the will to resist the inevitable and unalterable course for a woman of her station so she quietly accepted a proposal and married a fellow teacher at the M Street High School.

It took her several years, but she quietly arranged to adopt Temerity after several of their own children died. She never admitted to her husband that Temerity was her very own child, and if there was any resemblance, she passed it off as being related by distant kin.

As for Arthur, after Mary's sudden flight, he began to drink and to brood. When he received the anonymous letter announcing Mary's pregnancy, his drinking only increased. Langston tried to enlist him in his enforcement tactics for reluctant taxpayers, but Arthur could barely summon any enthusiasm to beat and threaten the people who ran afoul of his brother. If he drank a little more, he didn't think about his sadness. He didn't think about anything while he swung the heavy board at someone's kneecap, or their head. That's how he became so good at enforcing Langston's will and collecting debts, that he became something of the neighborhood boogeyman, at least for a little while.

In 1891, shortly after Mary's marriage, he was found dead in an alley off Beale Street, with a bullet in his back. No one could prove Robert Church was behind it, but no one could prove he wasn't, either.

After the death of her second child, all fight went out of Catherine. She died in her sleep at the age of 52.

Langston and the Law, 1890's

George and Jack were content to continue to work the land, adding the farm in a piecemeal fashion, as they each carved out a plot for their individual families. Langston's daughters, Daphne, Lucinda and Tamar seemed content to marry neighboring boys and start families of their own. Quickly, Langston's older children seemed to scatter to the four corners of the earth.

After the gruesome murder and mutilation of three black men who owned a successful grocery store in the Curve by a lynch mob headed by a seated judge, George, Jack and their wives and children joined a wagon train heading west. Along with several thousand other blacks, they walked alongside their wagons to find a new home out west. They settled on adjacent homesteads in a newly settled Oklahoma town, ironically enough, called Langston.

While Langston was sad to see his older sons leave Memphis, he hoped his boys would find a kind of freedom that was absent from the South. He himself was too entrenched in Shelby County to pack up and leave, even if had been the promised land itself. Later that same year, after Daphne's husband was killed in an accident, she became romantically entangled with Marion Johnson, a handsome young man from New York. Marion wanted to reunite with a branch of his family that had re-settled in Liberia in 1820 in exchange for their freedom from bondage. After surviving the rigors of transportation and resettlement, his family had become part of the ruling elite. A distant aunt, Amelia Johnson had written to invite Marion and the other remaining American relatives to move to Monrovia. Now that she had a child of her own, she wanted her son to have more family around. Daphne initially hesitated, but then quickly married Marion before taking her three kids with her to Monrovia. Of all the children by his two wives, it was Daphne's leaving that affected Langston the most. He knew that at such a great distance, he would never see his child again.

Lucinda and her husband moved to West Helena, AR shortly after that, leaving only Tamar and her family on the farm, along with Langston, his second wife, Dorothy, and their shared children, Lysander and Isaac.

It was his young son, Lysander, who had drive and ambition, and wasn't content to work the land. From his youngest days, as a toddler teetering after his father, Lysander was never satisfied. Unlike his own father, Frederick, Langston was determined not to let the ugliness of racism and prejudice hold his family back. He wouldn't let it destroy his hope or his family. That didn't mean it wasn't a continuous uphill battle. Sometimes, he looked in the small hand mirror he had given his first wife and railed at the injustice. He couldn't help to note that his skin was barely tan-tinged, but it separated him from the privilege he could have otherwise enjoyed if it were not. This imaginary, but very real division among men, was unfathomable for him at times, but, as much as it angered him, he was determined he wouldn't allow it to eat away at him like it had his father. Instead, he used it to propel himself forward. While he internally railed against the invisible line that separated men by color, he outwarded affected a calm and accepting demeanor. He had watched too many other men like himself pay the price for admitting their anger. Even Mr. Church, city hero, erstwhile rival, and his father's nemesis had paid the price. He'd been attacked and shot more than once. Buildings had burned and businesses had been destroyed, more than once over the years, but Robert Church had persevered.

Now Langston was seemingly becoming a convenient target for the courts. As the national panic set in and railroads floundered, much of the cotton industry ground to a halt. Railroads couldn't move the product as their unpaid workers went on strike, and mills went bankrupt before they could transform the cotton into cloth. Memphis' economic future was tied to cotton, so once again the city struggled to survive.

And so did Langston to some extent! Just as his fortunes had increased, the laws of justice came after him. It was as if the city's economic setbacks had forced the government to acknowledge his actions. For most of the so-called 'Gay 90's' Langston was in court. He was arrested for a series of crimes, including several cases of bribery. The charges were true, of course, but so missing the mark as to be laughable. For all that he had extorted much of Shelby County for the last several years, he was accused and convicted of receiving a bribe from William Harris for the small sum of $11.65. In that case, as in several others, in exchange for the bribe, he used his position as magistrate to drop criminal charges against several defendants. He was charged and convicted in this case while awaiting charges in yet another bribery case. While he was sentenced to 3 years imprisonment, the case was then thrown out by friendly Judge Moss. He was retried with his attorney B. F. Booth steadfast in his client's innocence. This time, the sentence was suspended. It was only a temporary reprieve as more and more Memphians came forward to accuse Langston of criminal behavior, but once they saw how 'bullet-proof' the now former magistrate had become from criminal liability, several of the claimants decided to pursue him in civil court.

While his father was fighting in court, Lysander was growing up watching the police come for his father. He and his younger brother, Isaac, grew to fear the arrival of the rough talking, often disheveled cops with names like O'Malley, Murphy, or Doyle. More often or not, they had a well-placed kick accompanied by a curse when they passed by the boys.

One day when Lysander was seven, and the police had come for his father again, one of the police officers yelled "Little nigger," while planting a kick to Isaac's backside, after he was too slow to move out of the policeman's path. While Isaac was nursing a kidney, that same officer leered at Dorothy, saying, "You look like you like them bucks, don't you, mammy. Seems like there's enough of them niglets running around to shows that you do," he said, exposing several broken and blackened stumps of rotting teeth. As he leaned towards her, she shrank away from him and the foul-stench emitted from the black hole he called a mouth.

"Ya'll sure you don't want to make nice with me, wench, and maybe make a little less trouble for your man?" he said, as his trio of fellow officers led Langston from the cabin in shackles. The other officers laughed as Langston signaled with a shake of his head and a glance for his wife and children to stay silent. Previously, some of the other officers had deferred to Langston due to his position as a magistrate, but recently, some of the police, particularly the Irish and immigrant cops from the poorer neighborhoods near his own, seemed to relish humiliating Langston in front of his family and neighbors. After the police had taken their father away, Lysander asked his mother with tears in his eyes, "Why? Why do they hate us so?"

Dorothy gathered up her two young sons and she told them. She told them about their grandparents who had been born into bondage, and that slaves were treated with less freedoms than those accorded most animals. She told them about war, conflict, and broken promises. She told them also about the greed and cold hearts that ruled many men, and the lack of the compassion that was endemic in the South, and among many white people.

She didn't have enough words to explain much more than that, as the conversation took a toll on her soul. She wasn't sure if the boys understood, but she knew that life would continue to teach them. She just prayed they would survive the lessons.

By the time he was ten, Lysander had figured out that he wanted to beat the system by going around it. As he had watched his father go through a series of legal challenges as County Squire, he couldn't help but note that the city's determination to punish his father seemed at odds with the high amount of crime that plagued Memphis. Whites could seemingly act with impunity, especially if it was against a black person. Lysander was too young to remember many of the crimes that occurred at the very beginning of that decade, but Langston wasn't. He watched as the whites were at it again, attacking, mutilating and lynching black men with little fear of possible consequences. But, then again, even the judge was implicit in the crimes. While Thomas Moss, Calvin McDowell, Henry Stewart and many others rotted in their graves, William Barrett, Judge Julius Debose, and his mob assassins remained free to continue their spree. The rest of the country finally sat up and took notice of the escalating amount of crime, and the runaway number of homicides. As Memphis was widely derided as 'Murder City' in outraged newspaper headlines across the United States, not much changed in the murder city itself.

For every moment of peace, there was a price his people paid for it. By the time, Langston came up with his plan, the century was almost over. For all that Frederick's dark prophesy remained true, Langston remained determined to beat it.

****

While Dorothy was doing her best to instill in Lysander and his younger brother a sense of urgency and ambition, her husband, Langston continued to be pursued thru the courts with multiple different lawsuits alleging fraud. As the 19th century ended, Langston's career as county squire ended too. Perhaps it was pushback from the poor whites who resented blacks in positions of power, but since Langston's district was based in the black neighborhoods of Shelby County, it was more likely that black voters had simply tired of his antics and continued charges of on-going corruption. Whatever it was, while he stayed out of jail, he was also forced back into life as a civilian and lost many of the perks of being a civil servant. Of course, he still had much of the wealth he and Dorothy had accumulated while he was in office. With much encouragement from his wife, he was also able to get past his one-sided feud with Robert Church. Enough so that he and his wife attended a political rally to see President Theodore Roosevelt speak. Or maybe it was just that by the turn of the century, Langston could forgive past grievances now that his mother, Catherine, was not whispering her venom in his ear. Whatever it was, Langston buried the axe deep enough that he was one of the initial depositors in Church's new bank, Solvent

Savings Bank and Trust. Or maybe he just didn't want his money in the hands of the lily-white.

Lysander, 1910

By 1910, Lysander had grown into a strong young man. As prohibition had settled into Memphis, he had moved into both bootlegging and distribution. A fine series of political networking and bribes made sure that the city never truly ran dry despite the political rhetoric. As his distribution network increased, Lysander had to recruit additional neighbors into distilling the liquid gold. Brisk sales meant that he always had coins jingling in the pockets of finely made suits. He saw the pride in his father's eyes at his modest successes and the increased attention from neighborhood girls. But it was the one girl who ignored his increased fortunes that intrigued him the most, Desdemona Fuller.

Desdemona Fuller seemed immune to the charisma of the light-skinned, well-dressed, and sharp young man. This only further sparked Lysander's interest. He ignored Desdemona's friends, who were only too happy to flirt and make coy eyes at Lysander as he waited outside the schoolroom for Desdemona to emerge in the afternoons. Finally, after two weeks of arranging his schedule so he could wait for Desdemona outside her class, Lysander grew frustrated and irritated. He brushed away the attentions of Merilee Williams to follow Desdemona as she left the school grounds. Despite still being in the schoolroom, Merliee already had a reputation for sharing her charms among South Memphis' young neer-do- well. Two of Lysander's homebrewing associates had recently crowed over Merilee's special talents. Whether this was idle chatter or absolute fact made no difference to Lysander.

As Desdemona continued to walk away, Lysander yelled in frustration, "Who do you think you are, Desdemona Fuller?" The kids in the schoolyard stopped their chatter to watch, as Desdemona halted in her tracks, and turned on her heels to face Lysander.

"Since you said my name, I think you know *exactly* who I am," Desdemona said haughtily. "So, you know," she continued, "that I am a lady, and I don't play around with *boys*." The way she said 'boys' with disdain angered the handsome, young man enough that he raised an eyebrow and then turned on his own heel to leave Desdemona and the rest of the schoolyard staring in the wake of his retreat.

"Well, now you've done it, Desdemona," Merilee teased. Merilee tried but couldn't quite hide her glee at the turn of events. Merilee was tired of the pale-skinned Desdemona getting all of the attention, while she heralded her virginity over Merilee and their friends. Everyone knew that Desdemona was a virgin, and that she was a devout Christian. Desdemona made sure that everyone knew that her virginity was linked to her divinity, her purity, and her faith. It made Merilee's blood boil inside even as she pretended to support Desdemona's unwavering pledge. It wasn't like Merilee had had the same privileges that Desdemona did. Merilee's mother, Abigail, owned a boarding house and took in laundry to make ends meet. If some of the borders and other special friends pitched in a little extra towards household expenses in exchange for Abigail's favors that just meant that maybe they had some meat for supper that week. If some of those borders began to eye Abigail's young daughters, then it was just expected that Abigail's daughters, including Merilee, keep their mouths shut and act grateful for the attention. It was only due to the generosity of one of her mama's "special friends" that Merilee was able to attend school at all.

It was only now that she was a teenager with her own regular suitors, that Merilee was able to push away the sweaty paws of the borders that kept their family afloat.

Desdemona turned to look at Merilee, while Merilee quickly composed her face into a bland expression. "Aw, I'm just kidding, Dessie. You know that Lysander Prince ain't got nothing on you. What about that handsome young doctor, Dr. Atkins? I saw him looking at you one day in church. He sure is something special," Merilee said, pushing down her feelings of resentment.

Desdemona and Merilee walked slowly down the street and chatted for another quarter hour before parting at the corner to head to their respective homes. Merilee to the ramshackle, slightly rundown, and rambling boarding house, and Desdemona to the tidy, if small home on Goodwyn Street.

Desdemona's family had bought the little clapboard house in 1900 when the family had moved to Memphis, and her father and brothers spent much of their time repairing and expanding the modest home to fit their expanding family. They probably could have afforded a bigger home, but her father had strong beliefs regarding wealth, and prosperity. He believed that modesty, education, and faith should be foremost in the black community and did not like to see conspicuous consumption among the community. His family was always well-fed, and dressed in clean clothing in good repair. His children were educated at private schools with additional tutoring in music, art and foreign languages. But, they were not, and would not be festooned with fancy silks, laces, jewels or gems. To her father, the Reverend Thomas Fuller, this was an affront to God. Her father was the principal of the Howe Institute, and steadfastly believed in the importance of education. He also believed that people should sacrifice their personal comfort for the sake of family.

Now that her oldest brother, Titus had married, his new bride had moved in too. Titus and her father had spent the last month enclosing the back porch while debating politics and scripture. Her mother, Mary Eliza, and her brother's wife, Felicity had gathered discarded newspapers and other materials to serve as insulation for the room. This was now the bridal suite for the couple. They packed the materials into the walls before her brother applied the plaster lathe concoction.

Desdemona couldn't help but notice that the still blushing bride had a bit of a rounded belly, so she knew that the new space would soon serve as a nursery too. She liked her brother's new, if bossy wife, but she couldn't wait until she could be out of the crowded house into her own place to live. The three, almost four bedroom house was bursting at the seams, especially with her twin brothers, Roland and Linus down the hall. At 12 years of age, they always seemed to be full of energy and pranks, while their stomachs always seemed to be empty. They shared the room next to hers, and sometimes it seemed like the very walls vibrated with their excess energy. She loved her wild little brothers, particularly Roland, even if they made her crazy sometimes. Even though they were twins, they were so different. Linus was more introspective and could only be talked into mischief by his boisterous and more outgoing twin, Roland. Roland for his part, delighted in making jokes and teasing Desdemona. His pranks were always light-hearted and good natured, which is why she didn't murder both of them outright. They had recently taken to teasing her about her ardent admirer, who they sometimes trailed after, as he persisted in approaching Desdemona with romantic overtures. They would make silly comments and roll their eyes behind his back as they watched Desdemona reject him over and over again. It almost made her feel sorry for Lysander Prince, she thought, even as a smile came to her lips thinking about it. But quickly, her mind shifted back to the crowded little house.

She bit her lip to stifle the sigh that arose in her chest as she thought about the tiny room she shared with her two younger sisters and her grandmother. It was so cramped already, and now there was going to be a new baby in the house, she thought. Maybe that's why her eyes lit up so much as she opened the door to enter the house, and saw Lysander Prince sitting on the well-worn but clean couch, flanked by her parents and wizened grandmother. He had a bouquet of wildflowers in his lap, slightly askew from his clenched fist. He sat ramrod straight and appeared ill at ease as her grandmother looked him over and made clicking sounds with her tongue.

Desdemona decided to take pity on the ardent suitor. Anyone who would run the gauntlet with her parents and her grandmother deserved a real chance, she supposed. It wasn't as if she wasn't interested in Lysander. She just didn't want to be another one of his playthings. But, if he was here in her living room, then she guessed that his intentions towards her were more than casual. After Lysander answered a few of her father's pointed questions, Desdemona's mother and grandmother nodded their heads in acceptance. Lysander turned to Desdemona and after a shy smile, he said, "How about if we head down to Mrs. Fisher's on Beale Street for some ice cream?"

Within three months of their impromptu ice cream date, Lysander was asking her father for her hand in marriage. While the Reverend and his wife thought it was a rapid courtship, once Lysander agreed to be baptized into his church, any doubts that Reverend Fuller had dissipated. The next month was taken over by Mary Eliza, her mother, and Desdemona's joyful, if hectic planning. Plans for Desdemona to continue her education were briefly put on hold until after the wedding. Mary Eliza had seen the looks the young couple had been exchanging and knew that this wedding couldn't be put off until after her graduation. Instead, the Reverend's students and an army of tutors came to the cozy house to instruct and quiz Desdemona in between fittings and other pre-wedding events. Maud Hooks and her mother, Vina Washington Peyton, spent much of the time on their knees with pins in their mouths as they worked on reworking one of Mary Eliza's best dresses into Desdemona's wedding gown. The champagne-colored, high-necked dress with a ruffled bodice and long sleeves, had been a gift from one of the wives of Reverend Fuller's most faithful congregants. She had ordered the custom-made gown from Worth's for her sister, but then, between the final fitting in Paris and the dress being shipped to Memphis, the sister had died. Unable to return the gown, and unwilling to keep it, Dr. Byas's tall, elegant wife was only too happy to gift it to the petite if slightly plump Mrs. Fuller. While Mary Eliza suspected the gift had more to do with the fact that Mrs. Byas's sister had been just over five feet in height. She was grateful all the same. She wondered how her husband would have felt about it if he had realized that the gown cost more than the home she was standing in. She knew she'd have to tell him, but worried that he'd want to sell the dress to finance construction of a new building at the Institute. Usually, she agreed with him, but this was their eldest daughter's wedding. Of course, the dress changed everything. With such a dress, a small, intimate religious ceremony was becoming more and more remote. Now, they'd have to include Dr. Byas and his family, along with the other prominent families of the congregation: Dr. Adams, Dr. Bailey, the esteemed Dr. Hairston, along with Mr. Pace, from the bank, Mr. Church, Mr. Farnandis, of the Knights of Pythias, Mr. Willis, and Mr. Covington, and the young Dr. Atkins. She had thought that maybe Dr. Atkins was going to approach Desdemona after services a couple of times, but it looked now as if Mary Eliza had misread his glances, she mused. Out of courtesy, she knew that she'd have to issue invitations to Edward Crump, who controlled the local police, if she wanted to avoid any problems. He was running for mayor, so it never hurt to stay in his good graces. It was doubtful that he'd appear at a negro wedding, but he'd certainly take note if he wasn't invited. Her husband was already planning on inviting the rest of the town clergy, along with Professor Handy and Professor Hamilton, one of the most ardent advocates for negro education in the city. Mary sighed as she thought about all the daunting tasks in front of her: food, a hairdresser, and finishing the invitations. Thank goodness, all of the arrangements related to the church would be taken care of. She'd always been happy to stay on the sidelines and out of the church society. Her husband had certainly had that part right. She looked again at the fantastically expensive and elegant Worth gown. Maybe they should sell it. Ah, but they couldn't, since it was a gift. She sighed again, deeply this time.

Maud felt a little intimidated by the project but bolstered by her mother's assistance. As a lifelong dressmaker, very little daunted Vina. With a nod and her mouth full of pins, Vina pulled in the waist of the dress by several inches to fit the wasp-waisted slim young girl. "You know, my husband is a photographer, Mrs.

Fuller," Maud ventured. She hesitated to interrupt the frenetic activities, but she knew Mary and Desdemona were in danger of being completely overwhelmed.

"Oh, bless you, Maud! I had completely forgotten all about a photographer. And your husband, Henry isn't just any photographer, he's one of the best in the city," Mary answered, relieved.

"Ooh, that's right," Desdemona said, "Julia Hooks is your mother-in-law! That must be something", she finished. She looked over at Maud, and there was a lot left unsaid.

"Oh, are you interested in music?" Maud answered, nodding to show that she understood the unasked questions.

"I was at one time," Desdemona answered. Her grandmother, Louisa, who had been listening so quietly that the rest of the occupants of the living room had forgotten her presence suddenly boomed out her question, "Is she still married to that cursed man who killed her sister? I could never understand choosing your man over your own blood," she finished. She didn't seem to notice her daughter, Mary, flush with embarrassment.

"Well, you know, she runs a detention center for wayward boys now," Maud answered carefully.

Like Louisa, Vina had no compunction about saying what she thought, "Yes, she's still with that heartless bastard! I hope one day he gets what he deserves. Claiming to be one of the righteous and causing such an awful tragedy," she finished.

"Now, of course, Reverend Fuller would never do such a thing, and shame of poor child of god like that," she added.

"Amen" said the ladies in the room before everyone went back to their respective tasks.

****

The wedding was beautiful. It may not have been the social event of the year for all Memphians, but among the black community, it dominated the gossip and social scene for several months. Despite their sometimes turbulent friendship, Merilee had a prominent role in Desdemona's wedding. It was at the ceremony that she met the handsome and dashing young Dr. Deloney. The relationship wouldn't last between Merilee and the good doctor, but for one spring day in 1911, anything seemed possible.

By the time the wedding became last year's news, the Lysander Prince family was already expecting their first child. Shortly after that, Lysander's one time hero and sometimes nemesis, Robert Church Sr., died. His grieving widow, Anna, wasted no time in widow's weeds before she managed to ensure that neither of her husband's older children received a dime. She diverted the enormity of their inheritances to herself and that of her son, Robert Jr.

She disinherited her only daughter, Annette, when she discovered her daughter's proclivities for other women after entering her daughter's room unannounced. She attempted to force Annette into a life of religious solitude and contemplation with no success. For this, Annette was unable to forgive, and she spent the rest of her life working as a schoolteacher in Jackson, Tennessee, away from her family's judgment.

Desdemona was nursing her daughter, Harriet, when word of Robert Church's passing reached her ears. Strangely, her husband seemed unaffected, but her father-in-law, Langston, openly celebrated. After she and Lysander named their next child, a boy, after his father, Langston, they grew closer as a family. The senior Langston is often on hand with his wife, Dorothy, to see his grandson, Langston Henry say his first words, take his first steps, and complete the other rites of babyhood. The rumblings of war grew louder in Europe following the assignation of Duke Franz Ferdinand in a faraway land. It seemed a million miles away from Memphis.

By the time Little Harriet is toddling, Desdemona is pregnant again with her third child. War swept across Europe, into the Ottoman empire, creeping into the Pacific, Africa and parts of Asia. Poison gas attacks and trench warfare dominated but President Wilson remained steadfast against the war. Then unrest began in Russia as catastrophic war losses compounded food shortages. The local paper proclaimed a new way to shop as the Piggly Wiggly Grocery Store opened. Against the backdrop of international events, citizens could no longer put their heads in the sand, and continue to carry on as if nothing was happening.

Russian soldiers refused to fight a foreign war as their country fell apart. Desdemona could only rock her babies to sleep and attempt to comfort them, even as more and more disturbing news arrived. Shortly after, it all hit too close to home one night at Sunday supper. She had invited her parents, mainly so that her mother could entertain the children for a few hours, but they arrived with an earnest young man in tow.

"This is Georgie Lee," her mother started.

"No, let me introduce future Army officer, George Washington Lee," her father interrupted. "He's getting ready to head off to France, so we wanted him to have a nice home cooked meal before he goes. He used to work at the Gayoso Hotel before he headed off to Officer Training School up north, in Iowa. You know, your brother, Roland, is planning to go with him" her father finished.

Desdemona was a little shocked to see that the fresh-faced young man looked to be her age. She also couldn't believe that her baby brother was old enough to go off to play soldier and carry a gun. It didn't surprise her much. Roland had always been the first to volunteer, the first to join in. She imagined his enthusiasm and felt a little disappointed that he wasn't there to tell her himself. Roland was out, probably soothing a bevy of little girls' hearts, she thought. He had grown from a lovable scamp into a local heartthrob. She was glad that Linus hadn't changed. He was still interested in books, and school. He was planning on becoming a Reverend like his father and was working several part-time jobs to raise some money to start his own church nearby. He was too independent to want to take over his father's ministry, especially since their father showed no signs of slowing down. Desdemona sighed and brought her attention back to her guests.

She felt as old as Methuselah with two small children running around. She felt a bit self-conscious about the rounded belly that was only beginning to announce that baby number 3 was on his way.

All thoughts of her returning to school have been permanently put aside as she juggled a life filled with back-to-back pregnancies, diapers, breastfeeding, cooking, cleaning, and running a household while pleasing an eternally amorous husband.

One day, her mother, Mary arrived for their regular coffee date with a stranger in tow. The unknown woman is severe looking, with her hair pulled back tightly. Her clothing is neat and clean, in muted colors, and minimal frills. She is wearing a long, dark, canvas skirt, and a plain white blouse, high necked and long sleeves. She has a jacket that matches the skirt tucked over her arm. Serviceable black leather boots peek out from beneath her skirt. Desdemona is trying to decide if the woman is a traveling missionary as she gathers up the coffee tray in the kitchen.

As she prepares to pour the coffee, her mother introduces her companion. "Desdemona, this is *Doctor* Francis Kneeland. She lives down on St. Paul Avenue. She just recently joined our congregation."

Doctor Kneeland looks directly into Desdemona's face with something akin to expectation. As Desdemona begins the usual expected small talk, but Doctor Kneeland stops her, saying, "I know this isn't really appropriate for a social call, but I was talking to your mother the other day, and I wanted to meet you, and to bring you a copy of this." She drew a small book out of her leather bag. The book was entitled, "What every mother should know."

"It was written by a nurse, but it's actually quite good," Doctor Kneeland explained as Desdemona glanced at the title. The doctor also talked about using breastfeeding to space her pregnancies, but Desdemona didn't believe in outmoded practices of prolonged breastfeeding. She knew that modern women gave their babies formula to boost their nutrition and health, so she ignored most of what Doctor Kneeland said, while nodding and pouring more coffee.

Desdemona felt irritated at her mother for insinuating that her parenting skills were lacking. Later, as she sat and read thru the book, she felt outright fury. Her husband had insisted on installing a telephone when they moved into the small home on Pendleton Street. She grabbed up the received and spoke to the operator to have herself connected to her father at the Institute. Her parents didn't have a phone at home, and she wasn't quite ready to speak to her mother yet. She knew her father would take her side. "Daddy," she wailed, "Momma gave me a *disgusting* book by that immoral Sanger woman about family limitation! Why would she do that? I am an excellent mother."

Even the Reverend with his conservative values and heartfelt convictions had been dismayed by the rapidity of Desdemona's family growth, but he was equally outraged, horrified and disgusted by his wife's actions. However, despite his daughter's urging, he limited his reaction to this private family matter. Not a word was ever said to his newest congregant, or to the congregation as a whole. He did, however, have a long conversation with his wife, Mary, when he got home that evening.

He surprised himself by agreeing with many of her arguments, as he was deeply concerned as to the effects of nonstop pregnancy and childbirth would have on his darling, and beloved, eldest daughter. He promised his wife he would have a discussion with both Desdemona and her husband, as their pastor, about this issue, but early the next morning while at the office, he received a panicked call from Lysander.

"She lost the baby, and she won't stop bleeding! That Doctor Kneeland is here, but Desdemona won't let her help. I am going to have to take her to Hairston Hospital!" Lysander said, sounding more urgent and upset than the Reverend had ever heard.

"What do you mean she won't let the doctor treat her? She's your wife, don't let her refuse!" Reverend Fuller argued.

"Okay, okay, I will keep trying," Lysander promised, "but I have to go. She needs me now. I will call you back once we get to the hospital."

Reverend Fuller hung up the phone and then stared at his hands for a while. The day lengthened and he stayed in his office, with the door closed, while he prepared to leave for the hospital. He packed a small bag, with his trusted bible, and the oil of anointing. He carefully placed one of his neatly folded vestments into the bag. Then he sat and waited for Lysander to call.

Just as he was beginning to pace his office, near noontime, Lysander called back, to tell him that the bleeding had stopped and that Desdemona, was weak, but safe at home. She had been distraught about the loss of their child, but after a sleeping draft, was resting quietly. As the reverend offered to come with his wife to look after Desdemona, Lysander cut him off.

"No. Desdemona was close to death, and I was close to losing them both. She made it very clear to me that she does not wish to see *your wife*," Lysander said, sounding upset himself.

****

Harriet, 1917

"I was a Leap Year baby, and it seems to me that I have been leaping ever since."

Augusta Savage, 2019

"My granddaddy says my aunt is an African princess," her small voice said proudly. She was on the playground, playing with several girls from her class. Roberta had just shown everyone her brand new set of jacks, and now the rest of the girls were looking at Roberta with something akin to awe. Harriet felt like she had to show that she was important too.

"Really? And how comes you here in Memphis?" her best friend, Cora said, curiosity and excitement overcoming her suspicion. Some of the other girls weren't really her friends, and they would have taken any excuse to taunt Harriet, but they paused the game of jacks to wait for Harriet's answer.

A student teacher walking past, catching part of the conversation, also slowed her stride to listen. The girls were too occupied waiting on Harriet to notice. Roberta, with her jacks now forgotten, was just waiting to pounce on whatever answer Harriet offered.

"My aunt Daphne, she's from Memphis. She's my daddy's older sister," Harriet said, confident after her grandfather had explained the connection to her. "When she was here, she married a man whose family was from a country in Africa, and they were royalty there. After they got married, they took a big boat over there, and she became a princess. She has a whole room full of pretty dresses, shiny shoes, and fancy jewelry! She even rides in a big carriage!" Harriet said confidently.

Miss Evelyn Sillers had heard enough. The young student teacher strode forward and grabbed Harriet by the ear. "Now, young lady, I've heard enough of these tall tales. You know it's a sin to lie to your classmates like this." She began to pull a startled Harriet towards the schoolroom.

Harriet remained surprisingly composed for a six-year-old. "No, Miss Sillers, my aunt really is a princess!" she insisted.

The young, inexperienced, white teacher flushed. She wasn't going to let her authority be challenged, least of all by a colored child. "If you don't stop telling these lies, I'll take the paddle to you girl! There ain't no such thing as a nigger princess. You don't know much of anything! Fine clothes, jewels, and fancy carriages. Don't you know that all the colored people over there are just a bunch of dirty, naked savages?" Miss Sillers railed at the defiant child.

Harriet remained determined. "But she is a princess, and I can prove it!" Out of her pocket came a much cherished, slightly faded photograph. It showed two open air carriages, filled with dignified looking black people in formal turn-of-the-century clothing. In the photo, the carriages were surrounded by a street lined with crowds of cheering black people in a variety of styles of dress. Their mouths were open in the photo as they cheered, and many in the crowd held up some flags. The focus of the photo was on the occupants of the second carriage.

"That's my auntie, right there in the second carriage, the one with the baby," Harriet offered earnestly, her young face looking up at Miss Sillers.

"How dare you!" Miss Sillers screeched before taking the photo and tearing it down the middle, rending the precious photograph in two. Then, before Harriet could react, with her mouth still open in the shape of an O, Miss Sillers grabbed her upper arm with her left hand. She dragged Harriet away from the playground, into the schoolroom, where a leather strap hung from the wall. Harriet reached out with her other arm to grab the beloved photo as she was being pulled away. Ms. Sillers's face was scarlet with rage, and she brought down the strap against Harriet's bare legs.

Harriet began fighting, and struggling to get away, which only infuriated the young teacher more. "Damn you, nigger, stand still," she yelled.

A startled Harriet did. She had never been spoken to like that. When she stopped fighting to look at Miss Sillers, Miss Sillers used the opportunity to strike two more blows against the little girl's legs. Harriet couldn't keep back a scream.

"What is going on in here?" boomed Mrs. Humphrey. Mrs. Humphrey was Harriet's regular teacher and was generally strict but kind to her students. She went by the title of Mrs. despite being an unmarried woman in her 40's. She was white, tall, stout, and slightly plain with a fair complexion that was prone to burn. Mrs. Humphrey had been teaching at the negro schoolhouse since she was a student teacher herself back when it had been at the cramped building on Orleans Street.

Mrs. Humphrey's parents had been stout abolitionists, and protestant ministers. They had moved from Ohio to Memphis shortly after the Union occupation of the city, to set up schools for colored children. Her mother had been the headmaster at this very school when Mrs. Humphrey was a child.

Miss Sillers stopped mid-stroke from bringing down a fourth blow on the little girl. She brushed back a lock of hair which had escaped her tightly twisted bun. She was panting with effort, and as she regained her breath, she said, "I was just," puff, puff, "teaching this nigger child," puff, puff, "that she can't go around telling lies, willy-nilly." she said, as she regained her composure.

"Now, Harriet," Mrs. Humphrey said sternly, "you've always been such a well-behaved child. What in the world has gotten into you?"

Harriet was so relieved to see Mrs. Humphrey that she burst into tears. "I wasn't lying Mrs. Humphrey, I wasn't! She's just a mean lady. I told her the truth! My aunt is an African princess – and I even showed her a picture as proof."

Mrs. Humphrey reached down to retrieve the cherished family heirloom that Harriet produced from a pocket in her dress. It was torn into two pieces. She looked at it briefly before laying the two pieces on a desk. "Now," she said soothingly, "that's a nice photo, Harriet." She continued in a calm, steady voice, "but, are you sure that's your family, and that it's in Africa? I don't know where it is, but I can tell you that it doesn't look like Africa. It's really hot there, and these people are wearing too many clothes."

She looked at the pretty child and continued, "I don't think that is your family, Harriet. I don't know who told you that wild tale, but they really got your goat, I think," her voice kindly.

She continued, "I am sorry to say this, Harriet, but your family came from slaves. A long time ago, people brought your family here to sell them, and well, frankly, because of that, your family didn't even have its own last name, much less a bunch of baubles. In fact, your last name is probably taken from the people that owned you. I don't know any Prince families around here, but that just means that maybe your folks came from Mississippi, like Miss Sillers," Mrs. Humphreys said with a pointed look at the young student teacher.

Harriet looked crushed as she silently took the two pieces of the photo from the desk and placed it carefully back in the pocket of her dress. Her whole face had crumpled up when Mrs. Humphrey was talking. Mrs. Humphrey felt a pang of regret, but it was best to tell the truth about these things, she thought. She glanced over at the student teacher and felt the urge to slap Miss Sillers for the petty smirk she saw on her face.

"Now, Harriet, you still have ten minutes to play before we start class again. Go on out to the yard she said, smoothing down Harriet's braids almost unconsciously. Harriet really was a nice child. This whole episode is just a shame, she thought. She waited until Harriet left before she turned back to Miss Sillers.

Mrs. Humphrey took a really good look at Miss Sillers. Evelyn was exceedingly fair skinned, with thin, strawberry blonde hair, and pale lashes that disappeared against her pale skin. She was heavily freckled with small deep set and watery blue eyes. Her mouth often looked pinched, like it did right now, as she pursed her lips, looking dissatisfied. This hid her crooked teeth and overlapping canine teeth that gave her a bit of a wolfish look at times. Miss Sillers looked back at Mrs. Humphrey and stood up a little straighter. "Why, she looks sly," Mrs. Humphrey thought, "she thinks she's getting away with this."

"How old are you, Miss Sillers?" Mrs. Humphrey asked in a cool, calm tone.

"Nineteen, ma'am," she answered almost bobbing her head in her eagerness to show her maturity. Evelyn was a student at the Ward-Belmont College in Nashville. She came from a prominent family in Northern Mississippi.

"And do you think a nineteen-year-old woman should be picking on and mistreating a six-year-old child?" Mrs. Humphrey asked, with absolute ice in her voice.

Miss Sillers jutted out her chin, and answered insolently, "That child was putting on airs, more so than any dumb nigger has a right to. I was just teaching her the error of her ways."

"And do you think that's what this job is?" Mrs. Humphrey said, sternly. She was too enraged to allow Miss Sillers to answer before continuing.

"Our job is not to judge, lest we be judged. Our job is to take these sons and daughters of Ham, for they have been cursed by God, and to bring these wayward and simple souls to the Lord. If you should so dedicate your life in this fashion, so will be your heavenly reward".

"If you do not have the virtues required to serve our Lord, it is best that we know that now, and discharge you from said service, and that is what I am doing. Return now to Nashville and I will speak with Dean Cox and Professor Hefley about your unsuitability. Go now, gather your things, and leave," she finished.

Miss Sillers momentarily looked stricken, and Mrs. Humphreys felt a moment of compassion. "Evelyn, dear," she said, putting her hand on Miss Siller's sleeve, "Not every young woman is meant to have a career. Maybe you just aren't suited to working with children," she finished kindly.

Miss Sillers looked affronted. "I'm vice-president of my year," she said haughtily, "maybe you are just an old crumb tabby!" She angrily grabbed her umbrella, and her scarf before stalking off. Mrs. Humphrey sat down at her desk and pulled out a piece of parchment and began to write a letter to the LeMoyne Christian Association, seeking a qualified student teacher to assist her at the schoolhouse. With that, Mrs. Humphreys put the incident behind her, as she placed the completed letter into an envelope. Then she went to the schoolhouse doorway to call for her charges to return to class.

****

That evening, before evening chores, Harriet approached her grandfather, Langston. Since his son's wife had almost died a few months ago, Langston and his wife had taken to coming around Lysander's house more frequently. Desdemona acted like nothing had happened, but her face carried a grief that left her eyes glistening and her heart remained heavy. She would turn away if her own family was mentioned, so Dorothy and Langston had stepped in to provide the young family with support. Langston had been surprised by the precociousness of their eldest daughter Harriet and liked to spend time with the sometimes overly proper, yet highly intelligent child.

"Grandfather," Harriet said formally, "why did you tell me that we had royalty in our family?" Her face and eyes were reddened as if she'd been crying.

Langston, who was now in his early 60's, remained a fine figure of a man, but he sensed a firestorm beneath the formality, so he kept his face calm and impassive as he answered, "Now, dear moppet, what is the problem?"

He paused for a moment as he watched his little granddaughter wipe away the vestiges of tears as she recited the events of the day and drew the torn photograph out of her dress pocket. She stared at the floor, ashamed as he took the two halves of the precious image. "I just took it to school to show my friends," she sniffed, fighting back new tears. She felt terrible that the family picture had been damaged.

Langston could see that she was already upset, so he didn't let her darling granddaughter see how wounded he felt seeing the photograph rent in two.

Instead, he traveled back to the cold dreary Saturday in January of 1896, when he received a surprise visitor. When he opened the door, he saw a very prim and proper looking woman standing on the threshold, unaccompanied. She had a thick woolen shawl pulled tightly around her as defense against the cold dampness that seemed to seep right into a person's marrow. She looked up expectantly at him, and he found himself inviting her in before he knew what he was doing. She settled herself on the settee in the small parlor as he lit additional lanterns and called to his wife to brew some tea. Finally, after what seemed like an eternity, after she shook off the damp, the woman began to speak and offer an introduction.

"My, my it's damp and chill out there today," she said. "It seems particularly so after two years in the hot and humid climes of Africa," she continued, as Dorothy entered the parlor with a tray of tea. She seemed to be waiting for some sort of reaction from the Princes. Once Dorothy completed the tea service, she sat next to her husband across from the strange woman.

"Oh, excuse me, but I am jumping ahead," the strange woman said with a bit of an embarrassed laugh. "I am just pleased and a bit overcome by my visit here today." She coughed into a delicate linen handkerchief and then quickly crumpled it into her palm.

She did not look a bit overcome, Dorothy thought, as she looked over the woman from head to toe. Pale, perhaps, and a bit too thin, but not overcome. She looked at her husband with an unpleasant question in her mind.

He raised one eyebrow at her and looked a bit shocked, as if he had read Dorothy's mind. They both then returned their focus to the stranger on the settee.

Finally, after taking a sip of the warm brew, which seemed to fortify her, the strange woman, again spoke, "Oh dear me, I did it again. I humbly apologize. My name is Doctor Georgia Patton, and I recently returned from a two-year trip to Liberia. I am here to bring salutations and news from Mrs. Marion Johnson. That's your daughter, Daphne, I believe."

That was when she had reached into a worn leather Boulevard bag and produced the photograph that he now so lovely cradled. "This is your new granddaughter," Georgia said, "Florida Monrovia Johnson," as she pointed to the infant in his daughter's arms. Tears came to his eyes as he thought about his long dead wife, Florida, and how she would have loved to see her namesake.

As he came back to the present, he said to his prim little granddaughter, , "Yes, that's my darling daughter, Daphne,"as he smoothed the torn edges, "And she is part of an important African political dynasty. It's not royalty, really, but more like our country with presidents except that there are only a few people that run the country. She married the nephew of one president, and later her own daughter, Florida, married the president a few years ago. Daphne's daughter is the baby in this picture," he answered.

"We can take the photo to the Hooks photography shop and see if they can repair it," he said to soothe the young girl. Harriet nodded hopefully but would not be soothed.

"But why didn't they believe me, grandfather?" Harriet asked in a small voice that speared his soul.

Langston didn't have an answer for the heartbroken child.

****

Dorothy was in the kitchen helping Desdemona to clean up after dinner. It had been become part of their routine, for her to assist the younger woman in the evenings before bed during their frequent visits.

"Dessie, I'd like to ask you something," she said as she dried a dish. Her lovely daughter-in-law looked up, with a wary expression on her face. Dorothy didn't want to press her daughter-in-law, but in this instance, she felt she had to.

"Have you talked to your mother since the accident?" she asked. Desdemona's face turned to stone as she shook her head no. Dorothy pressed on, "you know you should. She's your mother and she's worried about you."

The look that Desdemona gave Dorothy was enough to stop her heart. Her lovely, sweet countenance was completely transformed into something hideous and filled with hate. Her face twisted into a sneer of rage, as she answered back, "That! Witch! Killed! My! Baby!"

Dorothy was taken aback, and aghast. "How long have you been thinking this? It's been years since your miscarriage. You know it isn't true!" She looked at Desdemona with sadness and said, "She's your mother, all she's ever done is love you."

Desdemona just shook her head no, her mouth a cruel thin line. She challenged Dorothy with her eyes, as she jutted her chin out before spewing out her pain, "I haven't been able to keep a baby since she cursed me. I've lost three babies since my darling little one went away. All I ever wanted was to give my husband a big house full of babies and she made it so I can't even do that!"

Looking at the stubborn set of Desdemona's jaw, Dorothy became angry herself, saying "Dessie! I am ashamed of you! I think of you as my own child. You know better than that – you come from God-fearing folks. How dare you blame your mother for your tragedy! She's not a witch, she doesn't have magic powers. She's just a woman who loves her child. It was God who determined what happened to you – and we don't get to know the reasons why."

Dorothy was fuming now, and she continued, "Maybe that child wasn't ready for the world. Maybe the Lord didn't think the world was ready for that child. We don't know. But it's certain that we do know that your mother had mothing to do with it! As for any other miscarriages, that's very tragic but certainly no one's fault. Sometimes life just doesn't turn out the way we planned."

Desdemona said nothing, and turned away. She was finished with this conversation. She began to wipe the kitchen counter in a back-and-forth motion with her back to Dorothy.

"You can't really believe this?" Dorothy finally gasped, in exasperation, staring at Desdemona's rigid carriage.

Desdemona stopped wiping the countertop, and in a calculated and slow motion, turned and looked at Dorothy. With an emotionless voice and calm cold logic, she stated, "How else do you explain it? She gives me a book about *'family limitation'* and brings a doctor to the house, and that very day, I lose my child? I don't see how it could be anything else. God didn't bring that filthy book to my house."

Dorothy took a deep breath and let out an enormous sigh. "My dear, dear child! Don't you see that perhaps God was working through your mother? That he placed that doctor in your path, so that he would be able to aid you in your time of need? God is the only one who could have known what was about to happen, so then yes, he did set that book in your path. And for good reason! Don't you know that your poor mother was just worried about you, and your health. Having so many babies, so fast! It causes problems to happen, and now they have. Your mother was just trying to protect you from this." Despite her frustration, Dorothy's eyes were kind and filled with compassion for her daughter-in-law as she spoke. She reached out and took Dessie's hands in hers and looking her directly in the eye.

She took another deep breath before continuing. "Secondly, young lady, you need to take stock of yourself and remember something. I don't care how angry or sad you are – family is everything! Family is all that we really have or will ever have! This is exactly when you need your family!" Dorothy was so upset that she had to pause and take a breath to stay calm before continuing.

"How dare you turn your back on your family! Who do you think you are? That's the real sin here. That you think that you have the right to turn your back on your mother, the woman who gave birth to you and raised you, just because things don't go your way. That's what the rest of us call life – and it's these struggles that are why, no matter what, we have to stay together as a family."

Dorothy didn't pause for breath this time, as she continued, "Maybe you didn't know that growing up as a Fuller, though I have a hard time thinking that the Reverend would omit something like that. But here, in the Prince family, we stand together and we stay together, because family is what we have, even when we had nothing more than our names. So, if you are going to be part of the Prince family, then you had better change your ways," Dorothy finished.

Desdemona had a thousand angry retorts, but she bit them back and swallowed them whole when Dorothy came forward and enclosed her in her arms, pulling her head against her soft bosom. The smell of magnolias and laundry soap enveloped Desdemona and she felt safe. She nodded against Dorothy's chest, and stayed there for several minutes, as she cried out her grief. Dorothy stroked her hair and kept one arm around her.

****

March 1919

Desdemona caught her breath as she opened the screen door. The young man in the army union seemed vaguely familiar. He had a look of sadness on his face that took her breath away, and she suddenly felt frightened.

"May I help you?" she asked after a moment when he didn't speak. He coughed and cleared his throat and straightened his jacket.

"I don't know if you remember me, Mrs. Prince but my name is George Washington Lee. We met once before here at your house," he said. He paused again, seeming to gather his courage.

"I just came from your parents' house," he started. He stopped as he saw Desdemona's face harden. "Umm," he continued, "your mother told me to stop by here personally. She said you would want to talk to me. I was your brother's commanding officer in the 920th division. We served together in France, and I was there when he was mortally wounded," he finished. He didn't know why the hard look in her glossy eyes intimidated him more than his commanding officers had, but it did.

She finally stepped back and opened the front door to allow him to enter. She busied herself in the kitchen for a moment as he settled himself on the settee in the parlor. She used the precious time to gather her composure as she prepared a cup of the still hot morning coffee for her visitor.

After she completed the ritual, and Officer Lee was slowly sipping the dark brew, she slowly lowered herself into a nearby chair, feeling as if her limbs had lost all their bones and were now just floppy pieces of flesh. She felt a renewed grief at his presence. Her parents had notified her of his death, of course, but with their estrangement, it had been limited to a short note. She had refused to attend any of the memorial ceremonies, as if refusing to attend and accept the loss meant that Roland was out there somewhere, in France, breaking local girls' hearts and performing pranks. This made it all too real. She listened intently as Officer Lee began speaking again, as he slowly unfolded the course of events leading to her brother's death. She forced herself to focus on small details to keep herself from falling apart. She wished Lysander was here to help her through this, and in this moment, cursed him for his absence.

"What did you say about the cart and the women?" she asked again, confused as Officer Lee explained about battlefield radiographs.

"These things, there are called X-rays," he said, "and they let the doctors look inside of people. After the shell hit the trench, and Roland was injured, they used this machine to look at his wounds," he replied. He didn't say that when Roland was pulled out of the trench, he was so covered in dirt, mud, and blood that it was impossible to see his injuries. There were some obvious pieces of shrapnel that had shredded his extremities and were protruding grotesquely as the young infantryman screamed relentlessly, but they couldn't see any damage to his torso. Half of his face had been blown off, making his screaming, punctuated by gurgling and bubbling, a most horrible site. Officer Lee still had nightmares about Roland, but he kept that to himself.

He held back these details and continued, "the x-ray showed that he had some large fragments lodged in his abdomen. The doctors rushed your brother to surgery, but he didn't make it," he finished. He didn't tell her that her brother had survived the surgery, and had returned to the field hospital ward, heavily bandaged from head to toe, but that his abdominal wound had festered and turned gangrenous, with the tell-tale stench of approaching death. She needed to be spared that, he rationalized. Roland had moaned and suffered for two days before a kindly

French surgeon and his nurse had taken pity on his devastated form. The nurse had gently spoon-fed laudanum into his ruined mouth until he had slipped into a coma, and his writhing, and moaning stopped. Shortly after, Roland had slipped away entirely, and Officer Lee had taken a pen and paper to notify his family of his passing, using a more sanitized version highlighting Roland's bravery, loyalty, and sacrifice for his nation. Officer Lee wished that he could sanitize his memories the same way. He hoped that by coming here and speaking to Roland's favorite sister, some of the memories could be laid to rest.

But Desdemona sensed the truth, or at least appeared to suspect that her brother's death hadn't been as quick or clean as he'd laid it out. He could see it in her glistening, dark eyes. He was suddenly in a hurry to leave, before she could ask him something that would shatter his control. He'd done what he'd promised himself he would do, so now it was time to go.

As he stood to leave, Desdemona said, "but why did it take you so long to come here?"

George looked at her, with sympathy in his gaze. "I'm very sorry for your loss ma'am, but I just returned to Memphis yesterday."

After she showed the officer to the door, Desdemona broke down completely. She thought about calling her husband or her mother for comfort, but as she sobbed she thought, 'this is my pain alone.' At the same time, she resented them for not being there as she sat rocking on the floor, tears streaming as she thought of Roland, his bright sunny smile, his infectious laugh, and eternally upbeat nature. 'Why do they always take the joy from the world', she thought bitterly. After she finished crying for her beloved brother, she cried for her lost babies. When she was too tired to cry any longer, she pushed herself up to her feet, dusted off her hands, and washed her face. Then she went to the kitchen and began chopping vegetables to make the family dinner. Harriet and Langston would be home from school soon.

That evening, just as she was cleaning up after dinner, her mother came by. She came to the kitchen door and let herself in as Desdemona was drying dishes. She didn't say anything, but just opened her arms, walked forward, and embraced Desdemona right where she stood by the sink. She held Desdemona for several long minutes until Desdemona took her arms from around her and stepped back. Desdemona looked at her mother, and said, "Thank you." Then she turned around and left the kitchen. Mary Eliza watched her retreat before turning around and leaving through the kitchen door.

****

Mary Eliza Fuller and her daughter, Desdemona, never regained the closeness they had previously had, but when Mary Eliza died of breast cancer in 1925, Desdemona was at her bedside.

Book Three: Lysander, Desdemona and the spectre of death 1930 - 1932

By 1930, Lysander had realized that the way to wealth and success for his family wasn't through politics or public office. He didn't have his father's drive for public recognition, but for all that he lacked that ambition, he didn't lack the desire for prosperity or security. One day, while helping his youngest child with their homework, Lysander decided to take his cue from Benjamin Franklin. That night, as his wife sat at her dressing table as they prepared for bed, he turned to her and said, "Nothing can be said to be certain but death and taxes."

Dessie, who was applying cold cream to her face, said, "excuse me?" and turned around to face Lysander. Lysander who had removed his shirt and tie, was sitting on the bed and reaching down to unhook his sock garters, as he repeated, "Death and taxes. No one escapes either."

Now that he had Dessie's rapt attention, he stopped undressing to give his wife his complete attention as he explained. "I've been thinking about it, my beloved, and I want to open a funeral home. I've already talked to a guy named Walter Wills, up in Cleveland who is willing to teach me all about the business. He says it won't take more than a couple of months."

Desdemona stopped brushing her hair, brush still mid-air. "Cleveland? Why do you have to go all the way up north for something like that? And a funeral home?" Desdemona looked closely at his face, looking for a hint of his crooked grin that was the hallmark sign that he was putting her on. He did that sometimes. He liked to say things just to startle her. But in the years since they married, he was also the only one who could pull her out of her grief when they'd lost a child, and then again, when her family was affected by numerous tragedies. Most recently her brother, Linus, had been senselessly murdered by the Petting Party Bandit.

Linus had been on a date when the couple had been attacked by Charles Barr. Linus had died after being shot several times trying to protect his longtime girlfriend, Zelda Foster. Desdemona had nearly become unhinged at hearing of his death, and to this day, she blamed Boss Crump for his murder. Barr had been working for the political kingpin when the string of slayings linked to Charles Barr had occurred. A year later, when her baby sister, Denise, hung herself, only Lysander's dedicated care had kept her from being institutionalized. She had been almost catatonic for weeks, listless and almost comatose at times. Lysander along with his aging and now widowed mother, Dorothy, and his half-sister, Tamar, had provided her with round-the-clock care and support, while other relatives took in their children temporarily. It was Lysander's unwavering love that helped Desdemona fight her way back to the surface. She was still plagued with melancholia at times, but as time passed, she seemed to settle back into their quiet, normal, if unassuming life.

As she looked into the face of the man who had loved and stood by her through the hard times, she was amused to play into his latest prank. With that in mind, she waited patiently for the punchline. Instead, Lysander launched into what must have been a well-practiced salesman's pitch before answering her initial questions. Finally, as he wound down, he said, "I've got to go to Cleveland because that's where Mr. Wills is. He has the biggest funeral home owned by a negro in the whole state of Ohio, so he knows what he's doing. He's also the only one that answered my letters asking about the funeral home business. He's offered to apprentice me, as long as I commit to helping him six days a week during my training. He is even offering room and board."

After Desdemona took a few minutes moment to seriously consider everything he was saying, she agreed, surprising Lysander by saying, "but only if you contact Mr. Wills and he agrees that Langston Henry can come learn too. But don't stay gone too long, I need help keep an eye on Harriet. I swear that girl runs wild, "she finished, changing the subject.

Lysander smiled now that the issue was settled and said with a flourish, as he climbed into bed, "Everybody dies. You never know. Maybe one day the body we will be burying, will be mine." Desdemona shuddered at the thought.

****

Within just a few weeks, Lysander and Langston Henry were headed north on the bus to Cleveland to study with Mr. Wills. While Langston Henry hadn't been pleased to hear his mother's suggestion, when reminded of his finial duty, he said goodbye to his sometime girlfriend, Rhonda. She was a sixteen-year-old, with rich brown skin and buxom beauty who had started turning heads at the age of 12. She'd already left the schoolroom and she wanted to grow up and play house as fast as she could. For Langston, it was easier to leave the city than to leave her sweet smile and loving heart. So, he packed his bag without protest. He was, after all, a dutiful son. It was also a chance for adventure outside of Memphis and away from everything he'd ever known.

The sun was just beginning to set as he stepped up into the Smith Motorcoach. Behind his father, the tall lanky 16-year-old asked, with what sounded like trepidation, "Dad, have you ever been up north?" Lysander waited until they had both made their way to seats in the colored section at the back of the bus before answering. He remained quiet, with his eyes downward as they slipped into the few seats available in that section. Several rows in front of the division remained empty. Lysander stowed their small suitcases overhead, but kept a small burlap knapsack in his lap, along with their winter coats which would serve as blankets during the trip in the poorly heated bus. Once settled, he answered in low tones, "Son, I have never been farther away from Memphis than Corinth, Mississippi. All I know is that it is cold up North."

Langston Henry leaned close to hear his dad. They were both dressed in their heaviest sweaters, despite the only mildly cool weather, in order to better utilize the space in their small bags. As the bus pulled away from the Memphis downtown to head northeast towards Evansville, Indiana, both Princes looked out the window as they left behind the only home they'd ever known. For the older Prince, it was with much trepidation. For the younger, barely contained excitement. The senior Prince worried about the family he left behind, while Langston was only too happy to shed himself of the clingy girl next door. It was time for him to be a man and take on the world, he thought. He leaned his head against the window, as the dark highway was punctuated every so often with a small spattering of light; headlights from passing cars, the occasional lonely house, or the lights of small cities in the distance.

****

"Now, wake up boy!"

Gruff shaking accompanied the loud voices that pierced into his consciousness, bringing Lysander instantly awake. He looked over and quickly nudged his son awake too before the two shadowy figures in front of him could reach over and touch his son. He shielded his eyes with a hand against the glare of the flashlight aimed at his face, and nudged his sleepy son again, to caution him to remain silent.

Around him, several other negro passengers had been similarly disturbed, and like himself, all waited silently. Small clouds of condensation showed the quickening of breath and heightened anxiety among the silent passengers.

"Where you going, boy?" asked the loud voice attached to a big shadowy figure. The harsh heat of sour breath hit his face like a slap.

"Ohio, sir," Lysander answered with his eyes downcast. He kept his voice quiet, respectful, and resisted the urge to stand up straight to his full height of 6'2".

"And what are you niggers going to do in Ohio?" said the second voice with a snigger. Lysander made a silent prayer that Langston Henry stayed quiet, like he'd instructed before they'd left Memphis. As Langston started to answer, the first shadow elbowed him in the sternum, saying "Not you, I want to hear the young nigger answer."

"We're going to see my uncle, sir," Langston Henry answered as they'd rehearsed before leaving. Lysander was grateful that his son spoke quietly, and calmly even as he felt angry himself. He careful schooled his features to remain bland and neutral. The two men moved on to the next passengers. Lysander nudged Langston to stay at attention just as Langston started to relax.

The men went passenger by passenger, asking questions, demanding identification in some cases, and even searching through coat pockets, purses, and valises. As they reached the end of the row, they used one of the flashlights to poke a heavyset, dark skinned, middle-aged man.

"Hey, don't blow your wig, copper," the man complained in a mild tone. Before Langston even realized what was happening, the two men had forced the man off the bus. There were several dull thuds and one loud crack, followed by the sound of glass breaking and the loss of one of the flashlight beams. Then a laughing voice called out, "Welcome to Kentucky, niggers!"

Langston Henry looked towards the front of the bus as the driver re-entered. He saw what looked like an average white family looking back: a father, mother and two small children. The mother looked at the passengers in the back section of the bus in horror, and the father made a face of disgust, then anger as his younger child started to cry.

The bus driver started the engine, and the bus took off, leaving the middle-aged passenger behind. Lysander put his arm around Langston and they sat erect with their necks straight and faces forward as the bus pulled back onto the lonely highway.

****

The next six months passed quickly, as Lysander and Langston learned the mortuary business. For Lysander, he tried to learn as much as possible, working extra days and hours with Mr. Wills.

Mr. Wills for his part welcomed the Princes to the business and their dinner table as if they were indeed family. The thought made Lysander chuckle as he watched Mr. Willis's fourteen-year-old granddaughter, Loretta, peep shyly at Langston from underneath her long, thick, black lashes. The lashes framed those big, brown eyes that looked adoringly in his son's direction. For his part, while enjoying her childish admiration, Langston heeded his father's words of caution and stayed a respectful distance from the bashful Loretta. This would prove wise, particularly after Lysander received a letter from his wife, just weeks before their trip was scheduled to end. Lysander kept the contents to himself, but knew that there was a lot more than a new business waiting for the Princes when they returned home.

In fact, it was Desdemona, and a very heavily pregnant Rhonda and her father that awaited their arrival in Memphis. But despite this, Langston Henry refused to be dragged to the alter. Instead, after dodging a literal shotgun wedding, the Princes, father and son, got to work opening and operating their new funeral home. It's success was a foregone conclusion; as the second funeral home catering to the black population, after T.H. Hays and Sons, in a city best described by a northern journalist as Murder City, USA. After a few short months, but plenty of back breaking labor, blood, sweat and tears, business was booming.

But unfortunately, Lysander's prediction came true all too soon, and in 1932, after a massive heart attack, it was Langston Henry who prepared him to be buried at Mt. Zion cemetery in the Prince Chapel. While Lysander had taken after his grandfather, Frederick in matters spiritual, Catherine, the family matriarch, had overseen the construction of the family chapel before her own death in 1891. Lysander was laid to rest, not far from his father and mother, and grandparents. A tiny urn containing the remains of the tiny lost child was placed in the casket before Langston and his mother, Desdemona, surprisingly strong, dry-eyed and clear headed, laid their beloved Lysander to rest.

After his death, to everyone's surprise, Desdemona took the reins of the funeral home business, with her son flanking her. The business grew and grew, and Desdemona bloomed with new authority. Still youthful and attractive, she fended off numerous marriage proposals. She was too busy enjoying her independence to consider another serious romantic relationship. Besides, she still missed Lysander so much. He was the only reason she'd held together so far to keep his dream going.

****

Langston Henry & Bernice, 1934 - 1940

After a couple of years of running the funeral home full-time with his mother, marriage and fatherhood didn't seem like such a terrible proposition. But then again, it may have been because Bernice had the sweetest smile east of the Mississippi. Langston Henry had met Bernice at the Peabody hotel where she was a pastry maker. He was there to interview a young man who was working as a lobby assistant. The business was expanding, and Lysander Prince & Sons needed more help.

He didn't find an employee that day. The young man never showed up and he was left to cool his heels in the alley behind the Peabody for over an hour. That's when he met Bernice Davis, who knocked him off his feet when she suddenly swung open a door from the kitchen to the alley. Langston hadn't even noticed the door. She had a large basket of trash in her hands that was taller than she was, and she just barreled out the door at a determined march. It wasn't until she heard a loud grunt and connected with a solid body that she'd even realized what she'd done. Even then, she'd barely had time to blurt her apologizes and brush some stray food scraps off of Langston before she'd had to race back into the kitchen to finish the pastries for the dinner service. Langston hadn't even gotten her name, but he did get a glimpse of a hazel eyed, freckle-faced girl blushing to the roots of her frizzy, light brown hair. He hurriedly brushed himself off, and then waited in the alley for the next employee to appear. He'd hoped against hope that the hazel-eyed girl would return, but he settled for a chambermaid who was able to give him a name in exchange for his physical description of the little steamroller.

After his father died, his mom became obsessed with learning to drive the old Ford that they had bought second hand. That is, until the day she had to hand crank the car in a sudden downpour. Then sodden and dripping, she'd had to steer the beast on slick streets, while shivering, because there was limited roofing. That had cooled her enthusiasm pretty quickly, leaving the 19-year-old

Langston Henry to pilot the old Ford around town. He liked to cruise downtown Beale Street, and then, sneak thru the Pinch. His mother would have had his head, if she'd known, but that's what made it fun! Now he used the Ford with a purpose. He would wait outside the Peabody every evening for Bernice to leave work. She wouldn't let him give her a ride home in the car, but she would let him walk her home. They started off talking about silly things, but then progressed to talking about dreams, wishes, and hopes. These can often be equally silly, at that age, but both of them had experienced enough tragedies and pain to have the kind of dreams that actually mean something. As they talked every evening, and then talked some more, in open view of her parents on the porch, they talked about their hopes, which became shared hopes. Not for the usual material things, but for a better world, for a small piece of happiness to call their own. Gradually, much more gradually in Bernice's case, they came to see that the best way to achieve this modest portion of happiness, love, and support was together. It wasn't so much of a whirlwind romance, as it was a slow, rolling boil. When Bernice finally consented to go to the movies with Langston at the Palace theater, ostensibly to see another Fay Wray screamer, Bernice's family already considered him kin. So much so, that all the subterfuge just to see the latest Mae West film was almost comical. By the time the couple had made it through to "I'm no Angel" in the Fall of 1933, the attraction was undeniable, but if Bernice's family had already accepted Langston Henry as one of their own, Bernice was barely known to Desdemona. She certainly didn't know the depth of their feelings, or the frequency of her son's attentions.

In the March of 1934, when the young couple snuck off in the old Ford to Arkansas to get married, only part of the couple's family was surprised. The bigger surprise was that Langston Henry suddenly got busy being a husband and father. As busy as he was with the funeral home, he still managed to ensure that Bernice began to birth babies annually. No one was happier than Bernice's mother-in-law, Desdemona, who shared in her joy with each and every new baby. When the oldest son, and namesake died at 3, only Desdemona could comfort Bernice. She knew exactly what to say, because she knew the pain of loss. She was there for Bernice over the next fifteen years; for all of the births, as well as two more losses. Every time Bernice added to the family, Desdemona's heart swelled. This now, this giant, wonderful, chaotic, noisy family filled the hole in her heart.

As for Bernice, Desdemona and her endless outpouring of love and support made all the difference. Before the babies, Desdemona had been cool, and standoffish. Now, Bernice was one of them and a prized member at that, for her continued production of the Prince line. Langston had a sister, it was true, but Harriet wasn't spoken of in polite company.

If Bernice was aware of the frequent cards and letters that Langston had been hiding away in a box in the back of the closet, she never let on. She certainly knew about them after they got married, yet she never once asked. If she knew why she continued to hide the unopened letters after his death, she never once gave a clue.

Harriet, 1928 - 1944

The whimsical and charmingly formal child became livelier as the European war wound down, her beloved grandfather died, and the great pandemic of death eased its grip on the city at the beginning of 1920. It wasn't the dreaded Yellowjack, but the Spanish lady spread fear that infected the adults around her. Then just as she desperately needed her mother to help her make sense of the world, Desdemona descended into her own hell in the midst of multiple tragedies. This revolving cycle of fear, grief, and catastrophe loosened something deep within her psyche. Harriet could only watch. The sweet but proper child had learned that consequences were not always the result of specific actions, but more a quirk of fate. That being the case, Harriet slowly slipped towards decadence and extravagance just as the entire nation was doing the same. As millions of teens and adults mused about whether they had "It" and danced the black bottom to new jazz tunes, it was easy for Harriet to get lost in one of Memphis' network of speak-easies and private clubs. It was certainly easier than getting her mother's attention.

Prohibition had theoretically hit Memphis a decade earlier than everyone else, and thus Memphians were better at hiding and celebrating their vice. Harriet was at heart, a good girl, so when her Kortrecht High school classmates were slipping down to Beale Street, sneaking bathtub gin, and learning the Charleston, the Black Bottom, and the Shimmy, Harriet studied hard, helped her family and spent time with Grandmother Dorothy.

She wasn't interested in boys, and she didn't dream about marriage and babies. She loved to sing in the choir, and to go to the movies with her grandmother. They both loved the new musicals, especially the ones with Maurice Chevalier. By the time that she moved to the new Booker T. Washington School, she had become an avid fan of Josephine Baker after seeing a late-night, adult only showing on Beale Street. In fact, that had been her biggest act of rebellion to date. She had been intrigued, thrilled, and inspired to see a fellow negro on screen in a leading role. Soon after, when several scouts sent by King Vidor came to town, and appeared at her choir practice with news of auditions for a new musical, Harriet was ecstatic. Unfortunately, she knew her parents wouldn't be. Her mother had grown strict and somewhat distant during her childhood, and her father was seemingly always preoccupied with her mother. They seemed to have little time, or love left over for her. Her younger brother was busy with his own friends, and their closeness as small children did not continue into adolescence and young adulthood.

Initially, Harriet had turned to her beloved grandfather, who always made time for her. Then after he died, when she was seven, her grandmother moved in. Her grandmother took on the role of a parent, and Harriet would go straight to see her after school, to share her stories, and current news and events. Grandmother Dorothy would always stop what she was doing and make time for her. Even now, it was Grandmother Dorothy that had slipped her the coins for the movie. Her grandmother was almost 60 but she remained a vital part of the Prince family. Harriet wanted to tell her grandmother about the audition because she knew that her grandmother would support her, but she also knew that her family thought that actresses were low-class women. She didn't want to put her grandmother in a difficult position, so she kept news of the audition from her.

Instead, Harriet and two other girls from choir decided to go to the auditions together. Harriet didn't know the other girls that well, but she didn't feel quite brave enough to go alone, so she was happy to band together for the trip down to Beale Street. The auditions were being held in the Daisy theater in the early evening. As Harriet was walking down to Beale Street one of the girls, Ethel Mae, who was a year younger than Harriet, turned to her and said, "I don't know why you're going to this audition. Didn't you hear them say that it's for negros only?" Ethel's dark brown eyes were hard, and her face was twisted in a sneer. She put her hands on her generous hips and waited for Harriet's reply.

Harriet was taken aback. She had encountered this attitude before, but she was surprised at being confronted like this. She looked at the other girl and waited for her to have her say. It was two against one. It always was. "The other girl, Pearl, shrugged her shoulders, and said, "well, this is one of the only times someone is asking for a negro cast. You are going to show up and take one of our places. It's not really fair when you can just go to Hollywood like the white girls and audition there."

Harriet felt crushed, and then furious. "I know who I am, Ethel Mae Johnson and Pearl Watkins! I am a fine actress and an excellent singer. But what about you? If you don't get a part, Ethel, then maybe it's because you are as wide as a barn door and can barely hold a note. Funny," she sniffed, "but I thought fat girls were supposed to know how to sing."

She turned and looked at the other girl, with great disdain, saying, "And you, Pearl, you know, actresses need to know how to act? You certainly don't!" she spat out before marching the rest of the way down Beale Street to the audition.

In the end, all of them, along with 600 others, got parts as extras and bit players, although Harriet was almost rejected for "not looking negro enough." But she was cast in a bit part and carried it off beautifully. She was encouraged when Nina Mae McKinney sought her out to complement her on her acting. Despite being King Vidor's pet project, the limited budget meant that the film was completed and in the can in just a few weeks. It was the director's first sound picture and he had loaded it to the gills with songs and musical numbers. On the last day of filming in Memphis, Harriet was both elated and sad. She was elated after being told that she should come to Hollywood for a MGM contract, but sad to see the cast and crew leave.

That night, as the director and the cast celebrated on Beale Street, the bootleg liquor flowed and members of the Memphis political elite, of all colors came out to celebrate the big-time Hollywood director who had brought Marion Davies, Lillian Gish, and John Gilbert to the screen as he set his sights on their hometown of Memphis. Nina Mae Mckinney was the female lead, and she was just so breath-takingly beautiful. Harriet was in awe of her, and the other professional actors on the set but it was Victoria Spivey's singing that haunted her. Despite living in a city that was already famous for its music, Harriet had never been exposed to the inner workings of the entertainment business.

It was the first time that Harriet and most of the other colored cast members had been in a mixed social setting with the likes of Mayor Overton, Boss Crump, and Guston Fitzhugh brushing elbows with local negro child actors Half Pint and Gin Rickey, as well as the adult male lead, Daniel Haynes. It was mid-November in 1928, when the last scene had been filmed on the old steamer, the El Capitan, and King Vidor's cast and crew set out for Culver City. The racial lines dividing the city had been, at least temporarily, erased as the glamour and glitter of Hollywood, bathtub gin, and the roaring 20's drowned out traditional southern segregation. Despite the encouragement she had been given, Harriet wasn't part of the main cast, so she didn't get to accompany the crew to Hollywood for the final editing and film release. It had been a life changing experience all the same, especially for a somewhat sheltered and naïve girl from a good family, like Harriet. During local filming with the Hollywood crew, Harriet and her young, pretty, light-skinned counterparts had unprecedented freedom in Memphis. They spent the evenings crashing debutante balls at the Tennessee Club on the arms of erstwhile uncles, drinking at the Monarch Club, and dancing at the many, many clubs that had been evading the city's temperance movement since 1909.

The older generations, white and negro, were united in their outrage at this scandalous and libertine behavior. But, all too soon, Jim Crow, the Depression, and the ire of William F. Zumbrum pushed any ideas of racial tolerance into the background, where it would remain for almost another 40 years. In the meantime, Harriet and the other young women learned about what happens to unchaperoned and intoxicated young females. For some, there were more consequences than others.

Mercy Hospital, 1929
"This doesn't have to define you," the kindhearted young doctor said to the young woman who had her back to him. She faced the wall, with her knees drawn up against her chest. She looked so heartbreakingly young, and lost, he thought.
"You are a healthy, young girl, when you are ready, there's no reason you can't have another baby," he said to the silent figure. He could see tears leaking out of her eyes, though she cried silently.
The young physician stepped further into the room, and surprising even himself, sat on the edge of her bed. He needed to get through to her. The nurses said she had stopped speaking and eating. He reached out a hand and touched her shoulder over her gown. She startled but didn't otherwise react.
"This could be a new beginning for you. This isn't the end," he said, trying to project a voice with more confidence than he had. He felt like he was failing his young patient. He had seen several of these young girls come in, lost and broken. He didn't want to see this girl like he had seen some of the others, self-destructive in their pain.
"Please," he said, his voice almost breaking, as exhaustion from a long 36-hour shift mixed with a sense of hopelessness that seemed to emanate off his patient and infect his soul, "please, let me help you." He saw her eyes flicker with interest, and he suddenly felt a spark of hope. He began speaking rapidly in a soft, soothing voice, as he laid out his suggestions for her to rebuild her life. Despite her pain, she sat up and listened with silent attention.

24 hours earlier
Since she had given birth to the baby, she had withdrawn into herself. She was adamant that her family not be contacted, and she refused to name the child's father. She had been admitted, in labor, and had labored for two long days before delivering a small, but perfectly formed son. She remained strong and defiant during the long 48-hour period as she struggled to birth the child. It wasn't until a well-known local politician, Mr. E. H. Crump himself, accompanied by a stout and unsmiling, white woman,

identified as a social worker from the Tennessee Children's Home Society showed up that she crumpled. As Mr. Crump and the bespeckled social worker, Ms. Tann, threatened and pressured Harriet, she began to withdraw into herself.
"Now, this child, this child is almost white," Ms Tann said with interest. "I can find him parents out west that will never know any different. Don't you want that for this child? Do you think that you can provide better for this child?" she badgered.

Mr. Crump looked at the newborn child dispassionately, and began to berate the young woman, saying, "Do you think I owe you anything for this? Do you? Do you think this makes you special somehow? I don't suppose you think you are the first slut to try and hang a child on me!" he said, with his voice rising. Harriet turned on her side, away from her unwanted visitors, and cradled the tiny baby in her arms. She began to make cooing sounds to the baby, to block out the voices around her. Frustrated, the social worker had made a huffing sound and then indicated to the older, portly, white man to meet her outside the room. Harriet's crooning and cooing drowned out the muffled voices of the two in the hallway outside. She stayed on her side, crooning and cooing until the nurse came by later that day to take the baby back to the nursery. She didn't want to hand him over, but the stern matron in the freshly starched uniform wasn't giving her any options. She obediently handed the nurse her young son, and then tried to forget the earlier confrontation.
****

Chez Bricktop, Paris 1932-1938

The words of the young doctor echoed in Harriet's head. At his urging, Harriet had enrolled in the nursing program at Mercy Hospital. She didn't really want to be a nurse at the time, but it seemed to be a good solution that would allow her a measure of freedom and financial independence. After she had become pregnant in 1929, her brother had driven her from the family home, and she had never crawled back. Now, as a nurse, she didn't ever have to. The work was hard, and physical with long hours that helped keep her too busy to think about her regrets. The pay was meager, but by sharing a space with several other nurses, she had been able to save money to pursue her real goal of escaping Memphis.

At first, she didn't know where she wanted to go. She just knew she wanted out, and away from all the judgement and prejudice. She wanted to get away from all the expectations. But as she listened to her more sophisticated roommate, Ellie talk, an idea formed. Ellie was a northern transplant from New York. She had come to Memphis to see family, and never left. She had her own unspoken tragedies and grief, that led her to stay in the South instead of returning to her small apartment in Harlem. That didn't mean that Ellie didn't speak about her neighborhood in wistful terms. She entertained Harriet and the other nurses with stories about seeing Jelly Roll Morton, Adelaide Hall, and Noble Sissle in clubs and on Broadway. But, it was Josephine Baker that really sparked Harriet's interest. She had been introduced to jazz after hearing about Florence Mills and had been devastated by her death. It was so different from W. C Handy and the music of the Delta. Josephine Baker really captured her attention, with her audacity, and her sophistication, singing in French, wearing risqué costumes, and performing for huge crowds in Europe.

Harriet kept her dreams to herself and worked diligently at the hospital, and as a private duty nurse to make extra money. Then in the summer of 1932, Ellie announced that she was returning to New York for a few months. Harriet quickly asked to accompany her. Ellie might only be going to New York, but for Harriet it was her jumping off point to something bigger. She only had $75 dollars of the $102-dollar fare for the SS Leviathan, but Harriet knew if she didn't go to New York with Ellie now, she might not ever make it. As she hesitantly confessed her plans to Ellie, she expected ridicule or scorn. She was surprised when Ellie encouraged her, saying, she could help. She also advised Harriet to pack her clean and serviceable nursing uniforms in her small suitcase among her best dresses.

One late August day, Ellie stood with Harriet on Pier 86 in Manhattan as they waited for the ship's surgeon to arrive. Dr. Frank Stewart was a stern and serious looking gentleman as he strode up the pier to meet the two ladies. Ellie had helped Harriet with special attention paid to her hair and clothing. She had carefully relaxed and straightened Harriet's hair into the latest style of the day. The chemicals burned Harriet's scalp raw, but she was so anxious for the plan to work, that she never even complained during the long comb-out process. Ellie meticulously styled her hair in the soft elegant waves, and then dusted

Harriet's face with a light powder. She carefully placed a hat at a jaunty angle and handed Harriet her white gloves. Harriet checked that her seams were straight one last time in the mirror before they left the house to catch the train. Ellie had carefully coached her on her demeanor, and stood by and slightly behind Harriet as if she was merely a companion and not a peer.

Ellie faded into the background as the doctor gave Harriet a long once-over. Then, seemingly satisfied with her presentation, Dr. Stewart began to quiz her on her nursing experience and qualifications. As advised by Ellie, Harriet used Baptist Memorial Hospital over the smaller negro hospital to establish her bona fides. The ship's surgeon seemed satisfied, and after speaking with Commodore Randall and the Chief Steward, David Robertson, Harriet received passage to Cherbourg in exchange for her nursing services on the transatlantic passage. As an unmarried, third-class passenger, she would be roomed with another single woman during the crossing. However, at the last minute, Miss Dirouhi Adjikevorkian requested a private companion in her cabin.

Miss Adjikevorkian, a first-class passenger, was delighted to have a nurse sharing her cabin for the duration of the trip as a respite from her assigned chaperone, Sister Xaveria Molt. As Sister Molt had discovered that several other sisters from a Benedictine order in Chicago were also traveling to Europe, she was happy to be relieved of her duties, and had quickly moved to join her fellow nuns in their more modest accommodations.

Harriet stayed busy and entertained by the other crew and passengers on the SS Leviathan. The five-day journey to Southampton passed quickly with a surprising number of visits to the ship surgeon's office with everything from minor ailments like indigestion, constipation or headache to requests for sleeping draughts, tonics, and other formulas for a variety of injuries, particularly among the younger and more rambunctious travelers. Dr. Stewart muttered, under his breath about deaths, serious injuries, and other calamities, but the trip passed fairly uneventfully. After the first port of call, the ship continued to

Cherbourg, France where Harriet disembarked, in the company of Miss Adjikevorkian. She was startled, but touched, when Miss Adjikevorkian impulsively gave her a large hug before they went their separate ways. She quickly made her way to the Cherbourg train station and used some of the precious francs Dr. Stewart had pressed into her hand that morning to buy a ticket for the next train to Paris. She slept fitfully on the train but was exhausted but excited once she arrived, as she walked the streets of Paris.

She made her way to 66 Rue Pigalle. The night before she had stayed up with the Brett baby all night. Professor and Mrs. Brett were a nice enough couple but were panic stricken listening to their child barking his little lungs out. Harriet had stayed with the baby in the tiny little washroom in the medical office making a steam room for the boy. She gently rubbed his back to soothe the feverish child to sleep while the doctor hooked up the vapo-preselene humidifier, next to a small bassinet. Just before dawn, a sweaty and soaked Harriet trudged back to her room, after watching the baby sleep peacefully. Dr. Stewart had assured her he would monitor the baby for the rest of the morning, as the ship began docking procedures. She left the little office hopeful but feet-dragging tired. She had another burst of energy as they disembarked. She was eager to start her new life! She walked purposefully down Rue Pigalle, with a firm grip on her small suitcase. She tried to look more confident than she felt as she passed thru the slightly seedy neighborhood lined with nightclubs, brothels, bars, and other entertainments. These were interspersed with lively cafes, art studios and several small theaters.

It was still early, just past eleven, but the famous Chez Bricktop was open, if empty. A lone bartender stood behind the bar, drying glasses with a frayed dishtowel. Harriet put her small suitcase down before approaching the man who looked up as her heels clack-clacked. He raised an eyebrow and smiled at Harriet, putting down the dishtowel and leaning forward against the bar.

She introduced herself and asked if he knew of a respectable rooming house nearby. "Excusez-moi?" he said, looking at her blankly. Her face crumbled and her body seemed to collapse in on itself. She burst into tears.

"Now stop that sweetheart," he said, feeling sorry. "I was just kidding. I pegged you for an American the moment you walked in," said the bartender, in a soft accented English that carried the sounds of island accented French. He was tall, well-built and attractive, with his tight curly hair pomaded and parted to the side. He had a small, thin mustache that accented his strong jaw and pearly white teeth. He was in shirt sleeves, which were rolled to the forearm, showing strong, muscular arms, and grey slacks with a long apron tied around his waist and extending to the floor.

"But you are right – I don't speak French! I saved money to come here for 2 years, and I didn't learn any French!" she wailed as exhaustion overwhelmed her emotions. She suddenly saw all the glaring holes in her audacious plan, and she felt crushed and defeated.

The man came from around the bar and put his arms around Harriet. "It's all right now little mademoiselle. It's all right. You can sit down and rest," he said in soothing tones as he helped her to a chair. He fished a handkerchief out of his pocket and offered it to Harriet, who used it to wipe tears from her eyes, "But, if you've come for the party, it's gone away."

She knew she should be ashamed of her weakness, but she was too tired. She looked up at him, her face pale and wan from exhaustion and said, "Would you please tell me how to get to Chez Josephine?"

He looked a bit surprised for a moment, then caught himself. "You are on the right street. It was just past the windmill at Moulin, but it's not there now. She finished *La Joie de Paris* and leaves for London soon." He internally flinched as her eyes welled with tears again. She wasn't the first one of his fellow countrymen to come into Chez Bricktop looking for more than a drink, but her dazed and innocent appearance affected him somehow. He felt compelled to help the young woman, even if he didn't know why.

For her part, Harriet was taken aback with the open concern she saw on the man's face. She wasn't expecting anyone to care, but, after seeing his face, she left down her guard completely. Within minutes, the handsome, negro man with the rich, chocolate-colored skin, and clear white smile, was untying his apron and introducing himself as Joe Alex. He explained that he'd originally come to Paris from Martinique. He had arrived shortly before Caroline Dudley Reagan with her new American dance retinue. Josephine Baker and seven other performers had been brought specifically to be part of a new revue in Paris.

"I wasn't initially part of the stage show. I was just an extra body they hired, but I ended up being in the show," he said with a nonchalant shrug. "We thought it was going to be a new production to showcase our talents, but really it was just another opportunity for a rich, white woman to show-off a group of 'Noir'," he said using the French word for negro. He looked distinctly annoyed as he continued, "so they put us in a show called *'La revue negre'* if you can believe that," he said shaking his head, "but no one banked on Josephine!" he finished.

Harriet nodded, intrigued. She'd spent most of her life either avoiding whites or navigating the complexities of a shared space with a race that didn't understand the concept of sharing, only dominating. Her face lit up as he explained how Josephine Baker had used this opportunity to propel all of them out of the life of a chorus dancer. "We still perform," he explained, "but now it's only for our own benefit. Josephine thinks that the French treat us better here." he ended, leaving his own opinion unsaid.

Harriet's face was shining, she looked so eager, and she leaned forward to hear more. He had seen that look before, and he needed to gently bring her back to earth. "Madamoiselle," he started –

"No, it's Harriet," she quickly corrected as she wiped away the last bits of tears using a corner of the handkerchief.

"Now, Harriet, you look just plumb exhausted, and hungry to me," Joe Alex said. Let me stash your suitcase behind the bar and take you for a coffee and a croissant," he continued. "We have the best, little, café just down the street." he continued on, as Harriet let his words wash over her. She handed over the suitcase and listened to his melodious tones as he talked on about the food, and the neighborhood.

Harriet may have felt exhausted and as rumpled as her cotton dress, but her eyes came alive as she walked the street with Joe Alex. When they arrived at the café, she did a double take as they sat down in the busy café at a table near several other groups of diners. Joe Alex had seen that expression before, particularly on the faces of Americans. He waited patiently for Harriet to speak.

"So we can just sit anywhere?" she asked. He nodded patiently.

"And we can eat in any restaurant we want?" she asked.

"Any restaurant you can afford," he answered. He didn't mention the private, elite venues that catered only to the ultra-elite. He knew was she was asking. She had a look on her face of deep satisfaction that he didn't want to disturb. She would learn the truth soon enough, but he had seen this before, especially in Americans from the segregated South. It wouldn't take her long to realize that just because there were no actual signs saying, 'Whites Only," didn't mean that the French or Parisians didn't practice their own kind of discrimination, but he wanted her to have this moment to savor. While they settled down to a small repast of coffee, and lacey, light pastries, he peppered the young girl with questions as he studied her delicate face. He'd met many young girls like Harriet before, but she intrigued him. She carried with her an air of great sorrow, accompanied by an equal amount of determination and strength. He looked into her large, hazel eyes and was surprised to feel a sense of almost paternal concern.

It wasn't until a few weeks later when two things happened that made Harriet realize how fate (and Joe Alex) had smiled down on her. She was waiting tables at Chez Bricktop, when an elegant party came in to settle in a large corner table of the club. As her eyes were drawn to the lively group, she heard Madame Bricktop herself cursing quite animatedly in English at a young girl who had trailed in after the group. "Now, get out, you stupid girl! I don't run a charity for displaced and starstruck negros!" the proprietor yelled at the retreating figure. Joe Alex, at the bar, paused in preparing drinks to catch Harriet's eye, winking at her.

Then, Madame "Bricktop" Smith turned her attention to Harriet, snapping her fingers, saying, "Standup straight Harriet, and get moving! Don't you see that table that just arrived?" Then Bricktop herself sashayed in the same direction, welcoming the group in a magnanimous and boisterous fashion, as she retrieved a magnum of champagne from the bar.

In her rush to serve the table, it wasn't until Harriet looked up to take their orders that she saw she was face to face with her idol, the legendary Josephine Baker, at the table with several other people. She was speechless for a moment, taken back by the incredible youth of the young woman in front of her. For all the newsreels and shorts, she hadn't realized that the American dynamo was just a few years older than she was.

As she started at her idol, her pen and pad forgotten in her hand, a jovial, but portly, balding man with twinkling, blue eyes said in a heavily accented English, "Eh, Josie! You see that? Once again, a lovely fillie is struck by my awe-inspiring countenance." He laughed, breaking the spell that had left Harriet without words. Her idol answered the man in French, before turning to Harriet as saying, almost prophetically, "She's too cute for you, Henri!

You wouldn't know what to do with such a lovely," before ordering a martini, and turning toward her other shoulder to look at another man, who had a thick, black mustache and slicked back hair. He wore a fitted black tuxedo with glittering diamond cufflinks. Josephine looked at him with adoration in her eyes, as he leaned in close to whisper something in her ear, before caressing her long, elegant, swan neck with a kiss. Harriet felt spell-bound even watching the scene, and seeing her idol respond with a soft sigh, and then a quick laugh, as Harriet's boss moved in. The party greeted the proprietor with delighted greetings.

Her boss, a solidly build woman with red hair and an Appalachian accent, was there pouring generous glasses of champagne for everyone before settling into an open chair with a flourish. "Ah, my dear Count!" she said as she poured champagne into the mustached man's waiting glass. He bowed his head in exaggerated courtesy to Madame Smith, as she was formally known and met eyes with the reigning queen of the table and Parisian nightlife. They flashed each other a big fake smile, as she moved on to fill the glasses of the other joyous and boisterous members of the table. Madame Smith hated that slimy 'no account' count, but she adored Josephine, so she played the game.

Harriet collected the rest of the drink orders while she practiced a few words of her limited French vocabulary before rushing back to the bar, where Joe Alex was waiting.

As he prepared her order, Joe Alex said pithily, "well, you've certainly had a spot of luck, Henriette", addressing her and using his French name for her. Her face glowed as she answered, "Yes, you see her, she's so fantastique! She's amazing, so young and beautiful!" Harriet was in the throes of excitement. As he finished up the order, Joe Alex laughed.

"No, not her, my silly Henri! The jolly little man, the other Henri," he said. "He doesn't even know you are a nurse, and you have already attracted his interest, that is good!" he said to a bewildered Harriet. When Madame Smith beckoned to her,

Harriet was too preoccupied with managing the heavy tray of drinks to think much about Joe Alex's cryptic comments.

Before she could ponder his words any further several more patrons walked in. The club was shifting from an afternoon café into full blown, evening, jazz entertainment. She looked up with relief to see that the young couple at table 8 were finally leaving. They had nursed a couple of drinks each for several hours while the pretentious young man held court. He was the former stepson of a famous French writer who was mainly famous for carrying on a lusty affair with his stepmother. Since that infamous period, he had become a self-styled philosopher. He had recently been using Chez Bricktop in the afternoons to meet with his young American mistress, far from the prying eyes of his wife. The girlfriend was an energetic, bubbly, young woman with ash colored blonde hair. The blonde had christened the serious young man as 'Darling Bertie'. Her speech was often punctuated with laughter. The girlfriend would fawn over him while he lectured on and on. Sometimes they were accompanied by another couple, but as the evening wore on, the pretentious young man and the laughing blonde would slip away for a more private meeting. On their last visit to the club, the aggrandizing 'man of the people' attempted to rest his hand on Harriet's backside while she delivered another round of drinks. Harriet forgot the impertinent hand, or at least ignored it when she heard the girlfriend say to him, "This conversation is so boring that I think I am going to faint." Then the blonde woman stood up and made to leave. The hand was quickly removed from Harriet's backside, as 'Darling Bertie' made haste to intercept his girlfriend before she walked out. The woman shook his hand off her arm, grabbed her coat from the coat check, and stormed out. Since they had since returned together, they must have made up, Harriet mused. "Maybe he stopped boring her," Harriet said aloud.

This was just one of the things Harriet loved about working at Chez Bricktop. The work might have been menial in nature, but Harriet felt like she was getting a free education in arts and culture between the patrons and musicians who entertained there. It wasn't long before Harriet received a promotion of sorts. One night while a boisterous crowd was being entertained by *Arthur Briggs and His Black Boys*, the Prince of Wales, the Prince Aly Khan, and another man arrived with several elegantly dressed women. Bricktop greeted the Prince with great enthusiasm, while she personally led his party to a table that had been set aside specifically for the royals. Two of the beautiful, dark-haired women were mirror images of each other, with shiny black, marcelled curls, rich brown eyes, and long, luxurious fur coats over slinky satin gowns. One of the lovely ladies, had her small, gloved hand tucked in Prince David's elbow. When the couple came to the table, she was then seated between either of the rakish princes. Her twin flashed a her a sly glance, before taking a seat across from her sister, next to another elegantly dressed woman. The third woman had a slightly pinched looking appearance, with a long nose that was even more marked in contrast to her dark smooth bob with marcelled waves, and thin single line of hair in her precisely plucked brows. As Bricktop greeted one of the twins, saying, "and how is that darling little Gloria?" the woman with the sharp nose, thin lips, and pinched face said, somewhat waspishly to her handsome male companion, "Ernest, I need a drink, now!"

Ernest looked embarrassed at his wife's outburst before looking around for a waitress. His wife, in a nasally voice with a Baltimore accent which betrayed her North American origins, proceeded to call over to their hostess, in slightly slurred but demanding tones, "Girl, get me some gin and a fuzzy champagne." Bricktop looked irritated and angry, and snapped her fingers in Harriet's direction. Harriet hurried to the table.

"This is Harriet. She will take care you this evening," Bricktop said in crisp, cold tones before marching away. The Prince of Wales looked unabashed, while Ernest attempted to quiet his wife, who was even now trying to reach out and catch Harriet's sleeve. "Wally, don't worry, I'll get you a drink," Ernest placated his wife, as he attempted to get her to settled back into her chair.

"You-hoo," she sang out, catching the attention of the entire table. "Tel-ma! You and Gloooriiiiia are the best. Your sister Consuelo is so dull! I'm glad we left her back in London." Now her husband's face was bright red. Harriet hurried off to get the orders from the bar. Hopefully, the faster she got the woman a drink, the faster she would settle down. The band was already staring daggers in the direction of the prince's table. Personally, Harriet found the prince and all of his guests to be obnoxious, but she kept her thoughts to herself, and threw a sympathetic look to Arthur on stage. She was glad when the night was over, she thought, as she helped Joe Alex close up the club.

Joe Alex had a real talent for the mysterious, Harriet was discovering. They spent a lot of time together, but she still didn't know very much about him. Ever since that first day, when he swept her off to the local café, he had proved to be a real character and a loyal friend. Even now, she slept on a cheap, but charming bed with a chipped iron bed frame that he'd helped her find at a secondhand store. She'd found it, along with her tiny but immaculate apartment on Rue Delambre, with his help, one afternoon. Her French, while improving, wasn't yet up to the task of bartering, but Joe Alex, all smiles and laughter had gotten the crusty, dour-faced crone to agree to a ridiculously low price for the bed, a nightstand, as well as a tiny, drop-leaf table that now served as her dining room table. Dining room was an exaggeration for the space that was little more than a bedroom, with a tiny living room and miniscule kitchenette. She had a shared bath down the hall with three other apartments. It wasn't until after she was settled into her apartment the next afternoon, when he stopped by, that Harriet had a chance to ask Joe Alex about something she had been wondering about. She was in the tiny little area that served as a kitchen, boiling water for coffee, and setting out two of the delicate coffee cups that she had found earlier that morning while she was out buying staples. She kept her head down, and focused her attention on the delicately white cups with tiny blue flowers as she asked, her new and now dear friend, "Why do you work at Chez Bricktop? I have seen the advertisements around town, Joe. I have seen that you are famous here in your own right. You don't have to be tending bar."

He lifted an eyebrow at her before saying, "I work there when it suits me for the same reason that you do, for the community." He continued, "The street is lined with clubs and cafes. You could have stopped in at any number of them looking for Chez Josephine's, but you chose Chez Bricktop's for a reason. You wanted to be around people that would welcome you and accept you, and so do I." He looked almost challengingly at Harriet before picking up his coffee cup and changing the subject.

****

The marvelous and fascinating Josephine left town a few weeks later, but not before she had taken Harriet into her fold. At Bricktop's, Harriet continued to make friends, with fellow waitstaff, performers like the lovely Mabel who sang at the nightly shows, and the many fellow ex-pats who now seemed to almost huddle together after the mass exodus of Americans at the beginning of the depression. There were famous performers, artists, poets and novelists. This strange sort of kinship seemed at odds with Harriet's known reality at times. She could see why Josephine and many of her fellow performers found Paris to be magical. On her days off, when he was available, Joe delighted in taking her around the city. She could freely engage and was readily welcome to lively discussions in cafes, and clubs. On lazy Sundays, they would wander the city on foot. They would meander down the streets, taking their time, and enjoying the fresh air. It was beginning to turn colder, which only made the time more precious. There was nothing romantic between the duo, but their bond was becoming stronger every day. As they enjoyed an ice cream, Joe cajoled her down Rue de L'Odeon. They stopped at a storefront at number 12, and she used some of her precious funds. She joined the library at Shakespeare and Company, and they shared tea with Sylvia and her girlfriend, while she perused the small shop, and selected a small volume of poems to read. It wasn't an entirely idyllic fall, but it certainly seemed that way the day she bought a penny postcard and later mailed it to an address in Memphis.

On another rare evening off, Joe Alex, Mabel, and a couple other girls from work took her to see a show at the Grand Guigol Theater. She wasn't a big fan of plays but this macabre, visceral, and graphic show was a long-standing Paris tradition, and she loved it.

It might have continued this way indefinitely, but life has a funny way of changing. That winter, just before Christmas, Joe Alex was offered a lucrative touring contract that would send him to South America for a year, and the jolly, laughing 'Henri' with the bright sportscar began to return to see Harriet. At first, his visits seemed to be nothing out of the ordinary, as he arrived with groups of friends, sometimes requested her as their waitress. The third time this happened, Harriet felt a little uneasy.

She said so to Joe, who was doing one of his last shifts before leaving for Buenos Aires. She hesitated before doing so, but she had seen the diminutive, little Frenchman watching her somewhat intently. It frankly unnerved her. She was already devastated that Joe was leaving; she felt a hole opening in her heart but she refused to say it. She didn't want to say or do anything that would keep him from going. It was a high-profile tour, and he had turned down another such offer a month earlier. With the ongoing financial crisis, the offers had become few and far between, and she didn't want her dear friend to forgo such an opportunity.

Joe, who knew that Harriet was struggling to hide her feelings about his upcoming departure, looked over to where she indicated, and then laughed, saying, "Ah, yes, that is the delightfully rambunctious Henri Rene Leriche. I wanted him to meet you for some time."

With that, Joe stepped out from behind the bar, and escorted Harriet over to the small table where a widely gesticulating, plump man with twinkling, blue eyes was telling a story to his two companions, who were much more staid, and somber in appearance. As Joe made the introductions, the cherubic-like man interrupted saying, "Non, non, only sweet Josie may call me Henri! To the rest, it must be Rene or Dr. Leriche." With that dramatic and heartfelt outburst, even his sober companions flashed smiles.

With that, Dr. Leriche launched into a carefully prepared speech, "I have spoken with our dear friends, Joe Alex and the wonderful Josie, who inform me that you are a nurse from the United States. I am currently working both here in Paris and in the city of Strasbourg. I have a wonderful staff at the university clinic but I am just building my clinic practice here in Paris while I give a series of lectures. I was hoping to entreat you to come join me in the operating theater during my sojourns in this city."

Harriet suspected that Dr. Leriche's desire to hire her as an operating room nurse had less to do with any real need and more to do with satisfying the object of his adoration, the lovely and talented Ms. Baker. Josephine and Joe Alex had been united in their efforts to look after Harriet. But Dr. Leriche was less interested in doing favors for Joe Alex than he was for the lithe, lovely and exotic Josephine. He certainly knew from his close association with her that her heart was currently occupied with the slickly dressed and smooth-talking Count "Pepito" Abatino. Harriet felt overwhelmed, but after looking at Joe's anxious face, felt that she had to accept the offer. She didn't know much more than the basics of the operating room, but all of that was about to change.

****

It quickly became apparent that Joe Alex and Josephine had arranged for more than just another job for Harriet. They had also arranged for her smooth entry into the medical community of Paris. Dr. Leriche didn't operate in Paris that frequently but being introduced as "his" nurse gave Harriet entry into the medical community at large, and a social standing she wouldn't have had otherwise.

Like the ex-pat community that frequented Chez Bricktop and the Paris jazz scene, the community was a confusing mix of contradictions. Unlike the eclectic mix of artists, writers, philosophers, and their assorted rich patrons, Harriet and her blackness were not entirely embraced, but neither were they shunned. Here she was able to move in the larger French and American ex-patriot community, but it was confusing and bewildering in a way that made Harriet question all of the assumptions, norms, and societal rules she'd always known. While she knew that fame and money, such as that of famed jazz musicians and personalities had often created a partial racial pass into the company of the white elite, it was even more marked here in Paris. As a jazz club waitress here, she was welcomed with open arms by many of the illustrious patrons. Somehow, she didn't think that Man Ray, and his ilk would do the same in New York or in her hometown of Memphis. It was hard to wrap her head around.

It was even harder to wrap her mind around this same contradiction in the Parisian medical community. She was used to deeply segregated facilities, where negro doctors, nurses and patients were restricted to their own small, modest facilities while local whites had larger, state of the art facilities. Here, as Rene Leriche introduced her to the surgeons at the American Hospital in Paris, she almost would have welcomed open discrimination rather than the silent judgement of some of the surgeons' wives, and other American nurses. But, as a hospital catering to the American community in Paris, they couldn't afford to turn away a native speaker, even if her ever-so olive complexion and slight coarse textured curls hinted at her background. For her part, Harriet felt a growing resentment at being forced to endure these judgements. This slow, simmering anger was ever present, born of multiple generations of racial injustice, but this was the first time Harriet had allowed it to fully surface. It was always there, and it had always been there. It only grew stronger from the on-going insults and slights of local white society. Outwardly, she was calm, cool, and professional, but inwardly, it ate at her insides! It flared into heat in the pit of her stomach as she watched the ease at which her coworkers and their families embraced their whiteness, and their belief in their own superiority. They never seemed to question the rightness or fairness of this racial line. Here in Paris, it wasn't even spoken of, much less debated or discussed. Parisians seem to think that by denying it's existence, it would cease to exist. That this attitude might reinforce social inequity was also ignored. Harriet used this position of "ignorance is bliss" to continue her education. At the American Hospital of Paris, she took every opportunity to be shoulder-to-shoulder with the men who were at the forefront of medicine and surgery.

As a woman, she would have been hard-pressed to cross that threshold, but as Dr. Leriche's nurse, she was allowed the freedom to attend medical lectures at the College de France and the University of Strasbourg. As his nurse, she participated in ground-breaking surgeries. Harriet Prince stood in the operating theater shoulder to shoulder with many of the 20th century's greatest surgeons, including fellow Americans. William Halsted and Michael deBakery. If they found it odd to see the negro nurse from Memphis at Leriche's side, they kept silent. Rene Fontaine, Dr. Leriche's devoted disciple entertained himself during longer operations by quizzing the quietly attentive Harriet on anatomy and physiology. Dr. Leriche's blue eyes would twinkle as his erstwhile waitress demonstrated her intellect, answering accurately, and precisely in quiet but grammatically correct French.

She learned more than advanced physiology and the principles of vascular surgery in the operating room. She also learned a skill that would become critically important in the coming years; she learned how to administer anesthesia.

That summer, she temporarily left nursing to follow Bricktop to Biarritz, as part of her traveling staff. She and several other club staff stayed in a small, rented cottage, while Bricktop and her celebrity friends ensconced themselves in the Hotel du Palais. As the small, seaside resort town's population swelled with European aristocrats fleeing the doldrums of the depression, Harriet found herself rubbing elbows with displaced Russian nobles, along with the usual assortment of French counts and countesses. She also got used to seeing and serving the Prince of Wales and his entourage. But the summer days flew by. After enjoying the nightly opera of waves crashing against the shore, the quiet of the pre-dawn beach, and the luxury of her own private thoughts, it was time to return to Paris, yet again. She was quickly welcomed back into the operating room, where her quiet, studious nature and exact movements made her every surgeon's favorite.

While she was working with Dr. Leriche and his colleagues, both Josephine and Joe returned to Paris. Josephine returned somewhat devastated from a failed American tour. What was supposed to be a triumphant return was instead a crushing humiliation. Seeing her idol, mentor, and friend wounded in this way fed the anger that was slowly sapping Harriet's spirit. It was only with the filming of a new movie, here in Paris, that Josephine lost the sadness that haunted her eyes. Harriet was proud to serve as the on-set nurse, and laughingly protested as Josephine demanded Harriet's inclusion in several scenes that were crowded with uncredited extras.

Harriet filled her days working two jobs – at Chez Bricktop and at the hospital, which brought her closer to Josephine and the rest of the ex-pat community. It was her nursing training that brought her into the confidence of the various members. Her closed-lipped and broadminded, but caring, demeanor brought people to her one by one, in pairs, and small groups. Harriet was able to unlock many of the secrets of the human body for her friends in a way that medical establishment failed to do so. She also did it discreetly, which earned her the respect of her co-workers. She was a source of strength for Josephine during her 'monthly' troubles, as a series of miscarriages eroded Josephine's sense of womanhood.

Joe Alex's return was bittersweet also, for a different reason. After almost two and a half years away, he returned to tell her that he was permanently moving to South America, after finding a level of success that would be unobtainable in either the United States or Europe. He was taking some time before returning to Brazil because he had a lot of business and personal affairs to tie up before leaving again. This included Harriet, who he considered to be almost a daughter in his affections. He worried that she would be lonely, but in this, Harriet never sought any outside advice.

As for Harriet herself, while Josephine was singing of her two loves, Harriet was busy attending to everyone's needs. This gave her great satisfaction but there was a growing, gnawing hole in her heart. Her almost weekly letters and postcards to her family in Memphis continued to go unanswered. She could have made an expensive transatlantic phone call but held off, afraid of being rejected in real time. She could make excuses for the cards and letters, but, while the new technology made a telephone call possible, it didn't account for the emotional toll it could bring.

While she made a concerted effort at her friends' urging to experience joy, she had only a few brief romances. She found herself unable to trust her emotions. Once in a moment of vulnerability, soon after her arrival in Paris, she had leaned over and said wistfully to Mabel, as they watched Coco Chanel and her entourage arrive, "I wish I had her spirit de amor." Before Mabel could reply, Madame Bricktop herself, who was passing by to greet the new arrivals, said, "Non, non, Cherie! That is not love, to sleep with every rich man she can. That's just her business model." Coming from a sexual libertine like Bricktop, it was an astute observation. Nevertheless, Bricktop gave a warm welcome to the tanned, gaunt, woman who continued to sport cropped locks long after the rest of the world had moved on to marcelled waves and soft curls. Up close, her advancing age was apparent; from nicotine-stained fingers, to yellowing teeth, to sunspots on the displayed decolletage. But Coco still laughed and played the coquette sandwiched between the Duke of Westminster, aka her darling "Bunny," and his romantic rival, Paul Iribe, who was spending precious moments overseas, away from his beloved Hollywood sets.

Harriet threw herself into a brief, whirlwind, and passionate affair with an Italian violinist she met at the club. When he began to profess his love for her, she threw him out of her bed and her life. It all rang so false to her. The next year, in 1935, she saw him one day, on the street, holding the arm of a heavily pregnant woman named Sylvia, and felt nothing. This convinced her that she wasn't destined for the traditional life of marriage and family. She knew that Bricktop and Josie had their own romance, but she didn't feel that her passions swung in that direction either.

It was the next year, when Harriet was re-introduced to fellow American, Dr. Jackson and his laughing Swiss wife, Charlotte. Everyone called the tall, engaging and out-going, woman Toquette. It was impossible not to like Toquette as she engulfed Harriet in a warm embrace. As Harriet spoke with Jacksons, she felt an immediate affinity for the couple and their young son, Peter. So much so, that she had accepted their frequent invitations for her to join them on their country estate in Enghein. It was a lovely reunion after Harriet's first encounter with the serious, but kind Dr. Sumner Jackson several years before. She had briefly met Dr. Jackson early in her career at the hospital in Paris because an unfortunate Australian girl named Dorothy was caught in a lover's triangle. Mistakenly identified as American, she had been brought to the emergency room where she died of a gunshot wound to her head. In typical fashion, it was ruled a suicide once it was determined that her erstwhile lover was the very married, very wealthy, but dissolute heir to Coty perfumes. Both Harriet and the surgeon had been advised to forget the incident in order to obscure the taint of scandal that hung around the Coty heir due to his propensity for sexual adventures, public drunkenness, and drug overdoses. At the time, Dr. Jackson seemed terse but caring. She remembered the way the lines in his brow wrinkled with his concern for the young patient. She hadn't really gotten to know Dr. Jackson then, they had both been all business, with no time for pleasantries.

Now, in 1936, as Harriet was formally introduced to the good doctor and his family, things changed. Toquette, a nurse herself, quickly took Harriet under her wing in motherly fashion. This quick adoption into the Jackson family brought some ease to the inner turmoil caused by her estrangement from her own family. Unfortunately, just as Harriet was beginning to really settle in and find a sense of contentment with her newly assembled family and friends, a dark shadow began to cast itself over France and the rest of Europe. At first it was just lingering rumors that refused to go away, but then the Germans retook lands that had been ceded to France as part of reparations for the Great War. The was a sense of tension in France, that slowly eased away in the cafes, nightclubs, and cobbled streets. The talk in the operating room among the surgeons, many whom are veterans, became darker, as they frequently discussed geo-political matters in a depth and detail that Harriet had never heard before. As the Italians marched on Ethiopia, Harriet learned a whole new lexicon of military terminology and strategy. Economic unrest reached the narrow streets of Paris, as workers protested in the streets and merchants waged war against their employees. Coco Chanel, a frequent patron at the club, was one of the worst offenders. Harriet wanted to be surprised, but after waiting on the condescending and racist designer, she wasn't.

Josephine was gone again, and then with the death of Pepino, gone in another way. Harriet went to Beau-Chene to see Josephine several times after his passing and found her friend at loose ends each time. The witty, self-depreciating but ever-confident Josephine was missing. A lost little girl, Freda, stood in her place. Even as she pushed Harriet away, she embraced her. Harriet had difficulty soothing Josephine's loneliness, when she had no answers herself.

She had briefly dated a French composer but broke it off with Ray when she found out he had run out on his wife and child. She dated other artists, here and there, but it wasn't until a chance meeting during an evening session at the club when she met Szlama. He was with a group of people that came to hear Django Reinhardt and his jazz quintette. His eyes had followed her as she had served the customers, but she did her best to ignore him. Stephane and Harriet had remained on friendly terms after their brief affair years before, so when he invited her to sit and visit at the end of the night for a few minutes, after a nod from Bricktop, she was happy to do so. Stephane promptly introduced her to the severe looking Pole, and against her own better judgement, Harriet was immediately enraptured. She surprised herself by agreeing to meet him outside the club after it closed that night. She hurried to complete her tasks for the evening, and patted her hair into place, before slipping off her apron. She touched up her lipstick and grabbed her wrap before heading outside to meet him. Another server, Jeanette, caught her eye and winked as Harriet headed outside. She immediately started internally chastising herself for agreeing to meet a stranger so late in the evening. Then as she saw him in the light of the streetlamp outside, he looked up at her and smiled. A feeling of static electricity filled the air, in the cool, rain dampened street. She could almost feel her hair rising in the atmosphere. She continued walking towards the man and considered him objectively. He wasn't movie star handsome, but he was attractive in a more dark, intense, intellectual way. Still, he didn't appear to take himself too seriously, if his ready, but shy, smile was any indication. He had a pale complexion framed with dark hair. He had light brown eyes and thick dark brows. He was clean shaven, and lean but compactly built, like many Europeans. He stepped forward to meet her under the light and extended his hand. Again, surprising herself, Harriet took his hand. "Coffee?" he said in a strangely accented French. She nodded, and they walked down the street to an all-night café in a weirdly comfortable silence with just the noise of their shoes on the wet streets. They made inconsequential small talk as they drank coffee, with their hands, and bodies still touching. Harriet stopped questioning the connection between the two of them, and just accepted it. They finished coffee, and without a word, she stood and took his hand again. He dropped some francs on the table, and they hurried to her tiny flat.

They didn't talk until later, in the pale light of dawn, as he lay naked in her bed with her tucked with her back against his strong chest and her head beneath his chin. While he may not have been tall, he made her feel precious and protected. Then they talked and talked, each now baring their souls to each other. She talked about her jobs and her life back in Memphis. She talked about always feeling that she didn't and couldn't belong there. She talked about her loneliness too.

He, in turn, told her about his childhood in a small town outside Warsaw. He talked about leaving school to work and at a young age, realizing that he and his family were caught in a cycle of endless struggle. He rebelled against this nihilistic existence and joined a political group. He told her about being imprisoned when he was 22. He told her all of this in a calm, toneless fashion, with his face pressed against the locks of her hair, while stroking her arm. Harriet could feel the tension, and pain in his touch as he gentled smoothed his rough palm down her arm. His other arm was around her mid-section, holding her close, in a way that was re-assuring to them both.

He said some words in a language she didn't know. "*Du–shenyu*" he said as he stroked her hair. He turned her towards him and mumbled some other words she didn't know as he kissed and stroked her face. When he slipped out of the bed and began to get dressed, she silently told herself not to get upset. She chastised herself for allowing herself to get into this situation. When he left the room, she had too much pride to ask him to stay, and she was too ashamed to follow him to the door. She didn't hear the front door open, as she flung herself back into the bed, and told herself not to cry. She flung the blankets over her head and tried to pretend it didn't matter.

Soon small noises seeped into her protective cocoon. Then the wonderful, strong aroma of fresh coffee wafted into the tiny bedroom. With that, she emerged from her cocoon. She grabbed her robe from the back of the door, and wrapped it tightly around her, to ward off the morning chill in the cold apartment. He made her breakfast with swift sure movements, his bare feet making no noise on the wood floor as he brought two small plates to the tiny table. After they finished breakfast, he quickly boiled water to wash dishes, with the same efficient manner. They talked in low tones, with an easy familiarity that made it seem like he had always been a part of her life. Then he put on his socks and shoes, hugged her tightly, kissed her on the top of her head and left.

She didn't see him for a few days until he returned to the apartment. She had just gotten home from working at the hospital, and her legs were aching. When she opened the apartment door, he gave her a shy smile before entering. He saw the fatigue in her face, and before she could say anything, swept her up into his arms and carried her to the bedroom. He deposited her gently on the bed and doffed her shoes. Without asking, he began to massage her swollen feet. Harriet thought she would start crying with relief. She hadn't realized how tired and sore she was until that moment. He stopped for a moment to lean over and give her a kiss before he began massaging her feet once more. She began to tell him about her day, stopping at several points, and seeming to be surprised to find that he was actively listening. She didn't know what this was, but she needed it. When she finished telling him about her day, he surprised her by telling her that he had been out of town working in the railyards at Reims. They quickly fell into a routine of sorts, working at their respective jobs during the week, and coming together during the weekends. Sometimes he would take her to the Pletzl, a Jewish neighborhood in the 4th arrondissment, where he had been renting a room in a large boardinghouse. The Gerchinovitz family, that owned the boardinghouse, would invite the couple to dinner on Friday nights. The first few times, Harriet was overcome by the busy, noisy, and boisterous atmosphere of the home which was packed full to the rafters. But the Gerchinovitz family, especially their daughter Elise, and the numerous guests and boarders always went out of their way to make Harriet feel welcome, despite the chaos. Harriet came to look forward to the gatherings. Chairs were brought in from bedrooms, the garden, and down from the attic to make way for all of the people who crammed into the cozy house to eat. Mrs. Gerchinovitz would pile the plates with kreplach, fava beans, and the savory flavors of thousands of years blended in with traditional French cuisine. Wine would flow, along with stories, jokes, and fanciful tales. The 'pièce de résistance' was always Mrs. Gerchinovitz's chocolate almond cake which was served with a strong, aromatic espresso. The bitter taste of the coffee brought out the richness of the cake. During it all, there were loud discussions in multiple languages, including the one that Szlama would often murmur at her during moments of intimacy. During their visits, he taught her a few rudimentary phrases of Yiddish and Polish and the words to some of the songs that were sung during the evening. Then he would take her back to Rue Pigalle, just in time for her late-night shift at the club. He would be waiting for her outside the door of the club when her shift ended in the wee hours, and they would walk, hand-in-hand to the tiny apartment, which had become their shared home. Sometimes the sight of one of Szlama's shirts hanging in the bedroom would give her comfort during the week while he was away.

A few times, she took him to the Caribbean restaurants that Alex Joe had showed her, but these too were now struggling as the depression deepened its grip on France. The small American negro community was becoming increasingly tiny as jobs disappeared, clubs closed, and French labor laws restricted the numbers of foreigners allowed to be employed in any one location.

After a few months of this routine, Szlama returned from the small town of Longueau, near Amiens, in a strange and pensive mood. When she arrived home, he greeted her from the kitchen, where he was cooking, with an absentminded and distracted kiss on the forehead. He was subdued at dinner, and something inside Harriet wept. She had allowed herself to imagine a life with the gentle, yet fiery Pole. It wasn't the kind of life that others would ascribe to, as neither of them was inclined to traditional family life. Harriet's one experience with motherhood had left a bad taste in her mouth. Szlama seemed much the same, but they had their own sort of happiness, in their time together. Whether they were pursuing the usual romantic haunts of a city steeped in romance or spending time with friends in heated, intellectual discussions fueled by carafes of coffee and a haze of cigarette smoke, or the frantic lovemaking that punctuated their relationship, Harriet felt happy and contented. Each time they came together, there was a sense of urgency that they never discussed. It was the urgency that kept Harriet on guard for exactly this moment. Szlama calmly told her that he was going to Spain. She wanted to cry, she wanted to scream at him not to go but she didn't. She kept her pain bottled up inside, and only nodded. They spent the weekend pretending the parting wasn't a deep wound for them both. Just before he left for the train station, he asked if he might write, and again, she silently nodded. She couldn't speak and still maintain composure. He grasp her tightly in a hug that pressed her against the full-length of hi, and she could feel his heart beating wildly. Then he kissed her with unrestrained passion before he turned and ran to the platform for the train. Only after he entered the passenger car, and the train moved away from the station, did she give in to her tears. They were burning tracts down her face as she hurried back to the now desolate feeling apartment. No one at the hospital had known about Szlama so she kept herself blissfully busy at work, too busy to think about the pain of his leaving. Shortly after Szlama left, Bricktop, who had been struggling financially for the last few years, was forced to close the club entirely.

1936 ended, and 1937 began with Harriet spending more and more time in the operating room. She was gratified and heartened when her friend Josephine remarried and became a French citizen. She too, could not see herself returning to a country that didn't seem to want her, but at the same time, she couldn't entirely turn her back on her past.

1937 passed, with several of the neighborhood regulars missing, as they too headed to Spain as the civil war intensified. The talk of casualties and wartime injuries intensified. Harriet felt weary and frightened by the on-going and continuous ramblings of the operating theatre but also compelled to listen. A few letters had trickled in, but for the most part, she was still alone and lonely.

1938 was filled with much of the same, along with heated dinner discussions at the Jackson's apartment in the posh neighborhood on Avenue Foch. Many summer evenings were spent in the lush and lovely garden with the Jacksons, their friends, and colleagues. Harriet and Tat, Toquette's sister, would sit in a corner of the garden and laugh over the attempts all of the married couples made to provide suitors for the duo. Tat was relieved that Harriet had joined the group and was the newest victim for such match-making schemes. Harriet, now in her early 30's, viewed it all with a jaded eye. She dated casually here and there, usually musicians or other members of the small African American community in Montmarte but she was careful never to let her private life impinge on her reputation in the hospital.

She was also careful not to take things too far. She wasn't ready or willing to move on just yet, and she wasn't ready for any more entanglements. Coffee, dinner or an evening out was about all she could handle.

As things got increasingly tense in Europe, it seemed like everyone around her was urging her to return home. The Jacksons pulled her aside several times, and so did Bricktop and many of her friends in the neighborhood. Many of them returned to the United States themselves. Josephine never asked Harriet about leaving. Since receiving her French citizenship, Josephine had committed herself to her new nation, body and soul, and she expected it from everyone else around her.

Harriet gave serious thought to returning to the United States but just couldn't seem to make a decision. Then one day, shortly after the Germans invaded France, she came home to find Szlama waiting for her. He was thin, painfully so, almost emaciated and seemed weary, almost haunted, in a way she had never seen before. He looked at her differently, more intensely too, as if to memorize her face.

After a joyous reunion, as they lay in bed together, Szlama too, urged her to return home. She looked at him steadily and thought about all the unanswered cards and letters she had mailed to Memphis, as she told him that she was staying. She didn't tell him that she couldn't leave as long as he was part of her life.

He briefly attempted to dissuade her, but after seeing the set of her jaw, he stopped trying. After surviving a stay in the Gurs concentration camp, he couldn't bear to send her away.

Instead, he made a point of introducing her to Jewish doctors he knew. Now with the "phony war" over, and the 'Fall of France' accomplished inside of a month, Jewish physicians were forbidden to practice. The resistance had been hard at work forging identification cards to aid in their exodus from France. But these French physicians had refused to leave. Instead, they had formed a corridor to the northern coast, and served at a series of makeshift facilities that lined the route. Szlama was dedicated to helping his adopted nation repel the German invaders even if it meant he would be forced to leave Harriet again.

Harriet continued to work at the hospital during the strange period that came after France surrendered to the German armies. The Nazis also outlawed black people from working in France, and it was this, that pushed Dr. Jackson to send Harriet underground. He and her former surgeon, Dr. Leriche, did their best to protect her. Unfortunately, the aging Leriche was cautiously collaborating with Nazi officials and was unwilling to guarantee Harriet's safety despite his high position in the Vichy government.

Dr. Jackson was frantic to prevent any German ingress into the American hospital, but he worried endlessly about Harriet's safety. He encouraged her to go into hiding since she refused to leave. Now that France was occupied, she wasn't going home, and the Germans hatred for non-Aryan races was well-known. Szlama urged her to go north to Rouen to work at a secret hospital, with a group of resistance surgeons, so she quickly packed her things into two valises. The first bag was sent to Josephine's chateau de Milandes in the Dordogne Valley in Southwest France. It was within the section of France that remained under the puppet government of Petain, instead of the Germans. Josephine wasn't there but she'd make sure to safeguard Harriet's few small treasures. In the other valise, went more practical items, clean clothes, medical supplies, a hairbrush, and a small, leather-bound journal. Her American identity cards and passport were at the bottom of the bag she sent to the chateau. Szlama was coming to take her to the hidden route used by the resistance movement to travel within occupied France. He had provided her with false documents that identified her as a white, naturalized, French citizen.

Makeshift operating theater, Rouen, 1944

For the three years that Harriet had been in occupied France, she'd stayed quietly hopeful. She did her best to tamp down her anxieties and focus on the mission in front of her. At the beginning of her relocation to Rouen, the causalities had been minimal, and she'd served in more of a public health capacity for members of the resistance. Venereal disease, asthma, and other every day conditions kept her as busy as ever for the first year of occupation. But then the casualties started rolling in! The majority of the wounded weren't victims of the Germans, but of the widespread, and often inaccurate bombing by allied forces. The Germans were more likely to outright execute any foreign nationals they encountered, though torture of every day citizens was common too. As the legitimate hospitals and other facilities were destroyed over the course of months, the makeshift facility in a tunnel underneath one of Rouen's oldest churches began to serve more and more civilians.

Szlama had been able to come to Rouen on several occasions as part of his mission to bring supplies to the field hospital. Harriet and Szlama cherished the precious stolen hours. As much as the surgeons needed Harriet's assistance, no one begrudged the hard-working American nurse a few hours in the arms of her lover. If anything, they only wished to find the same solace, as the repeated bombing began to take it's toll on the populace and their morale.

In November of 1943, the scheduled supply drop with Szlama and his team didn't occur. Harriet was worried, but she had lived in a perpetual state of worry since the fighting had begun. She dedicated herself to administering anesthesia as she watched the delicate details of an operation to repair the ruined face of an eight-year-old boy caught in the crossfire outside the train station. Supplies began to run short as the days, then weeks, passed from the scheduled supply delivery. Without the usual deliveries, the tiny field hospital had little news from outside Rouen. Harriet's unease just kept growing, but with no information, she could do nothing but wait.

Months passed and new secret routes for supplies were established, and supplies began to trickle in, but there was little news. Winter held France in its grip. One icy day in late February, as Harriet was making notes in her journal, between operations, she felt a sharp pang of sadness. It overcame her, and she began to cry in earnest. One of the soldiers who was carrying in the next wounded, young man looked over at her with sympathy in his eyes. She quickly wiped away her tears and tried to shake off the sense of foreboding, as she helped the soldier transfer the young man to the makeshift operating room table. When the operation was over, and the patient was safely bandaged and placed in another area of the tunnel, Harriet retired to her makeshift bunk for a brief rest. She spent the time recording her feelings of deep despair before falling into a deep sleep. She slept so deeply that the surgeons were reluctant to rouse her when another casualty was brough in. Luckily the man was only superficially wounded, so they were able to get by without her.

Then one day in April, a courier was brought in a critically injured courier. Harriet recognized him from a previous meeting in Paris. As they worked to staunch the bleeding, he handed Harriet a poster. She quickly pushed it away, as she set to work trying to save his life. Unfortunately, her efforts were in vain, and she watched the light go out of his eyes while she still held pressure over a grievous wound on his abdomen. When the surgeon arrived to start the operation, she shook her head slowly. The surgeon looked down and sighed. That's when he noticed the bright red poster, that was partially stained with the courier's blood. When he saw the name and photo of Szlama on the propaganda poster about the execution of "traitors", he hurriedly crumpled it and pushed it behind a box of equipment. He could tell Harriet later. She didn't need to know right now, he thought.

That day, April 18th, the bombing of Rouen increased to a feverish pitch. The majority of the bombs hit civilian targets and other areas of dubious military value, leveling large areas of Northern France. Of the 500,000 tons of Allied bombs to hit France during the entirety of the war, the vast majority of this ordinance was dropped on the historic and lovely city of Rouen that day. As Harriet huddled with her patients against this "friendly fire" she thought about her patients. They were so young to be soldiers fighting such a miserable war, she thought. She held their hands as they called for their mothers over the deafening sounds of destruction.

Historical treasures such as the Notre Dame Cathedral of Rouen were not spared, nor was the Palace of Justice. As the bombs smashed the city's critical infrastructure, the ancient crypt beneath the church collapsed.

****

Book Four: Bernice & Barbara

Bernice 1954 -1956

Bernice knew it was time to talk to her daughters. It had been on her mind a lot in the last few days, ever since she saw the way some of the men's eyes had skimmed over her two oldest daughters last Saturday when they were downtown shopping. She put it off for several days as she struggled to put her thoughts into words. She was reminded again at evening choir practice, as she heard whispers about the daughters of some of the congregants. Her girls weren't mentioned, but one of Barbara's classmates was.

 She thought about her husband's great-grandmother, Catherine. She'd never met Catherine, but she was revered in the Prince family. She was also famous for speaking her mind, without hesitation. Even after all these years, many of her husband's elderly relatives would recall stories about the iron-willed matriarch at family get-togethers. She knew too, that the Prince family had already faced their share of trials and scandals. She thought of the stack of letters hidden away in her room, unopened. She walked to the dresser, and studied Catherine's steely-eyed gaze in an old, faded, family tintype placed next to a small keepsake box. The matriarch's erect posture and unwavering stare gave testimony to her fortitude and determination to protect her family. Her face, lined with grief, showed her perpetual pain at having failed to do so. Bernice knew that two of Catherine's children had died young, and the thought of outliving any of her children pained her. She didn't know if she would have been as strong as Catherine was. Her reputation was daunting! She also knew that raising children was not an easy task, particularly if you wanted them to thrive and uphold the family's values. It was too easy for children these days to be lured away by bad influences, what with the garbage on television and radio these days. Seemed like too many young men had cars, and too many young ladies were easily impressed by this. Life itself seemed almost too easy; it seemed like her children's generation didn't understand the hardships that had plagued her own childhood. She supposed much of that was her and her husband's fault when it came to their own children. She shook her head as she thought back to her own youth, the First World War and those early days of marriage during the depression. She thought of her classmates and childhood friends for a minute and sighed, before she mentally chastised herself for her procrastination.

She took a deep breath, steadied herself and went to her daughters' shared bedroom.

The cheery room was decorated with sunny yellow curtains, and crowded with a double bed, along with another twin bed, and a light blue, painted dresser that had been salvaged from the early days of their marriage. Battered, and used, the dresser had been painted and lovingly restored for the newlyweds, and then restored again over the years. Now it held a hodgepodge of clothing for the girls. The girl's artwork and class projects decorated the walls, from rudimentary crayon pictures in baby Bernie's favorite colors of carmine red and turquoise blue, to Joyce's more detailed and refined pen and ink sketches of neighbors and friends. She looked at all the innocent youth in that room, and wished again that the world was different.

Bernice gathered her four daughters in the master bedroom, where they sat on the edge of the bed, perched on her well-kept, soft pink, chenille, candlewick bedspread. Her girls ranged from a small toddler to a young woman on the blush of adulthood. It was time again for "the talk." Bernice's family had been having a similar talk with their daughters for as many generations as they'd been in this country. Bernice didn't know everything about the Prince family, but as she looked again at the stern, strong woman in the precious heirloom, Bernice knew Catherine would approve. Bernice knew her husband had been raised with similar words, even as he left this task to her. He didn't have Bernice's quiet strength and determination. He didn't have that same steel backbone that characterized the women, born, or married into this family did. Bernice hadn't been born a Prince, but she had accepted the mantle of responsibility the moment that he had put the ring on her finger.

"Today, we need to talk about something important, girls. Joyce, sit down next to your sisters and pay attention. Bernie, stop pulling Desdemona's braids and listen! Now Barbara, I know that you have heard some of this before, but you need to hear it again, so be quiet and pay attention," she said sharply, gaining her daughters' immediate attention. The girls stopped playing around and looked at Bernice expectantly. Bernice looked over her daughters, Barbara, at eighteen, was so studious and thoughtful, while Joyce, just barely fifteen, was more impulsive. Bernie, her six-year-old namesake, was a bundle of unbridled energy, while wee Desdemona, at four, was the baby of the family. That would soon change, with the baby Bernice was currently carrying, she thought as she stroked a hand over her rounded abdomen. The fetus kicked in response.

The girls straightened their posture and waited for Bernice to speak. Little Desdemona was barely more than a toddler, but she sat on Barbara's lap quietly and watched her mother.

Bernice took a deep breath, and hoped she was coherent. "There are too many people in this town that want us to fail. Some people, especially white people, want us to fail because our skin is too dark. They don't think we deserve the same life that they have. They hate us for being smart. They hate us because they can see with their own eyes that we aren't so very different from them. There are those that are jealous because we may be black, but the ladies in this family have always been known for their beauty. There are other people that resent us because have done well for ourselves. They fail to recognize hard work and only see lies. They think that we have somehow taken something that is not rightfully ours. There are just so many excuses that they have created to justify their hate for us.

"But they aren't alone in that. Among our own community there are also too many people that are so bitter with their lot in life, that they don't want us to survive either. There are those that hate us because our skin is too light. There are those that hate us because we have our farm. There are others that hate us because we will not bow our heads and accept the hand that we have been dealt. They believe that we should remain meek and quiet. They will even use the white man's book to try and subdue us. But that isn't what this family is!" she said.

Bernice thought about all the rejections she had faced, before continuing. She thought about Imogene Watkins and her smart little clique, and how they had done their best to shut out Bernice and her family from the social scene. Imogene's husband was the editor of the local paper, and Imogene wrote the social column. She was rumored to have written for Life magazine before returning home to Memphis. But it wasn't just Imogene, it was many of the ladies of South Memphis. They had pushed her out of the Debonair set when it started, stating that any woman with "that many" children just didn't qualify. Then they edged her out of the Merry Circle Charity and even the Housewives League. The head of the Housewives League couldn't even make eye contact while she sang out an excuse in a syrupy sweet voice. Bernice needed to prepare her daughters for this, so they wouldn't feel the same hurt and rejection that she had experienced over and over, throughout the years. She wanted to spare her children this.

At least it looked like her oldest, Barbara was breaking through; as a singer in the church choir, and an excellent student, she had been welcomed into the YMCA singing group, the Clique Social Club, and as a youth volunteer with the Alpha Kappa Alpha Sorority. Bernice hadn't allowed her to participate in the Rhomania Debutante Ball or become an Alpha sweetheart for a local fraternity. She was worried it might lead some of the church folk to talk. It wasn't enough that her girls were well-behaved, and virtuous. They needed to be above reproach. She took strength from her daughter's triumphs, before taking a breath and continuing.

"We are strong people, and we are a fierce people. We do not bend to the whims of others, and we do not sacrifice ourselves cheaply. We are not foreigners, and we are not outsiders. This is OUR land, and OUR country! This family has owned land here since we came to Tennessee and we are beholden to no one! Everything we have has been hard won, and hard earned, though our own labors. We do not owe anyone our allegiance or our gratitude for our freedom" she continued. "There are people that will try and befriend us for the sole aim of betraying us. Others want to use us, hurt us and abuse our good name. They think that they can infiltrate the Prince family and bring down the our proud family, down to their level, in the dirt. They think that they can shame us or bring disgrace upon our family. Many of them will do it under the guise of being a trusted friend, confidante, lover or protector. They will whisper sweet words and try to steal kisses. They will tell you silken but poisonous lies and false promises. They will say and do anything to destroy this family, and they will try to do this using you."

Her eyes bored into her eldest daughter's, "There have been many grave injustices that have been visited upon our family, and our people and it continues to this day. We do not forgive the perpetrators and we will not let them force us into submission. As the women of this family, an additional burden has been placed upon us – and additional injustices. We are not and will not be the playthings of the white man, or the white man's substitute. We aren't the whores of any man". Her daughters recoiled at her strong language, with Barbara looking deeply shocked.

Should we allow it, it will only lead to our destruction," she finished. She felt exhausted by her short lecture, and all the emotions and memories it brought welling to the surface. There was so much more she could say, she could even give cautionary tales, but she didn't dare dredge up the shameful family history.

Her oldest daughter, Barbara, flushed and nodded her head in acknowledgement. It was as if she could see Bernice's thoughts. Bernice's remaining daughters nodded as well. There was so much more that Bernice wanted to impart to her daughters, and to discuss, but it took too much out of her to do so. How do you explain the pain of being black in a country where the color of your skin was more important than the contents of your heart, or your head? How did you teach your children how to straddle two communities, both of which didn't and couldn't fully accept you? How to navigate the hostilities of both? To handle the pain of rejection? Furthermore, how do you teach your teenage daughters, that people would assume she had no virtue because of her race? That the same people that would sexualize her, would also be the first to shame or shun her?

Unfortunately, she knew that life would teach all of her daughters these devastating lessons. In the meantime, she would do what she could to keep her beautiful, precious babies safe.

****

Barbara, 1954

Bernice's oldest daughter, Barbara, was named after her maternal grandmother, who was rumored to have been in a long-term relationship with a white man. Barbara figured this was one of those poisonous lies that her mother was referring to but wasn't sure because it certainly wasn't talked about openly. She only knew it from eavesdropping on gossipy whispers at family gatherings. But rumor or not, Barbara took her mother's words to heart. It wasn't the first time that she'd heard that speech, or a similar one, but it was the first time, she'd really understood what the words meant. She thought about her family, their history, and her namesake, and the hardships they had endured. She thought about her paternal grandmother, Desdemona, for whom her younger sister was named.

Prince women had to be strong, even when society said they shouldn't be. Her grandmother, Desdemona, had single-handedly kept the family funeral home business going when Barbara's grandfather had died at an early age. She's done it despite the challenges of raising small children alone during the great depression. She felt ashamed as she thought about her friend, Nina Rae Miller, and her furtive meetings with a local politician.

Barbara had helped Nina to evade detection several times. Since Barbara had a reputation for being studious and serious, Nina's mom never questioned her too closely when Barbara accompanied Nina home to say that they were going to be studying at the Howe library. Nina's mom was probably just happy to think that Nina was going to crack a book, Barbara thought wryly. Nina wasn't known for being much of a student or a keen reader. If it wasn't a Hollywood glossy, Nina wasn't interested.

Nina was the granddaughter of one of the former pastors of the A.M.E. Zion church, who had sued Barbara's great-grandfather before either girl was born. Despite this history, the girls had become fast friends after meeting in the parlor of their teacher's house, where they were both enrolled in an afternoon course on etiquette and social graces. Both of their families were determined that Barbara and Nina would be presented at this year's debutante ball. Barbara was really excited about it and had been spending numerous afternoons practicing the strict etiquette that was required for presentation. She had even pressed her younger brother, Marvin, into practicing with her. As the oldest of the large brood, Barbara knew it was important to set an example for the rest of her siblings. Still, sometimes, it was just so awkward to curtsey and dance with her clumsy brother. He was all gangly arms and legs, and their other brothers would start clowning. Louie, Jack, and Richard would start teasing him, and Marvin would get so embarrassed that he'd just step all over her toes and ruin everything that they had been practicing. When that happened, she would get so mad that she would end up storming out her house and over to Nina's house. Nina's parents weren't as strict, so Nina and her brother, Anthony ran wild. Since Nina was being presented as a debutante in the same class as Barbara, Barbara's mother had relaxed her rigid rules about socializing after school and on weekends. Barbara was actually surprised because her mother's strict rules and regimens were legendary in their family. Her dad even joked sometimes by saluting her, and saying, "Aye, Aye, Ma'am."

Barbara had quickly exploited this new loophole. She would go over to Nina's and instead of practicing their curtsies, piano or their formal presentation, Nina would think of something more exciting to do. Sometimes, they would sneak down to the Summer Avenue drive-in. They would tell Nina's mom they were heading to the library, and then have the afternoon to themselves, free of parental interruptions or oversight.

Sometimes, Nina's brother, Anthony, and his friends would sneak them some liquor and cigarettes and they'd sit in their secret hideaway down by the river, watching fireflies, and shooting the breeze. Nina liked to talk about going to Chicago or Hollywood to make it big in show business, but even Barbara could see that it was a fanciful dream. Her parents often talked about Barbara going to college, and that sounded exciting to her. Barbara wasn't going to be the one to tell Nina that her starstruck aspirations were unlikely.

Recently, Barbara had joined Nina for cocktails at a local poker game. She'd thought it would be fun to dress up in one of Nina's satin strapless gowns and sip champagne like a lady of elegance and wealth. Despite being from a typical, upper-middle class family, Nina had a closet full of satin and silken fripperies and cheap, glittering gewgaws that were gifts from male admirers. Barbara's mom would have been outraged, but Nina's mom didn't seem to notice her daughter's new-found wardrobe. Or if she did, she didn't seem to want to address it. This never occurred to teenaged Barbara. (It wasn't until years later, as a mother herself, that she re-considered the situation. She had come home to Memphis for a brief visit, and heard about Nina's untimely death from an aggressive breast cancer, as she reminisced with friends. It brought back so many memories of their times together, including the night that had irreparably damaged their friendship.

The poker game was the catalyst. After endlessly cajoling Barbara, Nina had managed to convince Barbara to accompany her, with the promise of an elegant evening and a bit of "dress-up" for teenagers on the verge of adulthood. Instead of a sophisticated night on the town, acting like Grace Kelly or Lena Horne with a refined gentleman like Frank Sinatra, James Edwards or that handsome, charming Harry Belafonte, Barbara found herself being pawed and looked over like cheap, used, pawn shop merchandise, in a dark, smokey room in the back of a Beale Street club. It was more like Lana Turner, if the most recent issue of *Confidential* that Nina had devoured was anything to go by.

The men weren't handsome or debonair. They were paunchy, slovenly and greasy-looking with wrinkled shirts and stained ties. They were middle-aged and uncouth, spewing profanities from stained and yellowed teeth, as they gulped whiskey, spilled ashes from their cigars, and told crass jokes over five card Monty. The floor was sticky, and the club wasn't fancy. It had torn leatherette chairs and cracked Formica tables, with cigarette burns marring the surfaces. It was grimy and seedy, with a thick haze of blue smoke that made her want to cough and choke.

When one of Nina's paramour's associates spilled his drink on Barbara as he grabbed her arm and tried to pull her into his lap, she couldn't get out of there fast enough. Now, she remembered the incident with disgust, as she thought about how Nina had tried to shame her into staying. The memory solidified several ideas that had been rolling around in Barbara's mind for several weeks. The first was that Nina wasn't really her friend. Nina was a silly, sometimes vindictive, little slut that acted like she was from the Dixie Homes Housing Project. Nina wasn't a bad person per se, but Barbara suddenly realized that if she hung around Nina, she had nowhere to go but down. Despite her family's relative comfort, Nina's family didn't have the same values that Barbara's did. Barbara knew her mom was right about a lot of these things, and she didn't want to disappoint her. As she crept towards her back porch to sneak in her window, she decided that she would work harder at her studies. She wasn't a bad student, but she knew she could be a better one.

****

Bernice was relieved that a few weeks before her debutante ball, her daughter, Barbara, had an abrupt shift in attitude. Always a studious and obedient girl, Barbara had recently been experimenting in ways that Bernice didn't like. She knew Barbara had had a falling out with that cheap, little floozy, Nina, that had led to a breaking off of their friendship. Bernice didn't know exactly what had caused the disagreement, but she was determined that the girls stay at odds.

Since the disagreement, Barbara had been more diligent, and focused on her studies, and her debutante training. If she had to be reminded to smile more while practicing her waltz, and was noticeably laughing less, that was a small price to pay to keep her focused on her future. If only she could get Joyce to be more like Barbara, she thought, as she reached back to rub the small of her back. This pregnancy was taking a lot more out of her this time. She was so, so tired all the time, but mornings were the worst. Thank goodness the older kids helped corral the younger ones and get them off to school in the morning.

****

Joyce 1954

Joyce wasn't as receptive to her mother's message as Barbara. It angered her, frankly. She didn't care what other people thought. She didn't understand why her family didn't do something about it if it bothered them so much. Besides, why should they have to live differently from the whites anyway? She had heard that life was very different for blacks living up north. She was going to leave this stupid place as fast as she could. No one was going to tell her where she could sit, or what bathroom she could use. She wasn't going to be someone's maid either!

She couldn't wait to graduate high school and get out of Memphis. She wasn't going to be like her mom, that was sure! She would do more than have babies. It seemed like that's all her mom did, besides go to church, and clean the house. Joyce couldn't believe her mom was pregnant again. Wasn't she too old for that? Angry, ugly, thoughts ran through her mind for weeks. She bickered with her brothers and argued with her friends at school. She sat in the back of the classroom at school and became hostile. Inequities that she had always just accepted as unalterable, now rankled her.

Prior to this, she had lived her life away from white society in Memphis. They had their lives, and she had hers. Now, she began to focus in on the "other" Memphis. She took note of their restaurants, their clothes and their rules. She started to pay more attention to their culture. Her resentment grew. Now that she had really taken notice, she couldn't forget it. The "whites only" signs at the Beauty shop, and in the windows of downtown restaurants were like a rough sandpaper against her soul. The suspicious stares of white passengers on the trolley when she took her baby brother downtown to buy penny candy bored into her skin. The endless sea of white faces that peered down on her from billboards, and on the covers of magazines mocked her.

She remained irritable and angry until one evening, as she helped her sisters clear the dinner table. She suddenly snapped at her mom. Her mom had just finished scolding Joyce.

"Joyce, stand up straight now. Don't slouch. It doesn't look nice. You want people to see you as a nice, respectable, young lady, don't you?" her mother admonished.

Joyce visibly bristled at her mother's words then muttered under her breath, "Yeah, it's my slouching that embarrasses the family." She felt a burst of anger rise up inside of her, like a firestorm inside her stomach. She went to belch out this feeling, but the rage came instead.

Her mother raised an eyebrow, and opened her mouth, when Joyce abruptly interrupted and began yelling, "Why don't we leave this place, if they don't want us here? You keep saying that everyone wants to keep us down here – so why don't we go to New York or Chicago, then? I heard that they don't have all these stupid rules and laws to control us there. We should leave! Do you really think my posture, my clothes or anything else I do matters, when we aren't even allowed to try on clothes in a department store?" Joyce's chest was heaving with the force of her rage. Her face was twisted into an ugly sneer.

Barbara looked up sharply at her outburst and looked thoughtful. Bernice was taken aback by the venom in Joyce's voice. She had been sitting with her feet propped up, resting her tired legs for a few minutes before finishing washing the rest of the dishes. She felt at a disadvantage, as she was verbally attacked by her angry daughter. She struggled to her feet, pushing herself up awkwardly, limited by the ungainliness of her advanced pregnancy.

"Is that what you think, girl?" she said, with a deep weariness coloring her speech. "You think we should give up our home and our history because other people don't want us here? Where is your pride? You think we should let someone else chase us away from our land, our birthright? Your father's people helped build Memphis, but we should just leave that all behind, right? We should forget our self-respect and dignity too? All so we can sit where we want on the bus? Or use the dressing room at Goldsmiths?" she sighed heavily. She didn't know how to explain to her angry, teenage daughter that self-respect and self-worth were independent of the complicated racial policies of the South.

"So you think it's just a la-la land up in Chicago, where everyone loves everyone? You think if you take the bus up Highway 51, there's an invisible line you cross to get to racial harmony and respect?

She continued, "You think that the whites up there don't see us the same way that they do down here? Well, you'd be sadly mistaken, and sorely disappointed. They may not say it to your face up there, but they aren't any different. They don't want us in their neighborhoods, their schools, or their churches. They want us to be their maids, not their equals, just the same as any Mississippi cracker.

"Why don't you ask your dad about it? He spent some time living up there before we got married. He can tell you how it is. In the meantime, you ought to think long and hard about whether you'd really leave your heritage and your identity behind so easily. Because that doesn't say very much about you, or the values we've tried to instill in you." She turned her back to Joyce and trudged to the kitchen, without waiting for a reply. She started to tackle the mountain of dirty dishes, as silent tears rolled down her cheeks.

"Joyce, stop it! You are upsetting mama," Barbara chided.

Joyce looked at her sister, Barbara, in surprise as her mother left the room. She didn't expect the conservative and bookish Barbara to take her side, but she was still disappointed when Barbara started to admonish her.

Barbara didn't entirely disagree with Joyce. "It's not what you said, Joyce. It's how you said it. Mama doesn't deserve the disrespect. It's okay to ask why they never left, but not in that way," Barbara said in a conciliatory tone.

Joyce burst into tears, "You just don't understand! None of you understand! I'm not going to be like y'all! I'm not going to be like *her*," she said. "I'm not going to just have babies and spend my time on my knees for the Lord! I am going to do something with my life – and no one is going to stand in my way!" she finished before storming off dramatically towards the back of the house.

'Yeah, an actress, based on that performance," Marvin snorted, entering the room just in time to catch Joyce's statement. With that, the tense moment dissipated. Barbara accompanied Marvin to the kitchen to help her mom, as he searched for a snack.

"Son, how can you be hungry? We just finished dinner," Bernice teased as she handed Barbara a plate to dry and put away.

****

Joyce climbed the stairs to the attic and seethed. Even though it was cramped, hot, and stuffy, it was the only place Joyce could have any privacy in a house packed with people. She shared her room with her sisters, and even after her sister, Barbara, left for college this fall, she'd still have to share her room with both little Bernie and baby, Desdemona. Outnumbering the girls by almost two to one, her brothers claimed two of the bedrooms of the house. Her parents took up the remaining bedroom. The new baby would join her parents in their room as well. The house was practically bursting at the seams. There just wasn't room for a moody teenager.

In desperation, she had claimed the area behind several steamer trucks in the half-finished attic, as her own. She had re-arranged the assorted collection of old furnishings, clothing, and other forgotten belongings into a semblance of order to maximum her hidden spot. If the low-ceiling space hadn't been so cramped, and cluttered, she would have moved-in entirely. As it was, she was meticulous about keeping the small space clean and cobweb free. She always checked the small mouse traps that were set at the borders of an old rug she had salvaged from the trash. In addition to the rug that covered the 8 foot X 4-foot space, she had decorated *her* space with several cushions and pillows to make the area more comfortable.

There was a small, attic window, which gave the area some light and a whiff of fresh air, when she dared to crack it open. Now, it was bathed in moonlight. It had started out as a place for young

Joyce to hide her treasures from her troublesome brothers and their pranks, but it had grown into a place where the frustrated and angry young teen could brood, read forbidden romance novels, or simply hide away when she needed some time to herself, like now. She felt so stifled sometimes and she wasn't even sure exactly why. It was so hard to try and carve out a place for herself in this large, noisy and bustling family. Between baby Joey, and big sister, Barbara, Joyce was surrounded by multiple siblings, making it impossible for her to stand out. Barbara was too perfect, with good grades and all her little social clubs. Joyce struggled in math, even as she excelled in art and history, but it wasn't enough to make her standout. She wasn't interested in sewing or homemaking skills, and her secretarial skills were mediocre. At 15, she wasn't the slender beauty that her sister was. She was thicker, and built in a more sturdy fashion, like her mother. When her brother, Marvin, joked about her childbearing hips, she nearly cried. Despite all the perms, and pomades, her hair remained kinky and unmanageable. Her skin was blotchy and marred with a cascade of pimples at her hairline. Her mother tried to hide her wide hips in voluminous skirts that just made her look matronly. Compared to her sister's sleekly coiled coif, dewy, clear skin, and her fashionable and slim pencil skirts and twin sets, she knew she was the awkward, ugly, little sister. This was especially evident when she was forced to walk with her sister down the halls of Geeter High School. It was just another reminder that she didn't fit in, and it fed her discontent.

Her parents were pushing for college in a few years, but she didn't know what she wanted. She would have liked to work at WDIA, the local radio station but she knew her parents would never approve. She liked to sing, not the stuff from the church, but tunes from Johnny Ace, Dinah Washington, and Lena Horne. She spent a lot of time in the hot little attic writing poems and songs to express her feelings, but her songs didn't sound like Dinah or her other idols. Her songs were darker, angrier.

She felt invisible, except for when her parents were scolding her for another of her failures. Sometimes she thought about running away to Chicago or Detroit. She finished the song she was working on under the faint light of an old flashlight, before curling up in a ball. Later, she crept downstairs, into her room, climbing into bed with her little sister, Bernie. The young girl didn't stir, but her older sister, Barbara, in the bed on the other side of the room, opened her eyes "Joy, is that you?" she said in a half-whisper, half yawn. She then rolled over and went back to sleep before Joyce could answer. Joyce wished she could do the same, but sleep eluded her. She listened to the sounds and snores of her sisters while she laid still and waited for fatigue to overtake her.

****

Down the hall, reclining against their headboard, Bernice was talking to her husband in a low voice, while he rubbed her large belly. Langston loved to see Bernice full with his child. As he moved his hand, he felt the child inside move. He bent his head to kiss her belly, as she ran her hand thru his hair. Even now, when she felt like a melon ready to burst open, her husband made her feel beautiful, she thought. "Wait, wait, wait" she said, as he began to lift her nightgown to kiss her lower on her belly. She pushed on his shoulder for emphasis.

"What?" Langston said, bewildered.

"What are we going to do about Joyce?" she said. "And stop distracting me," she continued, as she pushed away his left hand, which was still making slow circles on her bare belly. She pushed down her nightgown and struggled to sit up straighter.

"What about Joyce?" he responded.

"She's just so angry," Bernice said before relaying the evening conversation to her husband, feeling slightly annoyed that sometimes, it felt like she did all the parenting. If her husband hadn't raced off to pick up a body for the funeral home after dinner, he might have been there when it happened.

"Do you want me to go wake her up and make her give account?" Langston said, with resignation in his voice. He hadn't noticed any change in Joyce's behavior, but he took his wife at her word.

Hearing this, Bernice felt again, as if she was parenting in a vacuum. Discipline was easy, instilling morals and values was hard. She knew her husband was working diligently to provide for the family, but sometimes she felt like he used his work to escape the trials and tribulations of having ten children under their small roof.

"I am afraid she is losing her way, Langston. We need to bring her back to the Lord," Bernice finished.

Langston thought for a minute before responding. "Darling wife, it's not the Lord we need to bring her back to. She is well churched, thanks to you and your dutiful teaching. It's this family, and our family business. She has shirked her responsibilities for too long. It's time that she comes to work at the funeral home after school like her brother, Marvin".

He continued, "We let Barbara out of her family responsibilities but that was different. Barbara doesn't have the time because of all her after-school studies and social clubs, but Joyce doesn't have that excuse. If she wants to mope around, she can mope around with the stiffs at the mortuary. They won't mind a bit," he said chuckling at his own joke. Problem solved; Langston's hands began to explore his wife once more. He waited for her to turn the lamp out, before pulling her into his arms and kissing her neck, which made her giggle like a young bride.

****

As 1954 continued on, Barbara prepared herself to leave home for college. She was the first in her family to do so, and there was a lot of pressure on her shoulders. Her brother, Marvin, who was just a year behind her, seemed immune to their mother's pressure. Instead, he spent the summer working at the funeral home and flirting with the girls from school. Barbara wondered if her brother had to endure the same lectures about protecting the family name, but she doubted it. Their mother might click her tongue at some of the girls he brought home, but she didn't seem upset by it. Barbara knew that if she brought a boy home, he better be the marrying kind, and she better be ready to get married. It wasn't fair, but she didn't expect her parents to change.

Joyce, on the other hand, withdrew into herself. She spent more and more time in the stuffy attic or out of the house, away from her mother's gaze. She didn't take her mother's lectures the same way that her sister did. She saw it as a sign of submission, and she wasn't going to submit to an unjust system. She was tired of being told what she could and couldn't do, and she was tired of following rules that weren't fair. She continued to write songs and poems in her journal and to look for a way out from under the family burden. When Johnny Ace died on Christmas Day, she became even more determined. She snuck out from under her mother's watchful eye to his funeral service at the Clayborn Temple. She made herself a promise that she would get out of Memphis and make something of herself.

Bernice could feel her daughter retreating away from her, but with the new baby, she didn't have the time or energy to confront her stubborn, stubborn child. She could only keep tabs on her the best she could and steer her out of trouble. She sometimes tasked Joyce with watching her younger siblings, just so she could keep her occupied. Her task became easier when Langston brought home a television that year, but Bernice would have preferred to have indoor plumbing. She had been urging him to use some of the profits from the funeral home to buy a house on Lauderdale Street for their large brood. Instead, she would just be grateful that Captain Midnight, Super Circus, and the Buster Brown Gang now kept Joyce and her younger siblings anchored to their seats on the couch.

Things settled down in the Prince house, and Bernice began to relax.

****

Bernice, August 1955

In the summer of 1955, Bernice was in the early stages of pregnancy, and was feeling nauseated and short tempered most of the time. Her usual endless patience had been replaced by frustration, as the younger kids became irritable in the sweltering heat. Bernice was tired of hearing the kids bicker, so early that morning, she packed up a bag filled with sandwiches and towels and rounded up the kids. It was barely 9 am but it was already a sticky hot morning with the thermometer edging past 90 degrees by the time she got everyone ready and out of the house. They headed to the Orange Mound neighborhood pool. Bernice had to remind herself of the refreshing water that was waiting for them as they trudged down the street in a single file line. The younger ones were rowdy, boisterous, and filled with an energy she could only envy. The older kids brought up the back of the line, making sure the younger ones didn't wander in the street, and she carried the baby.

She was glad that she had been able to get all the children vaccinated this year. The year before, her worries about a possible polio outbreak had kept the children home, even in the hottest weather.

This pregnancy seemed to be weighing heavier on her than the previous ones. She'd had a couple of miscarriages over the years, a stillbirth, and a crib death, but somehow, she knew this was going to be the last. She had just celebrated her 40th birthday, and her body felt weary. Her heart felt heavy knowing that she would never again bring life into the world after this, but this heaviness didn't last for long, as she played with her baby son, Joey. He splashed, and kicked, and giggled with glee. It reminded her of all the joy her children gave her and reminded her to be grateful to the glorious God who had given her such bounty. Thus satisfied, and with her nausea resolving, Bernice set out to enjoy the day with all of her children. They had a poolside picnic. She judged the kids makeshift, diving contests and watched the younger ones doze in the shade. She dozed off a little herself, to the sounds of children playing and laughing. She slept surprisingly well, waking as the air finally began to cool, and her son Jack leaned over her, dripping cool water droplets on her. The sky was a deep blush as she and the kids packed up their things and headed home. They were quieter on the way home, with exhaustion setting in, at the end of a relaxing, pleasant day. She smiled to herself, pleased to have had this moment with the children. Barbara was away at school already, and next week it was Marvin's turn. It was good to have this time with him before he left too.

The living room lights were blazing as they made their way up the street. Full twilight was just settling in as they walked up the front steps to the house. The kids entered first, with Bernice and the baby bringing up the rear. She stopped short when she saw the concerned and anxious look on her husband's face as she entered the house. He didn't look irritated that dinner hadn't been ready when he returned. He looked concerned, almost scared. She watched his face relax as he took in their appearance, the towels, and the sleepy baby. He didn't say anything right away but reached for the sleeping child. She gladly handed off the baby so she could quickly change out of her wet clothes and heat up supper. As she changed into a airy summer dress, she was glad that she had a raspberry gelatin mold congealing in the ice box for the kids' dessert along with the spam and egg casserole she'd made early that morning. She had an olive relish made with lime jello, celery, pickles, and stuffed olives to accompany the casserole. It was one of her husband's favorites.

She came back down into the kitchen and began to prepare supper. She wondered what was on her husband's mind. She knew it must be serious if he didn't want to mention it in front of the children. Now that the older kids were pitching in at the funeral home, there wasn't much that she and her husband didn't discuss in front of them. Langston thought it was important that the kids understand "the economics of real life," and she agreed. When their son, Richard, had decided last year that he wanted to be a professional baseball player, Langston had required Richard to work at the funeral home in order to earn money for his own baseball glove, baseball, and tickets to the local games at Martin Field. Bernice fully approved. She didn't want her children to grow up feeling entitled just because their family owned a business. She turned her thoughts back to the present.

As she heated the casserole on the stove, she warmed some leftover biscuits in the oven. As the kids came downstairs, one by one, after changing out of their swimsuits, the older ones came into the kitchen to help set the table. Even little Bernie helped with the silverware and her son, Bobby, brought the highchair to the table.

The children were uncharacteristically subdued at dinner. The sun and the heat had worn them out. Bernice knew they would sleep well, but Langston, still looked troubled, and he too was quiet. After an abbreviated prayer, there was no sound except the sounds of eating, the passing of dishes, and the scraping of silverware on plates. Very quickly, the children excused themselves. Marvin and Louis cleared the table, as Joyce started washing dishes. Jack led the younger kids upstairs to bed. It was if by tacit admission, they all knew something was wrong. By 8:30, all of the kids had finished up and traipsed off to bed. Bernice got up to make some coffee as Langston cleared the last few plates. They talked in hushed tones as she waited for the water to heat. Finally, after she poured the coffee and sat back down at the table, Langston began to speak. "Bernie, we need to watch the news. Something has happened." He turned on the television set, as she carried the cups into the living room. They waited in silence, sipping their coffees until the news came on, in Dick Hawley's crisp, rapid tones.

"In our top story tonight, the body of a Chicago youth who went missing the Mississippi Delta was found yesterday. The fourteen-year-old negro was last seen in the company of two white men, Roy Bryant and John William Milam, who abducted the boy from his uncle, Mose Wright's home in the middle of the night. The boy was weighed down with a heavy, gin fan and thrown into the Tallahatchie River. The body was found to have a bullet wound to the head along with injuries that appeared to have been made with an axe. Identification was made thru a piece of jewelry that had previously belonged to the young man's father. The boy is alleged to have whistled at Mr. Bryant's wife shortly before the abduction. Illinois governor, William Stratton, and Chicago Mayor, Richard Daley, are demanding a full investigation. The mayor is also asking that the federal government get involved. Currently, the boy's body is en route to Chicago for funeral and burial services by his family".

"WMCT has sent our own crew to Greenville, Mississippi to talk to the locals there, as well as to Money, Mississippi to talk to the relatives of the dead, negro boy. We will have that report for you tomorrow. In our next story, we will talk about the latest epidemic plaguing downtown Memphis, Jaywalkers."

Langston turned the television off and turned to Bernice. All the color had drained from her face. "Oh my God! How could this happen? He's just a boy. He's the same age as our darling Jack. Oh, my. Oh, dear Lord, his poor Mama!" she cried.

Langston put his arm around her to steady her. "Bernice, this case is going to be different, and I don't think it's going to be good. The folks in Chicago aren't going to let this rest. It may be just another dead negro to them folks down in Mississippi, but it's different up North. I don't think anyone is going to forget this," He paused.

"And while I think it's long overdue that they finally hold someone accountable for all the terrible things that happen to people down here, I don't think that's going to happen. I do think it's going to get awfully dangerous around here for a while. White folks are not going to accept people up north telling them what to do," he finished.

"But it's a child! He's somebody's baby!" Bernice exclaimed, heartbroken for the mother of this deceased child.

"Yes, he is," Langston said, "and I think that's the only reason why we are hearing about it at all. How many young, negro men have disappeared here in the Delta, over the years? So many," he said, gravely.

"So," he continued, "I want us to keep a very close eye on our boys. I know we've raised them right, but I think it might get very dangerous for young, negro men and boys in the coming days. The whites are going to want to push back after this. They always do," he finished, looking angry, frustrated, and emotionally exhausted.

With that, Langston took her hand, and they headed off to bed. Later, Bernice lay in bed, with Langston's hand comfortably around her rounded belly. She lay there silently, but she couldn't sleep. In the dark, quiet bedroom, with her husband's soft snores in the background, hot, bitter, silent tears washed down her face. Joyce's angry words came back to her.

Over the next few weeks, Bernice continued to grieve along with many in the black community. The death of Emmitt Till resonated deep inside her, as she felt the fear of every black mother. News footage showed lines snaking for blocks as mourners in Chicago waited to pay their respects to the grief-stricken Mamie Till. Women were seen fainting in the stifling heat of the crowded temple as they approached the ravaged body of a boy so close to Bernice's sons in age. She was proud of Emmitt's mother's unflinching honesty and grief. She was gratified to see that Mamie Till stayed unyielding, refusing to placate anyone, or to mourn in silence, hidden away. Mamie refused to allow her son and the horrors inflicted on him to be forgotten. Bernice felt a kindred spirit to this other mother. She didn't know if she would have the same grace, strength, and dignity if she had been in Mrs. Till's place. She prayed she never had to find out.

When the pictures were published in Jet magazine, she snuck a copy into the house. Away from the eyes of her children, she was crushed, infuriated, and devastated by the photos inside, showing the ruined face of what was once a smiling youth. It haunted her!

It only became worse, when the sham of a trial was conducted. In less time than it took for a movie matinee, the murderers walked free to the cheers of their white neighbors. It was no less destructive when the article published in early 1956 with the murderers bragging about their heinous crimes. When Bernice gave birth later that year, she informed her husband that the child was to be called Emmitt.

Bernice wasn't the only Prince to be deeply affected by the horrific and violent death of this young boy. Away at school, Barbara vowed then and there, never live in the south again.

Her younger sister, Joyce, stopped retreating to the attic to write her poems and songs. She stopped dreaming of tomorrow. Instead, in the middle of 1956, she boarded the *City of New Orleans* train with a small suitcase, a small amount of money, and her notebook filled with songs. In the pocket of her cloth coat she had two addresses scribbled on a slip of paper. She arrived in St. Louis, as a 16-year-old filled with false bravado. Instead of being a lost little girl, she was embarking on a great adventure. She headed to the first address, 4247 E. Maffitt Avenue, which was a stout-looking, older, brick building. An elderly African American female, who looked equally stout, was sweeping the sidewalk outside the building. Joyce straightened her posture, patted her hair into place, and discreetly adjusted her stockings as she stopped a few homes over. Once she was presentable, she approached the house. "Mrs. Matthews?" she asked, tentatively.

The elderly woman in a shapeless faded print dress looked up from her task and stopped sweeping. Joyce had never seen a dress in that style except in the old magazines at the library.

"I am," the woman answered, looking weary.

"Pearline Adams gave me your address. She said she is kin to you and Miss Mary. She thought you might be able to rent me a room here." She continued, saying, "My name is Joyce Green," using the alias she and Lorraine had agreed upon. Joyce was nervous but her voice was growing more confident as she spoke.

"Baby Pearlie? Down there in Memphis?" the woman asked.

As Joyce bobbed her head, and said, "Yes, ma'am," she watched the old woman's face transform. When she smiled with a gapped-toothed grin, her face relaxed and she looked decades younger. "How is that darling girl?" Mrs. Matthews asked, hopeful.

"Why, she is singing up front in the choir at the Clayborn Temple," Joyce recited, as Pearline had instructed. Joyce continued, "As a matter of fact, Pearline is planning on coming up here to stay in a couple months."

Mrs. Matthews looked delighted, then thoughtful, as she considered Joyce. She looked her over, and said, "How old are you, girl?"

"I'm eighteen," Joyce lied.

Mrs. Matthews raised an eyebrow, and said, "No, you're not. You may be a bit broad in the hips, but you look barely out of knee socks to me." She looked Joyce over again, saying, "Now, you expecting a baby, Miss Green?"

Joyce's jaw dropped. "No, no, Mrs. Matthews," she stammered, shocked by the inquiry. Her expression of dismay must have convinced Mrs. Matthews because, after making a "hmmm" noise deep in her throat, and looking Joyce over once again, Mrs. Matthews spoke.

"Well, I can rent you a bed in a shared room with my granddaughter, Mary. She's a bit older than you, but it's the only space I have left. If you stay here, there are rules. Do you understand that?" Mrs. Matthews said.

Joyce bobbed her head as Mrs. Matthews continued. "Now, Missy Green, you are underage. In this house, that means you go to school. So tomorrow we will march on over to the Sumner High School and get you enrolled. Furthermore, we are church-going folk, and if you live here, you are expected to attend Kennerly Temple services on Sundays. There's no smoking, drinking, or *co-habi-tating* in this house. Men are not allowed upstairs in the women's area at all. If you break any of these rules, you and your things will be out here on the street before the sun sets. Room and board for a shared room is 3 dollars every week and includes supper. There is a bathroom down the hall, and wash day is Thursday. If you are going to be late, or out all night, let me know before suppertime, so no food goes to waste. Got it?"

Joyce bobbed her head again and said, "Yes, ma'am." She reached into her pocket and pulled out three crumpled, one-dollar bills, which she handed to the elderly woman. Mrs. Matthews then led her inside on a quick tour of the boarding house and showed her to a narrow cot that shared space with a small twin bed in an immaculately kept room at the back of the house. The bed linens were worn and patched in places, and the walls were in want of paint, with a threadbare, rag, rug over bare wood floors. The wooden dresser shined with the scent of lemon oil. The wood floor was spotless, and the cot was made up tidily. Joyce thanked her host, before placing her suitcase underneath the cot. She headed down the hallway to the chilly bathroom and peered into the small, streaked mirror. She opened her purse and retrieved her Hi-Hat face powder. She then carefully applied raspberry crème lipstick to her plump lips. The make-up was a secret gift from her sister. Her mother would have never allowed it. Her older sister, Barbara, had been selling Lucky Heart and other cosmetics in her dorm to make some extra money. Joyce treasured the make-up and took pride in the fact that at least Barbara could see that she wasn't a kid anymore. She took one last look in the mirror, and after blowing her reflection a kiss, she headed downstairs and out of the house.

This time as she walked down the street, she strolled with purpose as she headed to the bus to take her across the river to 1312 Broadway in East St. Louis. The staff at Club Manhattan had just unlocked their doors when Joyce arrived. The owner of the club had been a talent scout in Memphis before relocating to St. Louis a few years ago. He had made his name in the Delta, both recording his own music, and recruiting musicians off Beale Street to make records for Sam Phillips, and their competition, Modern Records. In addition to his own club, the owner and his band, Kings of Rhythm, performed in various clubs on both sides of the Mississippi River. Joyce had heard rumors around Memphis that he and his wife now had their own studio. She knew this was the place to go if she wanted to record any of the songs that filled her notebooks. She entered the darkened club with her heart beating in her mouth.

The interior of the club was dimly lit back by the bar. There was a small stage directly across from the bar, which was better lit. There were tables in scattered groupings between the bar and the stage, and a young boy was wiping down the tables. Several members of the band were on the stage, chatting and laughing, while a skinny man of medium height, gave directions from the main floor in of front the stage. He was medium brown complected with a thin mustache. He moved with an intense energy that almost made him seem to shimmer, as he paced intently back and forth in a short course. Joyce was watching the man so intently that she didn't even notice where she was walking, until her hip bumped the back of the chair. The scrap of the chair against the hard floor caused the man, along with the people on stage, to peer past the stage lights into the darkened floor area where Joyce stood.

A man on the stage, with a saxophone in his hand, called out, "Are you here to audition as part of the stage show?"

At first, all Joyce could do was nod. It took her a moment, as the wiry, intense man on the main floor turned to look at her for her to squeak out a "Yes, sir!"

The people on stage laughed, and the man paused his pacing to look her up and down. He seemed to appreciate her fuller figure, looking at her in a way she hadn't seen a man do before. "Get on up there and show us what you can do," he barked.

Joyce started at his brusque tone, but hastened to scramble over to the stage. The man with the saxophone reached out a hand to lead her up the side stairs. Then he and the other band members positioned her off to a side area, that was marked with three evenly spaced X's on the ground. She stood there dumbly looking at the X's on the ground until the musicians started to play. Then almost instinctively, she started to move her hips and dance to the music.

"That will do," the man in front of the stage called out. "We do shows at least three nights a week, and you get paid ten dollars a week. On weekends we do shows across the river until 2 am, and then come back over here and perform until 5 am. Is that going to be a problem?"

"No," Joyce said in a near whisper as she gulped air.

"Now get on out of here and let us rehearse. I will expect to see you at this address on Virginia Place at 4:30 pm, Thursday," he said handing her a card. "That will give Lorraine time to get you fixed up and in costume," he finished.

"And plenty of time for Lorraine to eat her alive," the drummer called.

"Wait a minute!" one of the musicians called. "What's your name?"

"Missy Green" she answered, deciding that the less she used her real name, the better. If there was ever a time for Joyce Prince, daughter of the strict religious southern family to shed her identity, this was it. "Missy Green, I like that," she mused before being brought back to reality as the saxophone player said, "Well, Miss Missy Green, welcome to Ike Turner and the Kings of Rhythm."

Ecstatic, Joyce felt like skipping all the way back to the bus stop but restrained herself. She didn't want anyone looking out their windows to see her acting immature. This was just the first step to her new life. On the way back to the boardinghouse, she stopped by Woolworth's for a note card. She quickly scribbled a note to Barbara, telling her she was safe, and not to tell her parents where she was. She could trust Barbara on that. For all of their childhood arguments, her big sister was as loyal as they came. She handed 3 cents to the man across the counter, who promised to send it out with the morning mail. For another ten cents, the man behind the counter handed her an ice cream cone with two big scoops of vanilla ice cream. After she finished the cone, Joyce gave into temptation. This time she did skip all the way back to the boardinghouse.

In quick succession, Joyce's life fell into a routine. Classes during the week, homework during lunch, then a nap in the afternoon on the nights they had performances. She napped every chance she got, particularly on Saturdays, so that she wouldn't be too tired for church. Mrs. Matthews might not be crazy about her schedule, but she couldn't fault Joyce. She was always pleasant and polite. She paid her rent on time. She kept to herself, and she always told her in advance when she would miss supper. In fact, she missed supper so often, that Mrs. Matthews decided to start packing Joyce a lunch instead. Most of all, she never, ever missed church service.

She hadn't gotten a chance to ask Ike about looking at any of her songs yet, but she would. This summer, the band was going on the road – and Pearline was coming to St. Louis! She had already talked to Ike and Lorraine about adding Pearline to their routine, and with the way that Lorraine fired the girls on stage, Joyce was pretty sure that they would need somebody new by the time Pearline got here.

Lorraine didn't seem to have a problem with "Missy," but that's because Joyce was a little intimidated by the brooding, mercurial, Ike Turner. In fact, Lorraine seemed to have taken almost a maternal interest in Joyce, and in turn, Joyce would often help Lorraine with the kids during recording sessions. She wasn't needed then, since she was more of a dancer than any kind of back-up singer, and Lorraine could get wound up pretty tight when the kids were running around. Ike was always on edge if the band couldn't seem to get it perfect on the first take, so Missy and the kids tiptoed around Lorraine and Ike on these occasions.

By the next year, Joyce had become disillusioned with the Kings of Rhythm. After all this time, Ike still hadn't read any of her songs. He'd promised to, so many times, but he just kept putting her off. Then, just as he seemed to get interested in hearing what Joyce had to say, the Saxophone player's girlfriend, Ann, convinced him to let her sing in the show. She was devastated when after Ann did a rendition of "You know I love you," Ike made her lead vocalist. Soon after that, Ann was in the recording sessions with the band, while Lorraine and Joyce stayed outside and watched the kids. Ann even moved in with Ike and Lorraine.

She was even more devastated when one afternoon she caught Ann and Ike using her song notebook and making their own alterations. Before she knew it, they had stolen several stanzas from her notebook, and used them on a track called "Box Top." They also took several lines of her poetry for a song called "What can it be." She felt angry and betrayed, particularly since she felt like the melody they used cheapened the feelings in her lyrics.

 Later, when Ann's boyfriend, Ray, got in a fight with Ike and they both left the band, Joyce thought she'd get her chance, but Ike turned her down flat. It wasn't long before Ann was back, after giving birth to a baby boy, except that Lorraine had turned bitter, and suspicious, making it even more difficult for Joyce and Pearline to perform in the shows. Any tiny misstep was enough to get you dismissed these days. That was enough for Joyce, she knew she'd never get her chance if she stayed in St. Louis.

When the band travelled to Chicago that summer, she convinced Pearline to join her when she left the Kings of Rhythm. Joyce had an offer to sing back up with Buddy Guy and Muddy Waters. She liked Chicago, it had such a different feel than Memphis or St. Louis but the winters were brutal. The wind managed to cut through her heavy sweaters and coats as if they were tissue paper. The early darkness and the unrelenting cold of the Chicago winter made her feel sad and lonely. But soon enough, the initial promise of back-up singing had become tedious. No one wanted to let her show her range, or her talent. The nightly shows became a painful reminder that she wasn't quite good enough, or pretty enough for anyone to take her seriously. No one wanted to hear her songs. No one cared what she had to say. They just wanted her to sing back-up harmonies and dance on the stage. She was never invited to socialize with the band, so after each show, she trudged back to the dreary, old apartment building, and up several flights of stairs to her old, ugly and cramped studio apartment with peeling paint and water stains on the ceiling. She slept on a lumpy fold out couch, which was preferable to the old, stained mattress on the floor that Pearline had claimed shortly after they moved in.

Too often, now that Pearline had a new boyfriend, Joyce was alone in the tiny, cold apartment they shared, wondering what had happened to her dream.

After her friend, Pearline, attempted suicide after a failed romance with John Lee Hooker, she convinced Pearline that it was time to go home. It didn't take long to pack up her miserably few possessions.

On the train back to Memphis, Joyce and Pearline made a pact not to tell anyone about their interlude outside of Memphis. Pearline, for certain, had more to lose than Joyce, if word of her scandalous behavior reached Shelby County. As for Joyce, she wanted no reminders of her failed attempt at independence.

While her parents were stone-faced when they picked her up at the train station on a brisk, December morning in 1958, Joyce kept her mouth shut. She pulled her cloth coat tight against her, and she walked behind her father. His gait, stiff and formal. Her mother walked at her side, her mouth a disapproving straight line. There was no hug of welcome and no small talk during the short trip back to the family home. She didn't break the silence to ask for forgiveness and she offered no explanations. She entered into an uneasy truce with her parents as she crossed the threshold to their home in Memphis. She didn't even protest when they forbid her from seeing Pearline again.

No one was more surprised than Joyce when her application for Spring admission to Tennessee Agricultural & Industrial State College was accepted. Her parents seemed mollified by this, because she would be under the watchful eye of her two brothers who were enrolled there as well. Before she left Nashville, she placed the notebooks with her song lyrics in the trash.

****

Book Five: Bobby, Jack & Desdemona, 1968- 1975

There must be lights burning brighter somewhere
Got to be birds flying higher in a sky more blue
If I can dream of a better land
Where all my brothers walk hand in hand
Tell me why, oh why, oh why can't my dream come true

There must be peace and understanding sometime
Strong winds of promise that will blow away
All the doubt and fear
If I can dream of a warmer sun
Where hope keeps shining on everyone
Tell me why, oh why, oh why won't that sun appear

We're lost in a cloud
With too much rain
We're trapped in a world
That's troubled with pain
But as long as a man
Has the strength to dream
He can redeem his soul and fly

Deep in my heart there's a trembling question
Still I am sure that the answer's gonna come somehow
Out there in the dark, there's a beckoning candle
And while I can think, while I can talk
While I can stand, while I can walk
While I can dream, please let my dream
Come true, right now

"If I can dream" by Walter Earl Brown, 1968

Princes of Shelby County

Memphis, Tennessee – The Prince home, 1968

Bobby and his father, Langston, had their heads together at the dining room table when Bernice entered. They quickly looked up and fell silent as she brought in the tray with coffee and freshly baked pastries. She ignored the faintly guilty look on Bobby's face and felt her irritation rise as her husband and her son shut her out. Her husband and her 23-year-old son were making plans for another possible political run. Her two oldest sons were out in California now, and Jack was in Philadelphia. Bernice didn't care about politics except for trying to keep her sons, Bobby and Richard, out of the war. She was tired of all the political maneuvering anyway. After her husband's election loss in 1966, she thought that the family would get a break from all the campaigning, but it only seemed to energize them. It wasn't just that the community backed her husband's opponent, A. W. Willis. He was, after all, a fellow black man. But when the Tri-State Defender could endorse a panel of white men like Charles Burch, Drew Canale, and Fred Landau over candidates like her husband, she just had to shake her head. Her husband liked to say that it had more to do with the voting district, but when J.O. Patterson and Russell Sugarmon cruised to victory, she thought it was more than apparent that her husband personally failed to appeal to their neighbors. He was a good and thoughtful provider, but she didn't think he had the charisma necessary for public office. He couldn't engender the loyalty or devotion that Martin Luther King did, or even that of their own, local pastor. But she would continue to be the dutiful wife; she hosted endless Sunday dinners for influential members of the community and smiled until her face felt like it would crack. She did her best to rub elbows and make pleasantries with the wives of the power players her husband told her about, even when it was plainly apparent that they weren't interested in rubbing elbows with her. Finally, she put her foot down when her husband suggested that they leave the church named after his family to socialize with the more prominent members of the Clayborn Temple and the

Church of God in Christ. Her faith wasn't for sale, and it wasn't a popularity contest. She watched her husband and her son shut her out of their discussions of the Sanitation Strike and Mayor Loeb, which hurt her, but they couldn't stop her from being involved in her own way. Bernice joined with the other church members in sending bereavement casseroles to Verline Walker. She didn't like watching everyone play politics over the issue while a pregnant widow was struggling to feed her five kids.

She secretly supported her younger daughter, Desdemona, when she announced that she wanted to campaign for Dr. Dorothy Lavinia Brown's re-election. She felt a measure of Desdemona's disappointment when Bernice's husband forbade Desdemona from canvassing Memphis neighborhoods. Neither she nor Desdemona was mollified when he suggested Dessie work as a candy striper at the Collins Chapel Hospital, though she put on a brave face and encouraged her daughter to volunteer.

Bernice wasn't used to having these thoughts about her husband, but she resented being left out. She had been by his side every step of the way for almost thirty-five years now, and she had never felt so overlooked and dismissed before. She tried to see it as a bonding activity with their middle son. Ever since Langston had allowed Bobby to manage his election campaign, they had been as thick as thieves. She should have been pleased, but instead she was excluded. Once again, her husband brought J. O Patterson, Reverend Netters, and Frank Davis to break bread with the family. Once again, she reached out to their wives and daughters. She spent hours in the hot, stuffy, and outdated kitchen making the labor-intensive meals that her husband usually requested. She wiped a bit of sweat from her forehead with a handkerchief before returning to knead the dough for her grandmother's prized buttermilk biscuit recipe. It was part of a rich and wholesome meal of greens, creamy mashed potatoes, brown gravy, with brown sugar and mustard glazed ham. She had a pineapple upside-down cake cooling on the counter, and a platter with tomato aspic and crackers for an appetizer. Her husband and son liked to brag about her cooking, and the variety of guests at their home. They liked to say she was a fixture and the 'grand madame' of the Prince family political dinners, but she felt more like a piece of furniture or a section of the fading cabbage rose wallpaper. She was present, but not included in any more of the discussions beyond the usual banal pleasantries. These dinners weren't to advance Langston. This time, the family was backing her son, Bobby. She was proud of him; so strong, upright and handsome. Her pride helped her overlook his growing arrogance and the whiff of condescension she sometimes sensed emanating from him, particularly when he introduced her to his friends and colleagues. He was always respectful and loving, but he sometimes made her feel like she had failed him as a mother, somehow.

As the months passed and an incredible series of events unfolded within the city limits, Bernice felt tired. So, so tired! She was tired of seeing the stinking, reeking piles of garbage outside in the streets. These ever-growing mountains of trash threatened to engulf the family home, but she felt guilty thinking about her own comfort as the sanitation workers' families struggled.

She tried to keep the younger children home after the police attacked with mace and tear gas. She tried again as violent protests broke out at the neighboring Hamilton High. She watched; worried yet inspired as Martin Luther King declared, "You are demonstrating that we can stick together. You are demonstrating that we are all tied in a single garment of destiny, and that if one black person suffers, if one black person is down, we are all down." She agreed wholeheartedly, but that did little to quell the icy-cold fingers of fear that reached deep into her chest and squeezed her heart. She told herself to be brave and proud, but she couldn't shrug off her fears so easily.

She pleaded with her husband after the Payne boy from Parker Street was killed during the disturbances, and there were mass arrests on Beale Street, but he ignored her. She cried when her husband ignored the city-wide curfew and took her Bobby with him. She worried and cried with fear as the news carried reports of looting, showers of broken glass, and mass arrests.

She gathered the younger children around her, and stayed inside with the curtains closed, as her husband went out in the streets. She saw footage of local negro politicians being clubbed by police, and she cried. As the national guard poured into the city, and Martin Luther King spoke about the mountaintop, she could only pray that the violence would spare her family. In the end, Bernice's prayers were answered, and her family was unharmed as the city fell into chaos. That was little consolation as the collective dream of racial harmony died under an assassin's bullets outside the Lorraine Hotel.

In that moment, something inside Bernice broke, and would never be whole again. For her children, the death of Martin Luther King was a call to action that they could not ignore.

****

Port Authority Bus Terminal, June 1968

Desdemona or Decca as she preferred to be called, quickly stubbed out the cigarette as she heard Barbara calling her name. Impulsively, she turned to hug the uniformed marine standing near her. He had been on the same bus, sitting in the aisle across from her for most of the long journey. She had heard him tell a fellow passenger that he was headed back to Vietnam in a few days. Before she could lose her nerve, she kissed him straight on the mouth before letting go.

Then, without looking back at the slightly stunned marine, she grabbed the handle of her small suitcase, turned and re-entered to the bus station to find her sister. Barbara had a surprisingly loud, booming voice and Decca headed towards it.

She was quickly spotted by her older sister, and her brother-in-law, Clyde. As Clyde reached out to take her suitcase from her, her older sister, Barbara, embraced her. She saw a quick flash of disapproval on her staid brother-in-law's face as he looked over her fuchsia pink and bright orange paisley printed sleeveless mini-dress and matching pink patent leather ankle boots. She'd always gotten the impression that Clyde was a bit of a strait-laced Charlie wannabe, so she stayed mellow during his infuriating appraisal. She waited for him to make a comment, but he just compressed his lips into a thin line.

Barbara was a lot older than Decca, and a lot more sophisticated too, Decca thought, eying her sister's smart looking suit, fancy pumps, and matching handbag. Barbara had already left for college when Decca was just a young child, so she didn't really know her oldest sibling, but Decca knew that at 18, that she was ready to come to New York for a summer of fun and adventure. If her sister hadn't lived in the city, Decca knew there was no way her parents would have let her go. It was bad enough that they were pushing her go to the Tennessee Agricultural & Industrial State College in the Fall, but she wasn't going to let them ruin her summer too.

She'd wanted to go to Howard, but her mother was dead set against it. As the youngest daughter in the family, Decca probably could have cajoled her father into it, until her mother started making rumblings about "lack of supervision". Decca knew her mother was really talking about sex. Her mother had become increasingly preoccupied and concerned about the 'promiscuity of today's youth' as was discussed endlessly in her mother's church groups. In Decca's opinion, her mother was more interested in her non-existent sex life than she was, but her mother wasn't interested in entertaining Decca's thoughts on the topic. As far as her mother was concerned, if Decca went to the college in Nashville, her other brother and sister were enrolled there too, so Decca would remain under the watchful eye of her family. Her mother was so adamant that Decca was attending school in Nashville that she tossed Decca's acceptance letter from Howard right into the kitchen trash can. Decca had later snuck into the kitchen and retrieved the letter, which was covered with carrot peelings, and stained with coffee grinds. The letter, which she had careful wiped off, was now on the bottom of the suitcase her brother-in-law was carrying.

As they climbed on the bus that would take them straight down 8th Avenue – Central Park West to Harlem, Barbara looked at Decca sternly, saying, "You know, Momma sent me a three-page letter full of instructions and rules for your visit here this summer." Decca could feel her excitement fade, until Barbara winked at her.

"I'll read it to you when we get to the apartment, but honestly, Desdemona, you are headed off to college in a few months, so you need to get used to the world. Momma and Daddy kept us so sheltered at home that we don't know anything about the real world!" Barbara said frustrated. "I bet she kept you home from school and inside when everyone else was out there with Reverend King," Barbara finished, clearly exasperated.

"You got that right!" Decca answered somewhat bitterly. "And now I never will have the opportunity to be part of something so important. He's gone now," she said sadly. They were all silent for a moment. Dr. King had been assassinated in Memphis just a few short months ago, and the pain was still fresh.

"The world is changing, you know," Decca continued, "and I want to be part of that, as we make it better."

It was quiet for a moment, before Clyde spoke up and said, "You know, his wife came here a few weeks *after*, and we took the kids to Central Park to hear her speak. I don't know if the younger one will remember, but since he's gone now, I thought it was important for the girls to see that even if he's dead, the dream hasn't died. I don't know if they understood Coretta Scott King's words, but I sure did. She wasn't talking about our civil rights, but Vietnam, and somehow when I saw all those young soldiers at the bus station today, I realized it's one and the same. She said it then, but I didn't totally understand at first. Now I do."

It was the longest speech Decca had ever heard her sister's husband make. Even when they came back to Memphis during the holidays, Clyde had seemed quiet, if thoughtful. He had a mild and calm, if buttoned up manner, which was well-suited to his profession as a teacher. Decca wondered if it was because her loud, boisterous family tended to suck all the air out of the room. The family was well-behaved and orderly, but there were just so many of them, with the spouses and children of the older siblings in attendance. She knew that's how she felt most of the time, dwarfed and pushed aside, and permanently shunted to the children's table. She felt bad for accepting the rest of her family's assumptions about him, and silently vowed to keep more of an open mind. Besides, hadn't she learned that her parents and older brothers could be stubbornly set in their beliefs?

Decca was still smarting from her last confrontation with her parents. She couldn't understand why they wouldn't support her the way they supported all of her brothers. Even her baby brother, Emmitt, who was only 12, got more respect than she did. It was bad enough that her dad was obsessed with getting her older brother into politics, but now they were arranging for Emmitt to spend time with Reverend Abernathy because he mentioned being interested in religion. It was the same with her other brother, Joey, and of course, all the things they were doing to keep James and Bobby from being called up for a semester at *Saigon Tech*.

They wouldn't listen to her when she said she wanted to go to Howard, and they wouldn't let her march with the rest of Memphis. Her mother kept saying it was too dangerous. Her mom didn't even want her to wear mini-skirts, saying they were for 'ole dusty butts' and loose girls, even though all of her classmates were wearing them.

Nothing was too dangerous or scandalous for her brothers it seemed. Her parents turned a blind eye to all the mini-skirted young women traipsing around Bobby. Her dad kept eagerly encouraging her older brothers to go into local politics even after he lost the election when he ran for the Tennessee House of Representatives. He even let her brother, Bobby, manage his campaign. He didn't even make the primaries, but still. She knew that no one in her family would ever trust her with that kind of responsibility. They all just treated her like a baby, and Decca was tired of it.

Decca was astonished to see this new side of her sister. She had always seen Barbara as rather prim and proper on her visits home from college, and then law school. In fact, it was only at Barbara's wedding, when Decca was twelve that she had ever seen her sister as anything but composed and confident. On that day, young Decca had watched Barbara fiddle with her hem, as her mother tried to pin her veil in the dressing room. She had fiddled so much that their mother had taken Barbara's hands in hers, before sending Decca out into the hall, so she and Barbara could have a private talk.

While she was out in the hall, Decca saw several members of Clyde's family enter the small church that bore Decca's family's name.

Barbara and Clyde had been dating since they'd met in Nashville in one of their shared classes. In fact, Clyde had taken a teaching job near the law school to be around Barbara before they had decided to get married. Now they lived in New York City, with their two kids. Barbara worked at a private firm specializing in civil rights while Clyde taught at a public school in their neighborhood.

Decca was so excited, she was practically vibrating. She had been thrilled when they agreed to let her stay with them this summer. Her excitement didn't dim as they climbed the stairs to the small 6th floor apartment in an grey stone building sandwiched between two other, larger buildings that dwarfed the old, but elegant edifice on West 110th. While the stairwells and hallways were lit with dingy yellow, bare bulbs, and carpeted with thread-worn rugs, elegant wood trim and wrought iron windows gave testimony to the building's previous life as a Victorian mansion. As Decca watched Clyde lug her suitcase up the many flights of stairs, she was glad she had packed light. He caught his breath as Barbara opened the door to the apartment.

Now subdivided into many small apartments, only the grand fireplace and high ceilings in Barbara's and Clyde's apartment hinted at the elegant past of the limestone building.

The apartment, while small, was well ventilated, and neat as a pin. There were two tiny bedrooms, a shoebox of a kitchen, and a roomy living room. The fire escape served as a makeshift patio on hot summer nights, and a ceiling fan in the living room spun wildly. As they entered the apartment, Clyde slipped some money to the neighbor for watching the kids, and the neighbor returned to her own apartment. The two girls turned and looked at Decca with interest, as their father set her small suitcase down. The older girl, Shelia, was 8, while her younger sister, Rebecca was 5. Rebecca looked shyly at the ground when they were introduced, until prompted to shake hands by her father.

"Are you hungry? Would you like something to eat?" Barbara asked, while her two daughtered chorused, "We're hungry!"

"Yes, ma'am, Decca said, suddenly shy. "I'm just glad we aren't boycotting Wonder Bread anymore!"

Both Barbara and Clyde laughed. "Dessie! You aren't going to go near Wonder Bread while you are here. It would be a crime! You are in a huge city that is world-famous for food – and we are in Harlem, so the food doesn't get any better than that!" Barbara exclaimed.

Decca felt a sudden feeling of warmth and closeness at hearing her childhood nickname. She hadn't been called Dessie in such a long time. Only Barbara and Joyce, along with their mother had called her that – and they had both been away from home for a long time now.

While the girls gathered up their shoes, Clyde and Barbara discussed restaurants, in such a rapid patter that Decca couldn't follow. She gave up trying. Like her sister said, great food, no wonder bread. Finally, they settled on Sylvie's on Lenox Avenue, which was a leisurely 20-minute walk from their apartment. It felt good to get out of the apartment and take a look around. There was so much to see and hear and even smell as they headed down the street towards the restaurant, with the two kids in tow. Clyde and Barbara pointed out shops, restaurants, and businesses along the way. Decca couldn't remember feeling this happy in a long time. It felt like her entire life was starting – right now! She reached out an arm and wrapped it around her sister while they were walking. Barbara stopped, and Decca gave her an enormous hug.

Barbara was taken aback for a moment, and then touched. She felt content and relieved to be able to connect with her baby sister on a real level. She had been concerned that she wouldn't be able to relate to Desdemona, since they hadn't really grown up together. She was almost old enough to be her mother, and now, in this moment, her feelings towards her sister were protective, almost motherly.

Decca and Barbara fell back as Clyde scooped up their youngest daughter and put her on his back. His older daughter, Shelia took his left hand as they walked a short distance in front of Barbara and her sister. The girls chattered happily with their father, grateful for extra attention.

"So, what's the latest news from home? Mom writes, but her letters are always so boring. She recites the latest recipe from the Bisquick box. I find it hilarious since she's too frugal to actually buy Bisquick baking mix. She even sent me a recipe card for "homemade" Bisquick. Even her gossip is boring, because it's all about church activities and the *Merry-go-round* columns in the paper. I swear, with our last pastor having such a roving eye, she could do better than regurgitating Erma Lee Laws and her silly Co-ettes and the Housewives League," Barbara said laughing.

Decca laughed, saying, "well that's because she finally got someone to mention her in that stupid social column. I swear she must have sent everyone in the family a clipping of that picture showing her as the President of the Tennessee Funeral Directors Ladies Axillary!"

Barbara nodded, because, she had received a letter from their Mom with said clipping a few years back.

She continued, "Remember how irritated she would get when Emogene Watkins was writing the social page? She used to get so red in the face every time she mentioned the Debonair Set, or the VIP Social Club. You know she was just green with envy, but she'd die before she'd admit it. I am pretty sure that she pushed all of us into being debutantes and attending all of those ridiculous teas and charity balls just to get our names in that snobby column."

Decca continued, with a little snort, saying, "I swear, you are lucky you left Memphis. Just before I left, she made me go to three different events so I could *accidentally* bump into this Velma Jones. Once mom found out she was the regional director of the Alpha Kappa Alpha sorority, there was no way to stop her!"

Barbara raised an eyebrow, saying, "AKA, huh? Doesn't she know their reputation? The paper bag test?"

Decca shrugged, "I don't know. But aren't you an AKA?"

Now it was Barbara's turn to shrug, saying, "I did what I had to do to get where I am now. If that meant joining certain clubs, and meeting the right people, and making the right connections, then I did it. I needed all the help I could find to get my foot in the door. That was all I needed. That got me where I am today, where I live my life on my terms; where I want, doing what I want!"

Decca looked thoughtful, and said slowly, "Well, I sure don't want to attend that school in Nashville and work at the funeral home with Daddy."

As they walked down the block, Decca saw that several buildings had burned to the ground on this block. There were piles of burned timbers in some areas, with gutted frames of buildings, where efforts had been made to begin the cleanup. In others, the buildings remained in ruins, and the smell of smoke seemed to still linger in the air. Still others, showed signs of the beginning of reconstruction, but these buildings were few and far between.

Barbara looked closely at Desdemona and asked, "So what do you want to do?" She was interested to hear what this surprising baby sister of hers wanted to do with her life.

"Everything!" Decca exclaimed with enthusiasm, her smile lighting up her whole face. Barbara laughed, and said, "Well, that's quite a challenge."

"Oh, Barbara! There's just so much that I want to see, do, and experience! I feel like I've been trapped into this tiny, little life; school, church, babysitting, and family. I am pushed into trying to get into the right clubs, be a debutante, and go to the college that Mom and Dad want me to attend. They have this whole life planned out, only it's not mine! I know they love me, and that they want the best for me, but sometimes I think they only see us as a group of children, and not as individuals. I mean, it's different for Jack and Bobby because they are the favorites, but not for the rest of us. We are one of those stupid Bisquick recipes; same ingredients, same instructions." Decca seemed sad and deflated as she spoke, and she felt as mercurial as she seemed. One minute, the excitement of her trip filled her with exuberance, joy, and hope and in the next, she was crashing back to earth, remembering obligations and filial responsibility.

Barbara could understand and empathize the way few outsiders ever could. "It's okay, Dessie. I understand. We have all been there. Why do you think I ended up in New York? Or Joyce ran off to sing in nightclubs? I came here to forge my own path, and be a part of the future. I have kids and a family I adore, but you won't see me staying at home and holding church socials."

Dessie started to laugh, and then said, "Wait! What do you mean about Joyce? Boring old Joyce?"

Her older sister, Joyce, was married with babies, and was living just outside of Memphis in a rural community. It was hard for Decca to imagine her being much different from their mother. It seemed like she was mainly involved in raising her family and with church. The idea of her doing anything fun seemed improbable. She turned to her sister and opened her mouth, with her face full of questions.

Barbara saw the gleam in Decca's eyes and laughed. "Look, here we are at the restaurant! And nope, I am not going to answer any questions right now. That, my dear sister, is a story best told on another day." Barbara and Clyde laughed at the instant pout that took over Decca's face as Clyde held open the door for the girls to enter. Little Rebecca reached up and slipped her hand in Decca's as they entered the restaurant. When they all sat in the worn red leatherette booth, the girls crowded in around Decca, forcing their mother to sit across from her. Decca looked around the restaurant. It was small, with just six booths and several stools at the countertop, but it was busy, with a line of people waiting to pick up orders in grease-stained, white paper bags.

Decca didn't think any restaurant in New York could do fried chicken as good as Momma's, but the chicken was light, and crispy, and the mash potatoes were smooth and rich. During dinner she filled Barbara in with the news from home. "Well, it was first page news in the Tri-state Defender that Russell Sugarmon left his wife for a white woman," she said, dropping the biggest bombshell first.

"Oh my god!" Barbara exclaimed, "How mortifying!" Russell Sugarmon was a black community leader in Memphis, and "local boy made good", as a Harvard educated attorney who had recently won a seat in the Tennessee House of Representatives. His wife, Miriam, was a well-respected college professor with a PhD from John Hopkins. She was teaching foreign languages at Memphis State University, which had previously rejected her application for admission due to her race. They had four small children.

"Mama tried to hide the article, but it was terrible. It talked about him abusing her, not coming home, and moving into another apartment! It aired all of their dirty laundry! I felt terrible for her because everyone was whispering in church, but he walked around just like always," Decca said.

"I'll bet," Barbara muttered. Civil rights and dignity for all *MANkind*, she thought. Nothing ever really changed for women in the South, she thought. Even here in New York, she was having to fight to be listened to and respected. She was getting tired of the everyday sexism and discrimination at the law firm where she worked. Barbara was glad when Decca changed the subject to the Kappa Alpha Psi party at the Olympic Motor Inn. "I didn't want to go," she lamented, "but Momma made me because A. W. Willis and some other important people were going to be there. She made me curtsy to that Velma Jones and everything, but it turned out okay because she even let me have a date! Elmer Henderson brought me a corsage and everything! I didn't have to wear a hand-me-down dress, and I even met Honeyboy Thomas, and the head of the local NAACP!"

Barbara was enthralled and amused, listening to her sister. In one breath, she was excited about a date, a new dress and meeting a local DJ. "So you were excited to meet Maceo Walker?" Barbara asked.

Maceo Walker was the head of the local NAACP and had been instrumental, along with several others in getting Martin Luther King Jr. to come to Memphis for the sanitation strike that Spring.

"Yes, ma'am," Decca said, reverting to the usual form of address in Memphis. "I want to be like him. I want to help bring change. I don't know why I have to sit on the sidelines, when I could be helping!" she said with a burst of emphasis.

Decca was a little embarrassed about her outburst. She knew her sister was like the rest of her family and wasn't going to take her seriously. Everyone thought she was still a child. She turned her focus to her plate, determined not to cry. As she used a biscuit to sop up some leftover gravy, she thought about more mundane things as she waited for the heat to leave her cheeks. For one, she knew she would never mention Sylvia's restaurant in her letters home. There would be a war if she ever admitted how good the fried chicken here really was. She imagined writing such a letter to her family and felt her face cool, along with her emotions. She switched the topic again and began to talk about some of the young men that had recently died in Vietnam. On that somber note, the waitress came to offer dessert.

Feeling stuffed, she agreed to share a tiny sliver of peach pie with her two little nieces. Good food, the heat of the city, and a long day on the bus started to catch up with her despite her excitement. She was ready to sleep as soon as the meal was over, and by the looks of it, so were the girls. Barbara didn't argue about the expense when Clyde hailed a taxi, and they piled into the cab. Barbara watched as her daughters cuddled up to her baby sister, as they started to nod off on the short ride back to the apartment. It always amazed how quickly her daughters could fall asleep, and how innocent they looked; all the exuberance, and energy drained from their slumbering faces.

****

The next day, Decca woke as the sun was rising. The ceiling fan whistled and creaked above her, and she was grateful for the breeze to cut the hot, humid and still air. She carefully climbed out onto the fire escape to watch the activity in the alley below. She saw several rats scurry from one garbage can to the next, as a cat gave chase. The traffic from the street broke the stillness with a steady hum. Behind her, in the apartment, she began to hear signs of life; then soon, the sound of coffee perking on the ancient stove. A few minutes later, her brother-in-law thrust a mug of hot coffee out the window. They sipped coffee in companionable silence for a few moments, before he went to shower. Decca stayed out on the fire escape, deep in thought, until her sister and the girls came out into the kitchen.

****

"Dessie, we have to head to work. Clyde is taking the girls to school with him, and I am heading to the office before court. Here's a copy of the key. We should be back around 5:30 this evening. Here's some money in case you need to take a cab, go to a movie, or get some lunch. Don't worry, we will do something fun this weekend, okay?" Barbara said in a rush, handing Decca a crumpled two-dollar bill. With that, she raced out the door to catch the bus heading towards downtown. Shortly after she was followed by Clyde and the girls, as he juggled a thermos, his briefcase, and the girls' bag lunches. By 7:30 am, Decca had the apartment to herself.

She didn't waste any time finding her most fashionable mini dress. She carefully applied her make-up in the latest style, with bright blue shadow, and exaggerated liner. It gave her face an exotic cast, which was enhanced by the wrapped, high pony tail she arranged. It took her a while to straighten her hair for the popular style, but she was out the door and exploring the city before 9 am. That wasn't too early for the summer heat and humidity to start building a line of moisture along her lower back. She frowned to herself as she walked down the street, imagining the sheen on her cheeks and forehead. She kept going, window shopping and sight-seeing as she walked. She was pleased to see that the high humidity didn't seem to dampen the ardor of the male passersby, who all seemed to appreciate her trim figure, clear skin, and long legs. She smiled to herself and continued down the street, pretending to be unaware of their admiration.

She was swinging her arms and enjoying her adventure, when a store window caught her eye, and stopped her in her tracks. The clothes in the window were so different from what she was used to seeing in Memphis, it startled her. Everything at home seemed so insipid, and unsophisticated in the pastels and seersuckers of the South. Even the prints seemed faded and dull compared to what she was looking at now. The minidresses were shorter, the colors brighter, and the fabrics were alive with texture, unfamiliar patterns, and sheen. Despite the season, there was leather and suede fringe, and fluffy, fake fur in bright colors. There was a bright yellow dress that appeared to be made of big, yellow plastic hoops connected by tiny metal rings; a rainbow of patent leather accessories and tall boots, golden medallions and big hoop earrings; it was a dazzling, dizzying array She felt like it was fashion come to life. This was why she was here – to see and experience life in rich technicolor! No more sepia life for her. As her eyes wandered lovingly over all of the items, to take in all the beautiful colors and lovely patterns, she noticed a help wanted ad at the bottom of the window. She made the decision to apply just as a handsome, caramel-colored, young man opened the door to the store and invited her inside. That almost certainly worked in her favor because she was so enchanted with the store that she didn't have time to be nervous.

****

As she headed back from St. Nicholas Avenue, she felt like her feet barely touched the sidewalk. The feeling didn't fade that evening, when she told her sister over cartons of carry-out Chinese food. As she ate the tangy and unfamiliar strips of spicy, yet sweet chicken, she bubbled over with excitement.

When her brother-in-law asked what she did that day, it all spilled out in a smiling, happy, giggly rush, "I got a job today! I am the new salesgirl at the New Breed Fashion Boutique!" As her family looked at her in surprise, she filled in all the details. "It's a bit of a walk, but it's not too far. It's only two days a week. It's just so I can have some pin money, so I don't have to ask you for any. The store is run by a nice, married couple and they just opened it last year. Plus, they have the most gorgeous things - and I get a discount for working there!"

She looked at her sister and brother-in-law expectantly. Clyde looked impressed at her initiative, while Barbara seemed amused. "Trust my fashion-plate of a baby sister to get a job at the most happening store in Harlem on her first day!" she exclaimed. They celebrated that evening by going out to get an ice cream cone.

****

Decca was having a wonderful summer. She still didn't know what she was going to do about school in the fall. She hadn't told her parents or her sister that she was still planning to go to Washington, DC. She had secretly written back to Howard, stating that she would be attending. She had also placed a quick long-distance call from a payphone near the store, using all of her change, to call the admission's office and change her address to her sister's apartment. She figured she would have time to figure it out over the next few months.

In the meantime, she was enjoying her job. She wasn't just a salesgirl, she was also a part-time model. The owners of the store encouraged Decca to wear their clothing while she worked. The store was so hip these days, that anyone working in the store had to represent the New Breed look. With all of the celebrities, fashion reporters, and models hanging out in the store, what started out as a part-time job to make some extra money had morphed into a full-time life. Most of the people hanging around the store, like the models and actors, were just a few years older than Decca but they already had such exciting lives and careers. Decca was also surprised to see black girls, like Donyale Luna and Naomi Sims, as popular models in mainstream magazines. She was even more excited by some of the other Grandassa Models like Norsa Brath. They were undeniably beautiful to Decca, but she had never seen dark brown skin acknowledged as being beautiful in Memphis. She was ashamed to admit that she herself had never considered the idea of darker girls being beautiful. It wasn't just the glamorous models that left Decca enthralled. Everything and everyone she encountered at New Breed Fashion Boutique made her realize what a small, and limited perspective she had before coming to New York.

The owners, Jason and Mabel Benning, inspired her. She hadn't even known what a dashiki was until she entered their store.

Now Jason Benning, who also worked as a Professor of Negro Studies, was teaching her about the origins of their shared culture. It gave her a new sense of self to know more about her African roots. Many of the people who came by the store, came by to do more than shop for clothes. They were there to discuss black culture, and current events. They weren't content to accept their place in American society, separate from mainstream, white culture. They wanted to lead the change. Together with some of Kwame Brathwaite's models, Decca started to hang out with people who talked about all of the things that Decca's parents wouldn't discuss. They also treated Decca differently, in a way that sometimes hurt her feelings. Despite being told that she was beautiful her entire life, she was now told she wasn't dark or natural enough. Her long, sleek ponytail wasn't admired. It was ridiculed. She had been at a coffeehouse one evening after work with one of her new friends, Afeni, along with some other models, when they were joined by several others. Like Afeni, many of the newcomers had adopted African names and other nicknames. She was horrified when she was engaged deep in discussion with several local activists when a man named Sekou called her out for her light skin. She was quickly defended by several of her friends, but it was the first time that Decca had even been confronted with the idea that she might not be black enough. It made her feel uncomfortable in her own skin. She had never questioned her identity before, but now, Sekou and some of the others made her feel inauthentic. Her lack of knowledge of African history or her African heritage was also used against her. Far from driving her away from the movement, it only made Decca more passionate. So much so, that one late night, she lost her virginity to Afeni's friend ,Thomas, in the wee hours after leaving an after-hours club. They coupled quietly and quickly in the back bedroom of a small flat around the corner from the club. Afeni, Connie, Michael, and others were in the living room smoking grass while Decca was being introduced to the other side of her passionate nature with Thomas McCleary. It was over quickly, and afterward, she felt sticky, empty, and somewhat unfulfilled. She had never had such intense feelings before, and they didn't dissipate completely as she watched Thomas pull up his pants and tighten his belt. She felt confused and disappointed. Thomas looked up and flashed a grin at her as she pulled down her dress. She pushed down these feelings to smile back as she stood up a bit unsteadily, and made her way back out to where her friends awaited. After returning to the darkly lit living room, she quickly accepted the joint Connie handed her. She sat down next to her friends on a sagging, dark green, velvet couch, and stared at the lava lamp on a side table while she inhaled deeply. Thomas dropped an arm around her shoulders as he sat on the arm rest of the couch, slightly above her. It felt comfortable to her, so she didn't shrug it off. No one else in the room commented on the pairing, so Decca played it cool.

****

She never formally joined the Black Panthers, but she began to spend more and more time with Thomas, Michael, Connie, Afeni, Lumunba, Assata, and Afeni's sister, Glo. She volunteered for numerous community programs held by the party, and in just a few weeks, became a familiar face in the neighborhood. She became familiar with the people whose faces were now broadcast on the news as radicals and terrorists. It made her re-think everything she thought she knew, and it made her more determined than ever to forge her own path, her own way. She remained determined to go to Howard, and as the hot, humid days of summer passed, she became increasingly desperate.

While she had become closer to her sister, Barbara, she still wasn't sure that she could confide in her completely. She would share stories about store customers and such, but she didn't talk to her about all the new ideas she was exploring, or her acceptance to Howard. She turned to her brother-in-law instead. Clyde weas a teacher and an academic, so she felt like he would support her in her pursuit of higher education. She felt like he would understand her quest to broaden her horizons and develop her independence away from her family, and her parents. Early one weekday morning, as they continued their private coffee ritual, she broke the silence to broach the subject with him, while swearing him to secrecy. Over the coming weeks, she showed him the letters from Howard, and he made some calls on her behalf, to set up housing in the dormitory and other essentials.

They started to talk in the evenings, quietly and privately as Barbara cooked dinner in the tiny, hot kitchen. With the small black and white TV entertaining the children, Clyde and Decca would discuss the course catalog that he kept hidden for her. Barbara saw their heads close together on several occasions as she escaped the heat of the kitchen and felt uneasy. They always sprang apart quickly when they noticed her presence. Her sister's new-found sexuality didn't go unnoticed by Barbara either. She had turned a blind eye to much of Decca's partying and pretended to not smell the odor of cigarettes, grass or alcohol when Decca returned from some of her weekend adventures, but she was becoming increasingly alarmed by some of Decca's new friends. They looked rough, experienced, and jaded to Barbara's eyes, when they would stop by the apartment to pick up her baby sister. They didn't have Decca's naivete. They wore a lot of black. They had afros and an aggressiveness that even after her years in New York, Barbara was not used to.

Now, Decca wore her sexuality like a cape, it seemed to ooze out of her pores, like a perfume. Her skirts crept up even higher on her thighs as she whispered and talked intently with Barbara's husband on the couch.

There were only a few weeks left of Decca's New York summer. Clyde had made her realize that any plans to run away to Howard secretly were unrealistic. It was time for her to confide in her sister and enlist her assistance in convincing her parents to let her go to Howard. She thought about what she was going to say to Barbara all day at work. If her bosses noticed that she was distracted, they didn't say anything. Decca was a good worker, honest and sweet. They would miss her when summer ended.

Decca continued to rehearse her arguments during the walk back to the apartment after work. She climbed the flights of stairs with her heart pounding in her mouth. Her sister, Barbara, had been cool to her lately, and she knew if she couldn't convince Barbara, then she would never be able to convince her parents. She needed an ally. She stopped and caught her breath before putting her hand on the door to the apartment.

She prepared herself the best she could, took a deep breath, and opened the door.

****

Despite all her preparations and rehearsals, Decca was completely unprepared to see both of her parents in the living room. Off to the side, her small suitcase sat, packed to overflowing. Barbara failed to meet her eyes as her parents launched into a diatribe against her. Decca's heart sank when she saw the papers clenched tightly in her mother's hands. The Howard University logo was clearly visible on the crumpled letters. Decca recognized the letters from the housing department and financial aid, that had arrived here in New York after she had changed her address. She felt devastated by her sister's betrayal. She looked at Clyde with a question in her eyes. He was looking at his wife with fury. Barbara continued to look away from both Decca and Clyde, defiant yet ashamed.

Decca held up her hand to stop her mother's seemingly endless monologue. She walked over and picked up her suitcase, still silent. She looked at her father, beseechingly, and he gave a slight shrug. Deflated, betrayed, and profoundly disappointed, Decca turned her back on the group assembled in the living room. Wordlessly she trudged to the door with her suitcase and left the apartment. She didn't look back. She waited for her parents outside the apartment building and remained silent for the entire journey back to Memphis. She never forgave Barbara, and their relationship was never the same again.

A few weeks later, she attended her first college classes in Nashville, as a chastened and changed young woman. Her sister, Bernice, was in the same dorm while her brother, James, was across campus. She stayed obedient and quiet. She followed the curriculum recommended by her parents so she could come home and work in the family business after graduation. She began slowly, and privately to drink. A glass of wine or a small cordial after a long day of classes. It was the only thing that dulled the emptiness in her soul.

Desdemona 1969 - 1975

Her senior year, she met a charming, young man named William. He was bright and lively and all the things that Decca had been before the hollowness had settled inside. She married him at the age of twenty-two, and had a child she named Sophia Shakini that September. Soon after that, her husband began to hear voices, and they divorced. Now alone, with a small infant, Decca's drinking increased. It remained her private solace and went unnoticed by her few friends and family.

Things got ugly when her ex-husband got himself together and ran for state office in the mid-70's and her family publicly supported his opponent. They didn't seem to care how their actions affected Decca, her daughter, and her relationship with William.

It was almost amusing, when her brother Jack was arrested for drunk and disorderly conduct soon after, but Decca wasn't amused to see that once again, Jack could behave with impunity, immune from consequences, while her life continued to fall apart.

Later, William tried to reconcile with Decca, but his mental health remained fragile. Decca didn't think she could mother him and Sophia at the same time. She was barely keeping her own head above water. Sometimes, she wasn't sure that she was – she felt like she was flailing, kicking, and screaming as she struggled to stay afloat. She thought about it a lot as she drank during the afternoons as her daughter napped. She would stare at a dirty brown spot on the wall of her cramped Mississippi Avenue apartment, and feel the anger, along with numbness grow. If she drank enough, and fast enough, the numbness would win out over the anger – and she would just look at the spot, as cockroaches crawled in and out of the damned spot on the wall. Other days, anger won out – and she wondered why no one from her family came around to see her, or offer a hand. Where was her overbearing mother now, when she could use her help? While her montmer, Bernice, wasn't the doting type grandmother, couldn't she watch Sophie a couple of mornings so Decca could try and find a better job? If it wasn't for her ex-mother-in-law, Roseanne, and her babysitting, Decca never would have been able to get off welfare. She found that painfully ironic, when she remembered her family's private embarrassment over her welfare checks, while they loudly and publicly called for enhanced social programs. For Decca, the little house at 541 Gilleas Street was her own private social program; a daycare for her daughter, then pre-school, then after-school program, where Sophie received breakfast, lunch, snacks, and plenty of attention from a loving grandmother, Roseanne. Roseanne, who spent extra time teaching Sophie her colors, how to count, and helped the little girl learn to read. By the time Sophie had graduated to reading on her own, and beginning science projects, Decca's ex-husband had come back to live with his mother. He was heavily medicated, but still prone to violent outbursts. By that time that Decca had a good job working for a large insurance company so she could afford to move Sophie to an exclusive after-school program across town. She remained indebted and grateful to Roseanne, who never complained or commented on Decca's situation. If she thought Decca was a less than ideal mother, she never said anything. It was one of the easiest and least judgmental relationships Decca ever had. Roseanne listened, but never offered advice and seemed content to assist in child-rearing when Decca just couldn't seem to manage.

She never tried to facilitate a reconciliation between Decca and her son and seemed only too happy to be part of her granddaughter's life.

By the time Roseanna was murdered and dismembered by Decca's ex-husband in a psychotic rage, in 1983, Decca had switched to vodka. She had lost her job at the insurance company, and with it, her sense of self – and independence, away from her cloying, overbearing, and stifling family. She was forced to accept a position working for her brother. Vodka was her friend. It helped her get through the long days at the funeral home, and even longer Sunday dinners with her family. She had lost whatever pride and self-esteem she had when she was fired from the administrative position that she had worked so hard to attain. Working as a drudge in the family business was demeaning and humiliating. Worse than that, her family no longer bothered to disapprove of her, they just seemed to discount her entirely. They treated her like a ghost member of the family. She was there, but she didn't matter.

Now that she was in the eternal shadow of her brothers, Jack and Bobby and their political careers, she began to drink more openly. Why hide it, she thought bitterly. What did it matter, anyway?

****

Book Six: Jonah, Ember, and Robert Jr. the 1990's

It wasn't easy to grow up as a Prince in the 1980's and 1990's. By that time, the scandals of the previous generation of Princes had taken on mammoth proportions. No one was affected by this more than the children of Jack Prince and Robert Langston Prince. It didn't help that between marriages, divorces, mistresses, and girlfriends, Ember and Jonah were lost among an ever-expanding family of half-siblings and step-parents. Jonah's older brother, Robert, Jr. ,didn't have that problem; he was born with the silver-edged tongue of a serpent and the supreme confidence of a con man. Even as an adolescent, Bobby Jr. skipped the awkward stage and went right to heartthrob. While he seemed to breeze into young adulthood, Ember and Jonah stumbled.

LINKS 1990
Ember was so excited to be presented as a Links, Inc. debutante at the holiday cotillion. Links, Inc. was one of the city's exclusive organizations for prominent African Americans. Membership was elusive for all but the most connected and respected wealthy women in the community. Ember's invitation to participate in the event was a much coveted item amongst her peers, and their mothers. Ember has a beautiful new dress, and she's practiced for months. Her sister, Autumn, and her cousin, Courtney assist in the ceremony, but the focus is on Ember, and she relishes the attention. She feels beautiful and important today – and it's a wonderful feeling!

After she finishes her presentation, she wants to dance with her father, Jack Prince. He's been so busy campaigning and working that she feels like she never sees him. Now that her parents had gone through an ugly and public divorce, she saw him even less. But she knew he would never miss something as important as her debutante presentation. She scanned the room looking for her father. She saw her mother standing with Willie Herenton and Shantille Alexander's parents. She skirted around them, still looking for her father. She looks left and looks right and is getting ready to look outside when she feels a hand on her shoulder. She whirls around, only to face her mother, Marlene, who looks at her sadly and says "He's not here, baby. I'm sorry."

Ember wants to climb into her mother's arms like a child, but instead she lashes out in anger, "and that's all your fault!" Even as she says it, she knows it isn't true, but she can't seem to stop herself. She storms outside where she finds several of the debutante escorts smoking. She accepts a cigarette, and when an escort offers her his jacket, and a sip from a flask in the pocket, she accepts. It doesn't ease her disappointment, so she leans back into the young man's arms for some comfort. He's surprised but reacts quickly. He starts to try and flirt with her, but his teenage come-ons fail to impress her. She's had time to recover, and she realizes she doesn't want anything that he has to offer. She stubs out her cigarette, hands back his jacket, and heads back inside without saying a word.

Memphis State University, 1993

As Ember hurried out of the theater class, a tall, young man stepped into her path. "Ember? Ember Prince?" he asked.

Ember paused mid-stride to look up wearily at the tall, well-built man. It was probably another reporter asking about her dad's latest embarrassing incident. She was tired of her family being Memphis's own "Jerry Springer Show" with all their public squabbling and fights. When the questions didn't come immediately, she looked closer at the man who had addressed her.

He was dark complected, with skin the color of a rich espresso. He had black eyes, and pink lips with a blindingly white smile. One of his canines was slightly crooked and it somehow added to his charismatic appeal. He had a strong, deep voice that belied his youthful appearance. As he began to introduce himself to her, Ember had to force herself to pay attention. He had a lilting accent that was unlike anything she had heard before, and it was distracting her as she tried to place it.

"Wait, what?" she said, and then cringed at her gauche and awkward answer. She was usually known for being cool, collected, and for having a snappy comeback, especially with the local fast-talking wanna-be rappers and gangbangers. Now instead of the cool sophistication she was known for, she felt as gawky as a teenager wearing headgear to the prom. She felt her face flush, but to his credit, the tall, handsome, young man gave no indication that he noticed her discomfort. He held his hand out and said "My name is Emmanuel Johnson Tolbert. I am your distant cousin."

Ember was startled, but recovered quickly, saying, "Hey! What kind of come on is that?"

Emmanuel looked offended. "Do you not have a distant relative by the name of Daphne Prince?" he asked. Ember couldn't recall. She could barely keep all her cousins straight. She felt embarrassed to admit it. Instead, she said, "Do you mind coming with me? Let's go talk to my grandmother." She began to feel nervous about inviting a stranger into her car as they walked to the parking lot. She felt a sense of relief as she saw her sorority sister, Inetta, walking nearby. "Skee-wee," she said, using the sorority call. Inetta looked over and headed for Ember. Inetta was serious-minded, and a devout Christian, but she could also be whimsical and fun.

"Are you ready for some of my grandmother's home cooking?" she teased. With that, she convinced Inetta to join them. She quickly made introductions and ignored the side-eye Inetta gave Emmanuel. They climbed into the 1991 electric blue Ford Mustang and headed for her grandmother's house on Joubert Street.

Grandmother Bernice had gotten frailer in the years since her husband had died, but she remained a strict disciplinarian. This was tempered with love for her numerous grandchildren. Ember was one her favorites, because she always made time to see Grandmother Bernice. She would frequently stop by for lunch or a snack. She pretended to come for her cooking, but Bernice knew that her granddaughter was checking up on her. Since her husband had passed, multiple members of the family had tried to get her to move in with them, but Bernice fiercely clung to her independence. As she opened to the door to let Ember in, she wasn't surprised to see Inetta and a nicely dressed young man. Ember often brought friends, and Inetta was a frequent visitor.

After everyone was settled at the kitchen table with a slice of fresh pie, Ember said, "Grandmother, Emmanuel and I wanted to ask about some family history. He thinks we might be related". For a moment Bernice looked wary, but the expression passed so quickly on her face that Ember thought she must have imaged it.

Bernice's eyebrow raised, and then Emmanuel began to speak, with his precise diction, saying, "Well, ma'am, I am from Liberia, and I was told that one of my ancestors came from this family". With that, he pulled out a folded piece of paper. It turned out to be a handwritten family tree. He ran a finger down the branches, and stopped at one, saying, "Here. In 1893, Daphne Prince Allen of Memphis, Tennessee married Marion Johnson. They moved to Monrovia soon after. Daphne was the daughter of the first wife of your ancestor, Langston Prince. I believe she would be your husband's aunt, ma'am. Did he ever speak of her?"

Inetta's eyes shifted to Bernice, but Ember's eyes remained on Emmanuel.

Bernice looked acutely relieved for a moment, as if she'd been expecting something else, but when she answered she only sounded mildly perplexed. "No, no, he never spoke of an Aunt Daphne that I can recall, but his sister, Harriet, did."

Before Ember could ask who Harriet was, Emmanuel traced down the paper again, outlining his lineage, saying, "Daphne had two children. Her oldest daughter, Florida Monrovia Johnson was married twice. She had one child with each husband. Florida's oldest daughter, Victoria David Tubman is my grandmother. My grandmother married my grandfather, William Tolbert and they had eight children, including my dad,

Adolphus Benedict. So, we are cousins, many times removed," he finished. He looked over at Ember and said, "Daphne would have been your great-great aunt, if that helps make it a little clearer for you."

As they finished their pie, Ember was quiet and contemplative, while Inetta and Bernice peppered him with questions.

Emmanuel skirted over some of their questions but said enough to keep Ember's grandmother intrigued. He explained that his family had moved to New York in 1982, when he was still a child, but that he had spent much of his remaining childhood in Europe. He had been educated in private boarding schools, in France until graduating in 1988. He was now at Yale, working on his master's degree in international business and finance but had taken a semester program at Memphis State University to study with finance professionals from Fedex, International Paper, and other multi-national companies as part of Memphis State's well-known international business program. He had been waiting for an opportunity to look up his American relatives, so when someone on campus pointed out Ember, he had approached her. He laughed when Inetta asked if he was married, showing his white, even teeth. Ember found that she was fascinated with his mouth. His background seemed so exotic. She wished she'd been able to go to boarding school, to live in France, to wander the streets of Paris. It seemed so amazing, so romantic, she sighed to herself.

Her grandmother suddenly clapped her hands, and said, "Okay folks. Well, I have got to get to church soon." Ember and Inetta got busy washing the plates and wiping the table, before preparing to leave. Ember wondered at her grandmother's sudden change in mood but gave her a hug and a kiss before leaving, with a promise to stop by later in the week.

The drive back to campus was lively with Inetta openly flirting with Emmanuel. Ember had to tamp down her irritation and remind herself that it was none of her business. She told herself it was just a protective instinct towards someone who was family, but the other thoughts she was having about Emmanuel weren't family-friendly, at all. After they dropped Emmanuel off at his car, Ember turned to Inetta and said saucily, "It seemed like you were enjoying yourself."

Inetta replied, "Good Lord! He's fine, but he's too much dark chocolate for me." Ember was a little startled by the response but kept her mouth shut. She had only been an Alpha Kappa Alpha for six months, but she knew the rumors around their membership criteria. There were old stories about the sorority restricting membership to light-skinned women, and women bleaching their skin to join. That certainly wasn't true for the Epsilon Epsilon Chapter, but Ember had heard enough stray comments to wonder, just the same. She dropped Inetta off at her apartment, still bothered by the thoughts running through her head.

She returned to her apartment, and after finishing her homework, mused about her "cousin" Emmanuel. She didn't know much about Liberia, except that a lot of cruise ships were registered there, but she vowed to brush up at the library so she could make intelligent conversation when she saw him again, because she was planning to see him again, dark chocolate or not.

After seeking out Emmanuel the next day, Ember and Emmanuel began spending quite a bit of time together. Slowly, he peeled back the layers of his past and shared himself with her. It wasn't the romantic story that she expected.

He told her about fleeing the country after his grandfather was murdered in a political uprising in 1980 and the death of his father, Adolphus shortly after. His father had sought refuge in an embassy, but the military came in after him and murdered him. His mother had fled to the Ivory Coast, leaving her young son to be cared for by one of his many aunts, uncles, and his devoted grandmother. They were held in custody for twenty months before finally being released to leave Liberia. It had been a terrifying and uncertain time, particularly for a young boy. He didn't understand how their life had changed so completely, so quickly. He didn't understand how strange men could hate his family so much, and how they could harm his beloved grandfather who was such a kind and generous man in his eyes. What happened to all the people who claimed to love him and their family?

While much of his family settled in New York, his grandmother snubbed her nose at the idea at the American educational system for her darling grandson. The death of her son had affected her deeply. He was quickly shunted off to a private boarding school just outside of Paris. Emmanuel had wanted to go to Eton, but his family abhorred the British and considered them uncultured. It was devastating for Emmanuel to learn that the people in his new country considered him to be an educated "savage" as he heard one professor describe him. Snide comments and taunts were whispered by his new classmates, as he tried to adjust to his new life, and to grieve for his former life, a continent away.

He was lonely and isolated at the school in the small town of Maison-Laffitte, and passed the days in either the school library, or riding horses on campus. Paris was just a few train stations away, so he would spend many weekends alone, exploring Paris and imagining his future. After he graduated from high school, he was determined to come to the United States to live. Once he completed a degree in Economics at Harvard, he started graduate study at the University of Pennsylvania, with further study at Yale.

He had been staying with his Aunt Evelyn in New York on his breaks from school, but she had been quite ill this year. He didn't want to impose on his uncle William, while he figured out what he was going to do with his life. When he saw the semester program in Memphis, he knew this was the opportunity he was looking for. He was intrigued by his American family; he had heard of them the entire time he was growing up. His grandparents would tell him stories at bedtime about Daphne, Marion, and their little family; who had crossed the sea in great ships to seek their freedom and fortune in Liberia. Even though the families had lost contact at the turn of the century, they stayed alive in the oral family history that was passed down in the nursery to each generation. Now that he was spending time with Ember, he was fascinated. He's been in France and the United States for the last 13 years, but he'd never experienced anything like Memphis, and the black community here. It was very different from Liberia, Paris or even New York. But he liked it, families seemed very close. There was a sense of camaraderie and shared purpose for the most part. The seemingly senseless crime was distressing. He knew what civil war looked like firsthand, and he still had graphic nightmares of soldiers bursting in doors and killing people. The fact that life was so cheap in peacetime Memphis was difficult to fathom. He didn't understand why his friends in Memphis accepted it as normal.

****

Ember soon realized that she would have to make the first move with Emmanuel. He was kind and considerate of her, but seemed hesitant to approach her romantically, even as she got a strong sense that he wanted to. One day, when they were sitting outside the field house enjoying the weak sun that had burst thru the clouds after a heavy downpour, she waited for a break in their conversation. Then she leaned forward and kissed him. She was enormously pleased and relieved when he immediately put his arms around her and began kissing her back. From that moment on, they were a couple, and Ember was floating on air.

Their relationship was different from the ones that had come before. For the first time, she felt like she was dating a mature, adult man and not an overgrown juvenile. He was intelligent and well-spoken, kind, compassionate, and sensitive without being weak or needy. He respected her, and treated her with dignity and honor.

It was distressing to her that despite this, she quickly found out that Inetta was not the only one who thought Emmanuel was too black. It seemed that many of her friends, and even her family thought he was "too dark" or "too African." She was crushed when her favorite aunt, Joyce, pulled her aside at a family picnic to tell her "Cool it with the African." Emmanuel was sitting with several of her cousins, who were laughing and telling jokes, and he seemed to be fitting in fine.

Ember was perplexed. "But Aunt Joyce, I love him. I think he's the one!" she said, thinking that maybe someone had seen them together and thought they were overly affectionate. She thought they had been discreet at the picnic, but there was a moment when they had snuck off in one of the rooms of Uncle Richard's enormous estate to make-out.

Aunt Joyce answered, "No, you silly girl! You can't get serious with the dark ones. You can date them for a while, but you have to be careful. You can't have any accidents. You can't get serious, and you certainly can't get married." Ember looked at her aunt as if she had grown a second head. She'd never realized that her aunt held those kinds of beliefs, and it was upsetting. She quickly ended the conversation and walked back to where Emmanuel was sitting. She offered to fix him a plate, just to occupy herself and try and forget the previous conversation.

She headed off to the kitchen where a long buffet spread was set out, protected from the heat of the warm, sunny day. As she entered the kitchen thru the laundry room, she heard familiar voices, and caught her name. She stopped in her tracks to listen more closely. She heard her grandmother's voice say, "Well, Joyce, did you handle it?"

Joyce answered, "I don't know why I am supposed to handle it. It's your daughter, Jack."

Ember heard her father's voice, "You know the girl and I have a strained relationship because of her mother. And I don't trust her mother, Marlene, not to put silly ideas in her head, just to spite me. You have a good relationship with the girl. She trusts you and looks up to you. That's why we asked you."

She heard Joyce reply, "Well, I did my best, but she has some ridiculous notion that she loves him. She probably already goes to sleep with visions of white picket fences and a ring on her finger. I talked to her, but I don't know what good it will do."

Ember held back tears, hearing her life dissected by people she thought loved her. She knew her dad was vain, but it still surprised her to hear him express such ugly attitudes. It hurt worse to hear that the rest of her family agreed with him. She felt like she had been slapped awake, into a new reality that defied all of what she had previously thought to be true.

She quietly opened the laundry door and slipped out. She made her way to Emmanuel and then made their excuses. She was grateful that Emmanuel took it in stride and didn't question her until they were in the car. She debated not telling him what had happened, but she didn't want lies to taint their relationship. She was crying as she recounted the story, with her hands gripped tightly on the steering wheel, knuckles pale from the effort. She looked at Emmanuel and his face was set like stone.

They had been planning to spend the rest of the weekend together in her apartment, in bed. She loved those times with him. They would lay on their backs, hands intertwined while they talked about their hopes, their dreams, their pasts, and their futures. They would be naked, yes, but it wasn't about their bodies, it was about their minds. "Drop me at my place," he said abruptly.

He didn't say anything else for the rest of the trip, and Ember didn't know what to say. She pulled the car to the curb outside his apartment building and turned the motor off. She turned to him, to talk, to try to do what she needed to do to fix this; this silence, this coldness.

But Emmanuel didn't invite her in; to his heart, his mind or his apartment. Instead, he looked at her, and very calmly and coldly said, "I would wonder that you don't see the irony here, but then again, I have learned that Americans never do. They never see the hypocrisy in their own actions but are so quick to judge everyone else."

"Your family," he almost spat, "is worried that we might make a dark baby, a dark baby that might disrupt the superiority of your light, bright – and let me say this clearly, *white* family." His voice dripped pure acid as he continued, "I am descended from proud Amero-Africans. Amero- Africans who built the nation of Liberia into what it is today. Strong people who took the chance to free themselves from the bondage of the United States. I am directly related to no less than *three* Presidents. Yet, your family who was bred with generations of your white '*masters*' [and he said the word mockingly] dare look down on my lineage? You who have lost all your roots, yet claim to be a proud black family?"

He paused, before saying, with a sneer in his voice, "I am the one who is disgusted. I am disgusted to find this is what has become of the proud Prince family." With that, he opened the car door and got out, shutting the door gently. He didn't look back, even as Ember called, "But wait. I love you! I don't care what they think."

She quickly got out of the car to run after him, but he ignored her. Finally, as she stood in front of him, with tears streaming down her face, saying, "I love you, I love you," he looked at her again.

"I am sorry that I have misled you, Ember. There could never be anything serious between us. I mean, you just aren't on the same level," he said with cold finality. With that, he sidestepped around her and continued to his apartment.

Ember felt a squeezing in her chest as tears came with ragged sobs. She forced herself to draw a shaking breath. She slowly walked back to her car, where she continued to cry with a flood of tears blurring her vision. Finally, when she could breathe again, she wiped her face with her t-shirt and started the car. It seemed like an endless drive home, as his words washed over her again and again. Once she arrived, she went straight into her room, and climbed under the covers. She wondered if she could use the comforter to block it all out, forever.

****

Jonah, Georgetown, 1993

"Forget that jerk, Ember. I don't know why we are even talking about it. We're here in DC, and I plan to party!" Jonah said emphatically as they walked to a small brownstone near the Georgetown campus to meet his older brother, Bobby Jr. Bobby Jr., predictably, was politicking throughout Washington D.C. and wanted them to attend a party with his politically connected friends. Ember thought he was just showing off but didn't have a good excuse to skip it. He was her well-favored cousin, but Ember thought he was a bit of an arrogant jerk. She wasn't really interested in attending, until Jonah mentioned that the popular actress, Darryl Hannah, might be there. She could have cared less, but she knew that her cousin, Jonah, worshipped his brother. Ember couldn't see why, but Jonah had always been a steadfast and loyal friend to Ember, so she pretended an enthusiasm she didn't feel to placate him.

When Jonah and Ember arrived, the party was in full swing. Ember was a little dismayed to see that most of the people were in their mid-thirties, at least. She didn't recognize anyone other than her cousin, Bobby Jr., with two scantily dressed women on his arms. They looked like high-class prostitutes. He welcomed her in, with expansive gestures, as if it was his mansion. He then began to introduce Ember and Jonah to a variety of people, including "the mandatory Kennedys." This turned out to be William Kennedy Smith and another of his cousins. William had recently been acquitted of sexual assault charges, but he still gave off a predatory vibe that made Ember almost visibly recoil. He was intoxicated and was openly fondling the woman at his side. To his credit, she seemed to be a willing participant. As Bobby showed them around, he seemed different… Not drunk, but overly animated, and enthusiastic. He introduced her to some former classmates from his days at St. Albans School, which was one of the most exclusive private schools in the country. She didn't know who Malcolm was, but even she was educated enough to know who John Rockefeller *the fifth* or Kermit Roosevelt, *the third* was, or at least who their families were. They seemed friendly enough, if bored by the goings-on. For all that her cousin Bobby seemed to be in his element, his friends emitted a strong sense of ennui. They made brief small talk before fading back into the crowd of partygoers.

After a quick tour, Bobby disappeared too, into a group of six or seven people having an animated discussion about whether the current stand-off with the Koreshians in Waco, Texas was related to the recent bombing of the World Trade Center. As the group debated back and forth, she lost sight of Bobby.

Ember surveyed the party. The house was elegantly appointed with luxurious furnishings, and thick, plush carpeting. There were marble topped end tables, and expensive-looking paintings in fine gold frames. On the mantle were several photographs showing the home's owners with President Clinton in the Oval Office as well as what appeared to be several social events. There were also photos with David Miscavage, in front of what appeared to be an alter, as well as Julia Roberts, Kevin Costner, and Ivana Trump.

As she suspected, many of the people she met were older, old even! It was a little disconcerting to Ember to see them partying like, and with college kids. Jonah didn't seem to notice and had one arm around Barbara Boxer as he listened to John Glenn regale him with tales from his time as an astronaut. An older, grey-haired white guy named Tom tried to get cozy with Ember and steered her towards a back bedroom. He was from one of those fly-over states. As Ember attempted to disengage herself from his grasp to return to the living room, she caught site of Bobby in the back bedroom, with several others. He was sitting on the bed, with his back to her. As she paused in the doorway, a heavily tanned, generically attractive, blond man in his forties, invited her in. Bobby turned around.

"Ah, Ember, look. Here's a *real deal* Kennedy," Bobby chorused as she approached. She was surprised to see that Bobby had a mirror in his lap and was laying out several lines of coke from what appeared to be a generous baggie. A somewhat sleazy looking guy named Gary, who said he was from California, urged Ember forward. There were several other women Ember's age, sitting on the edge of the bed, next to her cousin. Bobby looked directly at Ember, and winked, just before he bent his head and snorted a line up his left nostril with a rolled up twenty-dollar bill. He passed the mirror to the next person, and it continued. Greasy Gary refilled the plate with nice, straight lines of coke, when the plate came his way before snorting two long lines up his bronzed nostrils. He then gestured to Ember with a nod of his head. Patrick, the tanned man behind her, urged her forward. Before she could think about what she was doing, she was leaning over, with her hair pulled back, to snort a line. Within seconds, she was filled with a sense of exhilaration, and power. In that moment, she knew that all her hopes and dreams would be realized. Why wouldn't they be? She was Ember Prince!

Bobby, and two of the prettier women, arose from the bed and left the room, just as Ember's cousin, Jonah, entered. Jonah quickly assessed the scene, and with a practiced air, quickly partook. Almost immediately after, there was yelling and a stampede of people to the back exit, and the windows. Ember was momentarily stunned by the sudden burst of activity.

"Stop, police!" she heard among the din. None of the people in the room with her looked concerned as she turned to flee. Several cops entered and placed everyone in handcuffs. Several minutes later, Ember, Jonah, and several of the other young women were loaded into a police wagon. They were taken to the station and charged with cocaine possession. Some of the other women were also charged with prostitution. Ember never saw any of the other people who were in the room with them, including cousin Bobby, at the station. They were booked, with their photos and fingerprints taken. The whole process took several hours; Ember was exhausted and upset.

Then they were taken back to the holding cells which were separated by gender. Ember and four prostitutes were placed in a cell that contained about 20 other women. Most of the other occupants also looked to be working girls. Several of them looked Ember up and down, but no one bothered her as she sat on the edge of a long, wooden bench bolted to the floor.

Bobby didn't accept Jonah's calls from the jail. Ember suspected as much when she saw the jailer lead him back to the other holding cell, dejected. Ember called her dad's lawyer, Scott Crawford instead, and he had both of them out within the hour. He couldn't do much to plea down the offense because the officers on the raid were determined to at least make some of the charges stick, and the prosecutor felt the same. The cops were tired of hearing anti-drug rhetoric from the same politicians that they routinely found drunk or high. If they couldn't book Ted Kennedy, then they would settle for a couple of rich brats. Ember ended up with community service since it was her first offense, but Jonah had a juvenile record, so he ended up doing three months as part of President Clinton's "Get Tough on Crime" initiatives. Bobby got away with it, like always. He was their own family version of the "Teflon Don" that was in the headlines all the time. He always seemed to worm his way out of trouble, but Ember had no intention of forgiving him this time.

Ember, Los Angeles 1995

After leaving Memphis State after her arrest and another unfortunate campus incident, Ember headed west, to Hollywood to be an actress. With a little help from her increasingly absent and occupied father, she was able to save enough to rent an apartment in a dodgy part of North Hollywood. The less he saw Ember, the more likely Jack was to send money. Now that he had multiple families, with multiple women, he sent Ember money somewhat regularly. Of course, with so many paternal financial responsibilities, it wasn't a lot of money, but it was enough to get some groceries. That was fine with Ember since she wasn't planning on struggling forever. She just needed her one big break, to get out there in front of an audience, so they could see what she could do.

****

Grandmother Bernice had died last year, but with so many children, it had taken a while for the dust to settle. Several of the boys' wives had helped clean out and distribute Bernice's things. Ember's mother, Marlene, was still close to her former sisters-in-law. So, when Joyce had invited Marlene for coffee at the old Prince home on Jubert street, Marlene went. She thought maybe Joyce could use some help taking things to the dump, so she filled up the tank of the old truck before heading over there. As they sat at the old, battered, kitchen table, she expressed her condolences as Joyce sipped her coffee. Instead of a request for help, Joyce leaned over and pulled out something from underneath the table.

She was surprised when Joyce had pulled out an old Gerber's Department Store hat box that was wrapped with twine. As she slid the box over to Marlene, she said, "I think Ember should have this."

"What is it?" Marlene asked as her fingers played and twisted with one of the ends of the twine. The box smelled musty and had a heavy layer of dust.

Joyce looked around, to make sure that none of the other women, who were still upstairs, were around. "Just take it. It's a bunch of letters. I am not fully sure I understand myself. But," she shrugged and continued, "it's family history and your daughter should have it." Then she shrugged again and took a sip of her coffee cup. Marlene looked over the box at Joyce and considered it. She knew that Joyce and her daughter, Ember, had always been close over the years. In a big family like the Princes, it was important for a child to have an aunt or uncle that took a special interest in their life. It was too easy to get lost in the shuffle otherwise. With 11 brothers and sisters, her ex-husband's nieces and nephews ran into the dozens. Even after being married and divorced from the Prince family, Marlene still couldn't keep track of all the Prince off-spring. It meant a lot to her that Joyce had taken the time to continue to foster the bond between herself and Marlene's oldest child, especially now that Ember's father was doing his best to make as many "replacement" families as possible. She needed those family ties to pull Ember back to Memphis one day. She finished her coffee and chatted with Joyce for a few more minutes before she hugged her and left, with the old box underneath her arm. As curious as she was, she didn't untie the box until she got home. After she examined the contents, she silently agreed with Joyce. She slipped the lid back on the box and began to package it for the post office.

****

Ember felt sick as put down the phone receiver and looked around the old and worn North Hollywood apartment. The late afternoon sun cast a particularly yellowish glow on the dented formica table, and the curling and torn linoleum floor in the kitchen. Dust motes were illuminated in their glory, as a sliver of light streamed across the worn brown and beige striped couch. It looked like a fleabag apartment because it was a fleabag apartment, but it was all she could afford right now. After her last two roommates bailed, Ember had been forced to move to a seedier neighborhood in North Hollywood, where she could afford her own apartment. Most of her furniture was from the Salvation Army and she felt lucky to have found it. The last roommate had cleaned her out while she was away at a casting call. She had come home to find the place empty except for her dirty clothes hamper. She felt fortunate that she hadn't had time to go to the laundromat recently, or she might not have even had that. Apparently, her thieving ex-roommate drew the line at stealing her dirty underwear.

Her father's latest trophy wife had just called to tell her that they would be visiting Los Angeles later that week. Ember knew it was just another opportunity for her dad to do his best to knock her down a peg, and he certainly would once he saw this place. It had been a long time since she'd been daddy's little princess. With all of her father's constant womanizing, some of his mistresses were younger than she was.

She wondered if his wife, Tamara, had heard the latest rumors that were swirling around Memphis about a certain pregnant staffer in her father's office. If she hadn't, maybe she'd keep that in her back pocket if things became too unpleasant during their visit. In this family, love was weaponized, so you always showed up armed for battle. She already knew that her father was disappointed in her for dropping out of school and leaving Memphis, but she wasn't interested in either the family funeral home business or politics. She wanted to be in show business, and she knew she had talent.

Her mom, Marlene, understood her. She knew why it was so important that she make a name for herself outside of Memphis, away from the family business. She understood why she needed to show everyone that she could do it, and that it wasn't the Prince legacy carrying her along. Of course, her mom always understood her best. As she thought about calling her mom, a knock sounded at the door. She hung the phone back up in the kitchen and headed to the door. The postman stood there with a box and a form for her to sign. She signed quickly and brought the box inside. She said "thanks" over her shoulder as she used her hip to close the door.

She sat down cross-legged on the dun-colored carpet and excitedly unwrapped the package. Beneath the brown paper, and inside another cardboard box, a note card was attached to an old hat box for a store that no longer existed. It was wrapped in old twine that was unraveling. Ember pulled the twine, and it came undone easily. She lifted the lid and peered inside.

Inside the box were bundles and bundles of letters and postcards. Each group of letters were bound by a length of twine. Most of the letters did not appear to be opened. However, there was one envelope that was slightly bigger than the rest, with a neat slit in the envelope, showing that it had been opened. It had beautiful looping handwriting on the front, addressed to 'The Family of Harriet Prince.' The return address was an enormous looping J. followed by a much smaller name in the same looping script. The address was indecipherable but the multiple stamps on the envelope indicated it had been mailed from overseas. Ember was intrigued. She somehow felt like whatever was inside that letter was going to change her somehow. She laughed at herself for her silly thoughts and shrugged her shoulders, but the strange feeling wouldn't disperse. She got to her feet and went to the kitchen for a glass of water, castigating herself for being ridiculous the entire time. She got the glass out of the cabinet and held it under the tap. Even as she gulped down the water, the sense of unease remained. She placed the glass on the short, chipped countertop that also served as a breakfast bar and returned to the tiny living room.

"Stop it," she chided herself as she settled back down on the carpet. She picked up the opened letter again and lifted the flap. The envelope felt slightly heavy. The letter was dated July 1944, and despite the age, the ink was dark and easily legible. As she opened the letter, she saw there were two small, faded photographs within the pages. She began to reach for the photographs when the words on the page, caught her attention.

"To the family of my dear friend, Harriet Prince," she read. *"It is with great sadness and a very heavy heart that I write to inform you that Harriet is no more. While I can offer no definitive proof of her demise, it is almost certain that she has been killed.*

I know that she wrote to you frequently, so you must be aware of her courageous work in the north of France. She went to areas where even I, with my guards and entourage, did not dare. For more than a year, she has been working at an underground hospital in Rouen, aiding the wounded citizens of the city and numerous members of the resistance. She also helped to hide and treat wounded, Allied airman, many of them Americans, who were shot down over German controlled areas of our country.

Sadly, I recently received word that she and the other members of the resistance hospital were killed in the bombing back in April. Unfortunately, until recently, there was no way for me to confirm this news. However, I have just returned from Rouen, and the city has been devastated. The entire hospital which was in the catacombs beneath the ancient Notre Dame cathedral has been destroyed. The tunnel and the crypt beneath the church collapsed during a wave of heavy bombing by Allied forces.

After walking the grounds myself, I must conclude, that there was no chance for survival. It is certain now that Harriet and all the brave souls she worked with have most certainly perished, and lie permanently entombed beneath the ruins of the church. I hope that the fact that she died in heroic service to humanity and fighting against the evils of Adolf Hitler brings you some small comfort. She was a hero to all of us that knew her, and much loved by many.

Your servant,

J. Baker

Josephine Baker

P.S. She left this photograph with me for safekeeping before she left for Rouen. It was her most precious possession.

Ember looked at the letter in her hand and read it again. Then she put it back in the envelope and looked at the small photographs, then realized that it was two torn halves of an old, old photograph. The outfits of the people in the photograph looked decades older than the 1940's. It was a photograph of people in an open carriage, with a woman with an infant in the center of the photo, surrounded by several other people. The woman wore a high-necked frilly blouse, and a very large hat, with a bow. The baby was dressed in a long white dress. There was some faded writing on the back of the photo in a barely legible copperplate style script. The brown ink said, "Daphne with Florida, 1894".

It took Ember a moment to realize what it all meant, but she carefully put the photo aside on the small coffee table. She felt sad for a moment as she remembered Emmanuel and his handwritten family tree. She had really loved that man. She sighed, then she reached for the first packet of unopened letters in the box. She spent the rest of the evening engrossed. When she finally reached for the last letter, she was surprised to see the bright light of the streetlights coming through the blinds. She felt her stomach rumble and looked at her watch, realizing, with surprise, that it was midnight. Several hours had passed while she had been engaged in unraveling the story contained within. She took a breath, and then carefully placed all of the letters back into the hat box. She stood up slowly stretching her legs, feeling a tingle as she did so. She wondered why she had never heard of Harriet before, and why so many of the letters had been unopened. It made her feel sad and lonely to think about.

She took the hat box to the small bedroom and placed it in the closet. Then she made a second trip, with the photograph held carefully in her hand, and placed it on her battered and scarred dresser. Task completed, she returned to the kitchen and began to make herself a sandwich for supper.

****

She didn't have a scheduled audition the next day, so instead of her usual routine of calling her agent, haunting the studio lots, and reading the trade papers for casting calls, she headed out to a copy shop with the photo pieces in a clean envelope. She left the envelope with the clerk. Then she headed to McDonalds for some coffee. When she returned 30 minutes later, she was thrilled to hand over one of her worn five-dollar bills in exchange for the now repaired photograph. She didn't know why she felt compelled, but she went by the Salvation Army thrift store and found a used photo frame for a quarter. With her prizes in hand, she went back to the apartment to scour the help wanted ads for additional work. She set the framed photograph on her dresser and looked at it again. She didn't understand why, but looking at the photo gave her a sense of peace and comfort. She wished she had a photo of Harriet.

She did weekend work as a bartender at a gay bar on Sunset, but she was always looking for additional short-term work to help her get by until she could land a big, juicy part. She was disappointed that she had to turn down an offer to work a catered event that weekend, but her dad was coming. She hadn't seen him in a long time and she missed him. She had so many memories of her dad when she was small, but ever since the divorce, she almost never saw him.

****

Her father and his new wife didn't disappoint. They were inside her apartment for less than five minutes before they were bickering and arguing with each other. In between condescending comments, the pain they inflicted on each other was obvious. Ember could swear her father's new wife was drunk. Before Ember knew what was happening, Tamara was arguing and cursing at her.

"So, what is this bitch doing with all the money you are sending?" Tamara yelled, "it certainly isn't for this dump."

'All the money?' Ember thought. The checks weren't that often nor very large. In fact, the last check had been for thirty dollars, about the same as the checks she got every year from her maternal grandmother.

"This is why our babies can't have nice things! Because you are sending all the money to this spoiled brat? So, she can sit on her ass all day and pretend to be an *actress,*" Tamara said with a snotty tone in her voice.

"It's for *my* child!" he father said ardently, angrily! "You don't get to dictate how I spend money on my child!" he finished, not looking at Ember.

Ember suddenly understood what was really going on and she felt profoundly sad, and disappointed. I don't know why I expected my dad to change, she thought. I don't know why I actually thought this visit was about me, she thought as her heart felt heavy. She suddenly felt exhausted, on the verge of collapse. She managed to fake her way through the rest of the very short visit. She wasn't surprised when Tamara demanded to leave a few minutes after that due to a "terrible, terrible migraine." Ember could only imagine what the hangover was going to be like tomorrow. She almost wished she could be there when Tamara found out where the money was really going.

****

Several months later, Ember didn't need to be there to know that Tamara found out where the money was going. Everyone in Memphis knew, once Tamara drove her car into her husband's mistress's house. Soon after that, a long editorial in the local paper calling her dad, Don Juan Prince was published, detailing many of the sordid details that her father had kept hidden. It also extensively detailed his use of public funds to maintain his numerous mistresses, girlfriends, and other sexual partners. After receiving a clipping anonymously in the mail, Ember could only be grateful she was two thousand miles away. She commiserated with her cousin, Jonah, who reported that his older brother, Bobby, was embroiled in much of the same. Jonah and Ember had remained close ever since they had been arrested together, while their cousin got off Scott-free.

Book Seven: Rebuilding the Legacy 2005
Jack, Robert and Desdemona

All of Bernice's grown children were gathered in the old mansion on Raines Road. It had been Richard's home prior to his untimely death a few years earlier. Now, in the midst of several lawsuits, his estate was preparing to sell the property before it could be seized as part of any settlement. Barbara had come down from New York to help coordinate this emergency family meeting. The large living room seemed almost cavernous due to the sparse furnishings. Most of Richard's belongings had long since been dispersed with just a few pieces of furniture remaining in the antebellum style home that sat on a 20-acre estate.

"Why are we meeting here? This place is practically empty," Desdemona complained. "There's not even something to drink," she continued.

Barbara pointed over to a large, red, picnic cooler in the corner of the room, "Make yourself at home, Decca," she said, with a pointed eye roll.

Jack spoke up, "We are meeting here to make sure that no one else is listening!" he said pointedly. As the recent victim of an FBI sting, Jack wasn't being paranoid when he imagined hidden microphones in his home or office. He was now facing a prison term for fraud.

While no one in the family directly addressed the fraud allegations or the recent indictment, Barbara again began to start the meeting, saying, "As you know, Jack will be losing his seat in the Tennessee Senate. This seat has been in the Prince family since 1971, and we can't let it end up outside of the family."

Jack looked away as she spoke, muttering, "and I was the one in that seat all of those years."

Robert abruptly took control of the meeting, saying, "Barbara, *you don't even live here.* You can't vote and you can't run for office. I don't even know why you are here. *Thank you for bringing the snacks*, but I can handle it from here."

Barbara looked aghast at being dismissed thusly by her baby brother. She swallowed several of her responses after she looked at her other siblings, most of whom were studiously avoiding her gaze. Only Decca would meet her eyes. So shunned, she sat down quietly at the edge of the couch, seeming to sink into its depths.

"Now, as I was saying, we need to work quickly to consolidate power for the family. We can't let the seat fall into the hands of outsiders. Now, I have done *my* duty, and then I handed over *my* seat to my son, Bobby," Robert said smugly.

Jack nodded in acknowledgement. Robert continued, "Richard did his time in office, until he died, and Emmitt too."

Emmitt nodded and interrupted, "Once was enough for me".

"Marvin and Louie live out of state like me, so they aren't eligible either," Barbara said, in an attempt at redemption.

"Barb, you wouldn't be a candidate even if you lived down the street," Jack spat, in disgust.

"Wait! Wait! Wait!" Bernice called, interrupting before the siblings could start bickering.

Robert spoke up once again, "Now I think it's time for Joe or Byron to step up and into Jack's shoes."

Decca looked up from her drink and spat, "Wait! What? Joe and Emmitt are the babies! Byron has no interest in politics and Emmitt had his stint. What about me? Or Joyce? Joyce could move back to the district and run."

Jack just looked over and started laughing. His brothers seemed to share his amusement.

Decca felt frustrated and angry. "Well, what's so wrong with me? I would be a good candidate. I don't have a bunch of dirty laundry, either!" she said, raising an eyebrow at Jack.

Barbara felt obligated to back her sister. "Yes, I think Desdemona would be an excellent candidate." She waited for her brothers to try and find some reason why she wasn't. They wouldn't openly say what they really thought, which was that women should stay at home, cooking, cleaning and taking care of children. For all that the Prince clan claimed to have progressive family values, and believe in equal opportunities for all, that stance didn't extend to their own homes. There, the traditional teachings of home and hearth prevailed.

Everyone waited for Joe or Byron to speak up and offer their candidacy instead. After a few moments of silence, Decca looked triumphant.

Jack quickly dashed her hopes when he said, "Well, you can go ahead and run, but I wouldn't expect too much from it."

The meeting broke up fairly quickly after that. Decca, Barbara, and Joyce walked together as they left the house, with Bernice trailing behind.

"You see," Decca hissed, "they don't support me because I am a woman."

Joyce shrugged. She was a homemaker, and she was happy to stay at home, take care of her kids, and sing in the church choir. The whole idea of a political empire was foreign to her. She didn't know why they couldn't be satisfied with what they had.

Barbara looked at Decca and said, "I am just glad to see that you want to participate in something. It seemed like we had lost you for a while."

Decca looked up, shocked, and said, "I don't know what you mean, I've been here. I've been working for the family business, but," she said sarcastically, "I guess you wouldn't know all that up in New York."

"Decca, I am trying to be supportive," Barbara said with a big sigh. Then she turned away to walk to her car, while Bernice, Joyce and Decca all walked to Joyce's car.

****

That fall, Decca managed to win the election by the narrowest of margins, 13 votes, but she did so without her more famous brothers at her side. They were noticeably absent from her campaign, but good for a newsworthy quote when hunted down by reporters. When news of campaign irregularities including dead voters, fake names, and ballot stuffing came to light, citizens of Shelby County just sighed. It was more of the same with the Prince family. Apathetic about on-going corruption, voters returned Decca to office even after state officials nullified the previous election. Unsurprisingly to the people who knew the family, Decca voted along the lines of Tennessee conservatives, despite representing the Democratic party. She voted against aid to needy families. She voted against women's reproductive rights, and she voted against her own values. She sat out many of the more important votes, and she became an important face in the "Right-To-Life" movement. She co-sponsored a bill to reject equity measures to fight poverty as part of a United Nations initiative and seemed to take pride in doing so. She pushed open carry and other handgun initiatives, voting to allow guns in public spaces including parks. She had an active political life at first, but politics didn't turn out to be the lifeline she had hoped.

Instead of filling the deep hole in Decca's soul, her new political position was more about making deals, and satisfying lobbies. She wanted to serve the public but was reduced to serving her family's self-interest. So, she drank to fill the hole, with some success. By a few years into her second term, her absenteeism was becoming a problem. She blamed anemia, fatigue, and some vague medical complaints, but it was really the drinking and the stress that was taking its toll.

So much so, that in just a few years' time, she was secretly hospitalized in acute on chronic liver failure. She was fortunate in that no one at Vanderbilt Medical Center leaked her secret.

Fortunate too that Vanderbilt had recently started an acute liver dialysis program, that helped bridge Decca until doctors could convince her estranged daughter into donating part of her liver. Her daughter, Sophia, who was now a licensed minister, with her own young family felt torn and manipulated. She loved her mother, of course, but that didn't erase all the years of drunken abuse she'd endured at her mother's hands, while the rest of the family remained blissfully oblivious to her plight. After her paternal grandmother's murder, she'd had only the Prince side of the family, and they were content to let her stay with her mother, even when her mother couldn't care for her. By the time she was ten, she was consistently caring for her mother and herself. Now, doctors were asking her to do it again – to give away a part of herself to save her mother. After consulting with her husband, and her God, she consented and went thru the painful process of donating a portion of her liver. In return, her mother made endless promises to return to the faith and abstain from drinking forever more.

Distressingly, "forever more" turned out to only be a year. Shortly after that, her mother was arrested for public intoxication and assault after falling over a barstool. Yet again, the rest of the Prince family disavowed Desdemona and left her to her misery.

By that time, the two youngest male Prince siblings had entered the political sphere, so there was no need for Decca, after all. In fact, two of her biggest political losses were to her brothers, souring Decca against her family, again.

****

Ember: New Year's Day, 2022

Ever since she'd woken up next to the disgraced, scandal-ridden, and flatulent Hunter Baron, Ember knew she'd finally hit rock bottom. She had flirted with disaster so many times before, but that moment was truly the lowest she'd felt in her entire life. It was worse than her brief foray into films in Hollywood when she learned how thin-skinned she really was. She always thought of herself as tough and resilient because she'd had to be in this family. The Prince family didn't take any prisoners; and her dad was the worst scoundrel of the lot. He'd made her feel disposable and easily replaceable her entire life, but that was nothing compared to central casting.

They thought nothing of telling you to your face that you were "too old and too ethnic." They didn't care about your feelings when they told you that your butt was too big and your boobs were too small. Then there were the times she'd auditioned for less mainstream films. That's when they told her that she "wasn't black enough." They didn't threaten to replace you if you hesitated to do a nude scene. They just waited until you came back from the lunch break and introduced you to your replacement. Then, they escorted you off the lot, like you were a criminal, not a dignified woman who didn't want to act in pornographic scenes that were last minute on-set changes to a marginal script on a low budget project. She'd come home to Memphis then, wounded, with her tail between her legs. She thought that was as low as she could go, lower that failing out of Memphis State, and lower than being blacklisted by her sorority, but it turned out her escapade with Hunter Baron was the very bottom of a pit filled with a lifetime of missteps and failures. The worst part of it all was that she didn't remember any of it. You would think that your greatest mistake would come with some internal warnings, but apparently, it didn't.

That wasn't to say that she'd listen. She'd ignored the voice in her head so many times before. It was the voice that had told her not to drop out of college, the voice that said she shouldn't try cocaine with her cousin at that political party in D.C. That internal voice that asked, 'Was she sure she wanted to do this?' She'd certainly heard that voice cautioning her before she had rushed headlong out to California. But she knew, she would have heeded the voice this time. But she never heard it.

The entire night was a blur. She remembered getting dressed to go out that evening and meet some friends. They were planning to go to the Blue Monkey and then out to Winchester to one of the new clubs to dance, but she didn't remember any of that. The next memory she had was waking up nude, hungover, and sore, with Hunter Baron beside her.

****

Veronica, March 17th, 2022

Veronica gritted her teeth and prayed as she turned the key in the door of the Parkway apartment. She looked down the hallway before quietly slipping into the apartment. She had been calling for the last two days to make sure that no one was home. Thank goodness, the owner was old-fashioned enough that he insisted on maintaining a landline.

As she eased the door open slowly, Veronica caught a quick whiff of the unappetizing aroma of rotting garbage. She sighed, "typical". She muttered under her breath, "Of course, he didn't take out the garbage before leaving town." Anyway, it wasn't her problem anymore. She continued down the hallway past the living room, where she noticed the massive, colorful David Lynch painting depicting downtown Memphis was hanging askew. A small porcelain figurine lay on its side on the heavy, faded, and worn Oriental carpet. An array of clothing was strewn over the couch, along with the remnants of what looked like several days' worth of nighttime snacks. Several kernels of blackened popcorn spilled out of a microwave popcorn bag. A wine glass lay on its side, surrounded by a dried pool of red wine. Veronica hurried past. She wanted to get in and get out as quickly as possible. She didn't want to chance an encounter, and thus a confrontation, if she could avoid it. She just wanted to grab a bag of her things and leave.

As she made her way toward the closed bedroom door, she heard a faint humming sound. It sounded like a thrum, thrum sound. She was racking her brain to figure out what she was hearing, the sound became a bit louder with every step towards the bedroom door. Somehow, the smell of rotting garbage had started to waft back towards the bedroom it seemed. She felt a breeze and noticed that several windows were open. For some reason, she had a feeling of trepidation as she turned the bedroom knob. She felt like turning and fleeing. Her heart was beating loud in her ears. It drowned out the thrum-thrum sound.

As she pushed open the door, a breeze brought the odor straight to her nose full-blast. She was gagging, her eyes watering, as she simultaneously took in the sight of thousands of flies. Flies coming in the windows, flies flying around the room, and flies covering a dead body. She started screaming before she even realized she had opened her mouth. She wanted to run in horror, but her legs didn't seem to work. It was like they wanted to make sure that she got a memory-searing look at the scene before they finally allowed her to run out of the apartment, her screams becoming shriller and shriller. In a remote part of her brain, the part that was still thinking rationally, she realized that she didn't have to worry about having a confrontation with her ex anymore.

****

Casey Lyon Agner looked up from the corpse to nod at homicide detective, Sgt. Rex Lester, as he entered the scene. Sergeant Lester acknowledged Casey, then grunted as he took in the scene. Most of the flies had initially dissipated once the crime scene experts had began setting up, but seemed to circle back around, as flies still hovered and buzzed around their heads.

The entire room was splattered with dried blood. It appeared to arch out from the wheelchair to the farthest parts of the room. The front part of the seat of the wheelchair showed a bloody outline of hips, and a very large, dried, maroon-colored stain spread out from beneath the body on the floor.

The corpse lay face down in a hunched over position at the foot of the wheelchair. It looked like the body had fallen forward out of the wheelchair around the time of death. Casey circled around the room taking photographs from all angles. The medical examiner was new and seemed taciturn and serious. His predecessor had been excellent, but she'd had a lighter side too. She knew that a smile or a small wisecrack would lessen the tension at the scene without diminishing any of her skill. It was too early to tell with Dr. Robbins.

Dr. Andrew Robbins looked up from where he was kneeling on a tarp on the floor. "Ok, folks, let's roll him over and see what did him in." He spoke with the easy mid-western lilt that belied his roots in Hackensack, New Jersey.

Casey raised the camera back to her eye, so she missed the collective looks of surprise as Dr. Robbins and another forensic expert, Robert Haley, turned him over. The body flopped over easily with minimal effort despite the team's efforts to roll him gently.

She quickly focused her camera on the scene at hand and took several wide-angle shots of the scene before closing in on the body. It didn't take long to be an experienced crime scene technician in Memphis and Casey was a well-seasoned professional. She'd been at the scene of some of the worst homicides in Memphis, and some of the most tragic, like the recent killing of several teenagers at a gas station by Graceland, or the murder of many of Memphis' hometown rappers in the seemingly endless turf war. Still, the scene Casey was looking at thru the lens still took her aback. In fact, Casey had to move the camera away from her face for a moment to be sure that she was really seeing what she saw in the camera's eyepiece.

What remained of the infamous playboy, Hunter Baron, lay on his back. He had a wide gash extending deep into his neck and almost severing his head. There was a dried piece of tissue hanging down from the center of the wound. Casey knew there was a specific term for what she was seeing, but she couldn't dredge it from the depths of her memory. Instead, as she took in the injury to his neck, she noted the presence of maggots squirming in and out of the gash. She took a few more photos before adjusting the lens for a close-up, for a better detailed look at the wound, and the insect activity. Lividity had set in, and while rigor mortis had already come and gone, the purple discoloration on his forehead, nose, cheeks and chin was fixed. This extensive discoloration along with the advancing state of decomposition made his ethnicity almost impossible to determine. The long, greyish-white, and unkempt locks matched those of the man in several of the photographs around the apartment.

"Couldn't happen to a more deserving guy, eh, Casey," Robert Haley said. Both Robert and Casey had been prosecution witnesses in the recently deceased's murder trial. But Hunter Baron had been acquitted of the matricide of his 93-year-old mother, and free to inherit her multi-million-dollar estate. It looked like someone beside the prosecution disagreed with that verdict.

By then Casey had taken sufficient photos of the scene. It was time to move on to the rest of the apartment. Casey would photograph anything that seemed out of place. Unfortunately, in such a messy apartment like this, it was difficult to tell what / if anything was out of the ordinary. Casey would just go room to room and take as many pictures as she needed to capture the scene and tell the story. She headed out of the bedroom, taking pictures of the hallway, showing portraits and artwork to be askew, along with some scuffs on the walls and some of the bottoms of the doors. There was visible hair and other debris in the dirty carpet, so she took close-ups. She didn't know how long the hair, lint and other crumbs of dirt, food and unknown bits had been there, but that wasn't part of her job. It was someone else's job, at the crime lab, to sort thru all the detritus to figure out what mattered. It looked like the apartment's owner vacuumed and otherwise cleaned rarely, if at all, so Casey certainly didn't envy the lab technician who was saddled with processing this scene.

In some ways, the kitchen was its own crime scene, Casey thought wryly. This job is giving me a twisted sense of humor, she thought as she photographed filthy dishes, with mold growing on them, and a rank kitchen trash can that was overflowing with rotted food, empty food wrappers, and take-out containers. Several empty bottles of liquor were placed on the floor by the trash container. An empty bottle of Bordeaux wine with a pink curling ribbon still wrapped around the neck was mingled in with empty vodka bottles. A bottle of high-end whiskey had fallen over and there was a very small, dried, golden brown spot of whiskey on the sticky, white tiled floor.

Flies swarmed around the sink, as well as spilled piles of seemingly every food item ever consumed in the last six months. There was a package of Southern brand cane sugar laying on its side, with a small mound of sugar spilled out. Next to it, a dirty spoon, with a dried, dark, coffee-colored stain beneath it. A small carton of milk sat forgotten on the counter nearby. Dirty coffee cups were scattered throughout the kitchen and dining area, and on end tables in the living room. All of them had a thick crystalized crust in the bottom.

Sprinkles of pepper and other spices dotted the area around the burners along with thick globs of hardened grease. She looked up and noticed the inside of the oven hood was fully encased and caked in grease. It looked like years of deep-fried chicken, hamburgers, and okras worth of grease. It looked like more grease than even the famous Dyer's Burgers Restaurant could claim. For some reason, this made her stomach roll more than the decomposing corpse in the bedroom. She took the last few pictures of the kitchen area before she hastily made her way to the next area of the apartment.

****

Ember, March 2022

Three months had gone by, and Ember was doing her best to put "the regrettable New Year's incident" behind her. She was sitting in the main conference room at campaign headquarters; working with her press secretary, John, on some new ideas for an ad campaign when the police showed up in her office. It was just after five o'clock and her administrative assistant, Trenivius, had already left for the day. As plain clothes detectives introduced themselves, Ember inwardly sighed, "what had her father done now?" she wondered. She jerked back to attention as she heard the words homicide division. She looked over sharply at the two detectives. Sergeant Rex Allen Lester was a solidly built, very tall, serious looking, Caucasian man who appeared to be in his early fifties. Ember would have been surprised to know that he was known for his easy smiles and dry humor. There was no smile on his face now. He was well-dressed and well-kept looking but there was nothing extravagant or notable about his outfit except for worn but clean cowboy boots peeping out beneath his trousers. He dwarfed his partner, Detective Renee Payne, who was an average-sized, light-skinned, African-American female. She was precise about her appearance, Ember mentally noted. She wore a closely tailored, light pink suit made of a fabric with a slight sheen. It was paired with a Kelly-green silk blouse with green sequin trim around the neckline. Seeing the specific color combination, Ember's mouth went dry. She looked up at the detective's face, which was unlined and expertly made up. Her thick ebony hair was pulled back into box braids worked into an elegant chignon. Small gold drop earrings accented with white pearls dotted her ears, matching a pearl bracelet peeking out from under her jacket cuff. A large emerald and gold enameled colored pin graced her jacket label. The entire look was finished off with no nonsense, but stylish flats in a matching green, and a pink-colored, smart looking handbag decorated with a Kelly-green ivy leaf. As Ember had expected, the handbag had an adornment attached to the metal ring that connected the strap to the bag itself. The adornment was a Greek emblem made of tiny stones in the colors of pink and green. Ember inwardly groaned. Renee appeared amused by Ember's perusal as Ember's gaze finally met her eyes. John didn't seem to notice the exchange, but Sergeant Lester watched her reaction closely. It seemed like it had taken an eternity to Ember, but apparently it had just been a few seconds.

"Homicide?" Ember and John said almost simultaneously, with bewilderment. "Of whom?" John asked. Even in a pinch, he never forgot his grammar, Ember thought. She almost smiled at the thought, before snapping back to reality. She tried to think about the recent homicides reported on the news but drew a blank. Nothing had happened in the last few days that stuck in her mind. Unfortunately, just too many people were killed in Memphis on a regular basis. A thought slowly occurred to her, but she kept silent. The only recent murder of note that she would recall was someone she didn't want to think about at all. Besides, she couldn't think of a reason why the police would want to talk to her about it.

Renee watched Ember's face closely and she could see several expressions flit across her face, just before Sgt. Lester answered. When Rex said, "Hunter Baron," Renee could swear she saw Ember crumple inside, for just a moment, before she looked up again and invited them to sit.

"Officers, please take a seat." Ember said sweetly. She continued, "but I must say, before you get too comfortable that I don't know anything about it. I certainly have no idea why you would want to talk to me about Hunter Baron," she finished.

After sitting down carefully, Renee crossed her legs slowly, pointedly, and clicked her tongue before saying, almost lazily, "That so? Because I can think of at least one compelling reason we want to talk to you." She smiled like the cat that ate the canary.

Rex watched the interchange with interest. He hadn't expected his partner to go in for the kill quite so quickly. He'd planned to start off much more slowly, with some seemingly innocuous questions before homing in on his suspect. However, whatever Renee had going, it seemed to be working. He saw a bead of sweat form on Ember's hairline while her press secretary looked at her questioningly.

Ember paused for a moment to collect herself. Distant memories of her, on her knees, blind-folded, reciting a poem flashed thru her brain. "A day of an Alpha Kappa Alpha Woman, A day of an Alpha Kappa Alpha woman is a day well spent! An AKA woman is always ready to lead, especially when it comes to meeting others' needs…" She remembered feeling humiliated as she faltered, while angry distant voices at the periphery of her memory mocked her. Then the poem slowly trailed off in her mind as Ember came back to the present.

Then she remembered who she was.

"I am Ember Prince!", she thought, "from a long line of Princes. We rule Shelby County!" With that she sat up a little straighter and looked Renee dead in the eye, and said with a crisp, but soft voice, that breathed authority, arrogance, and generations of perseverance and triumph, "I'm sorry but you will have to speak to my attorney. We are very busy here and don't have time for frivolous interruptions." Thus, she dismissed the detectives before turning back and giving her full attention to John, and the presentation that had been quickly set aside on their arrival. John blinked but followed her lead.

Renee stared at her for a moment with disbelief before quickly getting to her feet. She was astounded by the suspect's abrupt 180 degree in behavior. She opened her mouth, but Rex looked at her sharply, and quickly took her arm, steering her away from the suspect. Renee glared at him for a moment, and turned back to Ember and said, "Don't worry, we will be back Ms. Prince to talk more about this frivolous matter." Her voice dripped sarcasm on the word frivolous. Then she turned back to Sgt. Lester, and she stormed out of the building with the door slamming shut behind them.

Ember waited until she saw the cruiser pull out of the parking lot before she turned to John and said, "Let's call it a night." He agreed and went to gather his things. Ember waited until she got in her office to make the call.

"Daddy? Daddy, it's Ember and I need your help," she said in a small voice. Gone was the confidence and bravado from her earlier interaction. Now, she was just a scared little girl who needed her dad and his undivided attention. She held the phone to her ear, listening for a minute before she broke down in tears. She warbled a goodbye and hung up.

****

Ember's heart was in her throat as she walked down the long hallway to her dad's office. She followed his secretary, who was just one of the many attractive and lissome young women that he surrounded himself with. His constant and voracious womanizing was more well-known than his political positions or policies at this point, and he'd been in politics since before she was born. He'd also served time for federal charges that included bribery, witness tampering/ intimidation and extortion just a few years ago but was still expected to re-take his old senate seat in the next election. He was Shelby County, and Tennessee's version of Marion Barry. Like Marion Barry, he also knew the value of a good legal defense, because only God knew how many other crimes he had gotten away with. Ember knew that the FBI and state authorities had been investigating him for various crimes since she was a child, and this was the only thing they'd ever managed to convict him on. So, she wasn't terribly surprised to find Lee Filderman, a prominent defense attorney waiting for her in her dad's office. He was one of the few attorneys to be able to keep up with her dad without ending up in jail. He survived because he was incorruptible. He was also unlike one of his predecessors, Michael Scholl who was caught lying to the FBI.

He'd been on retainer with her family since he was a junior associate, still wet behind the ears. Of course, back then, he was the file toting gopher for Scott Crawford, before he'd been disbarred for being part of a narco-trafficking ring. Scott Crawford hadn't been much older than Lee, but the firm had partnered them together so he could show Lee the ropes. The firm didn't know that Scott Crawford had decided that the gangster life suited him much better than Men's Warehouse suits, and it wasn't long before he was riding around in fancy cars, adored with gold chains, expensive watches and cheap but flashy women. As a protegee of Russell Sugermon, Lee Filderman wanted to do anything but live the life of a gangster thug. He'd watched Scott Crawford flame out, while he made sure to do his homework. For all of his wanna-be Tony Montana aspirations, Scott Crawford had been an ace litigator. Now, Scott Crawford was doing 25 years to life for being involved in premeditated assassination of a rival trafficker, and Lee Filderman had inherited several of Crawford's high-profile families, who needed a defense attorney on retainer.

While Ember was relieved to see Lee, dressed in his typical flamboyant manner, in a Brooks Brother jacket and waistcoat, partnered with camel colored corduroy pants and matching leather shoes, she was deflated to see that her father was absent. She refused to ask where he was. Her father knew she was here. If he wanted to see her, he would. She was surprised to see that John Wellborn, her father's private security agent, was there, sitting off to the side in one of the more comfortable, stuffed chairs that were framed with a small coffee table and some art prints depicting Martin Luther King giving his speech at the Clayborn Temple. Some kitschy mall style African art completed the look. No doubt, the swaying secretary or her dad's third wife had picked that out, she thought smugly, before taking a seat in one of two the rigid wooden straight back chairs that were arranged in front of the massive cherry wood desk in her dad's office. It was one of her dad's classic tactics, to make supplicants to his office feel on edge and uncomfortable as they visited him to ask for favors. His own chair, currently occupied by Lee Filderman, was a luxurious padded leather chair with a high back designed to give him an imperial presence. It was a custom design, by a local company, and wouldn't have been out of place on a movie set about despot rulers or narcotrafficking empires.

Lee Filderman made a small sound as he attempted to scoot the throne-like chair closer to the desk, as he leaned forward towards a large yellow legal pad that was covered in a looping scrawl. From across the desk, Ember couldn't decipher the doctor-like script. "Well, Ember," Lee said, as he turned to a fresh page on the large yellow pad, "we are here to discuss your little problem."

John Wellborn sat up a little straighter if that was even possible. The fifty-something crewcut Caucasian man had an erect military bearing, that spoke to his origins as retired government agent. Rumors abounded that John's previous career with one of the three-lettered agencies had involved a large amount of 'wet work' in several lesser-known Latin American and Arab countries but it had never been discussed openly in the office to Ember's knowledge. His impassive face gave no clue as to the veracity of the stories that swirled around him. He looked directly at Ember, as to read her. His own face was completely inscrutable, but she felt judged to be somehow unworthy all the same.

She looked back at Lee and waited for him to continue. "Your father tells me that you are being investigated as a suspect in the murder of Hunter Lee Baron," he said in a grave voice. No trace of his demeaner gave away the fact that he had previously initiated a spirited defense in Mr. Baron's own murder trial. Lee's participation in Hunter Baron's trial had unceremoniously ended shortly after his appendix ruptured, landing him in the hospital for several days as his junior associates and a notorious local ambulance chaser, Kelly Darrow, fought an elegant duel with the prosecutor's office that resulted in Hunter's acquittal. As if to rebuke him for the lost opportunity, Lee's surgical scar twinged.

Lee paused and looked directly at Ember. "As you may know, I have been your father's legal advisor for many years," he said as he indicated to a crisp one-dollar bill, that Ember hadn't noticed on the desk. "Now, before we discuss private and potentially privileged matters, I would like you to retain me as well," he finished.

Ember nodded and pushed the dollar bill back towards Lee, and added her own crumpled five dollar bill to it, saying, "I would like to retain your services, Mr. Filderman." She wondered if this was for the benefit of the small, hidden, security cameras, and for Mr. Wellborn, who sat silently watching.

Lee then pushed a typewritten document towards Ember. "Please sign this agreement retaining my services," he said. Ember did so with a flourish, already tired of the cloak-and-dagger style game.

"Now start from the beginning," Lee advised once the signed document was back in his possession. As Ember began telling Lee about the police visit to her office, John leaned forward. Lee held up his hand, "Stop!" He said. "I don't need to hear this. I need to hear when you started sleeping with him," he clarified, his voice crisp but not curt as he looked over at her, waiting expectantly.

Ember was taken aback, and recoiled physically as though slapped, as she looked at Lee. She thought she detected a hint of sympathy in his warm brown eyes. Her face began to flame as she lost her composure. "I didn't have a.. a.. a.. relationship with Hunter," she said, almost stammering in her shame. "It was just an accident," she continued, "and I don't even remember how it happened." She felt eighteen again, like she was being called on the carpet for one of her youthful university skirmishes. She was suddenly glad her father hadn't shown up. Then her mind briefly drifted, had her father skipped the meeting to save her from the embarrassment of talking about this in front of him? He would certainly understand, she thought, considering the myriad of scandals and escapades he'd been through. She looked up at Lee and nodded her comprehension before starting again. She took a deep breath.

This time she detailed everything, starting with a brief interlude with Hunter in the 1990's in a storeroom at the "616" nightclub downtown. She admitted to the cocaine and the other drugs before moving ahead to her most recent encounter with the now deceased, playboy scoundrel, stressing that she had changed since the most recent episode, and was now more fully committed to her political campaign and it's agenda aimed at social justice and police reform. Lee just raised an eyebrow and looked towards John.

John nodded, and stood up, handing Lee a jump drive, while saying to Ember, "Are you sure his murder had nothing to do with this?"

John's statement hung in the air, while Ember's mind whirled. She was shocked to see that both John and Lee thought that she was guilty and seemed to just be entertaining her version of events. Lee was busy inserting the jump drive into a small laptop he had produced from his briefcase, while Ember stared back at John, speechless.

As the laptop booted up, and Lee opened the file, Ember turned back towards the desk. She noticed that John had turned in his chair, slightly away from the desk, as if to give her privacy. Ember felt deeply uneasy as the two figures appeared on the screen, then mortified, angry and finally incredibly exposed and violated as she watched the grotesque tableaux play out on screen. Lee paused the lurid images, freezing a frame showing a vacant-eyed Ember staring unseeing at the ceiling as a seemingly physically able Hunter Baron labored over her. She had been artificially posed in an awkward position that seemed designed to only humiliate and expose her. She felt devastated as she sat there, and a tear rolled silently down her cheek. She thought she couldn't have been more stunned as she stared at the frozen image, until Lee spoke.

"So, we know he planned to blackmail you. Is that why you did it?" Lee asked.

****

Marnie, Sonoma, March 2022

I was having lunch with my best friend, Sofie, when I got the call from my editor, Cort Beckman. Ever since I'd met Sofie Burts at her store, Global Heart, we'd been fast friends. Her store was on the main promenade of the town square in the picturesque town of Sonoma. Her store was filled with cute and colorful textiles, jewelry and other items imported from all over the world. Turkish pottery, embellished India silks and handwoven Guatemalan cotton embroidery caught the eye, along with colorful gems, stones, candles, and just about every other eye-catching and handmade artisanal art form. We'd bonded over a shared appreciation for handmade traditional crafts and had immediately established our own tradition. Every Friday afternoon around 2 pm, we gathered at the small wine tasting room a few doors down to chat and relax. We liked to go early on Friday before the weekend tourists arrived to enjoy a local wine, a couple of tapas and to catch up on the latest town news and gossip. Sometimes, some of our other friends dropped in to hang out with us, but with Sofie and I, it was like we'd always known each other.

That certainly wasn't the case, since I had only moved to the area a little more than two years ago, after a series of devastating events had upended my reality, starting with the murder of my husband by the notorious, religious extremists, ISIS. After that happened, I ended up walking away from a career as an overseas correspondent that had spanned more than two decades. In that time, I'd become more familiar with the geography of Iran, Iraq, Syria, Kuwait and Afghanistan than that of my own hometown. I didn't really even have one hometown per se, I just usually claimed whatever was the most recent place I'd lived. I hadn't really put down roots anywhere, except in my old university town of Memphis, Tennessee. I'd come to Sonoma to start anew and had been doing my best to plant roots ever since. But life had a funny way of changing things, despite our best laid plans.

Now Cort was on the other end of the phone, upending these plans yet again. I'd been working on a new article highlighting the Buena Vista Winery and its unconventional founder this week for Wine and Cheese Magazine. I submitted my work to a variety of 'lifestyle & luxury' magazines, but I was on full-time staff at Wine and Cheese. However, my editor, Cort had a bad habit of springing surprises on me. I inwardly sighed as he started the conversation, not with a greeting, or a "How are you?" but with "I just got off the phone with Neil, and it looks like we've got another plum assignment for you!" Neil Chase was the head of the editorial staff at the San Jose Mercury and a close friend of Cort's. It looked like the adventures of the "Count of Buena Vista" would have to wait.

Last year, after Cort had discovered that the headlining suspect in a brutal matricide of a prominent, Southern, political family was my former boyfriend, they sent me to Memphis to cover the trial for a series of articles for the San Jose Mercury. The trial was so bizarre, with so many names, faces, surprise witnesses, and newly discovered secrets, along with an unexpected verdict, that it had ended up becoming a book. Just recently, the book had won several more awards for storytelling and journalism, and the Shelby County mayor, Lee Harris, had declared a day in November as "Marnie Gellhorn Day."

So, Cort had my full attention. Now, I like to pretend that I don't like the drama or attention that comes with a high-profile trial, but that was a lie of grand proportions. After over 20 years of helicoptering into danger zones, avoiding snipers, landmines, and other terrorist and guerrilla threats, I craved the adrenaline rush that used to kick-start my writing. I'd also be lying to myself if I didn't admit that sometimes I craved more adventure than writing lifestyle articles on the best place to vacation, the right cheese to pair with a 300-dollar shiraz or a limited-edition chardonnay, could offer. Writing articles on multi-million-dollar views of the beach houses of the rich and famous sometimes just brought home the inequities in our society. I'd made a career out of sharing the voices of the oppressed and marginalized, and now I was writing about the best place to find truffles. It seemed surreal at times.

"Ok, Cort," I said, "I'm listening." Sofie raised an eyebrow as she heard his name. She motioned to the waiter to refill our wine glasses, and then sat back looking amused, as I waited for Cort to fill me in.

"Marnie, you will never believe it! The daughter of the first family of Memphis has just been charged with the murder of our favorite scoundrel! Neil and I have already decided that you are going back there to cover everything that you can. She's only just been charged, so make sure you pack for a potentially long visit, and yeah, bring that darned cat of yours. The secretary is already on the phone with Pettigrew properties to arrange for your housing," he paused to take a breath. I knew Cort was excited because it all came out in a rushed exhalation.

He audibly took a breath and said, "Now give Sofie my best and get back to your apartment and start packing! Mallory will call you in an hour with the rest of the details," he finished before he hung up. I didn't know whether to be annoyed that he knew my personal habits so well, or just stunned as I sat back and thought about what he said. I saw Sofie looking at me with a question on her face, but first I had to think about this.

The daughter of the first family of Memphis. That was pretty specific, not too many families could claim such as title. He couldn't mean the Prince family, could he? Which daughter? That family had more offspring and relations that you could shake a stick at! There was only one daughter that really had any public presence, and that was Ember. It couldn't be! Ember and I were just a year or two apart during her short stint at Memphis State back in the 1990's. I hadn't know her well back then, but we'd certainly crossed paths several times. Even though the Memphis State enrollment was large, even back then, the on-campus crowd was pretty small.

"This is unbelievable," I muttered as I scrolled thru my phone trying to find a specific contact. Yogi would know! Yogi knew pretty much everything that went on in Memphis. I sent her a brief text and it seemed like the reply came back immediately. It confirmed exactly what I'd thought. I looked up at Sofie and reached for my wine glass as I said, "It looks like Hunter Baron has gone and gotten himself killed!"

Sofie wouldn't know the Prince family, but she certainly knew who Hunter Baron was after the massive trial coverage, my book, and all that came with it.

She raised her wine glass, and said, laughing, "It looks like you are back in business!" We touched glasses and drank to the toast, but the entire time my mind was racing. I looked up to apologize to Sofie for my inattention, but she was smiling, when she said, "What are you still doing here? It sounds like you have a big story to chase! Now go!"

As I placed Henri Arthur George into his travel case, I reviewed my mental checklist. I strapped him in, rolled down the window to the car, and then went back to double check that I had locked the door to my apartment at the Sonoma State Historical Park. My landlord, so to speak, who was on sabbatical just an hour south, had agreed to have a friend come by and water the plants while I was gone. I was hopeful that I would be back in just a few months. It still seemed incredible that, just a mere day after receiving the call from Cort, I was all packed up and hitting the road again.

If it hadn't been such a brutal and obvious murder, I might have missed the spectacle that was Hunter Baron III's final send-off, but then again, maybe not. In the Jewish religion, the deceased are supposed to be buried as quickly as possible, preferably before sundown on the day of death. With such a gaping and unnatural hole in his neck, Hunter's sendoff had been delayed for a detailed and thorough examination by the medical examiner's office. In fact, I heard later, that two medical examiners examined the body, with one being sent from Nashville as insurance, I guess. Then again, there were few people in Hunter's corner anymore to push for a speedy internment. He'd been expelled from the orthodox community in disgrace. Of course, Michelle Gates remained fanatically loyal, and Eric Cassius remained steadfast as well, but they would have been hard-pressed to push for a rapid interment on his behalf in these circumstances.

As it was, I raced down 395 thru Nevada to take I-20 to avoid any weather along the route. I drove like Lucifer himself was on my bumper. Luckily, in those tumbleweed states, the speed limit remained firmly within the "bat out of Hades" range. There was so little east-bound traffic for most of the way, I could have hitched a rocket to the chassis, and never passed another vehicle. I didn't relax until I reached Texas. As big as Texas was, it was also the start of the home stretch for me. It also meant that I had been in the car long enough that any burst of adrenaline I'd felt at the beginning of this assignment had dissipated. During the drive, I reflected, I talked to Henri, and I listened to about a hundred Nancy Grace podcasts. I couldn't stand her when she was on television, but for some reason, I found her podcasts to be the perfect driving companion, especially for the long dead stretches at the beginning of the trip. The long, lonely highway once I crossed into Nevada, then passed into Arizona, and New Mexico were punctuated with crime and tragedy as Nancy Grace and her guests revisited old homicides and reported on on-going trials and high-profile cases. I'd made the drive back to Memphis enough times from California by now to have my own idiosyncrasies about preferred routes, truck stops, and acceptable hotels. I'm not a germaphobe by nature. I mean I spent a lot of my life sleeping in army tents, or in the back of moving vehicles, but lately I had gotten to a point where the usual 1-star side-of-the-road roach motel wouldn't do. I'd started getting increasingly squeamish about sleeping on thin, cheap, worn-out, 10-thread count sheets, and rooms with cigarette burns, and sticky carpet. It was a little difficult, because those were the hotels that were most likely to welcome Henri. Then again, even Henri seemed a little squicked out by some of those places. Once, he started playing with something that was sticking out from beneath the bed at a motel 6 in Wyoming. Well, that's another story, but let's just say, there are no Motel 6's in my future, and I'll probably never drive thru Wyoming again, if I can help it.

Luckily, I was on an expense account, so I could treat us to at least the level of hotel where I didn't expect to find a chalk outline when I entered the room. It was kind of weird because I also wasn't comfortable with anything too nice either. I guess when you've been a jeans and khaki kind of girl your whole life, bedside turndown service, bellboys, and pillowtop mattresses made me feel equally awkward. I guess that was also lucky for the San Jose Mercury, since they were picking up the tab again.

Still, the best way to stay away from gross motels was to just hurry up and get there, so I added some extra miles one day, and managed to make it to Memphis a full day earlier than planned. My apartment with Pettigrew Rentals wasn't ready yet so I pulled out my phone after I parked in the Cupboard Restaurant's parking lot, across the street from Methodist Hospital's downtown campus. I scrolled through my contacts until I found the one I was looking for.

Thank goodness for Sandra! She was one of the few people I knew that wouldn't be hacked off by a sudden request for a sleepover, and she didn't mind cats. She lived over the border in Mississippi, so I decided to stop and do a couple of errands first. Luckily, the weather wasn't too hostile, so it was safe to leave Henri in the car with the windows down for a little while. He was in his travel carrier, sleeping, so I figured he would be content for a little while. I grabbed a couple to-go orders from Cupboard before sneaking over to the Methodist Medical Office parking, which allowed me to skip the massive garage, and the line that usually went with it. I opened the windows and parked in a covered part of the smaller garage, so Henri would stay cool before I quickly made my way inside to the bridge that takes you to the main hospital. The weather was on the cooler side but I wasn't taking any chances about him getting over heated. I double-checked the notes on my phone again, before I made my way to the 6th floor tower to surprise a dear friend.

My beloved friend, Yogi, had been admitted for heart surgery the next day. She'd had a kidney transplant some years ago and suffered from chronic rejection so they had admitted her early to place a dialysis line and dialyze her. I was especially nervous because the Methodist heart surgery program had a horrendous reputation. After its most capable surgeon had left back in 2018, it had been a series of unexperienced temporary surgeons, one after another. Once the death toll was high enough, the hospital would get a little nervous and move on to the next green surgeon. Some of them weren't even wet behind the ears. The next to last one had been let go after he was pulled over for a DUI, while he was on-call for emergencies. While the breathalyzer did confirm that he was drunk, it turned out that the real reason he'd been swerving down Union Avenue was related to the operating room nurse that had her head in his lap. It shouldn't have been funny, but the police dashcam videos showing her screaming and slapping her hands on the windows, the steering wheel, and the good doctor himself after her hair got caught in his zipper, were crazy enough that they made one of those police video shows. Incredibly enough, she still worked in the operating room.

I'd heard so many horror stories from my friend Jauclyn that I was panicking. On my last visit to Memphis, she swore over a glass of Sonoma's finest pinot grigio that the last surgeon had turned to her in the middle of a repair of emergent aortic dissection to ask her what was next, and not in a teaching kind of way. "Marnie, I swear, he really didn't know or didn't remember. I was completely freaked out! Even Dr. Burch, the anesthesiologist, was freaked out and you know, Reggie's always as calm as a cucumber!" Jauclyn said. She swore on the life of her unborn child that she wasn't exaggerating or making it up, which was completely unnecessary. As long as I've known Jauclyn, I've known she's not one for drama. Exaggeration wasn't her style. Deadpan was! So for her to be so rattled put me on edge. When I called Yogi, I tried to dampen my panic as she told me how "friendly and nice," the notoriously inept surgeon seemed. I ended up begging her to schedule an appointment with Dr. Scheottle instead. He was an older, elegant surgeon who still had abundant charisma. You could tell he really had been a ladies' man back in his day. He had that Hugh Hefner kind of aura even in his late 60's. More importantly, he was considered the best heart surgeon in Memphis, bar none. Of course, that wasn't saying a lot in a town where surgical qualifications usually meant something like your dad was a surgeon, and maybe he'd even been a professor at the local medical school, so if your grades weren't quite there, he could still give the school a little push. Hey, that's not an exaggeration! I knew a surgeon once who did exactly that to get his very mediocre, very spoiled, very entitled but not very bright princess into the University of Tennessee. That was after he'd spent $ 750,000 on private schools, tutors, repeat MCATS, and even a research fellowship at Hopkins, only to have the Dean of the medical school at Hopkins tell him that his daughter was more suited to be a preschool teacher. Ouch! Nothing against teachers at all, but you know he wasn't saying that lightly, and I heard the entire story from the princess's own lips. So, a little bit of panic on my end probably wasn't unreasonable. Besides, I'd recently done an investigative journalism piece for ProPublica on how bad doctors managed to skate their way past all of the cardboard hoops set out for them. It had been a follow-up piece after Netflix made a movie about another Memphis surgeon, the one nicknamed "Dr. Death," after he'd mutilated, paralyzed and even killed scores of trusting patients.

Now, as I sneaked around the corner to Yolanda's room, with food in hand, I could at least try to relax. She had the best, and she was scheduled for tomorrow morning. I'd be on pins and needles all day tomorrow, but for now, I'd cross off one thing at a time.

Yolanda's head was buried over her phone when I entered. She was frowning at the phone, so I asked, "What's wrong? Battery dying?"

Her head whipped up like I'd fired a shot. The telemetry monitor showed that her heart rate briefly spiked up to the 120's too. "Geez, Marnie! You scared my heart practically right out of my chest!" she said laughing.

"I was just checking my phone again, and wondering why you hadn't answered my last message," she said.

I'd turned off my phone during the walk over to the hospital, so she must have messaged me then. I apologized and then offered the to-go carton as proof of my sincerity. Her eyes lit up as she opened it: homestyle meatloaf, oven baked mac n' cheese and a hefty helping of spinach and greens. I wasn't going to completely wreck her hospital diet, after all. I'd even switched out the buttermilk, hand-rolled biscuits for an extra helping of the green stuff, but I didn't volunteer that to Yogi. I might lose a hand if she found out that I'd intentionally kept the Cupboard's famous biscuits from her. For all that she loved food, Yogi was still no bigger than a minute. She had that elegant, angular look that some runway models had. I wasn't that lucky. I usually ranged somewhere between scrawny chicken, and a bit of a fluffy butterball depending on the time of year, and what work looked like. Scrawny chicken might be a thing of the past! It tended to go with long, sleepless nights, 24-hour shellings and bombardments, cold coffee, and cheap cigarettes. I'd given up everything but the coffee since moving to Sonoma, and the weekly wine and cheese afternoons with Sofie hadn't helped. I was veering into butterball territory again. Lovely, loyal and frank as ever, Yogi only took about three seconds to point it out, before demanding to know what happened to her buttermilk biscuit. I shouldn't have found it so hilarious, but I did, and I burst out laughing. I laughed so hard my ribs ached and tears came out of my eyes as I fought for breath. I guess I was just so relieved to see Yogi looking so good, and so normal the afternoon before surgery.

It also made me pull out the second to-go container that I'd kept behind my back. This container held one generously sized, fluffy, buttermilk biscuit (instead of the usual 3 enormous ones that come with the meal… Southern cooking means generous portions, you know). We chatted a bit while she ate, then I gave her a big hug to race back to the car, where Henri was patiently waiting. As I left the room, I felt tears coming to the forefront. I walked faster because I didn't want Yolanda to see me cry. My job was to be strong and support her. I couldn't let her know that I was scared.

A sudden wave of fatigue overcame me as I pulled into Sandra's driveway. I had been running ever since Cort called me: packing, driving, driving, driving, and then rushing to the hospital. I was still worried and preoccupied about Yolanda but there was nothing that I could do at this point. I was in town, and she knew I cared, and that was what mattered. The rest of my sorority sisters and I would get together and make sure she had everything she needed – we were family, after all. Usually, it was Yolanda who took care of everyone: sending flowers and cards for special occasions, surprise gift cards, coordinating casserole and meal delivery schedules, and even collecting donations when disaster struck, and one of my sorority sisters' house burned down. I know there are a lot of silly stereotypes about sorority members being airheaded and superficial, but that stereotype couldn't be more wrong. I was grateful to have these women in my life.

Thinking of grateful, I was never more thrilled to see Sandra bounding out of the house to welcome me. Sandra Lester was a fireball of energy wrapped up in a tiny, delicate package. Barely topping five feet even in heels, and weighing around 95 pounds, the fair-haired, blue-eyed, diminutive artist from Monterrey, Mexico was someone that you just loved at first site. I met her at a social event several years ago and had just immediately adored her. She was charming, funny, and just bursting with enthusiasm and vitality. It had been far too long since I'd seen her, and now we'd have plenty of time to catch up. I felt tears prick at the corners of my eyes and felt like a sentimental old fool for just a moment before I was engulfed in a huge hug. It was hard to believe that this little dynamo was also the doting "abuela" to her daughter's chubby, little toddler, Emma.

As I grabbed Henri in his carrier, we were already talking a mile a minute in our own unique version of Spanglish. I had started learning Spanish when I moved to Sonoma, and I took every possible opportunity to practice with Sandra.

As we entered the enormous house, I thanked Sandra yet again for offering her hospitality. She looked at me and started laughing. "Actually," she said, "your being here is an act of fate. Rex has been working the Baron case, and when I called him at lunch time, he said he wanted to talk to you. He read those investigative pieces you did last year, and of course, we all read your reporting during the trial, so he's eager to run some details by you, to get your perspective. You knew the victim so well, he'd like you to be a consultant on the case. He said he was going to talk to Chief Davis and get the okay first."

My eyes flew open a bit. I had completely forgotten that her husband, Rex, worked as one of Memphis' homicide detectives. I'm not sure how I'd ever forgotten because he'd been a featured character on the reality series, "The First 48." Apparently, audiences couldn't get enough of the tall, wise-cracking, detective with the southern accent. "He's on that case?" I said, surprised. I hadn't even thought about it, but it was a fortunate development. I was glad to know he was running it by his captain and the chief first because I wouldn't want to do anything to jeopardize the case.

"Yes, I was surprised when they assigned him the case since he knew Baron, but the captain said because the victim was so well-known by so many people in Memphis, it would be almost impossible to find experienced detectives that didn't know the victim. Captain Hughes also thought that this casual acquaintance might actually help the detectives, by giving them better insight into possible motives", Sandra replied.

While we chatted, I could see Henri out of the corner of my eye, as he stalked and sniffed every corner of Sandra's home. Her house was quite large, so he was going to be occupied for a while. We continued chatting as I ran out to the car to get Henri's luggage (his litterbox, food, water bowl, favorite blanket and his "traveling" scratching post). Work or no work, Henri had to come first. It was certainly an adjustment for someone who had been independent for so long, I thought as I set up his essentials in the laundry room, so he'd be ready when he was done with his own investigation. Since I'd gotten Henri, I'd realized a lot of things; and the fact that cats came with various accessories was one of them. Since I'd figured out the magic combination, (and made sure to bring his fleecy blanket), Henri had become quite the experienced traveler.

Despite its large size, the Lester family home was comfortably and cozily decorated in muted shades of honey, caramel and café that added warmth to a home dominated by fourteen-foot ceilings and a maze of rooms. Instead of being cold and formal, Sandra had brought the house to life with a series of colorful paintings depicting life in Mexico. Spanish - Colonial style, black iron fixtures added to the effect. The house was a testament to Sandra's lineage, as Rex's recent television residuals wouldn't have even covered the electric bill from the blaze of chandeliers that lit every room. The house was entirely Sandra, and her legacy as one of just a few remaining, direct descendants of a long-ago alliance between an Aztec princess and a Spanish nobleman. It was this Spanish bloodline that enabled Sandra's forefathers to survive the myriad of diseases that had decimated much of the indigenous Mexican population, but it was the Aztec side that gave her ancestors the strength to conquer much of Monterrey. Using their Spanish connections, the Villarreal family expanded from the small pueblo of Nueva Leon into most of the territory in rich, mountainous terrain. This family wealth enabled Sandra and her sister, Claudia, to attend the best private schools as the daughters of aristocracy. With the finest tutors to round out their education, both Sandra and her sister spoke English with soft lilting voices colored with a European accent. The evidence of this upbring was everywhere in the home, from the fine furnishings to the hacienda style fixtures and cherished family heirlooms that decorated the mantle. I mused over this as I passed several painted portraits of Villareal family members on my way back to the kitchen.

As I entered the warm, and fragrant kitchen, I saw that Sandra had set out a couple of bottles of Dos Equis, along with some homemade ceviche and fresh tostadas. She had an expansive, open kitchen, with a large granite topped island, with bar stools scattered around the island. As I squeezed some fresh lime over the ceviche and the beer, I felt completely relaxed and at home. We stayed in the kitchen listening to the cheerful, lively, traditional Mexican music, chatting and snacking until her husband, Rex, came home.

He smiled, with his voice booming a greeting as he entered the kitchen with several files in hand. He put the files on the counter as Sandra handed him a cold beer. I know I've mentioned it before, but Rex Lester was a tall hunk of Southern cowboy. If this was a movie, he'd be from Texas, but since he's a real person, he's just a big ole country boy from Mississippi. If I had to guess, I'd say he was just a few inches shy of seven feet. He had the rugged look of an outdoorsman and looked like he would be at home doing all kinds of things; like wrestling and skinning animals in the wild, gutting fish with nothing but his teeth, surviving off the land, and any of those other tired redneck stereotypes. In reality, he was a well-educated, well-spoken, Ole Miss graduate, with 25 years of solving crimes. He was also an amateur pilot, with his own kit-built airplane in a nearby hanger. I like to think that the slow, lazy-sounding accent of rural Mississippi gave him an edge when he was interviewing suspects since it made many people underestimate him. All the same, I wouldn't want to have to face him in the interrogation room.

Sandra put him to work, lighting the grill, and preparing some juicy looking cuts of beef, along with some vegetables to roast. She got busy slicing and dicing for a green salad, while I set the table. The weather had warmed up that afternoon, so we prepared to eat on the deck. It was one of those evenings when you forget about everything but interesting conversations and enjoying each other's company. As I cleared the plates away after the delicious meal, and wiped down the table, the aroma of strong, freshly brewed coffee wafted outside from the kitchen window. Sandra brought out steaming cups of dark, rich coffee just as Rex returned with the case files.

"I hope you don't mind," he said as he set down the files. "Chief Davis said it was fine, as long as you don't leak any confidential details before the case is closed".

Just as I agreed that I wouldn't spill any of the information that the police were currently holding back from the media and general public, Rex opened one of the files and set out a series of color photographs. With even a casual glance, I wished they were black and white. I've seen a lot of horrible things overseas, but this was different.

Since Hunter Baron hadn't been found immediately, all of the blood splatter had dried to a dark, maroon-brown color. Decomposition was also readily apparent on the deceased in glorious, Kodak color. The dark red-brown color dominated most of the photos, especially photos showing the entire room from multiple vantage points. Splatters aimed in one direction arching out and reaching the walls, the bed and parts of the ceiling. Rex tapped a finger against one of the wide-angle photos of the crime scene, and said, "What's interesting here is that the crime technicians found layers of blood in some of the splatter on the walls and floor". He looked at me for a minute while he watched me work it out mentally. He added two photos showing close ups of the victim's face and neck. As I looked at the terrible gash in his neck, I said, "So this means, he was beaten, and possibly tortured before he was killed?" I continued, "This wound to the neck would have been almost immediately fatal."

Rex nodding approvingly, as he set down close-up photos of Hunter Baron's hands. These photos showed jagged, torn flesh on five of the nailbeds on one hand, which was hard to see due to the caked blood coating his hands. The photos also showed small, black circular areas on the inner aspect of his forearms.

"Any cigarette butts found at the immediate scene?" I asked. I could see a glimpse of an ashtray on the bedside table, overflowing with cigarette butts, but I didn't see any on the floor. I did see in another photo, what looked like ash on the carpet, but the carpets didn't look particularly clean, so there was no telling how long it might have been there. I wondered if a savage killer would use the victim's ashtray or not.

Rex answered, looking a bit dejected, "the lab is still processing several large collections of used cigarettes, but I suspect none of them were left by the killer. The apartment wasn't very clean, so it's taking the lab a lot longer to process trace evidence just because there is so much other debris to filter out. I can't even imagine how much stuff they picked up in the vacuum cleaner bags. The victim hadn't lived in that apartment very long, so it's surprising how filthy the place was," he said. "I guess he wasn't one for cleaning," he finished with a small shrug. I wasn't sure if that was deadpan humor or not, but I suspected it was, and saw a glimmer of a smirk that confirmed it. During Hunter Baron's murder trial a little over a year ago, witnesses and crime scene photos had shown his previous home to be essentially unlivable due to hoarding, and a level of filth that would have horrified the average crack-house patron. There had been a dramatic moment in the courthouse last year, when it was revealed that the accused had been eating, drinking, and living in the house just a few feet from his mother's rotting corpse. Several jurors had turned grey, a few reporters had rushed out, ostensibly to vomit, and one spectator had passed out during the testimony.

While the only rotting corpse in the Parkview apartment had been his own, it appears that Hunter Baron hadn't developed any new housekeeping habits since being acquitted of his mother's grisly murder.

We reviewed a few more crime scene photos before Rex laid down the last three photos with showmanship flourish, like a gambler showing his cards for the jackpot.

"This information hasn't been released, has it?" I asked cautiously.

"Nope, it sure hasn't," Rex confirmed. As I looked closer at the first photo, I saw a dull, dark colored, irregular shaped, almost jagged object laying on top of a pool of blood. Its shape was almost like a leaf, and it was made of a very thin material. It didn't glitter like gold or a precious metal. In the middle of the top of the rectangular, there was a gold-colored straight piece of metal projecting out. In the next photo, a paper ruler had been placed next to the rectangle to give the size. It appeared to be around 3 inches in length, and 2 inches wide.

In the next photo, the item was being lifted with the edge of a pen. The newly exposed posterior surface was dull with blood, but there was a small area of brightly colored, shiny material with an iridescence to it.

"Wait," I said. "Is that jewelry?"

Rex looked impressed, as he answered, "Yes, and the folks in the lab say it looks handmade, so it's not some mass-produced Chinese-made Walmart trash. It's the first real lead that we have! Now we are talking to local jewelers to see if they recognize it".

A thought occurred to me. "Any current suspects? I asked. "What's the rumor about Ember Prince being involved, somehow?" I finished.

Rex became a bit cagey, but admitted it freely. "Marnie, you know I trust you completely, but on this one, due to the parties involved and the evidence we have so far, I am going to have to keep this information close to the vest."

We talked a bit more, but I was feeling increasingly tired, and a bit disappointed. I wanted to make sure I made some notes before I fell asleep, so I excused myself. I grabbed what I needed from the car and headed up to bed, to find Henri already curled up on the bed in the guestroom where I was staying. He roused briefly after hearing me brush my teeth in the adjacent bathroom. I looked at his sleepy face, and his perturbed expression, and sympathized completely. It only took a moment for me to fall into a deep sleep…the kind where you feel like your body is slipping deep into the mattress and there is no use resisting. Henri spooned up against me, with his head tucked under my chin. Cozy and warm, and accompanied by the soothing, rhythmic sounds of soft purring, I felt myself slipping down deeper.

Unfortunately, I didn't stay in that deep, dreamless sleep very long. I woke up at 3 am, sweating and disoriented, with my heart racing after a series of dreams featuring jewelry dripping with blood. In one dream, I was at the entrance of a fancy charity event, already out of sorts, wearing dirty khakis, with a camera slung around my neck, in an ornate ballroom, with classical musicians performing. The crowd mainly had their backs to me as a group of guests watched others engaged in a waltz, but I could see a sea of lacquered hairstyles, and hear the swish of satin skirts, and the soft tap of shoes on the glossy marble floor. Authentic beeswax candles burned overhead in 18th century chandeliers adding to the heat, and stuffiness of the room. As I pushed myself forward further in the room, I felt a sense of shame for being so underdressed for such a formal occasion. The how, why, and what of the situation were suspended, as I watched the scene unfold as if I was a player in a first-person video game. As I passed a group of men in formal frock coats in rich velvets, and damask in a rainbow of colors, I smelled the sickly-sweet smell of pipe tobacco. I paused at the unfamiliar idea of smoking indoors until I caught a glimpse of the dancers as they passed by. That's when I saw that the elegantly dressed ladies, with their pomade, patches, and elbow length gloves. They were wearing ornate, heavy jewelry that was oozing and dripping blood. It dripped down from their earlobes onto their chests to meet the slow, red river oozing from necklaces and chokers down into the valley between their breasts. As I stared at bloody diamonds, emeralds, and pearls, my heart began to beat faster, and an idea started to form at the edge of my mind. Then I woke up, and it all started to dissipate, as even the most vivid dreams do. I felt worried and frustrated, as I reached out to stroke Henri, as my mind tried to tease out the thought that had flittered away. It somehow seemed really important.

****

That morning, I abandoned the pretense of sleep once I smelled fresh coffee wafting up the stairs. It was only 5:30 am, but Rex was leaving for work as I came downstairs. I helped myself to a cup of coffee and contemplated my day while I sipped the life-restoring brew. Then I raced upstairs to shower and dressed myself in a somber, charcoal, sweater dress of a finely knitted cotton, paired with fine leather boots in a soft burgundy-brown. I'd mainly chosen the boots because I had a big, fashionable, bag in the same leather. It was big enough to fit my notepad, my cellphone, an extra pair of pantyhose and all the other essentials without looking like a sloppy tote bag. The dress was relatively lightweight which suited the bipolar weather that frequently afflicted Memphis. As the sun rose, it looked solemn and overcast outside. I added a mini-umbrella to my bag. Now that I was ready to go, I could sit at my computer for a while and gather my thoughts. Once I was finished, I went downstairs to meet Sandra. She was dressed in an equally muted fashion. We decided to ride together since I would have to come back to collect Henri anyway.

I felt a little self-conscious as I entered the Levy – Cooper Chapel at the Temple Israel Cemetery. I wondered who had pushed for his internment here until I saw Anita sitting in the front, stoically, with a stiff, erect posture. Hunter, in his arrogance, would have wanted to be buried at the Baron Hirsch Cemetery, which he would have considered to be more 'authentically' Jewish. The cemetery and its associated congregation are also home to many of Memphis' wealthiest residents, but after the trial last year, he had been expelled from the Orthodox congregation he had long called home. In fact, much of the large Memphis Jewish community shunned him for attracting such negative publicity and attention. Anita was his ex-wife and mother to his only child, David. They had had a brief marriage marked by abuse. Anita had fled immediately after their son was born, taking the baby far from his dysfunctional and manipulative father. Still, he was her son's father, and for David's sake, she wanted him to have a proper Jewish burial. If she hadn't pushed, his body would probably still be lying in the medical examiner's office. Her son, David, sat to one side, with her new husband on the other. Both of the adults sat with their faces impassive, while David looked stricken. As Sandra greeted mutual friends in hushed tones, I slipped into a seat in the back of the chapel. I wasn't surprised to see Rex in the back corner surveying the crowd. I wondered who the other plainclothes officers in the crowd were.

The chapel filled up quickly, due to Hunter's notoriety. I saw a cameraman from channel 13 sneak in for just a moment before heading back outside where the rest of the crew, and several reporters waited. I pulled out my pen and notebook and took notes while I looked out at the crowd. It was definitely a far cry from the chaos that had characterized Hunter's circus of a trial, but there were still pockets of D-list celebrities. Steven Seagal made a dramatic entrance, looking like a grotesque, overstuffed version of himself. He was wearing a blue, Chinese patterned satin jacket that was too tight, making him look a bit like the chintz sofa my aunt had when I was a kid. Hunter would have liked seeing him here. When he was alive, he lived and breathed celebrity, name dropping and social climbing.

Soon Rachel Mathis was slipping into the pew with me, accompanied by her teenaged daughter, Iris. "I can't believe Uncle Hunter is dead," Iris said in the dramatic fashion prone to girls her age. To be fair, given the way he had died, it didn't seem that excessive, even as Rachel rolled her eyes at me. It wasn't over-the-top until she joined a couple of girls at the front of the chapel who were taking selfies with the coffin.

Rachel frowned as she watched them, which prompted her daughter to slink back to the pew and sit quietly as she scrolled through her phone. Our heads turned as a large cloud of veiled black entered, crying bitterly, and making small moans. Rachel looked over at me and mouthed, "Michelle Gates" and I nodded. I remembered Michelle quite well from the trial, and this actually seemed pretty par for the course, as strange as that sounds. At least someone was staying in character.

I knew the moment Veronica Triana entered the chapel. Well, scratch that! I knew the moment that Laura Triana Africano entered the chapel, because I could almost hear a symphony of necks cracking as every man in the place, and most of the women whipped their heads around to stare. Laura Triana Africano, quite frankly, was devastatingly beautiful. While certainly some of her impossible curves were due to the surgeon's knife, her face had been exquisitely sculpted by nature itself, with big doe eyes. It wasn't just her beauty: it was the skintight bandage dress with the overflowing cleavage, the visible thong line, and the 6-inch Lucite, platform heels, the perfectly coiffed, and curly ebony locks flowing down her back, the lusciously pouty and incredibly glossy, red lips stretched over blindingly white teeth. All of it topped off with a short jacket of silver fox, and a look of utter and total boredom. In comparison, her older sister, Veronica, the bereaved, live-in girlfriend, looked like the cheap Walmart knock off. There was a very strong family resemblance. She was pretty but not excessively so, and while parts of her anatomy looked inflatable, she was also just a bit overweight. Not so much that most Americans would ever notice, but then again, she did have the misfortune to be standing next to the much younger, prettier model. She didn't look bored, but she didn't look overwrought either. She looked embarrassed to see all the attention on her and her sister. She hesitated, as if to take a seat near the back of the chapel, when the black draped Michelle Gates came barreling over, to pull her towards the front. In comparison to the Triana sisters, all the heavy layers of black crepe, bombazine, and veil made Michelle look like she was wearing a chadaree. Of course, with Michelle's strong religious beliefs as a recent convert to a branch of ultra-orthodox Judaism, this may have been intentional. For all her newfound and fervent religious belief, it was not accompanied by an equal interest in education, so she often confused Halal and Kosher, Arab versus Israeli, and sometimes reverted back to her fundamentalist origins, particularly when doing her very public prayers. Veronica accompanied her, albeit reluctantly, while her sister sashayed back outside to smoke. For someone with so much infamy, the actual service was disgustingly bland and generic. The rabbi had been invited from out of town, and started his speech with, "I didn't know Hunter, but". The service only went downhill from there. Things didn't improve much when his friends came to the podium. For someone so well-known by everyone in Memphis, it appeared that no one knew him well enough to say anything original, heartfelt, or personal. The only time that changed was when his son, David, came up to the podium. Now a gangly teenager, David was accompanied by Anita, who stood just off to the side, which seemed to give David strength. "My dad was not a great man, but he was my dad. He wasn't much of a dad, but still he was mine. For much of my life, I felt like he saw me as only a possession, and that hurt me deeply. Most of the time, he only wanted to be in my life to try to harass and manipulate my mother. I don't know think that he knew what it was to really care about someone. If he did, he never showed it. But still, he was my dad," he started, stumbling at the beginning, but his voice grew stronger as he continued.

"So, when he reached out to me after my grandmother's death, I thought maybe, now that I was older, we could have a real father-son relationship, like I do with my stepdad. But he didn't want that! He only reached out to me to see if I would testify on his behalf at the trial – and I wouldn't. Not because I was angry or hurt, but because I couldn't! I really didn't know anything about him," David continued.

"After the trial ended, he never reached out again, except to tell me by voicemail that I was a selfish, arrogant, disrespectful child who didn't deserve to have him in my life," he stated baldly.

"And I agree. My mother and I didn't deserve to be forever connected to such a horrible sociopath! When I first heard that he died, I was crushed because I thought it meant I would never have the opportunity to rectify the relationship with my dad. However, on the trip to Memphis, I realized that was never going to happen anyway. This is the best outcome I could have hoped for and no one deserved it more," he finished. Then David stepped away from the podium, and escorted by his mom and stepfather, he slowly walked out. As they passed by his stepfather, Albert, leaned over and embraced him.

The chapel emptied soon after. No one had volunteered to host a repast, but Rachel and her husband stopped to invite several of us to come by their home for drinks. I don't know if Veronica, or any of Hunter's friends went to the graveside service that followed, but it seemed doubtful since Veronica ended up making a very brief appearance at Rachel's house. As Hunter's significant other, I think Rachel felt obligated to invite Veronica, and Veronica probably felt equally obligated to at least put in a token appearance.

Sandra and I gave a couple of Hunter's old friends a ride to Rachels' house. His friend, Alex, had come to the chapel via taxi, directly from the airport, so he and another old friend, Dean Baxter, came with us. Dean Baxter had his own peculiar sense of humor. He, along with some other drinking pals, had engineered a very odd prank during the trial that had attracted a lot of media attention at the time. I thought about asking him about it but realized that any answer he gave wouldn't be satisfactory. I knew that Rex would be meeting us at Rachel's house, so I was interested to see what sort of observations the two of us would come up with, especially after the funeral guests were well-lubricated. Rachel is known for her gracious hospitality, sense of design, and for always having a large supply of top shelf liquor for entertaining.

When we got to Rachel's house, we were surprised to see Hunter's son, David, was there, but Rachel explained that her daughter, Iris, had invited him and his parents to come. Iris and David had become friends one disastrous summer during the one and only occasion where Hunter attempted to parent. David had ended up staying with Iris's family for most of the summer, until Anita and Rachel hatched a hasty plan to send him to camp with Iris.

I cautiously went group to group, to see if I was welcome. While many people had likened my work to a cross between Dominick Dunne and Norman Mailer, plenty of other people, particularly

Memphians, just saw me as the modern-day Hedda Hopper, a vindictive shrew out to share local secrets with the rest of the world. They seemed to particularly resent the fact that I was working for a newspaper in California and revealing a sordid past with "a bunch of neo-liberal, commie folks!" It was a pleasure to see that, for the most part, that wasn't the case today, even with people who had real reasons to be wary of me. In fact, Jodi Louis came up to me and embraced me, before pulling me to a corner where several people were doing shots. Jodi and I hadn't been friends, but she'd had a bit of an emotional breakdown last year when she was talking to me about the abuse she had endured while in a relationship with the bereaved.

"Everyone," she said, introducing me, "this is the woman who gave me my life back. She helped me get rid of feelings that I had been carrying around for a long, long time." Then she turned to me, handed me a shot glass filled with whiskey, and held up her own glass for a toast.

"Wait, wait, wait!" said one of the members of the little group, who I didn't recognize. "Go get young David for this. It will do him some good."

Jodi Louis, Helen Shiite, and Nancy Weinstone went over to David, Anita, and Albert. I couldn't hear what they said, but they all promptly returned. Rebecca Weinstone took a clean plastic cup and poured in small amount of Pepsi, but Bruce Weinstone, still hale and hearty in his 80's, took the glass from her, and added a generous dollop of whiskey to it. "You were a man today, and if there's any better time than this for a bit of whiskey, then I just don't know when, "he said, extending the cup towards David. I looked at Anita and Albert, but they were in complete agreement.

"That's right son," Albert said.

The little group gathered around, as Jodi Louis raised her glass again and said, "Here's to knowing that the bastard is dead!"

"Here, Here!" Helen Shiite said.

In almost synchrony, the entire group raised their glasses and drank the shot in one go. I am embarrassed to say I sputtered and choked a little while young David did not. Then the members of the group, one by one, gave David a hug and handshake or a good-natured slap on the back. Then David and his parents returned to circulate among the other guests.

"Hope that does the kid some good," Jodi said. "No one should have to live with guilt because their parent was crap," she finished. The other people in the group nodded.

Bruce Weinstone said, "I'm only here to reassure myself he's dead! It may have been over 30 years ago, but I still remember when…Ouch!" He stopped himself as his wife elbowed him and looked pointedly at their daughter, Nancy.

"Mom, Dad, I'm 53 years old! What do you think you are protecting me from?" Nancy said with exasperation.

Bruce shook his head, and said, "No! Your mother is right. 100 years wouldn't be long enough." Then he remained closed mouthed on the subject. I knew the whole story, so I excused myself and wandered around a bit more, quietly eavesdropping as much as possible without being too obvious, or so I hoped. I didn't see when Veronica entered the house, but I saw her helping Sandra in the kitchen. I figured if I waited a few minutes, I might have a chance to talk to her a bit, and get some more information, sensitively, of course.

Sandra was busy in the kitchen helping the hostess brew coffee. As she prepared a tray with cups, saucers, spoons and cream, she reached back into the kitchen cabinet to find the sugar. She had to rise up on her tip-toes for her fingers to finally brush a small bag in the back of the shelf. Rachel saw her struggling and turned away from the coffee pot to assist her. She reached up easily and pulled out the green and white bag. She handed it to Sandra who opened it carefully and started to pour it into an elegant silver container. "*Louisiana's Best,*" it said in rolling script on the side of the Southern Cane brand bag. Rachel smiled at

Sandra as she poured the sugar into the bowl. "That sugar! That's pure Hunter. It's fitting to have it out for this. He always was real particular about brands, in a weird kind of snobbery. You couldn't just serve him store brand sugar. Or Heinz Ketchup, or French's Mustard. It always had to be some eclectic, out of the way, regional label. He had to think that it was better than what everyone else had. I forgot he had given me that bag after one of his trips to New Orleans. I swear that crazy fool had filled his trunk with sugar before he came back to Memphis." As she opened the bag of sugar, to pour some into the bowel, Rachel suddenly sobered as she remembered that Hunter had died, and a gruesome death at that. For all of the ugliness that had come out at the trial last year, she still had so many fun memories of her long friendship with Hunter, starting when they were kids. Sandra reached over to embrace Rachel, who was putting down the coffee tray.

Veronica, feeling a bit awkward perhaps, busied herself by picking up the tray and carrying it out to one of the buffet tables that was already groaning with food. As she moved to leave the kitchen, she brushed the end of the counter, sending the open bag of sugar tumbling to the ground, spraying granules of sugar all over the kitchen floor. Veronica's face looked stricken and I hastened to grab the little dust buster cordless vacuum that was hanging in the pantry. I'd been to Rachel's house so many times, it felt good to know where something was and help out. "No use crying over spilt sugar," Rachel said, wiping away tears, as Veronica grabbed a kitchen sponge to wipe down the floor. Rachel gave Veronica a brief embrace around her shoulders while I vacuumed away the mess. Sandra was already poking around Rachel's cabinets to find more sugar to place in the sugar bowl waiting on the counter. Veronica wiped her face with a napkin before picking up the tray again. I figured I'd catch her when she returned to the kitchen and see what I could find out. She seemed genuinely distraught. Maybe the cold demeaner I saw in the chapel was her way of coping. Anyway, she must know something that could help the case.

Sandra was now bustling around pouring the fresh coffee into insulated carafes. By the time the coffee was served, there were long shadows beneath the trees as the early spring day turned into an ever darker, grayer, gloomier, late afternoon.

Not much more happened at the quasi-reception. I looked around for Veronica, but it seemed like she'd made her appearance and left, so Sandra and I headed back to Olive Branch. Once we arrived, I gathered up my things, thanked her profusely, and Henri and I got in my car and headed to our new, if temporary, housing in midtown Memphis.

****

The two-bedroom, mid-century duplex on a quiet street just off Poplar Avenue was adorable like a dollhouse, with a bright, peppy colored paint, and a decorating scheme that highlighted Memphis landmarks. Unlike a traditional dollhouse, the mattress was thick and comfortable, and the apartment featured a giant screen TV, a dishwasher, and a washer/dryer combo. Henri settled in quickly after his usual detailed inspection.

Me, not so much! I was still troubled by a couple of things. I wanted to know the connection between Ember Prince and Hunter Baron. I knew they ran in the same circles, as heirs of the Memphis political scene, but I needed to find out what had pointed the police in her direction. Rex certainly seemed to think whatever it was had merit, and he wasn't someone who was quick to jump to conclusions. He was methodical, organized, logical and straight-forward in his thinking. All good things, I would think for a homicide detective. So, the information must be pretty compelling, but not definitive. If it was a smoking gun, so to speak, then Ember would already be in custody.

I was also troubled by some of the photos I saw. I wanted to hear what the pathologist thought. The murder seemed to have an organized crime feel to it, that no one was mentioning. Given what I knew about Hunter Baron, and his need for recognition, I wouldn't be completely surprised if he was mixed up in some pretty nasty things. He'd had a real taste for cocaine, gambling, and fast living in the past so it was always a distinct possibility. Despite his apparent (and newly inherited wealth), it was also rumored that he was still living beyond his means. He was rumored to be resorting to his old tricks; stiffing creditors, disputing legitimate transactions, floating payments from bank to bank, and opening numerous lines of credit with his inheritance as collateral.

He also had an inability to keep his opinions to himself, plus an inflated ego, and sense of self-importance. This too sometimes caused conflict. I'd seen him talk himself into fistfights before, and have to retreat in a hurry. The idea that his mouth might have written checks that his fists couldn't cash wasn't entirely ruled out either.

The earring at the scene raised a lot of questions, but the general state of disorder of this entire apartment complicated everything.

Something was still tugging at the corner of my mind. I brewed some fresh coffee and sat down at the table to review and make notes on the information I'd gathered.

****

Veronica, March 2022

As soon as she got inside the door of the crummy, little rental, Veronica threw down her purse and kicked off her heels. The bland, corporate style housing was, in her mind, depressing with its beige color scheme and industrial carpeting. Even the few pieces of decoration were dull and generic, motel-style art. It was the best she could do on short notice, while she tried to re-group and figure out the next step. She sighed and fought off the sudden urge to cry. Having to sit through the funeral as the "devoted girlfriend" was stressful enough. No one had known that she'd left Hunter a few days before his demise, and she thought it would look odd, and possibly suspicious to announce it when he was just found dead. That was bad enough!
Then there were all the unresolved feelings she was harboring. She didn't quite know how to deal with these conflicting emotions. By the time she'd broken up with Hunter, she hated him. I mean, she really hated him! He'd put her through six kinds of hell before she finally realized that she had to end it. When she'd finally gotten to that point, she found herself becoming angry, with a rage she didn't even know she was capable of mustering. She'd fervently wished he was dead! Now that he was, all the good memories started to flood her mind; memories of how charming he was at the beginning, memories of the flowers, the romantic evenings and all the effort he had put into the relationship. She was fighting to remind herself that these memories were deceptive. That's how Hunter

had presented himself when they first started dating, but that's certainly not who he actually was.

If that wasn't enough for any one person to deal with, then there was her baby sister, Laura. She was enough to make any sane person tear her hair out. Veronica took a couple of deep breaths to calm herself, she wanted to be in complete control when Laura returned from smoking her cigarette. God, that girl was infuriating! Look at what she'd worn to the funeral! She'd made a spectacle out of herself at an event for someone who was gruesomely murdered! It defied belief, but Laura had always done whatever she wanted, and she never seemed to face any consequences. In that way, she was just like their mother, Yesica Bassi.

Veronica took after her father; more serious, contemplative, and academic in nature. Her parents' marriage had been volcanic in nature. Quietly dormant for long periods of time, then slowly smoldering, only to erupt with a hot, vitriolic lava that affected everyone around them. She'd done her best not to emulate them, but then had ended up in a relationship with a master manipulator like Hunter. It made her question herself, and everything she believed. For so long, she had shunned the passionate, emotional part of her family and she had been embarrassed by her roots.

The Triana Family, Venezuela 1920's – 1990's
Veronica's father, Amador Cohen Triana, was the direct descendent of *marrenos* or the Jews that converted to Christianity during the Spanish Inquisition. This conversion usually wasn't really by choice. So, after fleeing Spain, his Triana ancestors reverted to their original faith.

Since the Jewish community tended to be insular, his family had intermarried among the fellow Jews in the Maracaibo community for centuries. Over the generations, unlike many of the neighboring Jews, his family had become well established in the larger Maracaibo community and Venezuelan society at large. After working as money lenders, over the generations, the family expanded into mining. The Triana family had owned and operated several diamond mines in the Amazonia region of Venezuela since 1915, and mining gold ore for even longer. Each generation of Triana's sent their sons down to the Amazonias to work in the mines as a rite of passage before assuming the reins. Over the years, the local indigenous tribes had become familiar with the various companies invading their land. As mine owners went, the Trianas were no more or less brutal than their numerous counterparts. However, they did offer local tribespeople premium day wages, as well as bonuses that consisted of valuable trade items that were transported to the remote region from the bustling city of Maracaibo. Thus, over several decades, the Triana family had a direct impact on the development of many of the tribes, including the Huottuja. The Huottuja were different than many of the surrounding tribes in that they insisted on maintaining their independence from the many groups that ingressed into the Amazonias. For the most part, the Huottuja eschewed the dangerous work of the mines, though some of the female members of the tribe supplemented their households by selling various food items to the workers. Veronica's maternal grandmother, Maiisa, was a full-blooded Huottuja, who had helped her mother, Aloma, with just such a task, selling prepared meals of fish, plantains, potatoes and other fruits and vegetables. The Huottuja and the other tribes had already learned that the foreign visitors would not purchase some of their favorite foods, like roasted snakes, crunchy insects and chewy larvae. However, they could find interested buyers for ebene, the tree resin that was a potent hallucinogen that their neighboring tribe, the Yanomani had introduced them to, generations ago, before the Europeans had arrived. For the most part, the workers at the Triana Mines relied on Aloma and her daughter to bring savory stews, soups, and roasted vegetables to the mouth of the mine to feed hungry miners every day.

During one such lunch break, fifteen-year-old Maiisa caught the eye of one of the mine supervisors. He later took her to wife and brought her to live at the small mining settlement. There she continued to cook, and with the help of her husband, Juan Africano Diaz, she opened a little shack-like restaurant.

By the time that Amador met Maiisa's own fifteen-year-old daughter, Yesica or "Bassi", as she was known among her tribal kin, the teenager had already been recruited into participating in a local beauty pageant. Amador had been appointed as one of the judges for the Miss Diamond Mine contest, which recruited girls from all over the Amazonia and Bolivar regions. The winner's family was traditionally given a month's supply of food staples and a length of embroidered cloth.

The contest had been started in the 1930's, and the initial prize had been a radio, but this had proved impractical after a native girl won the first year. The lack of electricity in her village had made the gift essentially nothing more than an awkward looking trophy. Later, by the late 1960's, as the area slowly developed, the winning contestant and her mother were offered a chance to come to Maracaibo to compete in larger competitions, along with a collection of prizes to assist the contestant in adapting to sophisticated city life.

When Yesica was crowned Miss Diamond Mine in 1968, she had won more than the competition. She had also won the affection of one of the rich sons of the owner of the second biggest mine in the region. While she may have not have been been sophisticated, Yesica was by no means stupid. Like many children in the area, she had attended the schools set up by missionaries and she had seen the small black and white televisions in the mining settlements and listened to the radios playing music in the afternoons. She knew there was more to life than the mine and her small village. She wasn't going to squander the opportunities that had been presented to her. She, Maiisa, and her father, Juan traveled to Maracaibo, where her father had lived as a boy, and she was immediately embraced by her father's family. An army of cousins, aunts and uncles embraced their beautiful young relative while her father re-acquainted himself with his family. The aunts and female cousins embarked on a serious and determined crash-course of modern fashion, beauty trends, and mainstream Venezuelan culture. Yesica embraced it all, while her mother watched, intimidated by the loud, boisterous family. Yesica was a quick study and to the amazement of the city of Maracaibo, but not her family, she swept through the local competitions and was crowded Miss Maracaibo of 1969, along with a slew of other titles. Her biggest victory culminated in being awarded second-runner up in the Miss Venezuela competition that same year. That was enough for Maiisa, even if it only lit a fire of ambition in her daughter, Yesica. Maiisa decided it was time for her and Juan to go home, but first they would see their daughter settled.

For all of her other qualities, Yesica remained a loyal and dutiful daughter. After having a long flirtation, it was only a short courtship before she converted to Judaism to marry the light-eyed, serious-minded, and intense second son of the Triana family. For Yesica, the pageants were over. Fourteen children followed, with Veronica being the fourth oldest (and first daughter) with Laura trailing far behind, being born several years after the next youngest sibling.

During that time, Amador's older brother, Elian, was killed during a routine mine inspection when the mine was attacked by the Ejército de Liberación Nacional, a Colombian rebel group looking for spoils to fund their revolutionary activity. The death of his beloved, first-born son pushed Amador's dad into a deep depression, and then retirement. Amador was forced to assume the reins of the entire company. The quiet, serious young man became even more serious overnight. Streaks of grey appeared in his hair at almost the same time. When one of his cousins suggested that the family begin using some of the materials from the mines to form their own exclusive jewelry store, he consented with a wave of his hand. Prior to that, most of their products were sold for industrial purposes. Now workers sorted the biggest and the best quality gems to send to the family and their team of jewelry designers. The same was done with the gold ore.

By 1983, the Triana name had become synonymous with wealth and glamour in Maracaibo. Their jewelry store had become an exclusive destination for people of means. As the store's reputation grew, it attracted talented jewelry designers from throughout Venezuela, and then, South America. As the company's success grew, Amador had to juggle the jewelry division as well as the mines themselves. Security had become a major issue in the aftermath of the attack, along with growing

instability in the region as the neighboring nation of Colombia struggled to contain the violence from their on-going civil war.
 It was a considerable relief when his eldest son, Mario, decided to attend the Universidad de Zuila to study geology and learn modern mining technology. His next two sons became apprentices to the head jewelry designer. Then Veronica, so serious and intellectual like her father, took her love of sums and business to major in finance and accounting. So like her father, she was. It was his son, Abraham, the nerdy, charming, beautiful and gentle, slim almost fey young man, who decided to embark of a course in economics. Once at school, the beautiful and kind boy was quickly befriended by Hugo Rafael, the only acknowledged son of their new President, and leader of the Fifth Republic. His father had come to power as part of a Socialist political party founded in the wake of a failed political coup several years earlier.

As the 1990's had ushered in a period of renewed Communist and Socialist activity in Latin America, and as the wave of nationalization swept thru Venezuela, the Triana family began making contingency plans. Like their ancestors, the *marrenos*, they would flee their home, if necessary. Surprisingly, it was Abraham and Hugo Rafael's burgeoning friendship that gave the Triana family the means to survive. Initially seen as a steadying and sober influence on the rowdier and more erratic Hugo, the Triana family was now invited to Caracas to La Casona, and Miraflores Palace.

At the same time, the Triana family mines remained untouched by nationalization and the Bolivian Revolution that was engulfing the country. However, when Hugo Rafael abruptly switched majors from Economics to Dance, and announced his bisexuality at a private, extended family gathering, his father felt that the gentle Abraham was to blame. Hugo Rafael was quickly removed from the university and disappeared from public life, as it was whispered among Venezuelan society that he'd been banished from the family. His father, former alter boy, military graduate, and the son of humble primary school teachers, cast out his son. As his son's fortunes tumbled, so did the Trianas. Government agencies now came calling. As the family packed their best and most valuable jewelry pieces into the hems and linings of their clothing, Amador made sure that his overseas accounts were intact. It took several years of painstaking planning, secrecy and caution, but eventually the Triana family was ready.

Finally, in 2008, as the family prepared to travel under false passports to escape detection, baby Laura made her stand. At 14, she had already inherited generous gifts of beauty from her mother. As the youngest, cosseted and spoiled, she had been the living doll that Yesica had always wanted. As a young toddler, Yesica had already begun Laura's initiation into the pageant world. Hair was highlighted and curved, lips were rouged, and the tottering child was dressed in skimpy outfits and taught suggestive poses. Now Laura was just a few years away from eligibility to start the series of competitions that would culminate in Miss Venezuela and possibly international competition, the pinnacle of which was Miss Universe. After she began a hunger strike to protest the move, in quiet desperation, and under the triumphant smile of his wife, Amador consented to allow her to stay in a private boarding school, with the understanding that she would stay under the strict eye of two of the family's Mossad trained bodyguards. Since Laura had been secretly flirting with one of the guards during the daily ride to school, she quickly consented to the terms. Amador only hoped that his wife hadn't underestimated the President's ire at their departure. He didn't like the idea of his youngest child being a pawn for a vindictive despot.

The Triana family relocated, and the President's fury passed. Laura, and her school roommate and best friend, Vanessa Goncalves, were enrolled in Maracaibo's finest and most elite pageant training program as they continued to rack up titles. They had a regimented system that kept them from being in direct competition, as Vanessa competed in the pageant rotation a year ahead of Laura. There were enough pageants that they could each obtain the necessary wins to progress forward. Together they underwent the knife to augment their slim bosoms and behinds with silicone implants. Together Laura and Vanessa would meet for groping sessions with the young bodyguards, while being careful not to get caught doing anything that might endanger or disqualify them from competing. Their efforts were not in vain, though they had certainly developed into vain young creatures with all this endless adoration. In 2010, Vanessa took the crown for Miss Venezuela.

When it came time for Laura, she failed to reach the pinnacle and was crowned first runner up behind Irene Esser Quintero from the rural town of Rio Caribe in Sucre. She was enraged to lose the crown to someone she considered a peasant, but all was not lost, as Alexander Lebedev, a Russian billionaire investor, was in the audience. The former KGB spy wasted no time in arranging an introduction, and like her mother, Laura was not one to miss an opportunity.

Alexander was a 52-year-old father of five. Despite his age, he was a tall and impressive specimen, with a net worth estimated at 1.1 billion. He was a self-made man, with a royal pedigree. His ancestors, like most Russian boyars at the time, spoke only French, and maintained a multitude of properties in the French countryside. For those reasons it was only logical for the Lebedoya family, to flee to France when Audrina Federina Lebedoyova saw the fate of her first cousin, Nicholas. Alexander spent much of his childhood in Burgundy being regaled with family stories by Great Aunt Audrina, as she relived the glories of the past. The rest of the family did their best to live in the present. It wasn't until Breszhnev was partially through his reign that Great Aunt Audrina died at the elderly age of 96. His father, Yvengeny, a respected professor, and the toast of the French academia used the opportunity to return to Mother Russia when Alex was only 10, changing the family name to Lebedev in an attempt to shed its heritage. Sadly, the Soviet Union had a long memory and a great distrust of the aristocracy. Yvengeny and his wife, Maria, were forced to scrape out an existence as lowly paid teachers in one of Moscow's poorer districts. They watched as their son was indoctrinated with Communist ideology and eventually the Russian Intelligence community, while the secret police continued to maintain lengthy files on his parents. While his parents lived in a cramped, two- room six floor walkup, Alex rose in the ranks and became an operative for the KGB in London. He specialized in the James Bond style of intrigue, where womanizing and pillow talk were his best tools against Margaret Thatcher's British Empire.

By the time he went to Maracaibo, he'd long since made the transition to private industry, aided by his long friendship with former fellow KGB officer, Vladimir Putin. Along the way, he'd formed additional alliances with Solntsevskaya Bratva, the Izmailovskaya gang, and other powerful players in Russian organized crime. Since most of the bigger players were under Putin's protection, there was very little risk involved, but plenty of benefits. After doing his best to strip the motherland of much of its native resources, he was now prepared to do the same in Venezuela. But first he'd start with Laura.

Laura almost immediately became his mistress with little to no pretense involved. Both Alex and Laura were extremely pragmatic and direct individuals, so it wasn't hard for them to come to an understanding. She became his companion and full-time consort while he conducted business in Venezuela and surrounding countries. She didn't ask questions, ever.

In 2012, when Irene Esser faltered during the Miss Universe competition despite being the front runner, coming in 3rd place, behind the winner, American Olivia Culpo, and Janine Tugonon, from the Phillipines for second place. Laura watched bitterly. She knew could have done better, but Irene had beaten her in the run-up to the main competition. Alex agreed, consoling her over the loss even as she prepared for her next big competition, The Miss Earth Pageant, where she was again, the back-up contestant to Irene. Later, Laura never questioned Irene's sudden disappearance on the eve before Miss Earth, ensuring Laura's place in the pageant.

Yet again Laura was beaten, this time by the Czech Republic, being awarded third place herself, as Miss Water. She didn't question it at all. She then proceeded to the next competition, Miss International, losing to Japan. Alex never said anything, but when he concluded his business, he installed her in a luxury apartment in an upscale neighborhood in Paris, with the deed in her name. She forgot about pageants because she no longer needed them.

Now it was ten years later and Laura knew Alex could tire of her at any time. So, she collected fine jewelry, cash and all the gifts he bestowed on her, with an eye towards her future. She'd come to see her older sister in Memphis to ask for financial advice, to help her maintain her nest egg. She knew Veronica didn't approve of her lifestyle, but she also knew her sister was a financial and investment wizard.

Veronica had flopped down into the cheap, overstuffed, ugly but immensely comfortable recliner in the living room, just as Laura entered the apartment. As she took another deep breath, Laura was texting at a rapid pace, walking towards the bathroom. She didn't look up from her phone. Without saying a thing to Veronica, she entered the bathroom, turned on the light and shut the door. Veronica felt relieved when she heard the click of the lock. Confrontation averted. Veronica didn't feel like she had the energy to deal with her little sister's drama.
She stiffened involuntarily ten minutes later, when she heard the lock pop as Laura turned the doorknob on the bathroom door. Laura walked out with her trademark confident stride, not a hair was out of place. She looked flawless and almost life-like as she headed towards the door. She called out, "See you later, loser!" and laughed as she stepped out the door. Her laughter cut off abruptly as the door slammed shut behind her.
Though Veronica felt so exhausted she thought she could barely move, she made her way to the living room window in time to see her sister climb into the back of a waiting SUV. The glossy black Escalade had black-tinted windows, and Veronica just barely caught a glimpse of the driver as he pulled away from the curb. It was the same man who had waited outside the chapel during the funeral service. Veronica shook her head and forced herself to the task at hand. She opened her laptop and composed her letter of resignation. She read over it twice, then satisfied, she hit send. International Paper could do without her. Her talents were wasted there anyway. That settled, she dragged herself to the bedroom and the sagging mattress within. She climbed into the bed fully dressed and closed her eyes. She could pack later. Right now she needed to rest.

****

Shelby County District Attorney's Office, April 2022

"The police will be making an arrest soon in the Baron murder, so everyone in Team Six, be ready. Jose, I am going to want you to take point on this. This is a high-profile case, and we can't afford any fuck ups on this one," Amy Weinrich, the district attorney stated, as she stood at the head of the large room and addressed her staff. Several staff members were startled by the unexpected profanity from the normally calm and collected attorney.

The district attorney looked pointedly around the room, and then narrowed her gaze at the petite blonde on the left side of the room. "Carrie, you can assist the clerks on this one." Several eyebrows lifted in the crowded conference room.

"As some of you already know, Ember Prince is our main suspect in this case. You know her family has a lot of influence, so we need to be on point for this. No breaches in procedures, no short cuts. If anything seems slipshod about this case, I want to hear about it *immediately*!" Amy finished. She then strode away from the podium and Jamie Kidd took over the briefing to review the status of the current cases on the criminal docket. Despite the large volume of cases, the teams quickly summarized their progress and the meeting ended 30 minutes later.

"Wow, that was rough," Jose Leon said sympathetically to Carrie as they filed out of the room, "and unfair," he added. He continued, "I've been doing this almost twenty years, and the evidence you presented on the Baron case was solid. You just can't predict how a jury is going to react. With all this conspiracy nonsense going around, nothing is a sure thing anymore."

Carrie appreciated the senior prosecutor's words. The district attorney, had stoked the flames of Carrie's humiliation. Carrie had been personally and professionally devastated when she'd lost her first big case last year; the sensational murder trial against the decedent.

"Well, since I was the lead prosecutor against him, it wouldn't be quite right if I took the lead against his assassin, now would it?" Carrie said with an attempt at bravado to hide her embarrassment. She was too old for tears, but not too old that she wouldn't call Grandma Caro as soon as she got home. Grandma Caro was blind now, and she'd had to move in with Carrie's aunt and uncle in North Carolina, but she was still Carrie's best listener.

"What's this big explosive evidence that the police have?" Carrie said, changing the subject.

Jose Leon said, "I'm not going to tell you, Carrie. I am going to show you." Carrie and the rest of Team Six proceeded to another conference room. When they arrived, one of the secretaries, Cristina Sykes, with her long black hair swinging, stood on the tips of her toes, and reached skyward, to grasp the handle of the viewing screen. Once the screen was in place, Jose Leon attached his laptop to the media center, while Cristina dimmed the lights. The video began to play.

As the video ended, Jose Leon said, "Well, I guess we have the motive now. That would surely sink a political campaign."

"But whose?" William Cranford said with a smirk. The decedent, Hunter Baron, was well known for his numerous outlandish and unsuccessful campaigns for local office. He liked to propose wild conspiracy theories and even wilder policies. Only the eternally barefoot, Prince Mongo, who claimed to be from the planet Zambodia, had more unsuccessful runs at local public office in Shelby County.

Forrest Edwards smirked back and said, "True enough, that was not a performance that I'd want to remember, much less record."

Susan Taylor was disgusted by the juvenile nature of the discussion and threw her legal notepad in his direction. Jose looked annoyed and slapped his palm on the table.

"No more juvenile antics! Weinrich has assigned me as point on this. Now, I want Susan and Carrie with me on this. The rest of you are devoted to research, and eventually, discovery. Cristina will hand you your assignments," Jose barked.

"Hey! We all heard Weinrich bench the rookie, so why are you now benching us?" William complained.

"First off, who here can tell me they never lost a major case, particularly in the beginning of their career?" Jose thundered. He waited a few moments, with the room in silence, before saying," That's what I thought. So don't let one of our own get churned under for something that has happened to all of us at least once." He raised an eyebrow and looked directly at William before continuing, "Secondly, none of you are benched. As you all know, very well, cases like this hinge on the research. We need to be sure this case is solid before we get into the courthouse."

"Now Susan, Carrie, let's go meet with the police and the judge," Jose said, before turning on his heel. "We need to see what they've got!" he finished.

****

Judge's Outer Office

"So, we've got motive down pat," Jose Leon stated, "but I want to have more before I present this to a judge. Do they have an eyewitness? Anyone that can put her at the scene? Did the neighbors hear anything? Was there a security camera? Did it show our suspect entering the building?"

Detective Lester looked uncomfortable as Detective Payne stepped forward. Rex wasn't sure that the evidence against Ember Prince was that strong, but he seemed to be the only one in the department with any doubts.

Detective Payne presented the lawyers with a set of grainy, still photographs showing the back of a woman in a dark coat, accompanied by a large man who appeared to have shielded his features from the camera. He appeared bulky but formless in the photograph, with a hat and scarf that obscured the rest of his features. "We also have a doorman who is willing to testify that he saw our subject enter the building three days before the body was discovered," she answered.

"Do we have any foreign DNA that we can test against the suspect? Anything else that places her at the scene?" the assistant district attorney asked.

"There's a lot of DNA in that apartment. So much so, that it would be almost impossible to sort it out. The apartment was so filthy that when the crime scene technicians vacuumed, it took two vacuum cleaner bags to contain all the debris. There is probably DNA from anyone who ever entered the apartment since the day the decedent bought it. I don't know how we can tie that to the suspect especially since we already have it on video that she's been in the apartment before", Rex argued.

"But, we have the earring!" Detective Payne said.

"However, we still haven't been able to definitively link it to her," Rex said, feeling exasperated. He felt like he was poking a pin in a child's balloon as he watched his partner's face deflate.

"It looks expensive, like something she would wear. I am sure we will find the other one once we get a warrant to search her house," Detective Payne argued.

"Any luck in finding the murder weapon?" Jose asked.

"Not yet, but the pathologist says it's probably a boxcutter or a similar type of weapon," Detective Payne answered.

"A dime a dozen then," the attorney sniffed.

"But, it's her! You know it's her!" Detective Payne argued, "You have enough for probable cause, and a search warrant. Then we can look for the earring, the weapon, and anything else that will link her to this."

Rex had to clench his fists, he was so frustrated with Detective Payne. He interjected, "Now, Renee, we still have some other suspects to check out. Let's get all our ducks in a row first."

Detective Payne glared at him, "What is it with you? Why are you defending this murderer? You want her to get away with it? For all we know, her family is already helping her get a fake passport so she can flee. Her neighbor said she saw her putting luggage in her trunk yesterday, and she seemed pretty cagey when we interviewed her. She's probably gone already!"

"Now you are just being ridiculous!" Rex answered.

"Wait! Do you honestly think she's a flight risk?" the attorney asked, startled.

"She certainly has the resources," Susan commented. Susan and Carrie had been quietly taking notes during the exchange.

Finally, Jose sighed, and said, "Okay. I'll present it to the judge and see if we can get an arrest warrant. Detective Payne, I'll need you to come with me and talk to the judge. Carrie, Susan, go let the team know how we are proceeding, and then come to the judge's chambers."

Thus dismissed, Rex turned on his heel and headed back to the precinct. He didn't like the way this case was heading, but apparently, he was the only one. He needed to review his notes again and try to track down some other leads.

****

Ember, Family Compound, a few hours later

"Lee, what am I supposed to do now?" Ember asked the family lawyer, as she reviewed the sordid images Hunter Baron had recorded without her knowledge. "This makes me look guilty! If I had known about this – I probably *would* have killed him," Ember said angrily.

"No, you wouldn't have," Lee Filderman said calmly. Very little ruffled the Prince's family attorney. He had, of course, been cleaning up Jack Prince's messes for a very long time. That was enough to ensure that very little surprised him. In fact, he wasn't even surprised when John, the head of security, ushered a plain clothed detective into Jack's office, where Lee had set up camp.

The detective, a very attractive African American woman, was dressed in pressed navy-colored slacks, a crisp cotton men's style tailored shirt, a lightweight matching blazer, and low heeled but fashionable shoes. Her badge was prominently clipped on her belt, emphasizing her small waist and shapely form. Lee's eyes lingered for a moment on her figure before meeting her eyes. The detective did not seem amused by his perusal as she placed an arrest warrant on the desk. She was accompanied by two uniformed officers that both seemed fresh out of the academy. One of them looked too young to shave, but both carried sidearms that were prominently displayed on their uniforms along with handcuffs.

Detective Renee Payne was annoyed but also charmed by the sleazy lawyer; even his slow-motion once over couldn't dampen her excitement at finally serving a warrant on one of those self-centered, double-dealing, dirtbag Princes. This time, they wouldn't get away with anything. Voters may forgive fraud, and corruption, but the murder of a wealthy white man? It looked like the Prince family would finally get their comeuppance. Detective Payne was more than pleased to be able to present a search and seizure warrant that covered the entire Jack Prince family compound in addition to the arrest warrant for Ember Prince. If Ember Prince thought that she could hide evidence at her dad's house, she was in for a surprise. Politician or not, she and her officers were going to tear this place apart but first, she was going to put that Ember Prince in cuffs.

"Detective, I'd like a chance to examine these warrants. I would also like to make arrangements for my client prior to her surrender. Frankly, we weren't prepared for this," Lee Filderman protested.

"Now, that's just not going to happen," Renee said with a curt laugh. "Either Ember Prince comes with me now, or y'all are going to have a real problem, explaining that she isn't a flight risk to Judge Ward because she's going to have to run otherwise." Detective Payne looked like she almost wanted Ember to try to evade arrest.

"How did you even know that Ms. Price was here? Have you been surveilling her?" Lee demanded.

Now Renee just smiled and said, "Come on, and get your client down here, or do you want me to see if we can add charges of evading arrest and obstructive of justice?"

Lee wanted to slap the smug young detective to get the smirk off her face. He wanted to remind her that this wasn't how the legal system worked, but he could see that she was just spoiling for a fight. With her two rookie companions, he worried that things could go sideways rather quickly. He decided that he would treat her the same as he'd treat a mentally disturbed client, making no sudden moves, no complicated speeches. Just go slow and steady, he thought.

For her part, Detective Payne felt a deep satisfaction as she leaned over to watch him dial the phone to call Ember, who was in another part of the house. He looked directly at Detective Payne as he spoke to Ember, speaking blandly, to not enrage the detective by tipping off Ember about what was about to happen.

Finally, she had that murdering bitch, she thought. She fingered the ivy leaf keyring in her pocket while she waited.

Ember looked perplexed when she saw the detective and the uniformed officers in her dad's office. She had been in another wing of the house, having an uncomfortable conversation with her father when Lee called her. The conversation had been particularly awkward and disconcerting since her father insisted on having it while lounging in his king-size bed in satin pajamas with his latest flavor of the month at his side. Her name was Ingrid, and she looked at least a decade younger than Ember. She was light-skinned, and half-Asian, with large honey brown eyes framed with thick lashes. She looked at Ember coyly from under her heavy lashes with languid eyes.

Ever since her father had divorced Tamara, it had been a continuous merry-go-round of young women in her father's office and his bedroom. Usually, it was a combination of both. He seemed to think he was the African American Hugh Hefner. Despite a conviction for embezzlement and misuse of funds, her father continued to use political donations and government funds as his own petty cash to pay for his companions. As Ember stared down the latest young thing, displaying pert breasts in the scanty lingerie, the woman returned a bored gaze at her before she pulled open a drawer next to the bed and pulled out an emery board. Ingrid made no attempt at modesty and seemed to delight in showing her g-string to Ember as she languidly rolled over on to her stomach to reach into the drawer. Her father made no excuses or apologies for Ingrid's presence and didn't seem inclined to get out of bed to address Ember. She felt humiliated to be begging for her father's attention, but she needed his help. She worked to maintain her composure. She refused to let that slut in her father's bed be witness to her shame. It was almost a relief to get Lee's call, so that she could escape this awkward situation. She hurried from her father's suite, down the stairs into the main foyer.

She knew something was going on because Lee was terse on the phone, but she wasn't prepared to see Renee Payne instructing a uniformed policeman to arrest her. It was hard to believe that they had been friends at one time.

"Wait a minute, wait a minute! Aren't you even going to ask me if I have an alibi?" Ember demanded, outraged.

"How do you even know if I was in Memphis when this guy died?" she continued.

"Well, Miz Prince, where were you when Hunter Baron III died?" Detective Payne asked, sarcastically.

"I don't know. When did he die?" Ember shot back, unable to believe that any of this had gotten so far.

"Don't play games with me, girl. Do you have an alibi or not?" Detective Payne shot back, aggressive, and seemingly hostile.

Ember got out her phone, seeming to ignore the detective for a minute, talking out loud, "So, the meeting y'all barged into with my campaign manager was on the 18th of March, and so I guess it was on the news that morning, so yeah," smiling a big grin, "I do have an alibi for March the 17th. That was a busy Thursday for me," she said as she scrolled thru her online calendar. "I went to Nashville early that morning to talk to some people about campaign finance and general campaign strategy. My campaign manager and my secretary came along with me. We stayed there until after lunch before racing back here because I had a last-minute fitting for some alterations to my costume for the Masquerade Ball that weekend at the Annesdale mansion. The seamstress is on Madison Avenue and she stayed open late to finish up with me. After that, I went home and changed before heading to cocktails with several members of the Memphis Junior League. I don't know how late we stayed out, but it was pretty late. I had to call an uber, so you can probably look up the driver and find out exactly what time he dropped me off," Ember finished smugly. "Oh, and I think some of the ladies from Junior League posted some pictures of us on Instagram. Will that do?"

For a minute, Detective Payne looked stunned, but then suspicion returned to her eyes as she said rudely, "Who ever said he died on the 17th?"

"Enough!" Lee interrupted. "This is the most vindictive and malicious prosecution I've ever seen! You haven't even asked if she had an alibi? What kind of clown show are you running? How did you even get an arrest warrant? Did you do any real investigation before deciding to target my client?" Then he turned to Ember and said, "Go ahead and go with these officers. I'll meet you at the station and see if I can get it sorted out."

****

As she was being led out, Lee looked at her and reminded, "Keep your mouth shut. No talking until I get there." Ember couldn't have been happier to comply.

Sandra and Rex Lester, Olive Branch, 2022

"I can't believe she did that!" Detective Lester fumed. "I told her that the evidence wasn't solid enough, and she went ahead to the prosecutor's office," he continued as he stormed into his house in Olive Branch. "Damn that girl!" he half muttered, then said, "Yeah, you know her lawyer is going to make hay out of this, and I don't blame him. Yeah! Yeah! I'll keep you informed," before ending the call.

Sandra has looked up from the jigsaw puzzle she was working on at his outburst. "Darling, everything alright?" she asked with concern evident on her face.

Rex took a deep breath and sighed, as he placed his badge and gun in a kitchen drawer before shedding his blazer. He looked at her dear, tiny wife, whom he had nicknamed 'Hobbit' due to the disparity in their sizes and did his best to flash a quick smile, but the hobbit wasn't fooled. For all her tiny size, next to his six-foot six frame, she could go toe-to-toe with him in an argument. If she felt he was keeping things from her, there would be an argument alright.

She came out from behind the little table and cocked an eye at him. She went to the fridge and without saying anything got out a cold beer and twisted it open before handing it to him. Then she began taking out the ingredients to make dinner. As he took a sip of the beer, Rex watched as Sandra began rinsing vegetables. She pulled out the cutting board and he began the nightly routine and began to tell her about his day. He watched her julienne a zucchini as he felt the stress roll off his back, almost like a wave, and his shoulders loosened up.

As Sandra handed him a mixing bowl filled with corn flour, he took the wooden spoon and mixed the batter. "Sandra, I am just so frustrated with this case. I don't feel like it's as much of a slam-dunk as everyone else seems to think it is. I still have a lot of questions, and very little evidence to actually link the crime to the suspect," Rex said. He took another sip of the beer, as Sandra heated the cast-iron tortilla press.

He handed her back the bowl of tortilla batter, as she said, "So what happened today?"

He kept his eyes on the press as she scooped a small amount on the now sizzling press. "Detective Payne went behind my back and got the duty sergeant to present the case to the prosecutors. Then they went to a judge and got an arrest warrant for Ember Prince," he answered.

"And you don't think she's guilty?" Sandra asked as she lowered the top of the press. She stopped what she was doing to look up at Rex and wait for his answer.

"Well, I'm not saying all that, Hobbit. I am just saying that what evidence we have doesn't necessarily support her as being the killer. I mean, the suspicion is there – and there's motive, but I just can't place her at the scene in the days before the body was discovered," Rex answered with his slow Mississippi drawl. Sandra looked thoughtful, scrunching her brow for a moment, before she said, "Shoot!" and rescued a fresh tortilla from the press that was beginning to smoke.

The thoughtful gaze continued during dinner when Sandra seemed distracted at times. Sandra had been watching her granddaughter, Emma, frequently while her daughter taught at the local elementary school. Their usual day care provider had been ill, and Sandra had readily swooped in to help her daughter, Danielle. They had the kind of close relationship that Rex often wished he had with his own children, but taking care of an active toddler could be exhausting, and as he looked around the living area, at the scattered crayons, and toys, Rex wondered if she might be overdoing it. Sandra had just gotten over a serious illness, and she continued to tire easily. She had, in fact, just recently been able to get back to painting and her other artistic activities. He liked to tease his little Hobbit, because that included her love of ever more complex jigsaw puzzles. He had been devastated when she had been too tired to do her favorite activities. He looked closely at her face while they ate, trying to see if he could detect any residual vestiges of her illness. Her color was a little high, he thought, but she'd just finished cooking. She had faint, dark circles under her eyes, but for the most part, she looked better than she had in months. Satisfied, he turned his attention to finishing the delicious dinner she had prepared.

When the meal was over, he surprised Sandra by shooing her out of the kitchen. He sent her back to her little table to work on her puzzle, while he rinsed dishes and stacked them in the dishwasher. He knew that she used the puzzles to work out other problems, and to relax. As he wiped down the kitchen table, like he'd seen her do a thousand times, he heard her calling him.

"Rex! Rex!" Sandra said in a low voice, "Bring me those pictures from the crime scene again," with a sense of urgency in her voice. As he went to collect his files, she continued on, "This has been bothering me for days, and I just haven't been able to put my finger on it until now. I need to take another look at some of those photos."

He handed her the photos and watched as she quickly flipped through the grisliest photos, showing the corpse and it's injuries. She stopped and pulled out three photos that showed the earring on the floor, and then another in the lab with a ruler next to it, showing the size. There was dried blood on the front of the earring, which had landed face down on the carpet, but the rest of the earring was clean, showing a metallic surface.

"So," Sandra started as she searched her vocabulary for what she wanted to say. She was usually readily fluent in English, but sometimes, when the thoughts were just racing in her brain, it took a moment for her mouth to catch up. When that happened, she would just spit it all out in Spanish and give her mind a moment to work it out. "Entonces, esto me estaba volviendo loca. Yo se de este diseño, o quiero decir, yo lo conozco, pero no exactamente. Parece indígena, pero no es Mejicano."

Rex didn't speak Spanish, not by a country mile, but he could understand a lot of it. "What you are saying, is that you recognize the pattern on this earring. It's some kind of design, but not Mexican?" he ventured.

"Si. Si. This has been bothering me for a long time. It's definitely a native design, like Mayan, but it's not anything I've seen in Mexico. I could swear I've seen something similar in a magazine recently. Go get your laptop, Rex. I have got to get this stupid earring design out of my head," she said.

Rex had seen that determined look on her face before. After he brought her the laptop, she set it on top of the puzzle she was currently working on, so he knew she was serious. He watched her search the internet with various terms for a while, before he found himself yawning. He looked at his watch, and stood, stretching. "Ready for bed, darling?" he said. He wasn't at all surprised when she demurred. He knew nothing would suit but for her to research until she either found something or ran out of things to search for. He gave her a kiss on the forehead, which she barely seemed to notice, before he padded down the hall and off to bed.

When Rex made his way to the kitchen the next morning for a cup of coffee, he wasn't surprised to find a half-pot of coffee already made, along with a strangely energized wife. She was peering into the laptop like it held the secrets of the universe while she made notes on a yellow legal pad. She didn't look up when he came in, but said, "Rex, you need to talk to your sergeant today. You need to go to Paris. If he won't pay for it, don't worry, I will. I have already contacted the people you need to talk to – and I've been looking into flights and hotels."

Rex looked over the rim of his coffee cup at his wife as if she'd grown another head. He came over to the table where she was sitting, in order to look over her shoulder. As she explained what she'd discovered, he realized she was right.

****

That evening Rex was packing his bag as Sandra sat perched on the edge of the bed. "Are you sure you don't want to go?" he asked. He figured since it was her idea, she should go with him. She was more of an investigator than anyone in the department. She had found something that no one else had, and it might provide direct evidence linking a suspect to Hunter Baron's killer.

"No, Rex. I know how hard it was to get the department to let you go, even with us shouldering a lot of the expenses. If I go, you will have a real hard time explaining that it wasn't a vacation, since that's what they all think anyway," Sandra answered, pragmatically.

****

The officers at the main precinct were stalling Lee and he didn't appreciate it. He had arrived to speak to both the duty sergeant and his client over 45 minutes ago, but the officers seemed pleased to keep him cooling his heels, instead of taking him to the general lock-up to see his client. He knew that a sheltered woman like Ember must have been traumatized by the whole thing. Since Ember had been led away in cuffs, Lee and his assistants had been hammer-calling Ember's staff to get a copy of her personal calendar, to see if they could present an air-tight alibi. Unfortunately, neither her campaign manager nor her secretary could provide secure alibis for the week preceding the discovery of the body. With the police refusing to provide a more specific time of death estimate, it was hard to pin down all his client's movements, particularly the nocturnal ones. As she had mentioned, with the upcoming election, she had been extremely busy with speaking engagements, planning meetings, soliciting donations, and kissing babies. The lack of a consistent romantic partner or roommate didn't help either, since there was no one to vouch for her, if she did manage to spend a quiet night at home.

If this nonsense with the police and the prosecution didn't stop, he was going to have to file a pre-trial motion to dismiss.

Marnie, Silky O' Sullivans

Silky's on Beale Street during the day was like a tired old whore, Marnie thought. Neither one looked good in the harsh light of day. All of the cluttered nooks and crannies that looked charming during the evening when the bar was rowdy and roaring with life, just looked dirty and neglected in the mid-morning light. Marnie wasn't keen on tippling this early in the day, but she had come to see one of the local regulars. She watched while the wait staff did the last-minute preparations to ready the establishment for the day. She sat quietly in the courtyard after being admitted by one of the busboys, as she waited for Robert Eggleston. She decided to seek him out after speaking to one of Hunter Baron's former neighbors, Willy Bearden. While Mr. Bearden was something of a local celebrity, as a documentary filmmaker covering local history, he was also an older gentleman with fairly specific habits. When not in the field filming, he spent enormous amounts of time in his apartment editing footage. His apartment and home office, in particular, shared a common wall with Hunter Baron. The conversation that followed was quite illuminating. While Mr. Bearden never heard anything that sounded akin to the gruesome murder, over the months that Hunter had been his neighbor, he had heard plenty. What was most notable to Marnie was that Mr. Bearden reported only cursory contact with the police in the aftermath of his killing. He reported to Marnie that over the course of several months, in addition to what sounded like almost weekly parties, he overheard several loud arguments. Mr. Bearden also reported that the eccentric photographer might have additional information to report, since Eggleston was not only Hunter's downstairs neighbor, but a close drinking companion as well. It was clear that Mr. Bearden held the photographer in contempt, but whether it was for his poorly disguised alcoholism or his close affiliation with Hunter Baron, he wouldn't say. He seemed embarrassed when Marnie asked.

Marnie fidgeted with her pen and notepad as she waited, reviewing her conversation with Willy Bearden in her mind, and checking her watch several times. After several coffee refills, and one bathroom stop, Marnie was preparing to leave after waiting for over 90 minutes with no sign of the elderly photographer. Just as she finished paying the waitress, she was approached by an attractive but frazzled looking red-haired woman who appeared to be in her early forties. "Ms. Gellhorn?" she asked in a confident voice.

As Marnie nodded, she awaited the woman's approach to the table. As she settled back down in her seat, the woman spoke again, "Mr. Eggleston, well, he's not coming. I'm his assistant, Trish, and his son sent me to talk to you." Trish perched herself with one buttock on the stool at the table, resting all of her weight on her left leg. Her right leg curled into the crossbar of the wooden stool.

Marnie tamped down her annoyance long enough to respond, "Oh, so his son isn't allowing him to come? Or is he Mr. Eggleston's social scheduler? Mr. Eggleston sure didn't mention it on the phone when I made this appointment."

Apparently, Marnie's attempt to hide her feelings had been less than successful, as Trish answered.

"Ms. Gellhorn. Well, I am so sorry, but as it is.. Well, Mr. Eggleston, he's pretty advanced in years and such. His memory isn't quite what it should be, you know, so yes, his son, has taken over his calendar in an attempt to prevent snafus like today. In fact, Mr. Eggleston didn't remember this appointment at all – and he was still in bed when I went by his apartment this morning, on the way here." Trish answered, looking embarrassed but a bit defiant too.

"Okay, then," Marnie said, with a gentle smile as she softened her words, "how about we re-schedule it then? Would you prefer that we meet at the apartment? We were only meeting here by his request. I am happy to do what I can to make it more convenient for everyone involved."

Now, it was Trish's turn to smile, as she said, "Well, Ms. Gellhorn, I just have to apologize, as Mr. Eggleston has reconsidered this interview. He doesn't feel like this interview has anything to add to his career, so he's decided to cancel it." Trish's face was smug as she looked at Marnie. Then she stood up briskly, and without shaking hands or further comment, turned and left the bar.

Marnie was left puzzled, as she quickly made notes on the conversation, before she too, left the bar.

The Lester residence, Olive Branch, Mississippi, 10 days later

After an exhausting 19 hours of travel, lay-overs and airport coffee, Rex Lester was finally home. His quick trip to Paris had ended up taking over a week, as he tracked down several leads from Sandra's initial Google searches. His legs felt like they weighed a thousand pounds each as he dropped his bags by the front door. The high-spirited beagle mix, Robin, leapt with joy to see him as Sandra came around the corner to welcome him. He reached down to scoop up his tiny wife in his arms, swinging her around, as he pushed away fatigue to greet her. After an extended welcome, Sandra ushered him to the kitchen table, while she made him a steaming hot cup of coffee.

"Do you want to sleep first?" she teased as she held out the coffee, knowing that he wouldn't be able to sleep until he discussed all the facts of the case with her.

"No, it's okay, Hobbit, but I have got to talk to the prosecutor. They are making a mistake," he said.

Prosecutor's' Office
After waiting outside the office for over 30 minutes, Rex Lester was getting frustrated. He tapped one of the toes of his cowboy boots on the floor, rhythmically as he waited, but he needed to talk to the District Attorney's office about the case.

He could hear phones ringing, multiple conversations and papers rustling from the sagging, faded Naugahyde couch that served as a waiting area. The scratched and dingy brass end tables were so old that they still had metal ashtray inserts in them. Rex wondered what would happen if someone pulled out a cigarette and attempted to use those old ashtrays. Would they even notice before they smelled the smoke?

Finally, an overweight, harried looking, middle-aged woman with teased hair looked up from her desk behind the partition separating the waiting area from the receptionists' desks.

"Hon, you can go on back to conference room G. They are waiting for you there, "she called, gesturing down a long hallway that was painted a sickly greyish yellow, that was punctuated with a series of mustard brown painted doors. Faint gray vinyl composite tile with green speckles alternated in a checkerboard pattern with a darker grey speckled tile. It reminded Rex of an old elementary school, but without the handmade drawings and art projects. It was, he thought, fundamentally depressing.

The third door was labeled Conference Room G. As he entered, one of the junior prosecutors was in mid-sentence. He stopped, looked at Rex critically, and said sarcastically, "So nice of you to join us." Rex looked over at the table to see his partner, Detective Payne sitting between two members of the prosecutor's office, with a smirk on her face. They had several boxes marked as "evidence" in the middle of the table and appeared to be reviewing the contents and making notes. Rex felt like he had been knee-capped seeing his partner there. She hadn't said a word to him about a meeting with the district attorney. She hadn't said anything when he called her earlier to discuss the results of his trip to France. In fact, she had made an excuse to end the call before he'd had a chance to brief her. He listened for a few minutes as they rehashed all of the circumstantial evidence they had before attempting to interject.

"I just got back from tracing down the origins of the earring found at the crime scene. As we surmised earlier, it's not a mass-market piece," he said.

There was a rustle of papers as one of the assistants shuffled through some papers, and interrupted, saying "See here. There was no foreign DNA retrieved from the earring post. The only DNA on that item was the victim's."

Mentally, Rex took a deep breath to keep from showing his irritation. "Yes, I know, but.." he said.

"Then, why are you bringing it up?" the young assistant said, interrupting him again.

This time Rex glared at the young man. "First off, DNA is great and all, but it's not everything. It wasn't even a routine part of our local investigations until 1999 or 2000. Secondly, we still don't do it right – we don't even have our own DNA lab here in Memphis, even though Nashville built theirs way back in 1997. We still send our DNA out to the state crime lab – which delays everything for weeks. That report in your hand; that's a preliminary report. They send that out before they try to do DNA amplification techniques, so initially there wasn't enough DNA to identify anyone but Hunter Baron, but in a few more weeks, we might hear something different." Rex looked over to see the more senior staff nodding in agreement.

"And lastly, sometimes it takes good old detective work to trace back these items to their owners. I've done that, and I am pretty darn sure that the owner of this earring is not Ember Price," Rex finished.

"That doesn't mean anything," said the young assistant, looking chastened, nonetheless.

"That house was filthy beyond belief," Detective Payne said. "That earring could have been there for months. We've seen the videos, we know he's had lots of women in and out of there," she said smugly.

"Well, did you identify the owner of the earring in one of the videos, then?" Rex shot back. He could tell by the looks on their faces that they hadn't even checked.

Rex was getting downright irritated now. They were going to sink this case before it even began. This was just sloppy! He tried again to voice his concerns, but the prosecutor at the front of the room, held up his hand in a stop motion in front of his face.

"I don't know why you've decided to be such a big booster in the Ember Prince fan club, Rex, but you know, she doesn't have a decent alibi," Detective Payne said nastily.

"I guess you haven't seen the latest evidence we were able to pull off the victim's computer," Renee continued. She looked at the conference table and picked up a letter. "We printed this out from his computer," she said, "and tracked the email address, which was sent from an anonymous proton email account. But the IP address, well, guess where it led," she sneered.

"Right to your little girlfriend's office," she finished triumphantly.

Rex took the letter and read it. He opened his mouth to question Renee but the prosecutor interrupted what would have been a nasty to and fro, saying "I get it, Rex. You don't think she's guilty, but you need to leave your personal feelings out of this case. No, no! I don't want to hear another word! If I need any more information from you, I'll ask."

Dumbfounded, Rex couldn't do anything but turn around and leave. As he left the building his sense of frustration, anger, and injustice grew. Instead of heading back to his office to review his notes and continue his investigation, he headed back to the police department to speak to his captain. Unsatisfied with her response, he placed his badge and his gun on her desk and stormed out. He could clean out his desk later. Right now, he had another stop to make.

****

Back in the conference room, the prosecutor was chastising Detective Payne.

"Is this personal for you too, Detective Payne? Is there something between you and the suspect? Or is this some kind of ego contest between you and Detective Lester? I am sure getting the feeling that there is more to your eager participation than just standard procedure. I mean, you were pushing for that arrest warrant pretty hard, and awfully early into the investigation. Did the suspect do something to piss you off? To get under your skin? The District Attorney's office is not here to help you with your personal vendettas. Also, this is not Law & Order or one of those damn television shows where you can trample all over the suspect's rights! So, I want you to be damned careful about what you are doing out there. If I get one more whiff of any funny stuff, you are going to regret it."

Detective Payne blinked back surprise and tears at the rebuke. She nodded, then set her chin, "Yes, sir. And I swear sir, there is nothing personal about this case. I just don't want to see a guilty person go free." Thus dismissed, she headed back to the station. It wasn't until she sat at her desk that she noticed the strange looks and the whispers around her. She was almost relieved when the captain summoned her to her office. She expected another reprimand, but was surprised when the captain informed her that her partner had taken a leave of absence.

"When is he coming back?" she asked secretly buoyed by the fact that her captain hadn't mentioned her rebuke from the DA. The captain shrugged her shoulders noncommittally.

"Is he coming back?" she persisted, now concerned. Rex could be a stubborn, old redneck sometimes, but he was a good partner overall. They just butted heads sometimes. He was too cautious and wasted too much time tracking down leads that turned out to be useless, when the answers were obvious sometimes.

The captain shrugged again.

She left the captain's office and went back to her desk, where she dialed Rex's cellphone. It went straight to voicemail.

****

Rex wrestled with himself but continued up Third Street to his destination. He knew he could face serious consequences for what he was doing, but that didn't deter him. He didn't have an appointment, but he didn't think it would matter as he opened the exterior door to the offices of Lee A. Filderman.

****

The months until the run up to the trial were filled with pre-trial motions, headline stories, and city-wide rumors. Marnie spent the time following up on whispers, hints and comments dropped in news stories, lawyers' speeches, editorial columns and radio interviews. The media was fascinated by the trial... It had all the elements of a made-for-TV movie; a rich playboy victim with his own scandalous past coupled with a Kennedy-esque defendant with their own Memphis Camelot. Everyone was ready to capitalize on it; from the "Baron" Burger filled with cheese and bacon and slathered with dark red barbeque sauce at Huey's, to the "Bloody Ember" mixed drink at the Indulge Lounge on Winchester, to the surprisingly catchy tune "In the Cell Next to Me" released by Pooh Shiesty from his prison cell in Miami. Ember Prince's family was equally eager to exploit all of the endless free press and they enlisted prominent political activists into their camp.

For Ember, it was one disaster after another. Her whole life was imploding as she faced the fight of her life. As much as she resented her family at times, she was thankful that with their influence and rich coffers, she would hopefully be able to make bail. She'd find out at her upcoming arraignment. She couldn't imagine being incarcerated as if she was already guilty just because she didn't have money or a family with influence like her own. It made her think of all the other defendants she had encountered after she was first arrested. She remembered too; all the petty taunts and comments of the booking officers and all of the other officers that seemed to just happen by as she was strip-searched and humiliated. She wondered if she was going to find a hidden camera video of that performance too, in the vast web of the internet. It was a traumatizing experience, to be violated by strangers who were all too happy to strip her of her dignity along with her clothes in a futile search for contraband. As she waited in the holding cell for her family to post bail, she looked at all the other women around her. Most of them were shades of black and brown. None of them looked affluent or even middle-class.

She had known all of these things, of course. It was impossible to live in American society and be ignorant of this great racial divide, and her side of it, but that was always on an intellectual level. Even after her father and uncles were arrested and incarcerated, it stayed at the periphery of her knowledge; it wasn't something talked about at Sunday dinner. Her father, on his infrequent visits, didn't talk about how dehumanizing it was, and he certainly never shared with her what prison was like. She wanted him to talk to her now – not as a bonding experience, but to prepare her for what might happen. She knew that public sentiment was running against her, and she knew that she might be going away for a long, long time. Her dad hired a new media consultant, who kept going on and on about how this experience could help propel Ember into office – and for a moment, Ember considered it. She turned away from the reality of the upcoming trial and focused on how she could serve the people, these people, if she was elected to office. For too long, the Prince family had only served themselves, and the public knew it. Now as she listened to her fellow inmates as they talked about their lives, their experiences saddened and appalled her. She had known that poverty, crime and drugs were rife in Memphis, but she had grown up insulated from much of the reality. She might drive through a "bad" neighborhood, but she never lived in one. She didn't listen to gunshots and have to wonder if one of her friends or neighbors had been hurt.

She had attended private schools, and White Station High School, which was a standout for public city schools. She'd had the opportunity and was encouraged both at school and at home to learn and to excel. She'd had a chance to go to college, without accumulating student loans, even if she hadn't graduated. She wasn't stupid or ignorant, but her family's wealth and success in politics had kept her cloistered from the daily miseries experienced by many Memphians. Her entry into the legal system had been her own awakening, and she was ashamed of her naïveté.

****

As Ember and Lee Filderman walked unobtrusively from the courtroom, in comfortable silence, both dressed in somber shades of grey. The arraignment had apparently escaped the press' notice, with the exception of the ever-present Marnie. A visibly relieved Ember hurried down the steps after Lee, as they headed to his office to de-brief. Amazingly, she was being released on her own recognizance as an upstanding member of Memphis society despite being charged with first degree murder. Apparently, the Prince name was good for something, especially since this Prince didn't have any sort of criminal record. She had to surrender her passport, but she would have done just about anything to get out of lockup.. surrendered a kidney, if necessary.

Hearing the charges read out loud in the courtroom was startling, almost unreal, but she stood there unflinching while they announced the charges. She didn't understand how she could be charged with three counts of murder when there was only one dead body, but that seemed like the least of her problems.

Now, being on bail and facing a murder trial, strangely invigorated her, if only because the only other alternative was to retreat into herself and incarcerate herself within her mind to block it all out. She wasn't allowed to travel under the terms of her release and had to wear an ankle bracelet to monitor her movements. She could still give speeches, and interviews. Her campaign team pushed her to use her notoriety, and that of her suspected victim, but Ember couldn't. The more she read, the more she became involved in all the conversations around the elections, the more disgusted she became. She wasn't interested in any of this petty power-brokering and talking heads. The issues that had plagued Memphis hadn't changed, no matter who was in office. None of her relatives had made a dent in any of it, even as they added to their own personal coffers. She didn't feel lost anymore, she felt driven…driven to get away from this family, and the heavy burden it placed on her! She wouldn't even be here, on trial for her freedom, if it wasn't for their endless corruption, greed and desire for attention. She had allowed the Prince name to influence her decisions for too long; she had almost become another cog in their wheel.

She faced down her father and each of his advisors, because all of them, even her campaign manager, didn't really work for Ember. They were invested in getting her into office, sure, but not because they believed in her as an individual. So, she faced them all, stone-faced as she announced that she was quitting the race. She didn't know what she was going to do next, but since there wouldn't be a next if she lost the trial, she stopped worrying about it.. and concentrated on saving herself. She was relying on Lee to get her out of this mess. Right now, he was the only person she trusted.

Meanwhile – Robert Prince, Jr.

"Are you tired?" he called to the crowd from a hastily set up podium on the steps of the courthouse. "I said, my friends, are you tired?"

The growing crowd roared in response. "I know that I am just so tired. Tired of this injustice! Tired of the persecution!" he called.

The crowd murmured in approval.

"I'm tired of racist institutions and society trying to de-rail a black man every chance they get!" he said, with increasing volume and force.

Cries of amen came from the crowd.

"First, they came for my daddy. Some of you folks here may remember that," he said.

"Took them a decade to do it, and he had a heart attack in the middle of it – but they came for him, over and over. They were trying to put another black man in the grave if they couldn't put him in prison."

"Yes sir," came the response.

"Then they came for my uncle," he said.

"Uh-huh," was the crowd led response.

"And don't forget Aunt Desdemona. They came for her too."

"Sure did," said the crowd.

"Then they came after my grandmother for loving a black man," he continued.

The crowd was silent.

"Now, here they are, trying to ruin the Prince name, once again. They see me climbing in the polls, and they can't have that. Me, a black man, here to succeed and speak for you. They don't want that to happen."

Calls from the audience "Amen, brother!" and "Speak your truth!" rang out.

"So now they are going after another Prince to drag us through the mud. Don't let them get away with that. This has nothing to do with my cousin, and everything to do with keeping a strong black man down!" he said with a flourish.

"But all of you here, you know you can believe in me. Remember that a vote for Bobby Prince is a vote for the black community," he finished.

****

Lee Filderman shut off the television, after the recorded televised "impromptu" political rally finished and smiled.

Ember felt mortified. This was so typical of her cousin, to grandstand for himself at every opportunity. He hadn't changed since the days back in Washington DC. Always out for himself, always spinning the narrative to suit himself, never mind the facts.

She felt incredulous watching him talk about his campaign. What about her life? Her freedom? Wouldn't it be more likely that any effort to discredit her, would be done to jeopardize her chance at an impartial jury? How did her trial become about him?

And this stuff about their grandmother being white? It was just ridiculous! But then again, probably no more ridiculous than expecting her cousin, Bobby, to publicly support her during all of this.

She looked at Lee, embarrassed, ashamed, and appalled.

"I am showing you this so that you won't be caught off guard. Your cousin gave that interview yesterday afternoon while we were in court. I knew you probably hadn't seen it yet. Now, don't get too upset. Ember, this is good news!" Lee exclaimed.

"I know it doesn't feel like it, but just remember that jurors watch the news. They aren't immune to the thoughts and prejudices that all of us have. If your cousin manages to sow some seeds of doubt in the community, and steers people away from the lurid aspects of the case with his antics, then that helps us. I know you won't like the comparison, but think about the O.J. Simpson trial and his acquittal!" he finished.

Ember nodded weakly. She knew that Lee was a trial expert, but it all felt so sordid and dirty.

"I just hate that people out there think that I am capable of something like this," she said.

"I've made my share of mistakes in my life, sure, but I've never done anything violent, ever. I just can't believe how quick people are to think I would murder someone! This entire scenario has been so awful. I keep waiting to wake up and find out it was all just a very bad dream," she finished.

Lee nodded and said, "It's okay to be upset, and it's okay to be angry, Ember. This has certainly been unfair, and when we are done with this trial, I hope we have grounds for a discrimination suit against the city. In the meantime, I want your Bobby, Tami Sawyer, and Mayor Herenton out there spreading dissention every day. I want them to hold rallies, give interviews and write editorials. I want to see them on Channel 5 News, I'd even like to see them on CNN talking about the case. One of the associates in my office went to LSU with Don Lemon. Maybe we can get him talking about the case."

He continued, "If we could get A. C. Wharton on our side, we have a chance that we might be able to move to get the case dismissed. He may be retired now, but with his reputation as such a law-and-order type, his support would be invaluable. Now, he and your dad haven't gotten along, traditionally, but maybe Wharton would respond if we reach out."

Ember didn't comment. Lee looked intently at her and gently put his hand on her arm. He felt paternal towards her even though there were only a dozen years between the two of them. He had watched her grow up, and occasionally stumble into the self-possessed, and lovely intelligent woman she was today.

"Ember," he said, more softly, "it's okay, honey. I know it's overwhelming, but tomorrow, we start your defense. I need you to go home, eat a good dinner, then relax and get a good night's sleep. Take a bath, get a massage, do yoga, or whatever you need to do to make sure you are well rested. Tomorrow is going to be taxing and I want you at your best." With that, Lee stood and escorted Ember out of the conference room. He led her to the back exit of his office, to avoid any possible reporters. He watched her get into her car before he went back to his office to finish preparing for the next day in court.

****

Book Eight - The People vs. Ember Prince

> *"It's your duty to answer questions. You don't have to run around giving out information."*
>
> *Perry Mason (Raymond Burr) in "The Case of the Moth-eaten Mink"*

It was a miserable, grey, stormy morning on the first day of the trial. Jury selection and all of the other preliminary, judicial movements had been completed. On the morning of opening statements, it was the kind of weather that made you want to reset your alarm and pull the covers back over your head. It was ugly, it was loud, with howling winds and pouring, pelting, incessant rain. It was dark outside as if night was reluctant to cede to the day. Marnie wondered if all of the jurors, the judge, and attorneys felt as reluctant to leave their cozy cocoons as she did. She was pretty sure that the defendant hadn't leapt out of bed, praising the glory of the morning.

Marnie wasn't entirely correct. Ember may not have been eager to face the nasty, wet conditions outside, nor the cold courtroom, but she wasn't hiding under the covers. She had awakened around 3 am, after a nasty clap of thunder woke her. She had been unable to sleep after that and had given up trying shortly afterward. She slid on her slippers and padded down the hall to the kitchen to brew some coffee.

After consuming several cups of dark, hot, very strong coffee and reading some old mail, Ember climbed into the shower. She gave herself a pep talk as the hot, steamy water washed over her. She tried to give herself a "game day" speech like one of the coaches in the most recent sports movie, but it fell flat. Instead, she compromised, and decided to let herself cry out her fears in the privacy of her bathroom. She cried until she felt empty, and her face felt hot and swollen. She cried as her nose ran, and she began to cough. She briefly jumped back in the shower, to wash it all down the drain.

She took her time that morning, to compose herself, to be calm, serene and beautiful. She dressed in the modest suit that Lee's team had recommended and carefully arranged her hair in a serious style, pulled up against her head. She softened the look with a few soft curls framing her face. She wanted to look serious but not schoolmarmish; studious but friendly, and likable but modest. She needed the jury to like her, or at least not dislike her, so they could hear her side of the story with an open mind. She knew how easy it was for people to judge based on appearances and to judge harshly. One of Lee's jury consultants had even advised Ember to get a small amount of Botox applied to the corners of her mouth, to "make her look more friendly." She had spent the rest of that afternoon examining her face in the mirror before deciding that maybe she did have a little too much "resting bitch face." She felt ridiculous making the appointment, but she also wasn't going to let her fate be decided by a couple of downward wrinkles at the corner of her mouth. As she inspected her appearance, she was glad she made the extra effort. As she continued gazing in the mirror, she thought about her uncles, her father and even her Aunt Decca. They had all sat as defendants in a Memphis courtroom, even in federal cases. Some of them had been found guilty, and her own father had served time, but none of them had faced down a murder charge before. How had they done it? She knew that her uncle had delayed his own federal trial with complaints of chest pains, and donned the same suit, day after day for two and a half months as he tried to portray himself as a humble working man. Not only had it worked, but his loyal supporters had helped him raise another million dollars during his trial. Then again, that was a political trial on financial terms. There was no bloody victim, no sympathetic story.

It would have been nice if they had shared some advice, Ember mused, though her dad would have said, "Just hope you look good in stripes" or something to that effect. As scared as she was, that idea had her cracking her first smile of the morning.

Despite all of her extra activities this morning, she was ready hours early, her stomach jumpy after too much caffeine.

****

Once the courtroom had been seated after Judge Ward entered, he proceeded with several administrative actions including a roll call of the jurors and alternates. He made comments of two pre-trial motions and then began a lengthy speech to the jurors as part of their instructions. Carrie Bryant was surprised at how monotone his voice was as he reviewed critical information, including the definition of reasonable doubt, and the right of the defendant to abstain from testifying. As he concluded his long-winded instructions, he reminded the jury, "I need for all of the jurors to disregard any consideration of potential penalties in the case, as that is immaterial to the consideration of guilt or innocence."

At the prosecution's table, Carrie Bryant tried to keep from trembling. She had been relegated to a 'fetch and carry' assistant for this trial by her boss, Amy Weinrich, but a virulent strain of a GI bug running through the prosecutor's office had deemed otherwise. With over half of the prosecutor's office chained to the bathroom, Carrie was once again assigned an active role in the case, as second assistant to Jose Leon.

She felt embarrassed to be frightened but her previous experience in Judge Chris Craft's courtroom had been an exercise in abject humiliation. Carrie was relieved that Judge Craft was not presiding over this case. It had been assigned to Judge Ward, who had a reputation for general fairness, though he reportedly could be hostile at times, to attorneys that annoyed him.

Carrie was relieved not to have Judge Craft's cutting and sarcastic comments in her ear, but as she listened to the judge drone on, Carrie was glad that she wasn't the defendant. She would hate to think that her life or potential freedom hung on the instructions given in such a long-winded, monotone, and mind-numbingly boring fashion.

Her colleague and main prosecutor for the case, Jose Leon, was calm and methodically reviewing his notes. He wore a navy-colored suit with a soft pink tie. While a couple pounds overweight, Jose was an attractive, middle-aged man, with a kind face. Carrie thought he seemed to go over well with the jury, after observing earlier interactions.

The prosecutions' first assistant attorney, Sabrina Price, came running in breathless and with a rain sprinkled face, just moments before the gallery was seated. Bailiff William Bronson turned to look at Carrie after leading the jurors into the jury box. He was looking more fit these days, she thought. It was as if he read her face, as he smiled and then winked at her. Seeing the familiar bailiff helped Carrie conqueror her fear of returning to the courtroom after such an ignoble defeat last year. Her favorite court reporter had retired a few months ago, but she'd welcome any friendly, familiar face she could find. Before she could think more about it, the judge had entered the chambers, and Jose Leon was starting his opening statement.

"Good morning, everyone!" Jose Leon addressed the jury. "Now I know that most of you don't know who I am, and that's a good thing. You are all good, god-fearing, law-abiding folks, so you had no need to know much about the district attorney's office until today. My name is Jose Leon, and I have an assistant district attorney here in Memphis. I have had the privilege of serving the citizens of this city in this capacity for the last 18 years. Prior to that, I attended the University of Memphis, both for undergraduate and law school. I am not a native Memphian, but I do love my adopted city, warts and all."

You may not have heard of me during my time here in Memphis, but you know, I bet you've heard all about the defendant here. I know I sure have," Jose Leon said.

Before he could continue, Lee Filderman was out of his chair. "Objection! This isn't a popularity contest, unfair characterization of the defendant." Lee knew that objections during opening arguments could be a dicey thing, but he couldn't allow the prosecution to initiate a full character assignation of his client without protest.

Judge Ward gave Lee a little side-eye and sighed. "So, that's how it's going to be," he said under his breath. Then he looked over at the waiting attorneys and said, clearly and evenly, "Overruled."

Jose turned back to the jury, with a shrug, as he began again, "Even as an outsider, I learned all about the Prince family. Is there anyone here that hasn't?" he asked rhetorically. "I mean, you don't have to live here long to see that they live life with impunity. They don't have to follow the rules that the rest of us do. I mean, they can use public monies to pay for mistresses, stuff ballot boxes, commit insurance fraud or any number of things – and basically get away with it. I mean, we've tried to prosecute before, but we all know how that goes. But now – this, this here is too much for anyone to overlook! This murder just goes to show what happens when you are raised to think that you can do whatever you want and answer to no one. This murder here is more than a cold-blooded, violent and vicious murder of a political opponent; it's the culmination of generations of the Prince family operating without consequences. Of course, the stakes got higher, because as you know, that's what happens when crimes go unpunished."

Jose turned at looked at Ember, who sat staring straight ahead, emotionless. "You know, there is a temptation to feel sorry for this young lady here. To lessen her responsibility a little bit because she just wasn't raised right like the rest of us, but we can't do that, now, because she is accused of murdering an innocent man, a man who was debilitated and wheelchair bound, unable to defend himself. But it's more than that, because we need to send a message that this kind of preferential treatment and lack of accountability is what allowed all of this mess to happen in the first place, to allow it get to a place where something like murder takes place. It was a lack of natural consequences and an emphasis on winning at all costs that brought us all here today – so we can't feel sorry for this pretty young lady here. We need to feel sorry for the victim, even if he wasn't always the most likable folk. "

"I know that's another temptation here – to excuse or somehow lessen this crime because our victim wasn't any kind of saint. But we would be forgetting our very duty as citizens of this great city, and the state of Tennessee, if we did that. We aren't here to sit in judgement of our victim or his lifestyle. Besides that, it wouldn't be Christian of us, at all. Instead, we are here to uphold the law, and keep our fellow neighbors safe, and take murderers off the street."

Now, our evidence will show that Ms. Ember Prince, well, she was a bit of a sore loser. She was in the middle of running this political race when she found out that her ex-lover had some dirt on her, per se. Not only was he going to share that dirt, but he was going to use it to win the election, because you see – he was more than just an ex, he was running against her. Ember just couldn't allow that. Whether it was being dumped romantically or losing the election – Ember wasn't going to allow that to happen.

I don't think it was the election as much as it was the heartbreak, but then I am a bit of an old-fashioned gentleman. I also have a hard time looking at such a grisly crime scene and thinking that this is all business. No, this scene was right personal, from the injuries inflicted on poor Mr. Baron to the very personal items that were left behind. This wasn't just an all's far in love and war, this was *Beware a woman scorned!* " Jose roared.

"We will prove that not only did Ember Raine Prince murder Hunter Lee Baron in the prime of his life, but that she did so in a malicious, cold, calculated, and pre-meditated manner. Now… we don't know if she might have had a bit of help, or if she did it single-handedly, but she's an evil-hearted killer, with no remorse, or regret. It's not for me to decide whether she deserves to pay the ultimate price for her crime, but I am here to see her punished to the fullest extent of the law! I am here to see that justice is served.

Carrie was a bit taken aback by his ferocity but impressed to see him in action. She never would have guessed that the polite, mild-mannered lawyer had such a theatrical side, especially with his "aww shucks," way of addressing the jury. This belied his reputation as a highly articulate summa cum laude graduate. She glanced back at the gallery and the jury to see how they were responding to her colleague. She quickly picked out the blonde head of the journalist, Marnie Gellhorn, bent over a notepad as she furiously took notes. Next to her was a court approved sketch artist.

In a attempt to limit the amount of media hoopla for this trial, Judge Ward had restricted cameras to outside the courtroom. Marnie, the sketch artist, and two other local reporters were the only media allowed inside.

When she looked at the jurors, they seemed to agree with Jose's sentiments. She looked over at Sabrina Price, first assistant, at the other end of the prosecutor's table and felt relieved. Together they had pored over the mountains of depositions, reports and other documents that helped build their case. They had both expressed doubts about the "slam-dunk" nature of the trial, contrary to many of the other staff in the prosecutor's office. Jose's strong opening statement and the jurors' response to it was reassuring.

With his usual charisma and flair, Lee Filderman made his way to stand in front of the jury. Unlike his low-key counterpart, Lee was dressed to impress, with a bespoke sharkskin suit in electric blue. The beautifully cut suit was paired with a soft pink shirt and a dark red tie. The custom tailoring saved the suit from garishness with its fine lines and draping. It may have been an eye-catching suit, but it was also a lovely one. As Lee approached, he caught the eye of one of the jurors, a middle-aged white woman on the cusp of obesity, brightly dyed copper curls and tortoise shell cat-eye glasses. He smiled brightly at her, and said, "Isn't it a lovely shade of blue?"

She blushed and giggled in response. Lee then addressed the group, in a booming voice. "Good morning, ladies and gentlemen. It's a fine day in Memphis today. The rain has stopped, the clouds have parted, and now the sun is just peeking out to greet us!"

Several jurors looked up at the clerestory windows of the courtroom as if to confirm his statements, and two older gentlemen nodded in reply.

"I know a little bit about all of you from the voir dire process, and your personal questionnaires. Now, I would like to tell you a little bit about us. I know that a lot of people don't like defense attorneys on principle, and I hope that these folks never need us. Like many lawyers, I've been on both sides of the fence, so to speak. I have worked in many areas of the law, and sometimes still do, though I dedicate the majority of my practice to criminal law. I've worked in this area for at least fifteen years and have been a lawyer for over 30 years. I own my own small practice, of which I am very proud. I am also proud to have this wonderful attorney at my side, Kisha Mack, as part of my practice. She's a well-trained lawyer in her own right with several years' experience, and a magna cum laude graduate of Ole Miss. She has done a lot of impressive things including publishing articles in legal journals and such, but most importantly, she has agreed to assist me on this case. In big cases, serious cases, like murder trials, we like to work as a team. We want to make sure our clients get the best legal defense available. The other reason there are two of is, is that a case like this, a first-degree murder case, has a tremendous amount of documentation, evidence, witness testimony, and other information, court filings, and such. It's too much for one person to manage. I don't think that a case should ever be won or lost on a technicality like a misplaced pleading or an uncontested motion. That's sloppy but it does happen, and not uncommonly. But my hope is that with Ms. Mack and I here to manage the flow of papers and information in this case, any final determinations or decisions that all of you will make will be based on facts and evidence, not on whether or not we've managed to keep up with the paperwork."

"I'd like to thank my colleague, Jose Leon, over there for such a fine introduction for my client. He surely knows many of the members of her family. But then again, that's not the same as knowing my client."

"Like many of us, she has some black sheep in her family. Or maybe, if you prefer, some bad apples. I mean, I have an uncle in my family who is quite the scoundrel; a bit of a gambler, a drinker and even a bit of a womanizer. Quite embarrassing for the rest of us, but not much like me. I, have to admit to being an unremarkable bore in comparison, not only all straight A's in school, but nary a speeding ticket. Ms. Ember Prince is much the same. A lovely, generous, smart, young woman, hard-working and loyal. She doesn't deserve to be tarred with the same brush – and it seems terribly unfair to me for her to be hounded by the police because of her familial connections. I mean, we can't pick our parents, now can we?"

"But we will set aside, the gross prejudice of this guilt by association type prosecution, to say a few words about this case in general," he continued.

"People always like to think that trials are full of surprise witnesses, newly discovered evidence and gotcha moments," Lee Filderman exclaimed, "But that's just not the case," he continued.

"A good case for either the prosecution or the defense is one that is well prepared, and well executed. Facts are delineated in a linear fashion, with evidence to support these facts. Various experts may be brought in to help show how the evidence demonstrates the facts of the case, but these experts are discussing known and proven scientific methods not voodoo spirits or hastily made-up guesses. All witnesses and evidence to be presented is available to both sides for examination prior to the trial. This gives both sides a chance to have evidence examined independently. If there is a footprint, a fingerprint or a piece of DNA at the crime scene, each side has an opportunity to have their own experts, labs, and forensic analysis. This helps prevent errors or a potential miscarriage of justice. It's important for jurors to remember that this is an essential part of the justice system, as the level of scientific evidence has improved over time."

"Now, do any of you like crime shows? I know I sure do. I learn a lot about evidence and crime watching these shows. Does that surprise you? Well, it shouldn't, because there are newer and better tests all the time," Lee said before continuing.

"Prior to the 1990's, there was no DNA evidence for example. Experts used to use other techniques to try and match a hair to a suspect - and it wasn't always correct. Other so-called forensic techniques have fallen out of favor, as defense experts have been able to prove that the information was not specific enough to tie it to one specific individual. Same thing with bullet casings, rifling marks and all that.

"Oh, I see some of you are nodding there in the gallery. Now, I knew I couldn't be the only one who enjoys those mysteries. It's like a thousand-piece puzzle isn't it," Lee said, watching as a few of the jurors nodded.

"And isn't it just a satisfying feeling to fit that last piece into the completed puzzle?" Lee said. An elderly lady with crochet in her lap, in the main gallery nodded so emphatically that Lee could almost see her thinking, "Yes, Sir."

"Now, not to belabor my love of television, and all that binge streaming we can do now – you know, spending a whole, quiet, Sunday afternoon watching episode after episode of *Forensic Files*," he continued, as the prosecutor looked bored, "but ever notice how in some of the older episodes there is a post-script at the end of the show?"

He paused for a slight moment. "And what does that post-script say most of the time?" he asked rhetorically.

"That's right." he answered himself. "Plenty of times, it's the editors of the program updating the results of the case. I know that many times, it's because our understanding of the value and reliability of evidence has changed, like when all those bite mark cases had to be thrown out once they proved that the so-called," here his voice became somewhat sarcastic, "*forensic dental expert* had been making it up as he went along! And that same *so-called expert* had taught hundreds of other dentists his faulty techniques, and *these so-called experts had testified in thousands of trials!*"

He stopped and took a deep breath, "and so there were a lot of innocent people that had been put in prison based on faulty expert testimony. That is why it's important that both sides have a chance to examine any potential evidence, and to have it analyzed by their own experts. Because, you know that the prosecutors' offices in those cases sure wasn't volunteering that their *so-called expert's education and expertise came from out of a cereal box now, were they?*"

Lee was pleased to see that a few of the jurors heads nodded along with his conclusion. The attorneys at the prosecutors table seemed to glare at him, and he relished it. He took a moment to straighten his tie, before continuing.

"But more important than possible faulty science in this trial, is the lack of any real evidence pointing towards my client. My client, whom as you know, has already faced a trial by the media. While the media may have shown their disdain for my client, and her family for their own political reasons, they sure haven't been able to focus on any evidence of my client's guilt…because there isn't any! The law says that a lack of evidence means not guilty. All of you here have agreed to hear the case with open minds, and no preconceived notions. So, when you hear the information related to this case, and if you agree that there is no clear and present evidence relating to my client, then you have agreed to do your legal duty and find her not guilty. You accepted this grave responsibility when you agreed to be part of the jury.

My client, who may have had a romantic encounter with the deceased in the past, has had no arguments, no on-going relationship, and no contact with the deceased prior to his untimely death. But," he said, holding up a finger for emphasis, "there were several others who DID have on-going relationships, conflicts and arguments with the deceased, Mr. Hunter Baron." He held up another finger, "yet you don't see them on trial here today – or on trial in the media."

He held up a third finger, "This morning, you listened to Judge Ward give you instructions. These instructions included the instruction that defendants do not need to prove their innocence. That is not how American courts work. The judge also instructed you that the defendant is not required to testify, and whether the defendant testifies or not, is no indication of guilt."

"Now, we don't need to prove who did kill Mr. Baron here today – that's pure Matlock style television drama, but we will go ahead and show that there is no evidence against my client."

"That's the take-away message I want all of you jurors to focus on during this trial. I want all of you to keep asking yourself, as the parade of witnesses, experts and testimony is presented, I want you thinking and asking, "where is the evidence?" he said, with his voice reaching a dramatic crescendo.

"And when you come to the same conclusion that I have – that there is no evidence of my client's guilt *nor any participation* in this crime at all, then you will find her innocent, here in this court of law, away from outside influence, media reporting and everything else. That is your solemn duty, and I am glad to have you all here with us today," he finished, with a small bow to the jurors.

Kisha Mack felt like cheering when Lee finished his opening. She was so proud of her boss. Marnie too, in the gallery taking notes, was blown away by the force of his opening statement. He had thrown down the gauntlet.

Judge Ward called a short recess after the opening statements, to speak to both attorneys in chambers. Once Jose Leon, Sabrina Price, Carrie Bryant, Kisha Mack, and Lee Filderman were in his chambers, Judge Ward unleashed a verbal barrage.

"Hey, now all of you, be quiet and listen!" His raised voice surprised the attorneys and he thundered, "I don't care about your political ambitions or your weekend hobbies, but I won't have all of these junior theatrics! Counselors Leon, Filderman, those performances of yours were disgraceful! Jose Leon, last I heard, you were born and raised in St. Paul, Minnesota, not Piedy Holler, Tennessee. You aren't Barney Fife or good ole Andy Taylor, so I better not hear you doing that whole 'Aunt Bee' routine again." The judge's face was taut and red-tinged with his anger.

He turned to face Lee Filderman, saying, "And you! You aren't Johnny Cochran either. You need to tone down your rhetoric, and probably your wardrobe too. I'll not have a mistrial on my hands because of the likes of you two clowns!"

Jose Leon looked chastened, but Lee Filderman seemed to get a twinkle in his eye when he said, "Yes, Your Honor." As the bailiff led the five of them back to the courtroom, Kisha could almost swear there was a new spring in Lee's step. He confirmed it when he leaned over and whispered, gleefully, "Did you hear that? He compared me to Johnny Cochran!" Kisha just rolled her eyes in response.

****

Judge Ward's demeanor on returning to the courtroom gave no hint as to his previous tongue lashing. He appeared almost bored as the prosecution called their first witness.

Marnie watched closely as the first prosecution witness took the stand, but then Detective Renee Payne seemed almost calculated to catch the eye as she sashayed over to the witness box. She was dressed in a very feminine, light-rose colored suit that seemed designed to contrast with her prominently placed police badge at her waist, along with the hint of a shoulder holster, (though presumably empty,) still reminded observers of the casual violence of law enforcement. The suit pants clung to every curve, while the jacket hung open, showing a skin-tight, floral printed, crisscross style blouse that emphasized her ample cleavage. A simple gold cross necklace, small diamond stud earrings and a delicate gold colored watch served as her only jewelry. Her shoes, at least were no-nonsense block pumps in a nude color. As she was sworn in, square shaped nails in a delicate French manicure rested on the worn, courthouse Bible.

Sabrina Price gently led her through introductions and background, as Ms. Payne explained to the judge and jury that she had been a police officer with Memphis Metropolitan Police Department for six years after graduating from Central High School and taking criminal justice courses online at Austin Peay State University.

"And how long have you been a detective in the homicide division?" Sabrina asked.

"Three years," Renee answered, smiling at the assistant district attorney.

"That seems quite fast – to make detective, isn't it?" Sabrina asked.

"Well, yes. It can take some people about a decade to make detective," Renee admitted proudly, "but I scored so well on the detective exam that they let me join the homicide division right away. Most people have to do a stint in burglary or narcotics first."

"Very impressive," Sabrina stated, knowing that the defense would rather not make petty seeming objections early in the case, while the jury was still getting to know everyone.

Now that they had established Detective Payne's bonafides, Sabrina quickly moved to the murder, asking, "When did you become acquainted with the victim, Hunter Lee Baron III?"

Detective Payne answered quickly, "I first encountered the decedent on the afternoon of March 17th, of this year, 2022. Emergency services had received a call a little while earlier after his girlfriend discovered him in his apartment. Very quickly after a patrolman viewed the scene, the homicide division was assigned to the case, and I got a call to come to the address."

"What was your immediate impression on arriving on the scene, Detective Payne?" Sabrina asked.

"My first impression was that it wasn't a fresh crime scene. There was an extensive amount of insect activity, and the body was not in the initial stages of decomposition," Renee answered.

"Would you explain a bit more what you mean by not in the 'initial stages'?" Sabrina asked using finger quotes. Out of the corner of her eye, she saw a juror smile at that. She also saw several audience members lean forward in anticipation of Detective Payne's response.

"Well, you could tell that the victim had been dead for a while. All of the blood at the crime scene was dry, and the corpse was discolored. The bacteria and insects had already started to feast on him, so the speak," Renee said, with a bit of relish.

"What other immediate impression did you have, Detective Payne?" Sabrina asked.

"That whoever killed Mr. Baron really hated him. This was a crime of hate. There was a lot of violence in this scene. Blood was everywhere, coating the room. It wasn't something easy like a gunshot wound," Detective Payne answered.

'Objection – calls for speculation!" the defense called. "A crime of hate? It seems like our detective is a bit dramatic herself or maybe a budding novelist, hmmm," Lee said with a nod of his head towards where Marnie and the other journalists were sitting.

"Your Honor," Sabrina answered, "Wouldn't a homicide detective know what she's describing? If she says it's a crime of hate, then I would assume she knows what she's talking about."

Lee directly addressed Sabrina, "That's just ridiculous! Couldn't you describe almost any homicide or assault as a crime of hate, then? I mean, it's not like bashing someone in the head during a robbery as a crime of love, now, is it? This terminology clutters the crime scene. Let the forensic examiner be the one to tell us about the injuries."

"Sustained," Judge Ward ruled, "the witness can describe the scene without making her own interpretations. Now proceed!"

"The crime scene was messier than most, Sir," Detective Payne said, addressing the judge directly. "There was a huge amount of blood, splattering the walls, coating the floors, and caked on every visible surface. A massive cluster of flies were also present, even after all the crime scene technicians were on site. They were swarming and buzzing in a way I've never seen on a body found indoors. We had to keep shoo-ing them away, but they would just circle around and return."

A few members of the audience looked squeamish at the idea. Sabrina took a minute to look at her notes, letting the jury think about the idea while she prepared to ask her next question.

"Is there anything else you could tell us that you noticed straight away about the crime scene?" she pressed, "Were there signs of forced entry into the apartment? Or signs of a struggle?"

Detective Payne answered carefully, "There wasn't any sign of forced entry. The front door was intact, and there were no signs of a struggle in the rest of the apartment. He was found in his bedroom, and it didn't look like he'd been dragged there or forced there by anyone. There was no blood or marks anywhere in the hallways or living room, for example. There was no broken glass or furniture knocked over. There were a couple of paintings that looked askew but there was nothing to suggest that they were crooked after being disturbed during a fight or struggle. It looked like he was ambushed in his private bedroom after inviting someone in." Detective Payne finished. Lee raised an eyebrow at her final remark but didn't bother to object. Instead, he leaned over some papers and made a hashmark next to something that Marnie couldn't see clearly.

"I would like to enter these six photographs of the crime scene, photographed on March 17, 2022 as exhibit A," Sabrina said, "but first I'd like Detective Payne to take a look at them, so she can testify as to whether these photographs are an accurate representation of the crime scene as she initially saw it."

"Now that the witness has affirmed that these photographs are an accurate representation of the crime scene as she saw it on the date that the murder was discovered, I would like her to review these photos with the jury," Sabrina stated in practiced legalese.

The defense offered no objection to the photos being entered in to evidence.

The bailiff, William Bronson, was tasked with pulling down a large screen that would allow the photos to be projected and demonstrate fine details. These initial six photos, despite their subject, were not particularly graphic. The first few photos showed the bedroom in its entirety from different angles. While the victim was visible in some of the shots, he was face down without readily apparent or obvious injury. The photos seemed almost sepia toned due to the large amount of dark brown/almost chocolatey black coloring splashed across the photographs, giving the photos a 1980's filmstock feel. It wasn't until Detective Payne reviewed the photographs on the big screen, that the enormity of the brownish splashes made their impact on the jury.

 As Detective Payne pointed out brown splatter on the ceiling, and walls, she explained that these patterns indicated arterial spray. As she pointed out the almost black blood pooling, the sketch artist rapidly worked with broad strokes of chalk. As the bailiff placed the last photograph on the display, a close-up of the empty, blood-soaked wheelchair, several audience members paled and the gallery became absolutely quiet... no coughs, no throat clearing, there was even an absence of the usual sounds of deep breathing.

Sabrina held back the more close-up and gory photographs of the victim, which she was saving for later testimony.

"That's a lot of blood, isn't it?" Sabrina asked.

"Well, I am sure you will talk to him later, but the medical examiner said that it was about 95% of the victim's entire blood volume right there on that floor," Detective Payne answered.

Sabrina was surprised that the defense didn't seem to be paying attention to or objecting to any of the testimony. She couldn't help glancing over, almost waiting for an interruption, but both Lee Filderman and his assistant, Kisha, appeared to be reviewing pre-trial paperwork and making regular notations.

"Detective Payne, when did Ms. Price emerge as a suspect in this case?" Sabrina asked.

Detective Price straightened her back almost imperceptibly and answered, "Ember Price emerged as a suspect rather early in our investigation. Typically, we look closer to home for our suspects first; meaning family and loved ones but given all of his former notoriety as well as his contentious political race, tips and evidence began to point in another direction within just a few days after the body was discovered."

"So, detective, you did investigate Hunter Baron's girlfriend and his ex-wife prior to focusing on Ms. Price?" Sabrina asked.

"Of course, we did! That's murder 101. We were able to confirm his ex-wife Anita's alibi within hours of the body being found and identified. She was at her home down in Florida, which was confirmed by her family, neighbors, and co-workers at the school where she works. We also confirmed it by checking her Sun-pass toll card and corresponding video. She never left the state for the period of several weeks before the murder. She only left town afterwards, to bring their son to the funeral here in Memphis."

"As for his current girlfriend, Veronica Triana, her employers were also able to confirm her comings and goings, both by direct observation, parking lot video, and key card access. We were also able to track some of her home activity via internet logins and social media use, so she was also eliminated as a suspect within a day or two."

"So, once you eliminated his current girlfriend and his ex-wife, Detective Payne, would you lead us thru some of these tips and evidence that you mentioned that made Ms. Prince a viable suspect?" Sabrina asked.

At the defense table, Kisha silently and unseen by jurors, touched Ember Prince's hand underneath the table. They both knew what was coming, and Kisha wanted Ember to appear relaxed and unconcerned while the prosecutor waved her dirty laundry around for the whole courtroom to see.

"There were several things that were of immediate note. First off, we found a piece of woman's jewelry at the death site. It was obvious that the jewelry had been left only recently, and most probably at the time of the murder. It appeared to be very similar to known jewelry owned by Ember Prince," she answered.

"We will go back to the jewelry in a moment, Detective Payne, but could you tell me about the other evidence you found, that implicated Ember Prince in this crime?"

"The notes and the video." Detective Payne answered. "We found a series of threatening notes addressed to Hunter in his bedroom, along with multiple pornographic videos. Ember was the star of one of these videos."

"Objection! Grossly prejudicial language, Your Honor! May I approach for a sidebar?"

Judge Ward agreed, and said, "You may approach." Lee Filderman and Jose Leon approached the judge's bench.

"Your Honor, describing my client as the star of these videos is grossly prejudicial. She and multiple other women were victimized by a predatory individual who filmed them without their knowledge. Furthermore, there is evidence that at least some of these women were drugged beforehand. In fact, if Hunter Baron wasn't dead, he'd probably be up on charges for this!" Lee Filderman said in an outraged, but quiet tone.

Jose Leon shrugged, "I can't control what a witness says. She said it, we didn't."

Judge Ward looked at both attorneys, then the jurors before stating, "That last statement will be stricken from the record. The objection is sustained."

"And, Mr. Leon, I expect your witnesses to respect the court and it's rules."

Judge Ward then directly addressed Detective Payne, "And, young lady, particularly as an officer of the law, I would expect you to have more sensitivity, judgement, and class in this regard. Is this how you treat all your suspects?"

"No, Your Honor," Detective Payne said, embarrassed to be chastised thusly.

"So, you believe that these notes, along with the video containing Ember Prince in a compromising position, incriminated Ms. Prince?" Sabrina asked.

"Not only that," Detective Payne answered, "but I believe the videos are directly tied to the motive for the crime. Mr. Baron was killed to prevent other people from seeing these videos, which would have destroyed Ms. Prince's political campaign."

"Do you have any proof of this?" Sabrina asked.

"Yes," Detective Payne answered looking very confident.

"What is the proof that these videos were the motive for this crime?" Sabrina asked.

"The notes." Detective Payne answered succinctly.

Sabrina Price approached the witness stand, so she could re-direct this case back to the suspect at hand. "Okay. Let's talk about these notes that you mentioned, Detective Payne. How many notes were they?"

"Well, there were actually two different kinds of notes," Detective Payne answered.

"Tell me about the first kind of note," Sabrina Price asked.

"The notes are a series of emails. The first set of emails are from the victim. He sent these emails to the campaign office of the suspect, Ms. Ember Prince," Detective Payne answered.

"How many notes or emails were there?" Sabrina asked.

"Three." Detective Payne answered.

"I would like to enter as Exhibit B, printed copies of emails sent to the campaign office of Ember Prince." Sabrina Price stated, handing several pieces of paper to the witness.

"So entered," Judge Ward answered.

"Detective Payne, would you please read the first of these emails to the suspect, Ember Prince?" Sabrina asked.

Objection! Facts not in evidence! The prosecution has not established that these emails were sent to the defendant. They have stated that the emails arrived to an email address of the campaign office. There is no proof that this was our client's email, or that she ever even saw these emails," Kisha Mack roared, surprising just about everyone in the courtroom.

"Sustained," Judge Ward ruled, "the prosecution should refrain from referring to these emails improperly unless and until proper evidence is established to prove otherwise."

Sabrina Price continued unperturbed, re-phrasing the question. "Detective Payne, would you read the first of the emails?"

"Dear sweet, delicious Ember," she started.

"Such a lovely, juicy time we had so not very long ago. I've been waiting for your call, dirty girl, so we can play again. If you don't remember all the fun we had, here's a link to a small reminder," she finished, with her face expressionless.

"Where did the link take you?" Sabrina asked the detective.

"When we followed the link, it took us to his Google drive with the video of Ember Prince in his bedroom." Detective Payne said cautiously. Renee didn't want to ignite the ire of the judge again.

"Was the email signed, Detective Payne?" Sabrina asked.

"Yes, it was signed, The Hunter, with a winking emoji." Renee answered.

"After reading this email, what was your professional assessment?" Sabrina asked.

"I thought this note was taunting her. He was threatening her with exposure." Detective Payne answered.

"What were the other two emails from the victim?" Sabrina asked.

"The second and third notes from Hunter Baron were demands for money. He wrote that if he didn't receive forty thousand dollars from Ember Prince before March 15th, that he was going to publish these videos to the web and send copies to everyone on her campaign donation roster. He said he had hacked her servers and would send copies to everyone she knew. He also threatened to immediately release the video if she went to the police." Detective Payne answered.

"The third email was a reminder of the deadline, with a list of the media organizations he planned to target, including CNN, Fox

News, and several local stations. He even attached a press release that he intended to include." Detective Payne stated, holding up a separate piece of paper.

"In your professional opinion, did this seem like a valid threat?" Sabrina asked.

"It certainly did!" Detective Payne answered.

"Do you think that this would be a motive for someone like Ember Prince to murder Hunter Baron?" Sabrina Price asked.

"Objection! Calls for speculation!" Kisha Mack called.

"Your Honor, this is about motive. These emails clearly establish motive, and we will prove that!" Sabrina Price retorted.

"Overruled, you may continue." Judge Ward ruled.

"Let me repeat the question." Sabrina said. "Now, Detective Payne, in your experience as a homicide detective, do you think that these notes, these emails would serve as a motive for Ember Prince to murder Hunter Baron?"

"Absolutely," Detective Payne answered.

"Do you have any proof of that?" Sabrina asked.

"Yes." Detective Payne answered, confidently.

"Tell me about your proof that the notes Hunter Baron sent served as motive for his murder?" Sabrina asked.

"Just look at the email replies." Detective Payne answered.

"Okay, Let's do that, shall we." Sabrina said with almost childlike enthusiasm.

"Your Honor, I'd like to enter these documents to exhibit B as B4, B5 and B6." Sabrina said, as she handed the documents to Detective Payne.

"What was the date of the first email sent from Hunter Baron?" Sabrina asked.

"March 1st at 2:06 am." Detective Payne answered.

"And when did the first reply arrive?" Sabrina Price asked.

"The first email reply arrived at 10:30 am on the same date." Detective Payne answered.

"Please read the reply." Sabrina answered.

"Blackmail is a class D felony in the state of Tennessee and carries a sentence of up to 12 years in jail. Are you certain that you want to continue this course?" Detective Payne recited.

"There is no salutation, nor signature on the email note." Detective Payne concluded.

"Can you review what happened next, Detective Payne?" Sabrina asked.

"The second email from Hunter Baron's computer arrived on March 4th at 8:45pm. This is the email that threatened to hack her servers. This email also indicated that the files had been potentially sent to one or more of the contacts from the Ember Prince donor list."

"So, between March 1st at 1030 in the morning up to March 4th – the police didn't receive a call or report regarding these threats?" Sabrina asked.

"No, and we suspect that's the reason for the gap between emails. Hunter Baron was calling her bluff. Once he realized that the police weren't coming to his door, he continued his campaign against Ember Prince." Detective Payne answered.

"Objection. This reply should be stricken. This is pure speculation on their part – she says so herself!" Kisha Mack argued.

"Overruled. Defense counsel, let me remind you, that you will have a chance to address each of these points during cross-examination, so wait your turn," Judge Ward ruled, looking sternly at Kisha. Chastened, Kisha looked at Lee who nodded. They couldn't afford to aggravate this judge any further.

"What happened next?" Sabrina asked, outwardly appearing to ignore the exchange, but inwardly cheering.

"An email was sent from the Ember Prince campaign office at 9:15 the same evening. In the email, she agrees to meet his demands, and asks for a few days to gather the money," Detective Payne answered.

Kisha wanted to object to the characterization as to the author of the emailed note – but she looked at Lee and kept her mouth shut.

"The third email from Hunter Baron arrived, a few days later, correct?"

"Yes," Detective Payne stated, "it arrived March 9th and appeared to be a reminder that he would expose her to the media if he didn't receive payment."

"And did the police receive any calls regarding these emails or threats during this period?" Sabrina asked.

"No, we did not." Detective Payne answered.

"There is one more reply to this email demand, isn't there?" Sabrina asked.

"Yes, the last email sent from Ember Prince's office was dated March 11th, and it discussed arranging a meeting place to complete the transaction." Detective Payne answered.

"Did the email give a time or place for the transaction?" Sabrina asked.

"Yes, in the email she stated that she would hand over the money that evening at 10pm. It did not mention a location," Detective Payne answered.

"And, when exactly was Hunter Baron killed?" Sabrina asked.

"We believe he was killed on the night of the 11th." Detective Payne answered.

Sabrina nodded slowly, looking at the jury.

"Did you seize and search any of the computers in Ember Prince's campaign office?" Sabrina asked.

"Yes, we did." Detective Payne answered.

"And did you find anything else of interest on these computers?" Sabrina asked.

"Yes, we found an additional note that corresponded to one we found on Hunter Baron's computer." Detective Payne answered.

"Would you please explain?" Sabrina asked.

"The first emails from the deceased, Hunter Baron, were sent directly from his email account to an account in the campaign office. The replies were sent directly from the campaign office email. But, the last note which we initially found on Hunter Baron's email inbox came from a separate account, a burner email account set up on proton mail," Detective Payne explained.

"So, just to clarify, because I am not a tech person," Sabrina said, with a bit of a wrinkled brow, "you found this email on BOTH computers. You found it in the victim's inbox, as well as a copy on the hard drive of one of the computers seized from the campaign office?" Sabrina asked.

"Yes." Detective Payne answered.

"Is there any reason that a copy of an email sent to Hunter Baron would be found on a campaign computer?" Sabrina Price asked.

"The only reason that a copy of this email would be found on the hard drive, is that the email was written and sent from the campaign office computer." the detective answered.

"We would like to enter a copy of this email as Exhibit B-7, Your Honor," Sabrina stated.

She handed a copy of the printed note to Detective Payne, stating, "Please read this note in its entirety, Detective Payne."

"Fuck you, you evil motherfucker. You will get what is coming to you, and soon you will be just another rancid pile of garbage," Detective Payne said with minimal inflection in her voice.

"No, no, no! I don't think you read that properly. Read it with spirit, detective!" Sabrina stated.

"Objection! Asked and answered. This isn't high school theater," Kisha Mack called.

"Overruled, I'll allow it," Judge Ward ruled.

"Now, give me some venom, some hate, Detective Payne. The jury needs to really hear how this note reads!" Sabrina said.

At the defense table, Kisha Mack looked annoyed but tried to maintain a bland expression. Lee Filderman succeeded in looking bored, and Ember maintained her neutral expression, while inside she was acutely interested.

"Fuck you, motherfucker!" Detective Payne lashed out in an almost yell, then looked embarrassed.

Sabrina indicated she should continue.

"You will get what you have coming to you," Detective Payne read thru gritted teeth, "and soon you will be just another pile of rancid garbage."

"Wonderful, wonderful!" Sabrina said, clapping her hands. "Now, what date was that email sent?"

"March 10th." Detective Payne answered.

"I see," Sabrina said, in measured tones, before saying, "the prosecution has no more questions for this witness."

Judge Ward looked at this watch, and stated, "it's 11:45. I think we should take an hour lunch break before the defense starts their cross-examination. Let's meet back at five minutes to one everyone, so we can start promptly at one pm." He banged the gavel, and rose from the bench quickly and left, while the bailiff was still calling for the audience to rise.

"I couldn't have said it better." Lee Filderman quipped, "We have an urgent call we need to make."

"We do?" Kisha said. "Of course we do." she answered herself laughing.

"First, pull that list of potential witnesses out of the file folder there, and let me check something," Lee stated.

"You mean this list of 379 people, including all of the prosecutions' witnesses, several employees in the district attorney's office, multiple members of law enforcement, my local postmaster, the entire extended Prince family, notable Memphis business associates and some so-called Instagram celebrities?" Kisha said with laughter in her voice, as she handed over a tightly typewritten list that extended for multiple pages.

"Yes, that list, exactly!" Lee said as he scanned the list looking for one name, in particular. He pointed to a name and address on the list, and said, "Kisha – I'll make sure you get lunch, but I need you to contact this person – and get a subpoena, if necessary. It won't necessarily mean anything, but I want you to have it in hand before you contact the consulate, and the foreign press if needed. They don't have to honor it, but I am hoping, in the name of international cooperation and public relations, that they will."

Kisha's eyebrows rose a little, as she looked at the name and address. She didn't recall the name except as a brief mention in one of the pre-trial interview notes, but she didn't remember any other details. She hustled off to get started on the task.

Marnie

Marnie watched the exchange between Lee and Kisha but couldn't hear what they were saying, as the people around her began to exit the courtroom. As she was leaving the courtroom, Marnie saw a middle-aged man she faintly recognized exiting the benches usually reserved for the family of the victim. He saw her looking at him and smiled. She caught up to him, and he introduced himself. "Um, Hi. I don't think you remember me; I was at the funeral. You're that journalist, that wrote the first book about Hunter Baron, right? My goodness, I am rambling," he said.

"I'm Marnie Gellhorn," I said, shaking his hand as we proceeded out of the courthouse.

"Oh, I am so sorry, I completely forgot to tell you my name. I'm Albert Fin. I married Anita, Hunter's ex-wife. I am here as part of a compromise between Anita and myself," he said.

"How about I buy you lunch from one of the food trucks outside – and you can tell me all about it," I offered.

"That would be lovely," Albert answered graciously. "This situation is kind of strange, so it helps to talk about it."

"It's a Thursday, so there will be a lot of food trucks to pick from. I bet that's the real reason the judge let us out so early." I said.

We went to a Mexican food truck, before stopping at a BBQ food truck so I could get some pulled pork. I would have rather had ribs because well, I always want the ribs, but I didn't think a barbecue smeared face and shirt would be a good look for my first day in the gallery. It's not like I could really enjoy ribs without making a mess, and believe me, I've tried.

We settled down at a bench in Court Square Park near the iconic fountain. The park was bustling with people as we approached the lunch hour, and it made for some fine people watching as we started to eat.

"So, I do remember you from the funeral, Albert. I remember feeling so bad for David because I knew he had such a complicated relationship with Hunter, but I was glad to see what a supportive father you were," I said.

"Yeah, that's kind of how I ended up here at the trial, in the family section, of all places," he answered. "It feels awkward because there was no love lost between Hunter and I, but I am here for David. That poor kid has so much baggage from Hunter. I mean, I think he figured out fairly early that he was really only a prop for Hunter, but it hasn't been easy. He acts like he's fine these days, but I know that he's struggling. This whole thing; his manipulative dad, absentee father, the trial over the death of his grandmother, and now the murder of his dad. All of this must be devastating but David doesn't want to talk about it," Albert said.

"I can't even imagine. It must be difficult on Anita too. I know he was an abusive spouse, but still, an untimely death just leaves things unsettled, re-opens old hurts," I answered.

"That's actually what this compromise is about. I really thought it would be good for David to come to the trial, and get some closure, but Anita thinks it would be too traumatizing. I think she is also concerned that a lot of really negative things are going to come out about Hunter, and she still trying to protect David." Albert stated.

"I'm not sure how much more damaging information can come out at this point," I answered. "I mean, after his trial last year, but then again, look at what they were talking about today. So, I guess I can see Anita's point", I conceded. I personally agreed more with Albert, but it wasn't my child.

"So, at least this way, I am taking notes, and I can answer some of David's questions, and maybe be a counterpoint to all the blurbs on the news. They just eat up the grisly aspects of it. I never forget that this is David's dad, so I think that will help. One day he will be old enough to read your articles, but right now, it's too easy for him to only see the most sensational stuff…the drivel that crowds the internet!" he answered.

"I hope my writings brings him some comfort one day, then," I answered, somewhat awkwardly.

"It will, It will. You humanized everyone in the story and that's important." he answered.

We finished our lunches in a comfortable silence while we people watched, before heading back to the courtroom.

It was a weird feeling for me, because I hadn't had to confront what my writing felt like for the people I wrote about in a long time. When I was a journalist overseas, most of the people I wrote about never even saw my stories. The few that did, often didn't speak English. But I was writing about war, conflict and human suffering, so most of the time, the people in my stories just wanted the world to know that they existed… that they loved, laughed, cried, felt pain, and suffered like everyone else.

This was a little different, and it bore thinking about. I was still deep in my thoughts as I entered the courtroom and sat in my seat. Maria Mack, the sketch artist showed me a few of her sketches from the morning session, including one of the defense attorney, Lee Filderman with an impish grin after one of his exchanges. It made me laugh, knowing that he was just getting started for the day.

First day of trial, defense cross-examination begins

"So, are you are a lifelong Memphian, Ms. Payne?" Lee said, asking some softball questions to establish himself as a gentleman to the jury.

"Yes, sir!" she stated crisply. Detective Payne had no intention of allowing this shyster to make her look silly.

"So am I. It's a beautiful city, isn't it?" he said, with a sigh.

"Yes, sir." she answered.

"Didn't you have any big-time career aspirations? I mean, I thought law enforcement officers always wanted the Los Angeles or New York beat, so to speak?" Lee asked.

Detective Payne looked at Lee, with an almost visible eye roll, as if he was the stupidest man alive, before answering with an almost frustrated sign. "No, that makes no sense. First off, the beat, as you called it, is for rookie cops doing neighborhood patrol. I tested out of basic patrol almost right away. Secondly, if you want to do big city homicide, then Memphis is the place. Better experience than Detroit, Chicago, even New York." she answered a touch huffily.

She wasn't looking at the jury when she answered, but Marnie was, and Marnie saw that Lee Filderman had scored a point. By letting her frustration show over such a minor issue, jurors were now wary of the young homicide detective. She also saw Kisha Mack seeming to follow along with Lee's cross-examination as she consulted notes on a legal pad, but the defense team didn't seem to be keeping score, at least not overtly. Very quickly, Lee Filderman moved on to his next point.

"You know, I have been making small notations throughout your testimony, little things here and there, that I wanted to ask you more about. I was going to move on to my next point but I think we need to address the elephant in the room first. I think we need to talk about the real reason my client is even in this courtroom today, and that's you and your *crime of hate* against her," Lee said.

"Objection, badgering the witness!" Jose Leon called.

"Overruled, I'll allow it." Judge Ward said.

"Let's start off with your contention that my client, Ember Prince, is a willing participant in these so-called adult films that the crime technicians found. Isn't it true that my client had no knowledge that she was being filmed?" Lee asked.

"That is what she claimed, but you know, she did used to claim to be an actress." Detective Payne answered sourly.

"On what evidence do you base this belief? Can she be seen mugging for the camera? Posing herself in more attractive angles? Making love to the camera, is what they call it in Hollywood? Is there any evidence that she even knew it was there?" Lee Filderman demanded.

"How should I know?" Detective Payne answered petulantly, "I'm not a film director."

"But you are a detective!" Lee answered shortly.

Lee Filderman appeared to be getting more and more frustrated with this witness, but in reality, he couldn't be more pleased with her demeanor. It made his contention of malicious prosecution all the more believable. In fact, the more he had to deal with this police detective, the more he began to believe it himself.

"I want a yes or no answer to my next questions, Detective Payne." he said, speaking slowly and deliberately.

"Does my client appear to be looking at the camera?" he asked.

"No." she answered.

"Does she appear like she could be altered, drunk or drugged? As in, Does she look uncoordinated, clumsy or unsteady?" he asked.

"I don't know." she answered.

"Did she look drowsy, or confused?" Lee asked.

"I don't know." she answered stubbornly.

"Isn't it true, that during a previous conversation, you voluntarily stated *that she looks really out-of-it, she looks like she can barely stand?*" he asked, quoting from his notes.

"I guess so then." she answered.

"Isn't it true that placement of the camera was deliberately hidden from anyone who might be entering the room?" he asked.

"Yeah." she answered.

"Isn't it true that several of the women that you have managed to identify on the videos report that they believe they were unwillingly drugged?" he asked, voice steady.

"Yes." she answered.

"And isn't it also true that none of these women had previously consented to have sexual relations with Mr. Baron?" he asked.

"Yes, I think so." she answered.

"It's also true, isn't it, that not one single woman identified on this series of disgusting videos had consented to being filmed?" he asked.

"Yes." she answered.

"Now, knowing all of this, didn't you, just here today, in this courtroom, suggest that my client was a willing and consenting participant?" he asked, voice rising slightly with indignation.

"Yes!" she answered, defiantly.

"So then why are you confused or unsure about the circumstances behind my client?" he asked. Before she could answer, he continued, "Or did you knowingly slander my client's reputation in a court of law, knowing that she is on trial for her very life?" Lee asked, his voice incredulous.

Several jurors leaned forward to await her response.

"I guess I was confused." she answered, looking at the floor.

"Well, let me clear that up for you, as my client has stated multiple times to you, in fact, in my presence, that she had no memory of ever even agreeing to go to Hunter Baron's apartment. She did not consent to any sort of sexual activity with Hunter Baron, nor would she ever consent for any kind of recordings of such acts. She didn't even know that there was a recording of such a thing until such information was discovered during this very investigation, in your pursuit of her as a suspect." he finished, shaking his head in disgust before continuing to question the witness. "Now, let's move on." he finished.

Detective Renee Payne, in her form-fitting and tailored feminine suit, remained silent and stoic during his scolding but she looked over angrily at the Prosecutor's table. Shouldn't they be objecting or something while this jerk was hassling her up here? She managed to look bored while she waited for his next question, shifting in the witness chair, and sliding back a bit into a more comfortable position.

"Detective Payne, how many other women from the videotapes did you interview?" Lee asked.

"We interviewed all of the women that we were able to identify. Eighteen, I believe," Renee Payne answered.

"How many of these women did you suspect of killing the victim?" Lee asked.

"None." Renee answered.

"But, if being on this video is my client's supposed motive for the murder, doesn't it make sense that other women could be equally suspect?" Lee pressed.

"We didn't find any of the other women to be suspect." Detective Payne answered.

"Why is that, Detective Payne?" Lee inquired.

"There were lots of reasons." Renee answered.

"Objection, Your Honor, witness is being nonresponsive!" Lee said.

Judge Ward addressed Detective Payne, "Answer the question."

"Sir, there were eighteen other women, and most of them didn't know anything about being filmed, thus no motive." Detective Payne answered.

"Wait. So, when these women said they had no idea they were filmed that meant that they had no motive, but when my client admitted to being in the dark about the filming, it somehow made her more of a suspect? How does that work?" Lee asked.

"Well, that's easy." Renee said, almost flippantly. "Your client is an actress. When she said she didn't know about the films, we didn't believe her."

"Why didn't you believe my client?" Lee asked.

"Objection, badgering, I mean, argumentative." Carrie called, still trying to get her confidence back.

"Badgering! How is it badgering to know why she has persecuted my client to the point that she's on trial defending herself from first degree murder charges?" Lee demanded.

"Overruled." Judge Ward ruled.

"We have it on good authority and evidence that Ember Prince knew about the videos before the murder." Detective Payne responded.

"Just like the other three women who knew about the films, Hunter Baron had attempted to blackmail my client. That's what you've been trying to avoid disclosing. Isn't it true that Hunter Baron attempted to blackmail and extort four women on these videos, not just my client?" Lee pressed, tired of her evasions.

"Yes," she admitted, "the victim did contact a couple of the women regarding the videos."

"Isn't it true that his attempt to blackmail my client was intercepted by her father's security officer?" Lee asked.

"That's what he claimed," Detective Payne answered, "but then we discovered the emails."

"He's happy to testify under oath, Detective. Would that change your mind?" Lee asked.

"Objection, argumentative. Your Honor, how is she supposed to answer that question!" Sabrina argued.

"Overruled, and honestly," Judge Ward answered, "I am getting tired of this petty back and forth."

"Detective Payne, if the head of security for the Jack Prince household testified under oath, would that convince you that Ember Prince had no knowledge of the blackmail attempt?" Lee said, practically gritting his teeth.

"I'm sorry, but no, it wouldn't," she answered.

"So you believe he would perjur himself –"

"Objection, argumentative! Asked and answered, Your Honor." Sabrina said.

"Sustained. Defense has made their point." Judge Ward ruled. "Now ask something else."

"Did you interrogate the other women who were being blackmailed by Hunter Baron?" Lee asked.

"The other women had solid alibis." Detective Payne answered. Lee sighed, shrugged his shoulders, and looked at the jury like, "See?" before approaching the witness stand again to look closely at Detective Payne. He paused in front of the witness stand and made direct eye contact with the young detective long enough for her to become uncomfortable and look away.

"Let's talk about these notes or emails you referred to earlier." Lee said. "You said you were able to see that several responses to a blackmail attempt were traced to a computer in my client's campaign headquarters. Was it her personal computer in her private office?" he asked.

"No." Detective Payne said.

"The laptop she frequently carried from home?" Lee asked.

"No." Detective Payne answered.

"Then, what computer was it?" Lee asked

"The email was found on the hard drive of one of the desktops in the reception area of the campaign quarters." Detective Payne answered.

"So, it was written on a computer in the area where the secretaries who answer the phones sit?" Lee said.

"Yes." she answered.

"Did you interview all of the secretaries and ask if they had written the email?" Lee asked.

"No." Detective Payne answered.

"But that email address was the main email contact for the campaign, correct? I have here that it was ElectEmberPrice@gmail.com." Lee asked.

"Yes, that's correct." Detective Payne said, stone-faced.

"Do you know how many individuals have access to this email account?" Lee asked.

"No." she answered, still defiant.

"The answer is six people: three secretaries and three volunteers. They rotate who answers and manages the inbox. It's even marked on the main white board in the office." Lee said.

"Is there a question?" Jose Leon interjected.

"Do you know who Trenivius Alexander is?" Lee asked.

"That's the suspect's personal assistant, I believe." Detective Payne answered, a bit petulantly.

"Did you know that Trenivius Alexander was assigned to answer emails on the day the first email arrived?" Lee asked.

"No!" Renee answered, now openly hostile.

"Would it surprise you to know that Trenivius Alexander later volunteered to take over the inbox duties for the general campaign email?" Lee persisted.

"I suppose so." Renee said sourly.

"Then again, as you said, you never interviewed Trenivius Alexander, correct? Lee asked.

"That's correct." Renee answered.

Lee looked at the jury before moving on.

"You said, according to my notes, Detective Payne, that it was an 'old, messy crime scene'. You also said that 'it was a crime of hate'. I know you said that because we argued a bit about it, but now I want to go back to that. So, in your opinion as a young homicide detective, the scene was a crime of hate. Did you base that on the amount of blood or the types of injuries sustained by the victim?" Lee asked.

Detective Payne visibly bristled as the defense attorney repeated the term 'crime of hate'. She was beginning to regret that she had coined the phrase. "There was a massive amount of blood on the scene." she said. "If you remember the photos, you can see what I am referring to." she answered.

"So, a large amount of blood equals a crime of hate?" Lee asked seemingly perplexed.

"What else made this a crime of hate? Was it the rest of the scene? As you testified, the remainder of the apartment showed no sign of struggle." Lee asked.

"The mechanism of murder – that was a definite sign of hate." Detective Payne replied.

"Now, let's say that I go along with this argument, Detective Payne. According to this, a gunshot wound to the back of the head, that's not hate – that's just business, right? But multiple stabbing wounds, that would be hate?" Lee asked.

"Yes." she said, nodding at the same time.

"And how many stab wounds did the victim have?" Lee asked.

"One." she answered.

Detective Payne was surprised when Lee shifted focus again, saying, "Now, let's go back to the messy part again. You said there were no signs of a struggle outside of the bedroom." He looked over at Judge Ward and addressed the court, "I'd like to admit a series of photographs taken by the crime scene photographers shortly after the body was discovered on March 17, 2023. These photographs show the general state of the apartment, and include the hallways, kitchen and other living areas. I would like to admit these photos into evidence as defense exhibit A after Detective Payne reviews these photos with us, if there are no objections."

Once again, Bailiff Bronson pulled down the large projection screen.

"Will you verify that these two photos are of the decedent's living room, Detective Payne?" the defense attorney questioned.

"Yes, this appears to be the living room of the victim, Hunter Baron III." she answered.

"Now, what's that large white item on the floor?" he asked.

"That appears to be a replica of Michelangelo's statue of Moses." she answered.

"Ah, a student of art! How lovely!" Lee said with a genuine smile. "Not the famous David but still a notable work indeed. Now, it looks to me like the statue is laying on its side. How do you think it got that way?" he asked.

"As you can see from the pictures, our victim wasn't much of a housekeeper. We think that the statue may have been laying there for anywhere from a couple of days to a week before he died. His neighbor reported that he had a loud get-together about a week before he was discovered. We expect that this statue and some of the other debris in the apartment was left over from the party and unrelated to his murder." she answered.

"But you checked the figurine, right? I mean, it looks like a handy implement to bash someone's skull in, to me." he pressed.

"Yes, one of our officers checked it for blood when they arrived on the scene." Detective Payne answered, with irritation seeping into her voice.

"Did he find any?" Lee asked.

"No, he didn't see any blood." she answered, now openly frustrated.

"So, did they take it to the lab?" Lee insisted.

"No. There was no sign it has been used as a weapon, so they didn't collect it for the lab." Detective Payne answered warily.

"Hmm. Well, that's interesting, because sometimes particles of stuff like blood can end up being really, really small. Too small to see with a naked eye even." Lee mused.

"Objection, speculation!" hollered the prosecuting attorney.

"But, is it speculation if I introduce this report into evidence?" Lee asked, rhetorically before continuing, "I mean, after reviewing these photographs, one of our private investigators contacted the apartment manager, and well, he just felt so strongly about it that he documented the full chain of custody, before he took several items from the apartment to a private lab. It's all documented in the letter we sent the prosecutor's office." Lee said innocently.

Judge Ward's eyes flashed with anger as he said, "I'll allow it, but keep the theatrics to a minimum, counselor. You've already been warned, next time it's contempt!"

"In that case, I'd like my assistant attorney, Ms. Mack, to introduce this lab report, dated March of this year, into evidence. First, let's have Detective Payne read the summary findings." Lee Filderman said before yielding the floor to Kisha Mack.

Kisha Mack stood and approached the bench, providing one copy of the document to the judge and then handing the second copy to Detective Payne.

"I object to this document being admitted into evidence," Jose Leon called out. "This is a violation of proper procedure," he added.

"Oh wait, I have something else for you too." Ms. Mack said to Jose Leon, as she handed him the receipt for a certified letter delivered to the Prosecutor's Office on March 28th. I have an affidavit from the postal worker who helped me prepare the letter as well." she said, handing him a third document.

She continued as the prosecutor looked over the documents he'd been handed, saying, "She witnessed and initialed the bottom of the letter, too. If you return to the first document, the letter, you will see the initials W.S.R on the bottom corner. That stands for Wilhemina Smith-Robinson, who is the head postmaster at the post office at 5821 Park Avenue. You know, the branch right by St. Francis Hospital. " Kisha finished, her heart beating wildly in her chest. She hoped she wasn't alienating the judge and committing career suicide. She handed the copies of the second and third documents to the Bailiff to bring to the judge.

Judge Ward, far from being annoyed with Kisha Mack, appeared impressed, stating, "You may proceed."

"Detective Payne, would you please read the lines at the top of the letter that outline the items submitted to the Delta 5 Forensics Laboratories in Roswell, Georgia?" Kisha asked sweetly.

"This letter is to acknowledge and review the results of the following items which were submitted for forensic analysis. These items are one Volterra alabaster statue of Italian origin, that is a replica of Michelangelo's Moses sculpture, one intact wine glass with a small amount of burgundy colored fluid enclosed separately, and six remainders of partially smoked cigarettes." Detective Payne recited.

"Now can you read the summary paragraph regarding the Moses sculpture?" Kisha asked, her voice pleasant and friendly as ever.

Detective Payne returned to the letter and began to recite, "There was a small amount of damage to the front of the sculpture's head, with minor chipping of the hairline. Small chips were also seen in the figurine's beard. Under a microscope, and with the application of luminol, microscopic flecks of blood were detected in the chipped areas with a Kastle-Meyer test. This was confirmed with a Teichmann test. The amount of blood detected and obtained was insufficient for full DNA analysis."

Detective Payne stopped reading aloud for a moment before being prompted to continue by Ms. Mack. "However," Detective Payne continued, "DNA and fingerprint analysis of the base of the statue detected several sets of fingerprints and two definitive sets of perspiration DNA, both male. One set of fingerprints and sweat DNA corresponded with the DNA of Hunter Lee Baron, which was submitted for comparison. The other DNA remains unidentified, but was of male chromosomes, and of Eastern Eurasian origin within the subset of Haplogroup N (M231). This unknown male DNA was also identified in 2 of the six cigarettes in the area around the filter." Detective Payne paused and took a breath before continuing, "The remaining four cigarettes contained DNA matching the DNA of the subject submitted for DNA comparison, Hunter Lee Baron." Detective Payne paused again, as her eyes widened and continued to scan the remainder of the letter.

"Detective Payne, I know this is a bit tedious, but I have just one more section I'd like you to read," Kisha said. "Would you please read the section regarding the wine glass?"

Detective Payne was hesitant, but began to read the last section, as instructed, "A Bordeaux style wine glass of Czechoslovakian origin was received along with 0.3cc of dark, burgundy colored fluid, which was contained in a separate, small container provided by our company. The contents of this container matched the dried contents found on the inside of the wine glass. Serial analysis of the dried residue and the liquid contents were identical in all characteristics, and appear to be from the same source, a 1997 French Bordeaux. This wine was found to have a high content of thallium salts which due to their nature and concentration, were almost certainly an intentional contamination. The concentration as determined by the liquid contents did not appear to exceed 10 mg in this small sample, but if extrapolated to 6 to 10 ounces as served in a glass of this shape and size, it would account for a 800 to 1200mg dose, which would be a sufficiently toxic and lethal dose for most adult males, without immediate and rapid treatment. After acute ingestion, the individual would have shown signs of toxicity within four to six hours." As Detective Payne paused, there were gasps from the gallery.

"In addition to the liquid contents, several fingerprints were found, including complete index and thumbprints for two distinct individuals with a partial palm print. Trace DNA was obtained from saliva on the rim of the glass. The fingerprints could not be fully identified, but the DNA again matched the male DNA previously submitted for comparison." she finished.

"Whew, that's quite a mouthful," Kisha said. "Thank you, Detective Payne, it's been a pleasure, but I have no more questions for you at this time." she smiled and added, "I would like to reserve the right to recall this witness."

As Kisha turned to go back to the defense table, she swore that Lee winked at her. If that was his way of giving her a thumbs up, she'd take it. She felt surprisingly light-hearted for being a defense attorney on the first day of a possible death penalty case.

Sabrina Price stood up at the prosecution's table and announced, "The prosecution would like to call our next witness, Dr. Andrew Robbins."

A balding, middle-aged man with greying brown fringes of hair, of average height, wearing a light tan suit with a muted tie made his way to the stand. He wore gold-rimmed, rounded spectacles, similar to those worn by John Lennon. This distinguished his otherwise average appearance. Instead of giving him a relaxed or mellow appearance, these eyeglasses confirmed his rather academic appearance. If casting for a movie, he would have been a great stand-in for a librarian or advanced physics professor, but that was due more to his serious, staid demeanor in the courtroom than any actual physical characteristic. Members of the gallery would have been greatly surprised to know that in addition to his extensive intellect and remarkable recall, he also demonstrated considerable wit, slightly on the dry side, but amusing to his friends and co-workers.

After being sworn in as the Shelby County Medical Examiner, Sabrina Price began to take him through the preliminary questions.

"Dr. Robbins, you are new here in Tennessee, aren't you?" she asked after he had given his name and credentials in the flat, unaccented tones of mid-Atlantic American English.

"Yes, I accepted this position after the unfortunate death of the previous medical examiner, Dr. Chancellor, last year. " Dr. Robbins answered.

"Where did you come from?" Sabrina asked, giving rise to the question in most of the audience's mind.

"Well, I was originally from New Jersey, of all places, but after graduating from Georgetown Medical School and completing my pathology residency, I have spent thirty years in San Diego, California," he answered.

"I was recruited here to replace Dr. Chancellor's absence. My kids are all grown up and out of the house, so my wife, Charlene and I thought that a move to Memphis would be wonderful." he said with a smile at the gallery.

"I know that my accent makes me hard to place," he added with a wry smile.

"How are you finding Memphis?" Sabrina asked, mostly to give the jury a bit more time to take the measure of the man before they delved into the meat and potatoes of the gruesome crime.

"It's amazing and intimidating." Dr. Robbins admitted. "In many ways, Memphis has such a glorious small-town feel: Sunday picnics, friendly neighbors, beautiful and stately historic homes, tree-lined avenues with veteran oaks – all the things of a John Grisham novel, and the small but lovely things that you just don't see out in California." he answered.

"Wow, Memphis is a big city too," he answered, "especially in my department. It's amazing what my predecessor was able to accomplish with such a busy city and medical examiner's office. Karen must have been an amazing person! I have so many more opportunities and resources here in Memphis than I did in San Diego." he finished.

"Well, that's just lovely to hear." Sabrina commented before asking, "How long had you been here before you were involved in this case?"

"I had been working here about 8 months before I was called to the crime scene at the Parkview Apartments." Dr. Robbins answered.

"What were your immediate impressions on entering the crime scene?" Sabrina Price asked.

"Well, I was surprised to see that the deceased wasn't an elderly person. I had thought that this apartment building was an assisted living facility." he answered.

Several of the jurors laughed. The Parkview Apartments were famous as an ultra-expensive, independent to assisted living facility for upper class seniors in Memphis. It had caused a bit of a stir when Hunter Baron had decided to purchase an apartment there. In his usual round-about-way, it had turned out that Hunter Baron had insider information on the fact that a group of real estate developers were heavily interested in the property. He had stood to make a very large profit if the massive renovation project went forward. It was ironic because Hunter Baron was widely known for his poor financial decisions, overspending, and massive credit card debt. This had been wiped out once he had received his full inheritance. Had he lived just a little while longer, he would have stood to receive a large buy out as the developers bought out the very few remaining residents who owned their individual units. The displacement of the senior citizens, and the continued gentrification and development of the mid-town area aimed at attracting young, working professionals had caused considerable controversy. The fact that out-of-state carpetbaggers had purchased the property escaped no one's notice.

Sabrina did not comment on these facts but continued her line of questioning.

"We've already seen some photographs of the crime scene, but I would now like to introduce a second series of photographs, ten in total, as exhibit B. These photographs show the victim at the crime scene as well as visual documentation of his injuries. I would like Dr. Robbins to walk us through these photographs during his testimony today," Sabrina said handing the photographs to Bailiff Bronson.

As was their usual procedure, the projection screen was lowered so that the entire courtroom could see the images in full detail.

"Dr. Robbins, would you describe for the court what we are seeing in this first photograph?" Sabrina asked.

"Certainly." Dr. Robbins answered. "In this first photograph, we are looking at a full-length view of the corpse of Hunter Baron. As you can see, he is facedown in what we call a prone position. His body isn't entirely flat on the ground, and this is because we believe that at the time he was killed, or while he was being killed, he fell out of his wheelchair. This is consistent with the blood splatter pattern that you can see here, where it arcs out, and here where it coats his wheelchair." He used a laser pointer to indicate the blood splatter on the oversized screen for the jury.

"If you look closely at the exact color of the blood, as well as the way it is spread on the ground beneath the body, it looks like he began bleeding, then fell or collapsed on the ground where he continued to bleed until he basically exsanguinated on the ground, facedown." Dr. Robbins explained.

"Can you see any visible injuries on the body in this photo?" Sabrina asked.

"There are some small injuries that appear to be some abrasions on the crown of his head, which are a bit difficult to see in this photo." Dr. Robbins answered.

"Do we know what caused these abrasions or scratches to his head?" Sabrina asked.

"We don't know definitively what caused these abrasions, but they don't appear to penetrate entirely thru the skin. There is minimal bleeding or bruising around the area." Dr. Robbins answered.

"During earlier testimony, it was suggested that an object like the statue in this photo (referring to exhibit A) may have caused injury to the deceased. Do you agree?" Sabrina asked.

Dr. Robbins examined the photo of the Moses statue for several seconds before answering, "Why, yes, that's an excellent catch by your investigators, especially since the statue appears relatively intact in this photo, and the deceased certainly didn't appear to sustain major injuries from it. Neither to the scalp, the skull or any other part of the body. We x-rayed the corpse during the autopsy and no injuries like a skull fracture were found. It may have grazed his head, but he certainly wasn't knocked out."

"What other injuries are visible in these photos?" Sabrina asked.

"In addition to the abrasions to the scalp, there are also several injuries visible to the dorsal surface or what we call the back of his hands. These circular lesions here." he said, as he indicated to the hands, "These are almost certainly burns, probably from something like a cigarette." Dr. Robbins answered.

Sabrina raised her eyebrows, saying, "So this would indicate what? That he was tortured before he was killed?"

Dr. Robbins answered, "Yes."

Now Sabrina's eyebrows appeared to be approaching her hairline. "Really?" she said, "And were there other signs of torture?"

Dr. Robbins looked at the jury as he answered, "Yes, as well as post-mortem mutilation. It appears that several of his fingernails were pulled off, in addition to the multiple cigarette burns."

"Did he have defensive injuries?" Sabrina asked.

"Oh yes! He was awake and fighting this!" Dr. Robbins answered. "Do you see these deep cuts in his palms, and the additional cigarette burns? He had his hands up trying to defend himself." Dr. Robbins finished.

"Was his actual cause of death due to torture?" Sabrina asked.

"I guess that depends on how you define torture," Dr. Robbins answered displaying a flash of the wit he was famous for. He continued, "His immediate and actual cause of death was from massive blood loss after his throat was cut, starting just beneath the left ear and extending to the other ear."

"And was there some additional mutilation done to the deceased neck?" Sabrina asked.

"Yes," Dr. Robbins answered, "his tongue was pulled out thru the incision in his neck. You can see it here in this close-up photo, but due to the state of decomposition, it might be hard for a lay person to identify." Several gallery members appeared to visibly recoil as he traced the edge of decomposing tongue as it passed thru the incision and shredded tissue in the victim's neck.

"Speaking of decomposition, what is your expert estimation of the approximate time of death?" Sabrina asked.

"I'm going to ramble for a minute, folks," Dr. Robbins said, "as I work backward to the time of death here so you can see how I came to my conclusion." Several jurors appeared to nod, approvingly.

"Hmm.. Mr. Baron was discovered around mid-day on March 17th, which was during that spell of 70 degree weather we had for about a week. Remember that? It came right after that snowstorm that dumped all that snow and jammed up I-40 on the 11th and 12th. All of the blood, the splatter on the walls and such, and even that thick saturation on the carpet beneath the body, was already coagulated or congealed and dried up. The technicians and I couldn't find a single area, even in that area right beneath the body, where any of that blood was still wet. That doesn't happen right away. Now there's this German expert, a forensic pathologist named Frank Ramsthaler, and as best that he and I could estimate, is that this quantity of blood, being around four to five liters in volume, in those weather conditions with the windows open, it would take probably 48 to 60 hours to dry so completely. Now, Dr. Ramsthaler, along with another doctor, named Dr. Fiona Smith in France, they wrote all the books on blood pooling, splatter, coagulation and drying times. Together we talked to Dr. Smith, and she agreed with our estimate. So that's one tool we used to estimate time of death," he finished.

Sabrina nodded to Bailiff Bronson who brought forth the whiteboard and some markers. After approval from the judge, Dr. Robbins approached the white board and made a series of columns.

He labeled the first one, "Blood saturated carpet – completely dry = 48 to 60 hours.

Then he turned back to the judge and began the second point, "Now, the next things we usual look at are the livor, rigor and temperature of the body. Anyone who watches tv knows these ones. But, they should also know that the ambient temperature affects the rate of decomposition. In this case, it probably slowed it just a little bit, since the daytime temperatures were in the 70s with an open window, but the nighttime lows still dropped down into the low 50's and upper 40's, like a mild refrigeration. On examination, there was no livor mortis or dark discoloration from blood settling in dependent areas, and the body had passed through full rigor or muscle stiffening, and it was now absent. The body temperature was equal to the ambient temperature of 75 degrees or almost 24 degrees centigrade. All of this tells us that it's been at least 24 to 36 hours, which is consistent," he says as he returns to the white board to write "Livor, Rigor, Temperature – at least 24 to 36 hours."

"One of the last things we look at is the state of decomposition and insect activity. In this case, it's pretty standard and we can use the basic body farm data from east Tennessee. He hasn't been immersed in water, we've already discussed the ambient temperature, so there is no rapid acceleration of decomposition. He did show signs of bodily discoloration, particularly around the abdomen that is quite advanced," Dr. Robbins says as he points to a photograph showing a bloated abdomen with greenish colored skin.

"That is bacteria at work, eating you from the inside out, basically," Dr. Robbins says, almost gleefully. "But then you get the flies, and man, they are quick."

Marnie looks around the courtroom and notices that a few of the gallery members including Albert are looking a bit queasy, or roughly the same greenish color as Hunter Baron's bloated gut.

Dr. Robbins pulls a photograph out of the stack and hands it to Bailiff Bronson for projection. "Now here, if you look at the eyes, you will see, that even though the body lay face down, there is ample evidence of larval masses around the neck wound, the tongue tissue extruding from the neck, and underneath the neck wound itself, extending onto the carpet. There is also evidence of maggot activity on the nail beds, around the mouth and eyes, along with beetle activity. There was quite a large maggot mass just inside the neck incision, which is why decomposition is more advanced here. In fact, if I had checked the body temperature at the wound site, in the maggot mass, it would have been several degrees warmer than the rest of the corpse," with the last sentences being almost an aside, as if he were a professor in a university course.

He continued his lecture, "As you can see here in the photo, there are beetles climbing in and out of the corpses' open mouth," he said.

Marnie noted that now several members of the gallery are looking a bit queasy, and Albert has gotten up and is heading out of the courtroom. She looks over at the jurors, and notices to her surprise that two of the younger jurors; one a very young computer programmer with multiple facial piercings, and a goth looking, twenty-three-year-old female community college student have looks of rapt attention. She doesn't remember the computer programmer's name from jury selection, but she does remember that the college student's name is Candace Spencer. Mainly because among her multiple visible tattoos is a tattoo of a green lollipop, making her think that to someone, the heavily inked girl with the stereotypical dyed black hair, black lipsticked, raccoon-eyed young woman is their darling baby, Candy. She briefly wonders about the young woman's major, but then directs her attention back to the witness. He's been taking the entire courtroom on a ride she thought.

"What is the estimate with all of this insect activity?" Sabrina prompts, while trying to avoid looking at the projected photographs.

"Well, combined with the incredibly putrid smell of decay that completely permeated the room and most of the apartment, and smell is one of the criteria for estimating time of death," he said, "with the beetle activity and the larvae mounds, I'd have to say three to five days. The heavy presence of flies in a pre-pupal and pupal stages makes me lean towards five days. Flies are pretty predictable, and they start landing on and laying eggs on dead bodies within a few minutes to hours after death. The window was open, giving flies and other insects ready access to the body right away. So, if we were to add this to our white board," he said, arising once again, to write, "Maggots, beetles = 3 to 5 days or 72 to 120 hours."

"Now, Dr, Robbins, I hate to disagree but a lot of these numbers don't match. Can you explain?" Sabrina asked.

"Certainly, Ms. Price." he answered, surprising her by addressing her directly and by name, "If you remember some of our time of death indicators are mainly used to measure death in hours, like livor and rigor mortis. We said that it was *at least* or a minimum of 24 to 36 hours. Blood drying time extended that interval to almost 3 days, but our insect activity gave us a more precise interval of three to five days. Lastly, if you notice how the corpse is dressed, in polar fleece pajama pants and a thick sweater, then I would place the death at some time on March 11th or 12th, or during the brief cold snap. It was in the mid-80s right before the snowstorm, and in the 70s, a day or two later."

Sabrina Price put her hands together and actually clapped for a moment before she caught herself. "I'm sorry," she stammered to the judge, "but his explanation was incredible. It was so informative yet easy to understand. It sure didn't sound like this when I interviewed him. I swear, I had to look things up in my thesaurus after the first time I talked to him."

Judge Ward looked amused but stated quite sternly, "Please contain yourself Ms. Price. Maintain your decorum and remember where you are."

At that moment, Sabrina Price remembered why her former boss, Kelly Darrow, used to joke that Lee Filderman had been censured a few years ago for calling Judge Ward, "a limp, humorless, and incompetent dick."

"Yes, Your Honor," she said stiffly and formally. She was tempted to curtsy, but contained herself, as 'Jerk' Ward advised. She could take crumpets with the Queen of England, she thought, and this jerk could kiss her ass, talking about maintaining decorum.

She turned back to Dr. Robbins and said, "I have no more questions. I would like to thank you for your enlightening and educational testimony today. It was very helpful." She didn't bother to look at Judge Ward to see what he thought.

"Ladies and gentlemen, It's 4:45 in the afternoon. Let's stop here today, and resume with the cross-examination of this witness in the morning." Judge Ward proclaimed.

Judge Ward couldn't dampen Sabrina's enthusiasm. This was the best day in court she'd ever had since she had decided she wanted to be a lawyer. She'd actually enjoyed herself, bantering with the witnesses, but she wasn't terribly surprised when her boss, Jose Leon, turned to the other assistant district attorney, Carrie Bryant, and said, "Okay, training wheels off again, you are up tomorrow."

In fact, Sabrina was pleased. She liked Carrie, but she'd had a bad break on the original Hunter Baron case, and the District Attorney, Amy Weinrich, had been punishing Carrie ever since. Leon was right. It was time for Carrie to get back in action, and away from the filing cabinets. Sabrina leaned over and squeezed Carrie's shoulder with excitement as they walked out of the courtroom to head back to the office for a quick strategy session before heading home.

****

"Some day, huh?" Kisha Mack offered as the defense team left the courthouse. Lee just groaned.

"Hey, none of that!" she said, "Overall, I think we did pretty well. That forensic torture stuff doesn't hurt us anyway. Who would ever believe that Ember Prince slits people's throats or pulls off fingernails? Even if you thought she was guilty, that's a bit of a hard sell. Besides, we crushed them with those lab results." she said, too exuberant for her boss to resist. Her optimism was contagious, especially since he was coming to believe that his client really was innocent.

Defense attorneys always talk about how everyone deserves a fair defense, and shy away from talking about or even thinking about the guilt or innocence of their clients. "It's not relevant!" they argue, and as good defense attorneys, we try to believe that ourselves, but that's not entirely true. In this case, Lee's sense of injustice was growing, and it was lighting a fire underneath him. He and Kisha carried the files to the trunk of his sedan and he went home, determined to dig through every possible document to be prepared for court tomorrow. He might as well pick up a pizza on the way home because he certainly wasn't going to have time to cook. He didn't ask Kisha to assist him because it was one of those instances when he wouldn't know what he was looking for until he actually laid eyes on it.

****

Ember accompanied Kisha and Lee out of the courthouse, but then abruptly separated from them to climb into a car waiting at the curb. It wasn't her dad or any other family. They had been noticeably absent today, but it was one of her dad's staff, John Wellborn. She wasn't in the mood to talk, but she did tell him, "John, please make sure someone sits in the gallery tomorrow." She didn't have to be a lawyer to know that it didn't look good for the famously tight-knit Prince family to fail to show up and support their wayward daughter. If anything, her cousin Bobby owed her, since he'd been using her misfortune as part of his personal election fundraising campaign. Her dad owed her too, for all the missed school plays, debutante balls, graduations and other occasions that he hadn't bothered to attend. Maybe he could round up part of the legion of half siblings she had out there and really pack the gallery she thought. As John made a turn, Ember interrupted. "No, John, I want to go to my apartment."

"Sure thing," he answered before turning the car around. They sat in comfortable silence until he pulled the car to a stop at the curb in front of her apartment building. She nodded her thanks before getting out and heading inside. She didn't bother to make dinner, but just went to the bathroom to run a bath.

Trial, Day Two

That stomach flu was the best thing that ever happened, even if Carrie's own stomach was in knots. Now that they were in the second day of testimony, it was too late for the district attorney to try and replace her. She was glad that the defense was starting with Dr. Robbins cross-examination this morning. It gave her a little more time to prepare herself.

****

"Hello, Dr. Robbins – and a belated welcome to our fair city!" Lee Filderman said jovially as he approached the witness box. The defense attorney was wearing another one of his sharp ensembles.

He seemed to have a real talent at walking the fine line between fashion and ostentation. Today's very dark blue, almost black, suit seemed sedate until you noticed the ivory damask waistcoat with fine gold embroidery. The gleam of a 22k Albert chain caught the eye. You could be almost certain that at some point today, Lee would be pulling a small pocket watch from the embroidered pocket of the garment. His decadent habits along with his easy-going nature made the defense counsel more approachable, more likeable. He had the boyish charm of the Matthew McConaughey of the 1990's without naked bongo playing. People liked him in spite of themselves. This seemingly innocuous trait was particularly important when negotiating treacherous or potentially damaging witness testimony.

Dr. Robbins smiled and nodded in reply.

"So, this may be silly, but I just had to ask," Lee said, "are you related to *the* Dr. Robbins who wrote *Robbins Pathology*? My neighbor Katie is a nurse, and I borrowed a copy from her the other day. She said it's basically the bible of your profession," Lee finished.

Dr. Robbins looked pleasantly surprised and pleased, as he answered, "Why, yes, I am. Dr. Stanley Robbins was my uncle, my favorite uncle, in fact. He's the reason that I am both a doctor and that I specialized in pathology."

"Hmm, it's a small world, that's a fact," Lee said, before launching into his cross-examination.

"But, you know, when I was looking through *Robbins Pathology*, I didn't see a chapter on torture. Did you see a lot of torture injuries in San Diego?" Lee Filderman asked.

At this, a gleam came into Dr. Robbin's eye, as he answered, "You have a valid point. I haven't performed that many autopsies with injuries that are suspected of torture. For that reason, I consulted Dr. Michael S. Pollanen of the Ontario Forensic Pathology Service and University of Toronto, Department of Laboratory Medicine and Pathobiology, as well as another colleague of his, Dr. Jorgen Thomson of Institute of Forensic Medicine, University of Southern Denmark. Both of these gentlemen have researched and published extensively on the topic of forensic evaluation in cases of both torture and deaths in custody for Amnesty International, the United Nations and other international organizations."

"Ouch," Lee Filderman said taking a step back, to the amusement of the jurors. "And you reviewed this case with both of these experts?"

"Yes, I did. We had several video conferences, before, during and after the autopsy. They also referred me to the Minnesota

Protocol which is the updated and revised United Nations manual on the effective prevention and investigation of extra-legal, arbitrary and summary executions. They were very helpful, and I found the manual quite informative. I can write down the title for you, so you can download it off the internet," Dr. Robbins answered. The good doctor's demeaner was so polite and cordial that Lee couldn't tell if he was being facetious or if he was being earnest in the reading suggestions.

"I am surprised that you didn't see the notation in my autopsy report, where I cited the manual and referred to my collaboration with Dr. Pollanen and Dr. Thomson," Dr. Robbins finished. This time, Lee strongly leaned towards factitious, but then he did recall seeing some small footnotes on the autopsy report, in a size 8 font. He internally cursed himself for failing to do his research, and for asking a question for which he didn't already know the answer. That was cross-examination 101.

He braced himself for the next series of questions, though he did know the answer to these.

"Is there a specific name or colloquial term for the neck wound inflicted on the victim?" Lee asked.

"Yes, it does have a very specific name - the Colombian necktie," Dr. Robbins answered.

"And, do you know why doctor, it carries this distinctive moniker?" Lee asked, looking interested.

"It is believed that this method of murder and post-mortem mutilation originated during a period of extreme upheaval in Colombia during a violent ten-year civil war in the late 1940's and 50's. It was used to send a message and intimidate the family, neighbors, and allies of the victims. It is one of several brutal methods of post-mortem mutilation used during this time." Dr. Robbins answered.

"Is this also associated with organized crime?" Lee asked.

"Unfortunately, any sort of technique of extreme brutality, extreme violence, or mutilation, is now associated with organized crime and narcotrafficking. It's almost as if it's a competition, particularly among the Mexican cartels," Dr. Robbins said. He added, looking sad and disgusted, "And yes, I did see some of that in San Diego. Much more than I wanted to."

"Unfortunately, Memphis hasn't been entirely spared by the Mexican cartels," Lee said, "though thankfully, we haven't experienced the worst of it. Our crime rate is bad enough," Lee commiserated. If it seemed strange for a defense attorney to be lamenting about the city's crime rate during a first-degree murder trial, no one seemed to comment on it.

"But, getting back to the situation at hand, wouldn't you say it's more common to see this kind of killing as part a gang related or drug related activity?" Lee asked.

"Well, certainly, though there is nothing that precludes an individual from participating in this." Dr. Robbins answered.

"An individual participating? So this couldn't be a one-person job, is what you are saying?" Lee pressed.

"Well, no. I think it would be very difficult for one person to incapacitate a victim that was the size, weight, and physical condition of Mr. Baron," Dr. Robbins answered.

"But, wasn't he found near a wheelchair?" Lee asked, addressing one of the prosecution's early contentions.

"Yes, but that appears to be either an affectation or a recent event," Dr. Robbins answered, explaining, "the corpse displayed fairly well-developed musculature in the lower extremities for someone that age. There was very minimal muscle wasting or atrophy that you would expect in a wheelchair dependent person."

"Okay, so let me just make sure I understand what you are saying. You are saying that it would be very difficult for a single person to subdue, restrain, and murder a 6 foot 1-inch-tall, middle-aged man weighting around 200 pounds in this fashion, correct?" Lee stated.

"Yes, that's correct." Dr. Robbins confirmed. "Slicing someone's throat requires a greater degree of physicality than a lay person might expect, especially if this person was awake and fighting, as the victim appeared to be."

"And you are also saying that you didn't see any signs that the victim was disabled, despite reported use of a wheelchair?" Lee asked.

"Yes, that is also correct." Dr. Robbins confirmed.

"Now, the prosecutor didn't mention this at all, but were there other reasons that the victim might have been feeling poorly, Dr. Robbins? There were some surprising toxicology results, weren't there?" Lee asked.

"I am glad you asked." Dr Robbins said. "It's actually quite interesting. I wasn't in the courtroom for prior witness testimony, but I understand you've already talked about the discovery of some thallium salts." Dr. Robbins said. The defense attorney and the prosecution witness had an interesting dynamic now, almost a bantering exchange.

"That's correct." Lee answered, a little bit unaccustomed to answering questions, instead of asking them.

"What did the victim's serum or blood toxicology show?" Lee asked.

"In addition to having positive results for both cocaine and THC, the active ingredient for marijuana, the deceased's blood samples showed the presence of not one, but two heavy metals!" Dr Robbins said dramatically.

Kisha wondered if the Judge could scold witnesses for theatrics, but Judge Ward seemed to be enjoying the testimony.

"What heavy metals were detected, Dr. Robbins?" Lee asked with exaggerated courtesy. With the prosecution witness doing a lot of the heavy lifting, Lee felt magnanimous.

"Well, in the blood samples, there was evidence of massive ingestion of thallium salts, presumably with the red wine as the source of ingestion, but there was also evidence of arsenic poisoning, and this is a bit trickier to evaluate. We ended up having to gather hair samples and toenail clippings for this. We couldn't examine the usual fingernails because, well, most of them were missing," Dr. Robbins said.

"Was there something different about the arsenic poisoning?" Lee asked.

"The arsenic poisoning wasn't all at once. Our victim had evidence of slow, chronic poisoning. It must have been over several months because we were able to detect arsenic in his hair. We could also see Mee's lines on both his toenails and the two fingernail samples we could find. The lab confirmed that these white horizontal lines on the nailbeds were the result of chronic arsenic ingestion." Dr. Robbins finished triumphantly.

At the prosecution's table, Sabrina Price leaned over slightly to whisper quietly into Carrie's ear, "This must be why the defense listed all of our witnesses on their witness list. Look how he's got the medical examiner in his corner!"

Despite her hushed tones, Judge Ward looked at her and frowned. She looked innocently at the Judge and batted her eyelashes slightly. Jose looked over at her, appalled.

The defense continued on, undisturbed. "Dr. Robbins, how would someone have chronic arsenic poisoning?" Lee asked.

"Well, there would have to be multiple ingestions. This doesn't happen from a one-time poisoning. Now, in rural areas, we sometimes see a very low level of chronic arsenic ingestion from people with well water because arsenic is a naturally occurring substance but it's usually very mild and not enough to sicken anyone. Our mass spectrometry showed that this chronic ingestion far exceeded that. This must have been an intentional poisoning." Dr. Robbins answered.

"Now, this might sound like a stupid question, doctor but I was playing amateur detective, trying to get all the pieces of this case. So, when I heard about the cocaine and THC, I went and talked to some officers I know in the narcotics division." Lee said. If there were a few snickers in the gallery, Lee ignored them. He had made his name as a defense attorney defending drug dealers, so he certainly had plenty of contact with multiple members of the narcotics squad. In fact, he had assisted on the defense of Craig Petties, a major narcotics dealer in Memphis.

Lee continued, "The officers mentioned that frequent cocaine use can lead to arsenic poisoning. Could that be the case here?"

"Highly unlikely!" Dr. Robbins snorted. "The serum levels were simply too high. He would have had to ingest toxic levels of cocaine on a regular basis." he answered. "While it appeared he was a chronic, recreational user, there is simply no physical or pathological evidence that he ingested massive amounts of cocaine on a routine basis." he finished.

Marnie looked back in the gallery to where Albert was sitting. She was glad that Hunter's son, David, wasn't present to hear some of this testimony. The most damaging things were the incidental things, she felt. Like hearing a doctor debating whether your father's frequent cocaine use could have contributed to his chronic arsenic poisoning.

She noticed that several lesser-known members of the Prince family were also in attendance. Dressed in Sunday church suits in luxurious fabrics, these Prince in-laws and distant cousins were best known for their periodic appearances at weddings, funerals, campaign events or any other time when strength was in the numbers. She didn't see any members of Ember's immediate family…certainly not her dad and latest stepmother. Ember's mother had died several years ago, but it didn't appear that her sister, Autumn, was in the gallery either. Marnie turned back to the witness stand as Lee continued to cross-examine the doctor who performed Hunter Baron's autopsy.

"So, in addition to having his throat cut, the deceased was being poisoned with two different poisons?" Lee asked, almost incredulous.

"Yes." Dr. Robbins answered.

"Now, in your professional opinion, Dr. Robbins, what is the likelihood that the same person is responsible for torturing, cutting the throat and administering these two poisons, one repeatedly, to the victim?" Lee asked. He saw a middle-aged male juror roll his eyes as he asked the question.

"I would rate that as being highly, highly improbable, almost impossible. The torture and the actual murder certainly went together, and it's even possible that he was initially poisoned with thallium by the same individual, but the arsenic poisoning, that was done over a period of time. That was done by someone who had frequent, regular contact with him," Dr. Robbins answered.

"In that case, wouldn't it be more likely that a lover, a roommate, a co-worker or someone like that was responsible for the arsenic poisoning?" Lee asked.

"Objection, calls for facts not in evidence!" Carrie said, bobbing up to her feet.

Both Judge Ward and the defense team looked at her strangely. She could feel her face turning red as heat traveled up her neck. "I mean, Speculative!"

"Overruled, on both counts." Judge Ward ruled. He then looked down at the junior attorney and said, "I am going to throw you a freebie. Anytime counselor Filderman opens his mouth, you can object on grounds of compound questions, almost guaranteed."

The entire court was surprised by this moment of levity, and it took a moment for the attorneys to recover.

"If I may proceed?" Lee asked the court.

"Go ahead, but she's on to you now," Judge Ward answered.

"Marla, could you read back the last question?" Lee asked the court reporter.

"In that case, wouldn't it be more likely that a lover, a roommate, a co-worker or someone like that was responsible for the arsenic poisoning?" Marla recited.

"Objection, calls for speculation." Carrie said.

"Overruled. I'll allow it." Judge Ward ruled.

Dr. Robbins answered, "Yes. When it comes to chronic poisoning, the rule of thumb is to look close to home."

"Would it surprise you to know that the deceased's serious girlfriend was never even considered a suspect?" Lee asked.

"Without knowing the circumstances, I can't really speak to it, but she should have been someone that the policed looked at closely," Dr. Robbins answered.

"Yes, indeed." Lee said, before stating, "I have no more questions for this witness, Your Honor."

Before Dr. Andrew Robbins could arise from the witness stand, Carrie addressed the court.

"Your Honor, the prosecution would like to re-direct this witness," Carrie Bryant stated.

"Proceed!" Judge Ward declared.

Carrie Bryant felt like she was walking on eggshells, and nothing over the course of the morning had done anything to diminish the feeling.

"Dr. Robbins, you testified earlier this morning, that the victim was found with significant levels of two heavy metals: thallium and arsenic. You also stated that the arsenic poisoning was chronic. Isn't it possible that the victim was using a wheelchair due to the effects of these poisons?" she asked.

"It's certainly possible. Arsenic poisoning can cause muscle cramping and numbness and tingling in the extremities, but the main effects are on the gastrointestinal system. However, if he was requiring the wheelchair due to muscle cramping or weakness, it would have been a very recent development. As I stated earlier, he had no evidence of muscle atrophy that you normally find in someone who is non-ambulatory or with limited walking ability," Dr. Robbins answered.

"Thank you for clarifying that, Dr. Robbins." Carrie said, addressing the witness.

"We have no further questions for this witness." Carrie addressed the court. Dr. Robbins arose, smiled at the jury and audience in the gallery before adjusting his suit jacket and leaving the courtroom.

"The prosecutor may call their next witness," Judge Ward said impatiently, with an obvious glance at his watch. It was only 10:30, so it was too early for him to call for a break for lunch. Despite having a degree in religion from the Memphis Theological Seminary, at times the 65-year-old judge struggled with maintaining his patience, and he certainly had never been able to claim any sort of state of grace. He was deep in his own re-election campaign, and despite being on the bench in this position since 2004, this year looked to be different in the aftermath of the nationwide Black Lives Matter protests. There was also the local case of Pamela Moses, which he had overseen just a few weeks prior. That was another noteworthy case of aggressive prosecution that made him wonder about what was going on behind the scenes in Amy Weinrich's office. In any case, he hoped to wrap up today's session in time for him to meet with his own campaign advisors. He focused his attention back on the case at hand and did his best to stifle his frustration.

Several more witnesses took the stand that day, including Robert Haley, a crime scene technician, as well as another lab expert, but there were no major findings that had not been testified previously by the first two witnesses. The fact that the state hadn't performed the tests necessary for the detection of thallium poisoning was more glaring than the tedious testimony reviewing the mass spectrometry and liquid chromatography examinations that were used to confirm the presence of arsenic in the deceased blood, hair and other tissues. It felt a little awkward to call the same people on the witness stand that she presented during her case against the decedent which had been her last major case. She still couldn't bring herself to refer to him as the victim because of that either, but the absolute worst part of her so-called comeback today was to see the jurors' eyes glaze over during the testimony. She tried not to let their visible boredom or apathy affect her. She didn't want to rush boring but important testimony because she felt uncomfortable. There were almost no objections from the defense during this portion of testimony, which was primarily procedural in nature.

At 12:02 Judge Ward called for a lunch time recess, while Casey Lyon Agnor's discussion about additional crime scene photos that had been admitted into evidence. They weren't critical photos, but they demonstrated the general conditions of the apartment, to help show that the police department wasn't negligent in their evidence processing. Casey Lyon had just finished discussing the kitchen trash contents, and the absence of a possible murder weapon on the scene, when the lunch recess was called.

****

Marnie watched as the defense team, along with their client, left the courtroom. Ember seemed more like another attorney in her muted suit of soft grey with a satiny white blouse with a floppy bow at the neck. She had sensible heels paired with flawless pantyhose and a knee length skirt. She wore very small, basic silver hoops in her ears, and makeup in natural shades that enhanced her olive complexion. She wore no other jewelry, just a plain watch.

Marnie wondered what the trio was talking about. She wished she could be a fly on the wall to overhear their opinion of this morning's testimony. She felt like the prosecutor had gained some ground with the jury this morning, and wondered if they felt the same.

****

As everyone filed out of the courtroom, Kisha looked at both Lee and Ember. "Whew, it's been a long morning!" she said.

Ember looked at her and answered before Lee could, "I hope the jurors found it as long and tedious as we did. Now, what's your plan for cross examination? You know that's not my earring!"

Lee smiled and said, "Don't worry about this afternoon. Kisha will be great. Besides, we have plenty of our own evidence to present, remember?"

"Now, who's buying? Oh no, wait, that's right – it's you, Ember!" Lee said in a moment of levity.

The smile on Ember's face told him that she appreciated his attempts at normalcy.

"Ah, another time, Ms. Prince. I hate to disappoint, but we already have sandwiches waiting in a conference room so we can go over some of the materials for this afternoon," Lee continued.

Ember wouldn't ever say that she enjoyed these trial conferences, but she certainly appreciated being part of them. She felt like Kisha and Lee appreciated her contributions, and she felt like they were committed to her defense in a way she might not have fathomed if she wasn't privy to all of their machinations on her behalf.

They continued to make their way to the conference room where one of Lee's office secretaries was waiting, with additional files and their lunch.

****

Once the defense team was firmly ensconced in the conference room with the door closed, Ember released some of the questions she'd been bottling up since the courtroom. Did her attorneys think she was losing? Should she reconsider the deal? What else could they do to show her innocence? They had talked about all of this before, but the questions had swirled around in her mind all morning as she listened to the testimony. Every time she realized that many of these experts, the police, members of the jury, and other people in the audience believed that she was somehow involved in all of this, she felt herself start to panic.

Kisha answered Ember's questions again, but Ember could only listen with half an ear, as the rest of her was distracted by the massive lub-dub of her heart speeding up as she thought about going to prison for the rest of her life. She came back to the present as she heard Kisha say something she hadn't expected.

"..And it's possible that we might end up needing you to testify to that," Kisha said, "but we are planning to have our own expert testimony to refute theirs."

This was the first time anyone had broached the idea of Ember testifying since the trial began and she was startled.

"But, as we said early on, that's only as a last resort." Lee said, "I really don't want to put you on the stand and give them the opportunity to smear your reputation any further. There are a couple of jurors that seem to be of the more conservative Christian type." Ember laughed mirthlessly. "Worse than accusing me of murder?" she asked before answering her own query. "No, no, you're right, I did see a couple of hypercritical looking biddies sitting there." She continued, disheartened, saying, "I hate to be convicted of murder just because they think I'm some kind of sexed up jezebel. It's ridiculous, but this is the South, so there's that." Ember said with a sad sigh.

"Ember, I don't plan to give these harpies a chance to have a go at you." Lee Filderman said, consoling her. "I think we are already making a pretty decent dent in their case – and we haven't even started presenting our case yet."

"Ember, that's why we are here strategizing," Kisha reminded her, "and you are a critical part of this process. Your input is essential." With that, they passed around a plate of sandwiches, fruit cups, and bottles of water. As they ate, they reviewed the earlier testimony for holes, errors and factual inconsistencies. By the end of lunch, Ember was feeling a new sense of optimism as they headed back to the courtroom.

****

As the defense team was returning to the courtroom, Jose stopped Lee Filderman in the hall with Sabrina Price and Carrie Bryant at his heels. "Hey, just so you and your client know, our offer for a plea deal expires as soon as we finish presenting our case." He raised an eyebrow as he continued, "You've seen how the case is going so you might want to advise your client to take the offer. A life sentence with possibility of parole after 30 years sure beats the death penalty." he offered.

Ember Prince looked as disgusted with the offer as she had the first time Lee had brought the offer to her. Before Lee could advise her to ignore it, she answered, angrily, "And that's an offer? For an innocent person? To go to prison for the rest of my life! Fuck you! I'll take my chances! I'm innocent and I'll not go to prison to make your workload easier!"

Jose Leon looked momentarily surprised by her vigor, before he turned to Lee and said, "Okay then, see you in the courtroom."

****

After the jurors returned from lunch, Carrie had the unpleasant prospect of watching juror #9 try to suck and pick parts of his lunch out of his teeth while she recalled Casey Lyon Agnor to the stand, to discuss one small but critical piece of evidence. She was glad she hadn't questioned her on the topic prior to the recess because she wanted the information fresh in the jurors' minds. She knew the case was off to an unremarkable, if not bad start, and she felt that this testimony might vindicate them.

She, like everyone else, had seen and heard the crimes of racism and politically motivated prosecution, during the protests and grandstanding outside the courthouse, which were being led by Ember Prince's cousin, Robert Prince Jr. The idea that she might be involved in such a miscarriage of justice was extremely upsetting to her. As a Caucasian woman from a small town in Mississippi, she was extremely sensitive to criticism or charges of racial prejudice particularly by the ignorant, inbred, redneck, white trash flavor. She hadn't realized how much this bothered her until the Black Lives Matters protests brought it all to the forefront. She believed that institutional racism existed, particularly in the justice system, but she desperately wanted to believe that she was part of the solution. Now that protesters were calling the prosecutor's office racist on the evening news, with actual protestor's placards with her name on it, she found it all deeply troubling. She needed the evidence to show that they were prosecuting the right suspect, for the right reason.

She consoled herself with the idea that if there was ever an opportunity for a sound bit, or a clip on the evening news, Robert Prince Jr. was there. He made sure to be center stage as much as possible, even if he couldn't be bothered to take his place in the courtroom gallery, Carrie thought. His presence outside the courthouse had less to do with racism and a lot to do with his election campaign. Word was that this was all a preliminary attempt before he attempted a run at the U.S. Senate as part of a lead up to the White House. She wondered how Ember Prince felt about her cousin's antics for a minute before returning her thoughts to the testimony at hand.

"Ms. Agnor," Carrie asked, "Would you identify this item for me?" Carrie held up the thumb drive labeled "Exhibit C" for the court to see.

"That appears to be the thumb drive containing files from a computer seized at the Jack Prince family home," Casey Lyon Agnor answered.

Carrie addressed the court, "I would like to enter this drive into evidence, as previously mentioned, exhibit C. Due to the nature of this evidence, we would like to clear the gallery before viewing."

"Objection, prejudicial!" Lee called. "Your Honor, we have already discussed in detail the existence of this adult material," Lee said. "We are willing to stipulate as to the contents of this drive without needing to exposure the jury to such prejudicial material," Lee argued.

"That's not entirely true." Carrie argued. "That's why it's important for the jurors to see the archives on this drive."

"Overruled. The prosecution may present the material." the judge ruled.

A small table with a television and laptop computer was wheeled into the courtroom. It was reminiscent to Carrie of elementary school, when the teachers would wheel in big, outdated, heavy televisions, with an old VCRs to watch either government mandated education, or an occasional Disney movie when they had a substitute teacher. She was almost expecting to hear "I'm just a bill, sitting on Capitol Hill," instead of the surprisingly high quality, high-definition video taken from Hunter Baron's secret cameras. The video started, and viewers could see the large unmade bed, and room strewn with clothing, trash, and other items that had previously been identified as the victim's bed room in other crime scene photos.

"As you can see from this video, this footage was taken in the bedroom of Hunter Baron," Carrie stated. Two figures ended the frame, with one being the tall figure of Hunter Baron. He was aggressively undressing a sleepy looking woman, who kept slumping towards the ground, until he finally dumped her, like a sack of potatoes onto the bed, where he proceeded to continue to undress her. Her eyes were closed, and Hunter appeared to turn her face in the camera's direction. Carrie paused the film at this point.

"I don't need to show the rest of this video, as Hunter Baron is not the person on trial. I think it's fair to say and agree to the defense's contention that it's obvious in this video that the female subject has been sedated somehow. Now, Ms. Agnor, you examined this file completely, and detected no signs of alternation, correct?" Carrie asked. After the film was paused, Carrie waited, as the audience was allowed to re-enter the gallery. She repeated the question for their benefit, once they were seated.

"Yes, ma'am. On my examination, the film appears entirely intact and unaltered after being downloaded to the laptop, and subsequently, the thumb drive." she answered.

"Was the chain of custody form intact when you received these items for evaluation?" Carrie asked.

"Yes, they were. I received them directly from Officer Demetrius Haley." she answered. "If you look here, on the form that accompanied the thumb drive, it contains his original signature, date and time, as well as location where collected." she finished.

"And did this laptop and thumb drive come from the crime scene at the victim's apartment?" Carrie asked.

"Objection, relevance, Your Honor!" Lee called in a futile attempt to stop what came next.

"Are you kidding right now?" Carrie asked, "You are well aware of the relevance." she finished.

"I am going to go with the kid on this one, Filderman, but nice try. Overruled. Counselor Bryant, your witness may answer," Judge Ward ruled.

"No, it didn't." Casey answered.

"According to the chain of custody form, where was the evidence found and collected?" Carrie asked.

"The evidence was collected from 909 Kensington St, in the Vollentine Evergreen Historic District in central Memphis," Casey answered.

"And, who lives at this address according to what is written on the chain of custody form?" Carrie asked.

"It says here that a Mr. Jack Prince is the owner of the property as well as the thumb drive and the laptop." Casey answered.

So, this would indicate that the owner of the laptop was well aware of Hunter Baron's activities prior to this trial, wouldn't it?" Carrie asked almost rhetorically.

"Yes, ma'am. I believe so." Casey answered.

"Thank you, Casey. Now, there is another piece of evidence I'd like to review with you." Carrie said, before turning to address the court, "I'd like to enter this as Exhibit E." She held up a small plastic bag that contained a single piece of jewelry.

"Exhibit E also includes these photos of the crime scene that contain images of the earring." Carrie finished.

"Before entering these photos as exhibit E, I would like to have this witness review these photos here, Your Honor," Carrie said. She waited for an objection from the defense but nothing was forthcoming.

"Now, Ms. Agner, would you tell me what these photos show?" Carrie asked, after handing the photographs to the Bailiff for projection.

"Here in Exhibit E, photo #1, you see a very large, saturated area of blood next to the bed, which seeps into the carpet underneath the bed. Just there, a few inches under the bed, within the saturated pool, is a small object," Casey said, using a laser pointer to circle the small item. In the photo the item is just barely visible as a small projection within a gelatinous pool of blood saturating the carpet. A small glint or reflection of metal from one side of the item is caught in the camera flash.

Carrie hands the next photo to the Bailiff.

"And what do you see here, in photo #2?" Carrie asked.

"In this close-up photo, the item becomes clearly identifiable as a piece of jewelry. You can see the ear post here sticking up. It's like buttered toast. The decorative side landed face down with the post sticking up." Casey said she indicated, to the earring post.

"Who examined this piece forensically?" Carrie asked.

"I did." Casey answered. "I retrieved it, labelled it, examined it, photographed it, and swabbed it for blood, and DNA."

"What is most striking about this item to you?" Carrie asked.

"The most striking and important thing about this earring is its position in the photographs, and the blood pattern on the jewelry." Casey answered.

"Would you please explain that more fully?" Carrie asked.

"Certainly. If you look here, in this photo, you will see that the earring appears to be laying on top of the blood saturating this rug. This is important to help determine when this earring ended up on the floor." Casey answered. "That's particularly important in cases such as this, where the crime scene has a lot of unrelated or pre-existing clutter." she added.

"Why is that significant?" Carrie asked.

"Since the earring is laying on top of the blood, we can determine that the earring didn't end up on this floor until after the victim's throat was cut. If it had been laying there before the homicide, the earring would be under the blood, or covered with blood. Instead, we see blood on the earring only on the side that was in contact with the large pool of blood that saturated the carpet," Casey replied.

"So, the fact that the earring was found in this area, and is not covered in blood means that the earring ended up on the carpet after the murder?" Casey asked.

"Yes. It had to have ended up on the carpet, just under the bed, after the victim's throat was cut." Casey confirmed.

"Are you able to tell anything else about when this earring ended up in the victim's blood?" Carrie asked.

"Yes. The earring ended up in the blood shortly after the victim's throat was cut. We know that because there is a significant amount of dried, crusted blood on the surface of the earring that was in contact with the bloody carpet. In fact, it coats the surface, as you can see here in this photo, almost obscuring the design on the jewelry. This would only happen if the earring landed in blood that was fresh and wet!" Casey answered. Carrie tensed internally, waiting for an objection that never came.

"Is there anything else you can tell me about this earring?" Carrie asked.

"Yes. This earring is not a mass market item," Casey answered.

"You mean, I can't go out and get a similar pair at Claire's or the mall?" Carrie asked.

"No, Ma'am. Certainly not! As you can see from these sequential photos, as we cleaned off a small portion of this earring, it revealed some very expensive materials. This part here is made of precious metals, primarily platinum." indicating the material framing a pinkish material. "And this section is 24 karat gold, which is actually quite rare in modern jewelry." Casey answered.

"That does sound expensive." Carrie answered. "What is this blue-green material? I don't know that I've seen something like that." Carrie inquired.

"Well, it's hard to even really seen it, here, but that is a very costly gemstone. I have a photograph here I'd like to project so you can see what this gem really looks like." Casey answered, handing over a professionally staged looking photograph of a jewel on a black velvet background.

'Wow, that is absolutely stunning! That's not an emerald or a sapphire." Carrie declared, as the photo was projected. "That's the same kind of stone as in this earring?" she asked.

"Yes. That stone is called Alexandrite. It's one of the most expensive gemstones on earth. It's worth many times more than a diamond." Casey answered.

"Why does that gem sound familiar?" Carrie half mused.

"Back in the 1980's and earlier, Alexandrite was commonly listed as the birthstone for June. However, as the price continued to rise, they changed the gemstone to something cheaper, namely Pearl and a semi-precious stone called Moonstone," Casey answered matter-of-factly.

Carrie suspected at least three June birthdays in the gallery as she saw heads nod in agreement to Casey's statement.

"How expensive is this Alexandrite? What would the stone in this earring cost, for example?" Carrie asked.

"Well, after speaking to multiple jewelers and doing some research on the internet, it appears that the gem in this earring would cost upwards of twenty thousand dollars," Casey answered.

"Twenty thousand dollars! Whew! And that's just one earring. Not too many Memphians can afford that, can they?" Carrie asked.

"No, Ma'am. This earring would certainly be out of reach for most people." Casey answered.

Ember quickly scribbled a note that she passed towards Kisha and Lee. It said, 'It must be my earring because it was expensive?' with several question marks after the question. Kisha nodded to acknowledge the note.

"This has been very enlightening, hasn't it?" Carrie asked rhetorically. "Ms. Agner, thank you very much for your testimony today." Carrie said, before addressing the judge, "The prosecution has no more questions for this witness."

Judge Ward glanced at his watch before stating, "Let's take a short recess for lunch before the defense begins their cross-examination."

****

If the defense wanted to challenge any of the evidence presented today, they had to do it during their cross-examination of Casey Lyon Agner. But Memphis was more of a small town than most people realized, and Ms. Agner was an experienced technician. It would take a ration of charm and finesse to question the well-respected and well-liked technician. For this, Lee preferred Kisha to take the lead.

Once Ms. Agner was back of the witness stand, Kisha approached, saying, "Good afternoon, Ms. Agner!"

Casey smiled, showing beautiful white teeth, and replied, "Good afternoon, Ma'am."

"I took some notes this morning, so I wouldn't waste your time asking you things you've already answered, but I also have a couple questions about things I didn't quite understand or somehow missed this morning. I'd like to review my list with you, if that's okay?" Out of the corner of her eye, Kisha saw a couple of jurors nod, as if they had been keeping their own list of questions.

Casey gave an affirmative response.

"Ms. Agner, this morning, you were talking about the discovery of an earring underneath the decedent's bed. You explained that the way the earring was found, and the pattern of blood on the earring indicated that the earring was not present before the murder, correct?" Kisha asked, warming up.

"Yes, Ma'am, that is correct." Casey answered.

"When you were examining this earring, were you able to isolate any DNA? From the post, perhaps?" Kisha asked.

"Yes." Casey answered, "Unfortunately, all of the blood samples taken from the earring post were all matched to the decedent, and presumably came from contact with the victim's blood splatter. The only foreign DNA that was retrieved from the earring was inconclusive."

"So, any speculation on the owner of the earrings, would be just that, speculation. Or do you have any proof of ownership of this earring?" Kisha asked.

"What do you mean by proof?" Casey retorted.

"Did you find the matching earring?" Kisha asked.

"No." Casey answered.

"Did you find a receipt or evidence of purchase of the earrings?" Kisha asked.

"No." Casey answered.

"What about photographs? Do you have any photographs of anyone wearing the earrings?" Kisha asked.

"No." Casey answered.

"Let's see. The biggest lead you have is this earring, and you don't have DNA, or any other proof of who it belongs to? Does that sound like an accurate summary of the situation?" Kisha said, bulldozing through before the prosecution could make an objection.

"Yes, Ma'am." said Casey who had expressed the exact same thoughts herself to Detective Payne.

"Judge, I have no more questions for this witness," Kisha said.

"Prosecution, please call your next witness." Judge Ward said, briskly.

"The prosecution calls Andres Ochoa Cristancho to the stand," Jose Leon stated. An attractive, well-groomed man in his late forties approached the witness stand. He was dressed in an inexpensive but clean and well-pressed navy suit, with a starched white shirt and a dark blue tie. He had worn Oxford dress shoes, which had been buffed to a high shine.

"Please state your name and occupation for the court," Jose Leon asked.

"My name is Andres Ochoa Cristancho, but I like to be called Andrew." the witness stated in cautious and carefully enunciated English which carried a soft pronunciation typical of some foreign accents. "I work at the Peabody Hotel now, but I used to be the doorman at the Parkland Apartments," he answered.

"Andrew, do you remember a tenant at the apartments named Hunter Baron?" Jose Leon asked.

"Yes. He was the youngest person that lived there. Everyone else was umm viejito, I mean senior citizen." he answered.

"That's very true," Jose Leon said, "but would you confirm if this is the picture of the person we are talking about?" Jose Leon handed Mr. Ochoa a publicity photo of Hunter Baron.

"Yes. That him." Mr. Ochoa answered.

"Do you remember when he was found dead?" Jose asked.

"Yes. It was just before the apartments closed for good. There were a lot of police and detectives." Mr. Ochoa answered.

"Did you notice if Mr. Baron had any visitors in the days before his body was found?" Jose Leon asked.

"Yes. I see a lady leaving, walking fast." he answered. "She came at ten o'clock at night, when I get ready to go home."

"Is she here in the courtroom today?" Leon asked, expectantly.

"Yes, I sees her." he answers.

"Would you point to her?" Leon asked, sure of himself.

Andres reaches out his arm, with a finger extended, and points to a lady in the first row of the gallery. Before Jose Leon realizes what has happened, the defense is on their feet. Lee Filderman states, "For the record, please note that the witness identified an African-American female sitting in the gallery. Please have it state for the record that this is not the defendant!"

"Are you sure? Estas Seguro?" Jose Leon asked, confused.

"Si, estoy seguro!" the witness answers adamantly.

Defeated, Jose Leon faces the judge, and states, "I have no more questions for this witness."

Lee Filderman approaches the witness and says, "Hello, Andrew," enunciating clearly and speaking a bit more slowly.

"Did Hunter Baron have any other visitors during your shift?" Lee asked.

"Yes. I think he is having small party. First come flowers, then a group of people, two big men and a lady in a fur coat and hat," Andres answered.

"Were the men white or black?" Lee asked.

"They were white; big, white men, almost two meters, I think." Andres said, with one hand above his head to indicate height.

"And the lady, did you see her?" he asked.

"Yes. She in big, beautiful, fur coat. I never seen such a coat in Colombia." Andres answered, in almost awe. "It was a long coat all the way down to her feet, in the color of dark coffee. It looked really soft. She had a soft furry hat that was the same. I remember because it was very cold outside."

"Was it one of the ladies sitting at this table here?" Lee asked. He indicated to the defense table, where Kisha Mack and Ember Prince sat, trying to remain calm while every eye in the courtroom turned in their direction.

"No, no, someone else." Andres answered.

"Are they in the courtroom today?" Lee persisted.

"No, not here." Andres answered.

"Now, Andrew, I am sorry to ask again, but this is very important. Are you sure the lady you saw with the two men, in the fur coat, isn't here in the courtroom, right now?" Lee said, trying not to hold his breath.

"Yes, I sure." Andres answered.

"Andrew, thank you very much for your time today." Lee said, before addressing the court. "I have no more questions." he stated.

"The witness may step down." the judge instructed before saying, "Prosecution, please call your next witness." in a brisk, impatient manner.

"The Prosecution rests." Jose Leon answered.

Kisha and Lee looked at each other, a bit startled. There were still a few witnesses on the prosecution witness list, and the prosecutors hadn't really presented any kind of smoking gun, so it was surprising that the prosecution was ending their presentation already, and especially on a losing note. Before Lee could say anything, Judge Ward emitted a deep grunt, almost a chuckle, bringing all eyes forward to the bench once more. The clock said 4:37, though it felt later to everyone who had sat thru the long hours of testimony.

As he sat there in his formal robes, Judge Ward looked at Bailiff Bronson before nodding. He reminded the jury not to discuss today's testimony, even amongst themselves, before dismissing the court for the day.

Lee appreciated the reprieve even though it had more to do with Judge Ward's 5:15 tee time at the Memphis Country Club, followed by drinks in the Clubhouse with some of his campaign backers. The Judge actually preferred the course at the Chickasaw Country Club, but he was expecting some large checks tonight, so he could afford to be expansive regarding the course. This general sense of well-being had spread over the course of the day, making Judge Ward's personality a little less. waspish and sarcastic than normal. He'd almost seemed …pleasant, Lee thought as he raced out to the car, hoping to get a jump on traffic. He was meeting with two critical defense witnesses this evening, to go over their testimony before they started tomorrow. He'd already asked Kisha to review several discovery documents this evening, in preparation for tomorrow.

****

As she passed the Bailiff on her way out of the courtroom, Ember was deep in thought. She was also angry. By the time she was in the parking lot, the keys were already in her hand, and she had already recited her argument for the next confrontation at her father's house.

****

The Defense presents their case

The next morning felt entirely too early for Kisha. She was pleasantly surprised when Lee pressed a hot cappuccino in a disposable cup in her hand as she met him outside his office. It was still dark when she had left her home in Whitehaven. Even now, it only six-thirty as Lee unlocked the office, and streaks of daylight were just beginning. Once in the office, after a quick run thru of the day's presentation, Lee and Kisha were ready to head over to the courthouse. Once Ember Prince arrived, the three of them left the office on foot. Lee liked the defense team to arrive together with the suspect, especially in high profile cases. He thought it presented a confident and cohesive picture to spectators and the media. He was pleased to see that Ember was wearing another subdued, but classically feminine outfit today. She looked very much like a demure and proper lady in the jacket dress, with taupe pantyhose and practical one-inch heels. He didn't need a jury consultant to tell him that stilettos were a fatal mistake with a conservative, Southern jury. He was also glad to see that she'd stuck with the very plain, small gold hoops, and understated jewelry. She didn't wear a cross, like many in the courtroom did, but he thought that might look too obvious to jurors. She hadn't been photographed in a cross on the campaign trail, so she shouldn't start now. Instead, the Barbara Bush style pearls were her only other adornment. A basic Casio watch was hidden by her jacket. It briefly crossed his mind, that even if her acting career had never taken off, she had obviously learned an awful lot about wardrobe and appearances during her years in Hollywood.

****

Ember tried not to think that morning, and to just keep one foot in front of the other. She tried to fill her mind with banal topics, so that her facial expression didn't vary. This strategy had come in handy during the prosecution's testimony as her reputation was tested, and the very gory photographs had filled the courtroom. She had been able to almost feel the stares and glares of members of the jury and the gallery while the medical examiner had testified. She knew it was critical that she kept her face straight ahead and didn't do anything that could be construed as guilt by the jury. There were several members of the jury that seemed like they would be eager to pounce on any potentially inappropriate facial expressions.

She didn't think it would be any easier today, so she was ready to mentally recite mathematics tables in her mind, if necessary.

She felt an unfamiliar feeling in her chest when she saw her father file in along with the rest of the gallery that morning. He was dressed in a subdued manner, in a dark suit, and had no entourage in tow. He caught her eye as he came in, and she felt like a small girl again, wanting to please her father. His eyes looked kind and caring when he looked at her, and that too reminded her of when she was a small child before everything had changed. When their family had really been their family.

****

"For our first witness, the defense would like to call Ms. Trenivius Alexander." Lee Filderman stated. Lee was dressed in a taupe colored, sharkskin suit. The sheen of the material gave it a golden hue in the torch style lighting. Sunshine was just beginning to penetrate the dark, wood paneled room. He paired it with a French cuffed, stiff white shirt, and a soft, champagne colored damask tie. There were no fancy waistcoats or pocket watches, but the rich brown leather of his John Lobb oxfords gleamed with fresh polish. The shade of his leather belt looked made to match. Deep blue lapis cuff links finished off his elegant look.

It was a shame Lee Filderman hadn't lived in an earlier age. He would have made an elegant and educated courtier to the Duke of Orleans, arguing l'Ancien Droit alongside intelligentsia like Henri François d'Aguesseau and François-Marie Arouet, in a full skirted coat of velvet, satin or silk. He would have cut a fine figure in waistcoats in cloth of silver or shot through with gold embroidery to contrast with elegant breeches, white silk stockings and a fine linen stock, but now, in Memphis, 2022, he still somehow had the class and bearing to look anything but dandyish. With his witness on the stand, Lee was in his element.

Trenivius Alexander appeared nervous on the stand. She was a young, African American woman with long dark brown braids, big brown eyes and beautiful, even, white teeth. She was nicely dressed in a royal blue sheath dress and matching jacket.

"Good morning, Ms. Alexander!" Lee said with enthusiasm, smiling at his witness.

Trenivius Alexander visibly relaxed with his greeting, saying, "Good morning, Sir." in response.

"Ms. Alexander, you have heard Detective Payne testify that the police found several emails going back and forth between the official election headquarters and Mr. Hunter Baron. These emails were in response to some threats made by Mr. Baron. Now, we can do a lot of back and forth, but that's just tiresome for our jury, especially this early in the morning, so I am just going to say it flat out. Some of these emails were traced to a computer at your desk. Did you write them?" Lee questioned. The jurors looked attentive to hearing her answer.

"Yes, I did." Trenivius Alexander answered.

"Why?" Lee asked, seemingly perplexed.

"I was trying to protect Ms. Ember, my boss." she answered.

"Did you ever show Ember the emails or tell her about them?" Lee asked.

"No!" she answered.

"Why not?" he asked gently.

"I knew it would embarrass and humiliate her, and that's what he wanted. If he really wanted the money, he would have sent it to her personal email, which isn't that hard to find." she answered.

"Did you notify the police or the Tennessee Bureau of Investigations?" Lee asked.

"No." Ms. Alexander said softly.

"Why not?" Lee pushed.

"You saw the emails. He said he would send the video to the whole world if I did. Besides, if I went to the police, it would have been reported on the local news. I wanted to handle this quietly and save Ember from any embarrassment. She's a good person! She doesn't deserve this!" she added, defiantly, while looking at the prosecutors.

"Did you talk to the police when they came to the office and seized the computers?" Lee asked.

"No. I waited for them to come ask me questions, but they never did." she answered. "They just showed the warrant, took the computers and left."

"Did the police ever attempt to contact you?" Lee asked.

"No! If I'd have known that they were going to find those emails, I would have gone to them myself." Trenivius Alexander said, looking upset.

"Now, I have one last question, Ms. Alexander." Lee said. "Why did the doorman, Andres Ochoa, identify you yesterday, here in open court, as the last person to visit Hunter Baron?"

Trenivius Alexander looked frightened as she answered. She hadn't expected to be identified yesterday, and she had been terrified when the subpoena arrived yesterday evening. She hesitated as she answered, "I went to the apartment that night, like he said, but no one answered the door when I knocked. That's when I realized I was making a mistake."

"What do you mean?" Lee asked.

"I had taken forty thousand dollars from the campaign account to pay Mr. Baron but as I walked to his apartment, I realized that made me as much of a thief as he was. When he didn't answer, I left right away and replaced the money in the account first thing in the morning." Trenivius Alexander answered.

"Did you do anything else?" Lee asked.

"Yes. I went to see Jack Prince and told him the whole story. I even showed him the emails." Trenivius Alexander answered.

"Do you know if the police ever asked about the bank transactions?" Lee asked.

"No, I don't think they ever did, but as I said, I never talked to anyone from the police. Only I and the campaign accountant had access to the campaign account. Ember isn't even a signatory on the account, so she couldn't have taken out any money." Trenivius Alexander volunteered.

"Ms. Alexander, thank you for your time." Lee said, gallantly. He turned and nodded to the prosecution, stating, "Prosecution, she is now your witness."

Carrie Bryant strode to the witness stand. She wore what she considered to be her "power suit" which was a bright red pants suit, paired with a square-toed heels in the same shade. It had been an impulse buy in a moment of weakness at Dillards, but now she felt it was worth every penny.

She smiled brightly at the witness, to disarm her. "Ms. Alexander, Are you covering for your boss, Ember Prince?"

Trenivius Alexander, who had been in the process of returning the smile, halted in her tracks. "No!" she answered.

"You do know that perjury or lying on the stand is a class A misdemeanor and is punishable by up to a year in jail." Carrie stated before continuing, "Now are you sure you aren't covering for Ember Prince?"

"No, I wouldn't do that!" Trenivius Alexander stated emphatically.

"Just like you wouldn't take money out of campaign funds?" Carrie asked.

"Objection! Badgering the witness!" Lee stated. "Your Honor, the witness has already testified as to the fact that she withdrew and replaced the money in the account in the same 18-hour period, which is reflected on the bank statements she has provided."

"Sustained. Particularly as it doesn't appear that the police were interested in these financial transactions. Counselor." Judge Ward said, addressing Carrie Bryant, "You can't start a fishing expedition at this late date just because the police failed to do their job."

"Yes, Your Honor," Carrie said, acknowledging Judge Ward.

"In that case, I have no more questions for Ms. Alexander." Carrie finished.

As she left the courtroom, Trenivius Alexander looked solemnly at Ember Prince, almost in apology. Ember Prince met her eyes and allowed just the faintest smile and nod at her loyal employee.

"The defense would like to call Mr. Rex Lester to the stand," Lee Filderman boomed.

"Good morning, Mr. Lester!" he said cheerfully. It was this slightly mischievous, jovial air of his that did more to convince the jury of his client's innocence than a lot of scientific gobbley gook. While the layperson's understanding of DNA was a lot more advanced than it had been in previous decades, the quibbling back and forth among experts and technicians still induced almost instant boredom and apathy. The fact that the defendant's counsel seemed fearlessly laid back and relaxed during a capital murder trial, meant a lot to the jurors, especially the older ones. The older jurors still believed that integrity could be foretold in a handshake or a man's word. Despite his reputation for high-profile cases, Lee Filderman didn't have a history of defending grossly guilty ones. There were no O.J. Simpsons in his legal closet. His biggest wins had come by exposing deep injustices and gross incompetence in the legal system.

This public opinion might have changed if fate had not intervened in dramatic fashion. Lee had initially been the lead counsel on a very controversial case the year before, when he was struck down with acute appendicitis. In that case, an almost certainly guilty and most unrepentant defendant had gone free, in one of the biggest scandals of the decade. It wasn't quite as juicy as the Memphis Trouser Affair of the mid-80's, which involved the Australian Prime Minister at the time, but it was close.

"Good morning!" Rex Lester replied in an equally robust tone, flavored with a thick Mississippi accent. Two jurors appeared to nod in approval of the exchange. In comparison to other witnesses, and members of the court, Mr. Lester sported a more relaxed appearance. This isn't to say that he wasn't well put together, but instead of dress shoes, he wore worn but clean leather boots. He wore impeccably clean but unmistakably classic bootcut denim Levi jeans, ironed with a crease down each leg, and anchored with a large oval silver belt buckle with a 2-inch piece of turquoise in the middle. He wore a white, oxford button-down shirt, and a beige sport coat with coffee brown suede accents on the shoulders. The only thing he was missing was his Stetson hat, and that was sitting on the seat of his Ford F-150.

"Mr. Lester, would you please introduce yourself to the jury, with your full name, spelling, and professional title and history?" Lee asked.

"My name is Rex Allen Lester, that's L-e-s-t-e-r, and I am currently a private detective. Until recently, I was a sergeant with the Memphis homicide division. I have over two decades experience in the homicide division alone, and twenty-eight years as a police officer in total. I have been involved and investigated over a hundred fifty cases in my career." he answered.

Several eyebrows raised with this introduction, and Lee Filderman was quick to act on this as he heard a loud whisper from the prosecutions table saying, "What the hell is this? What is he doing on the stand? Get me the defense witness list!" as Jose Leon hissed at his associates.

"28 years as a police officer! I bet you have some stories, man oh man!" Lee said, with the easy camaraderie that comes with interviewing people you know and respect. "You know, I bet you look familiar to some of these people in the courthouse today, nut were you ever on that show, the one that they filmed here in Memphis, *The First 48*, following the homicide division? It's been a while since it was on television." Lee said.

"Yes, Sir. I surely was. They started filming that series in Memphis just a few years after I transferred into Homicide. I was on a couple of episodes in season 6, with my old partner, Tony Mullins." Rex answered with a bit of humor in his voice.

"You said you were with the Homicide Division of the Memphis Police Department until just recently?" he asked. "And how recently would that be?"

"I took a leave of absence two weeks ago." Rex Lester answered.

"Oh, that's quite recent, practically yesterday! So, I guess you *are* familiar with everyone in the case?" Lee asked, nonchalantly.

"You could say that." Rex Lester answered, deadpan. "I was Renee Payne's partner on this case."

"Oh, my! Well, then it's safe to assume that you were intimately acquainted with the facts of this investigation. May I ask why you have taken a leave of absence?" Lee asked.

"There was a significant difference of opinion amongst myself and my former partner over the nature of the evidence. As I mentioned, I have over two decades of experience investigating homicides, and the evidence against *this* suspect in this case is circumstantial at best." Rex Lester answered.

"That's sounds quite serious!" Lee said, with an arched brow. "Did you attempt to discuss your concerns with anyone?"

"I attempted to address it with Detective Payne directly on several occasions. I felt she was rushing to get an arrest warrant without proper evidence. I went to the District Attorney's office for the same reason. Finally, the only thing I could do in good conscience was talk to you. I knew that coming to the defense team was career suicide, so I took a leave of absence before I approached you at your office." Rex answered.

"Why would you sacrifice your career for Ember Prince?" Lee Filderman asked.

"I didn't sacrifice anything for Ember Prince. I don't know her. I've only spoken to her about this case a handful of times. In many ways, this has very little to do with her. It's about my personal principles." Rex answered.

"I refuse to sacrifice my ethics, my sense of right and wrong and a long career dedicated to pursuing justice by sitting by and watching an injustice happen. It's better to leave than to become a bad cop." Rex finished. He saw the prosecutor, Jose Leon, stiffen at his words, but he refused to soften them. His career in law enforcement was over anyway because now he would be seen as a snitch in the department.

"That sounds like a really difficult decision. It must have been quite painful for you to show up on my doorstep." Lee said sympathetically.

"It was and it wasn't," Rex answered. "It's always painful when you realize the shortcomings and weaknesses of others. It's disturbing to think that you have dedicated a career based on honesty and integrity to see others in that same career that care more about making arrests and making a name for themselves. " Lee nodded for Rex to continue.

"Leaving the Memphis Police Department, well, it was probably time anyway. I graduated from the police academy when I was just 21 years old. I could have retired several years ago. I just wasn't ready to then. If this hadn't happened, I would have kept going for three or four more years, but I can't do it to just punch a clock. That's not who I am. It has to mean something." Rex finished.

"Well, I think it's a great loss for the department and our city to have someone with all your experience just walk away. Let's talk more about the things you saw, and why you came to me." Lee asked.

"Would you give me an example of something that you felt was improperly investigated, Sergeant Lester?" Lee said, using his former title to remind the jury of the expert nature of this witness's testimony.

"From the very beginning of this case, when the hidden camera and the videos were discovered, my former partner became obsessed with the idea that the videos were the motive for the killing. When she saw that Ember Prince was one of the women on the tapes, she became hyper-focused on her. I mean, we still haven't even identified all of the women on the tapes, much less confirmed alibis for them when I left two weeks ago. We knew he was blackmailing several of them, so in my mind, every single woman on that tape had motive." he answered.

"Detective Payne stated that all of the potential suspects have been vetted and cleared except for the defendant. Do you disagree with this assessment?" Lee asked.

"Unless she went back to tie up many loose ends, there is no way that Detective Payne eliminated all the possible suspects. I really doubt that she has had time to do so, because she has been in such a rush to push the District Attorney's Office into charging and arresting the defendant. Proper police procedure requires you to eliminate potential suspects before focusing in on others. You let the evidence lead you to the suspect. You don't tailor your interpretation of the evidence to fit a chosen suspect. Renee, as much as I think she has potential, has been deadset in her ambitions. She has been in such a hellfire hurry to arrest and convict a member of the Prince family. Heck, I think if old Grandmother Bernice Prince hadn't died, she'd be here in front of this jury," Rex finished.

Several older Memphians laughed, as they pictured the stalwart and staid Bernice in her prim and proper church clothes. She had been a legend in the African American community and had instilled both fear and discipline in a whole generation of young Memphians.

"Why do you think she has it out for the Prince family?" Lee Filderman asked.

"Objection! Calls for speculation! Mr. Lester doesn't know what Detective Payne was thinking. He's not a mind reader," Jose Leon argued.

"But he did work side-by-side with Detective Payne, which gives him insight into her attitudes, thoughts, and behaviors." Lee argued back.

"Overruled. Witness may answer." Judge Ward ruled.

"Daniel, will you read back the question to the witness?" Lee asked the court reporter.

""Why do you think she has it out for the Prince family?" Daniel recited.

"I don't think it's intentional. I think it's subconscious or what have you. I think that Renee, like many people in Memphis, is just fed up and frustrated with what she sees as the criminal antics of this particular family. She's not a malicious person, and she's certainly not a bad police officer. I just think she's let her personal feelings get in the way." Rex answered.

"That may be so. Politics can certainly stir people up, especially after these last few go-rounds." Lee agreed, with a couple of spectators laughing. "But," he said, getting back to business, "Would you give me another example of a disagreement you had with Detective Payne?" Lee asked.

"I had a real problem with how quicky she accepted Hunter Baron's girlfriend's alibi. They had a history of a turbulent relationship, and according to acquaintances and neighbors, she had recently moved out of his apartment, so things were definitely rocky in that relationship. By several accounts, she had cut him completely out of her life, changed her cell phone number, and was making plans to switch jobs. Neighbors, friends, co-workers, and even just passersby had commented on several public fights the couple had in the past. Yet, she's also the person who discovered the body. It doesn't quite sit right with me. I am not so sure I'd be so quick to dismiss her as a suspect just because her sister says they were home watching movies all night. It's not like two twelve-year-olds at a slumber party after all." Rex answered.

"So, Hunter Baron and his live-in girlfriend had recently broken off their relationship. Did you find anything else suspicious about this?" Lee asked.

"It's pretty suspicious to me that you have an apparent giant blow-up in a relationship with your significant other, or a possible spouse, but the grieving wife or ex-girlfriend, whichever it is, doesn't mention this at all to anyone. Instead, she plays the role of the grief-stricken loved one, except that she leaves the funeral early, and then ducks out of the reception." Rex answered.

"Wait! Wait! Wait! Sergeant Lester, did you say spouse?" Lee questioned.

"Several people reported that Hunter Baron and his girlfriend had eloped to Aruba, but I could find no evidence or documentation of a legal marriage. It may have been just a symbolic or religious ceremony, or maybe the paperwork was never filed. But I do know that several of her co-workers said that she certainly believed she was married, and had shown them photos of the event." Rex Lester answered.

"So, that would change things, wouldn't it? I mean, if they were married, legal or not. This new widow might be entitled to his financial assets, correct? That certainly seems like a motive." Lee finished.

"It's a strong motive, particularly given that Hunter Baron had himself recently inherited a fairly tidy sum on the death of his mother." Rex Lester answered.

"Was there anything else that you thought should have been investigated more thoroughly in regard to the possible Mrs. Baron?" Lee asked.

"It's suspicious to me that no one ever got a search warrant for her new apartment to look for, I don't know, *the matching earring or maybe a box of rat poison?*" he said, ending with some sarcasm.

"So, you feel that the case has been sloppy?" Lee asked. "Do you have another example of this?" Lee was enjoying watching his witness poke holes in the prosecution, in his warm Mississippi drawl, which sapped a bit of the venom out of his tone.

"I certainly do." Rex said, warming up to the topic. "I also think that if a piece of expensive jewelry is found at the crime scene, I'd suspect the girlfriend, at least until I tracked down more information on the jewelry." Rex answered.

"I understand you have some knowledge on this critical piece of evidence, the alexandrite and platinum earring that we heard so much about from the prosecution?" Lee commented.

"Sure. We heard all about the price of the gemstones, the presence of the victim's blood on one side of the earring, and their failure to get DNA from the post. But nothing about where the earring might have actually come from, or who the owner might be!" Rex answered.

He continued, "This jewelry is unique, in the pattern, the use of the materials and the execution. It's not something you see every day, even among high-end pieces. It has some features that are very distinctive to South American art, the way the metal is heated and formed into an iridescent sheet. The pattern, and the way the Alexandrite is inlaid, that too was suggestive of indigenous techniques."

"Indigeous? Do you mean like Native American? Like the Chickasaw?" Lee asked. The Chickasaw Nation had lived in the

Mississippi Delta until being forcibly relocated in the 1830's and marched on the Trail of Tears to Oklahoma. There was a local archaeological museum for the Chickasaw Nation in town that was a favorite for school field trips. Several members of the jurors looked acutely interested and leaned forward.

"Not Native American, like American Indian exactly. More like native to the Americas." Rex answered.

"I wasn't exactly sure what tribe or even what country, so I sought out experts. I went to online forums, chats, and video conferences with multiple jewelers, who were able to identify some of the techniques as unique to a particular type of jewelry made in Maracaibo, Venezuela by an up-and-coming artist working for a family of jewelers," Rex said.

"Wow! That is pretty specific, Sergeant Lester. Were you able to find a Memphis connection?" Lee asked.

"As a matter of fact, I found a couple of very interesting connections. The first one is that the biggest and most famous jewelers and gold traders in Maracaibo, Venezuela was the Triana Africano family. That's a Spanish-Jewish family that goes back over two hundred years in Venezuela. They originally came to escape the Spanish Inquisition, if you can believe that. Then they got into gold mining, among other things, in different parts of Venezuela. They became part of the elite Jewish community in Maracaibo," Rex was saying as Jose Leon called out,

"Objection! Relevance. We aren't here for a world history lesson, Your Honor."

Judge Ward looked visibly annoyed as he stated, "Overruled! I find that I am quite interested to hear about this Memphis connection myself."

"Please continue, Sergeant Lester," Judge Ward instructed.

"In the early 1980's Venezuela wasn't the place it is now. It was glamourous, wealthy, and exciting. Maracaibo was like a much classier Miami, and the Triana family, with their wealth, gold mines and fancy jewelry, they were rubbing elbows with everyone." Rex said.

"It was a big, happy, family too, with fourteen kids. One of the kids was friends with the politicos, and another was a pageant winner. A couple of kids ran the family business, and another was the accountant, and one of the kids was responsible for maintaining the jewelry store. This all collapses at the end of the 1990s but before that, while things were still good, one of the sons hires a young girl to train as a new jewelry artist. This new employee ends up being just phenomenally talented – doing really one-of-a-kind stuff and making a name for herself in Venezuela." Rex explained.

"Then she comes to Memphis?" Lee asked.

"No. She ended up going to Paris, where I tracked her down and interviewed her. Her name is Anna Karina Raga, she made the earring, and she's outside in the hallway waiting to testify." Rex finished.

"Well, with that. I have no more questions, but I reserve the right to recall this witness." Lee finished.

"Prosecution, your witness." Judge Ward called.

Jose Leon stood up deliberately and started a slow clap. "Bravo, Bravo!" he called sarcastically, "That's quite a show you and Mr. Filderman put on, *Mr.* Lester." he said as he approached the witness stand, "I should have known something was fishy when I saw your name on the defense's witness list."

"None of it would have been necessary if you had listened to me when I came to your office," Rex replied.

"So, this is bitter grapes because you want your own accolades, then?" Jose Leon said, his voice taking a harsh edge.

"Not at all, Sir! I don't think that wanting to see a crime solved is bitter grapes, do you?" Rex retorted.

Jose Leon ignored his taunt, and asked snidely, "When did you find the time to find this jeweler? I hope you didn't use department resources to fly all over Europe on some sort of holiday."

"It's funny that you'd think that. That's what my wife said you would say when she booked the plane ticket on her personal credit card. Since I found the witness who is going to solve this case, I think you owe my wife fourteen hundred dollars for my travel expenses." Rex replied.

"I used my vacation time for the trip, but I know you won't reimburse me for that. I figured keeping innocent people out of prison was a worthy enough cause." Rex Lester added.

Lee turned his head and saw smiles in the gallery. The Mississippi cowboy had his fans, it seemed. Jose Leon ought to tread lightly, he thought to himself. It was why he let Jose run with it, instead of objecting to his line of questioning. Let him alienate the jury with his hostility.

"Don't you think it's a wee bit exotic to have some foreign jeweler involved in a murder in Memphis, Tennessee?" Jose Leon asked sarcastically.

"Are you suggesting that we shouldn't investigate any evidence that leads us outside of Shelby County, Sir? I am not quite sure I understand your question," Rex Lester retorted, "but I suppose you can ask her yourself."

Jose Leon abruptly switched his line of questioning, and asked, "Did you resent having a younger, female partner when you *were* with the Memphis Police Department?' Jose Leon said, stressing the word 'were'.

"Is that your angle?" Rex said, laughing. "That's a shame, because I really enjoyed being a mentor and teaching the younger detectives the ropes. You know, they even gave me a plaque for it, was that last year, no, that was 2021, Mentor of the Year. In fact, I was nominated several times by fellow detectives, Deborah Carson, Paula Harris, and Connie Justice. Then there's Caroline Mason and Doreen Shelton. They are the ones, along with Bill Ashton, who originally showed me the ropes back when I moved over to Homicide." Rex answered.

"But, if you need me to be some kind of sexist redneck just because I'm from Mississippi, then that's your thing, not mine!" Rex Lester finished.

Jose Leon abruptly flushed with frustration, as he saw two jurors and several spectators glare at him. He took a deep breath before trying a different tactic.

"I commend you on your diligence, but I don't recollect you ever bringing any of this marriage stuff to me. I would have wanted that all sorted out before I ever went to the judge for an arrest warrant. So, when did you do all this research on the deceased's girlfriend?" Jose Leon asked, more kindly.

"I started it after the remaining building neighbor, a Mr. Bearden, mentioned that Hunter Baron's wife had moved out. I thought it was a mistake, until I interviewed some of her former colleagues at International Paper and talked to one of the doormen at his apartment building. They all confirmed that the deceased was introducing her as his wife prior to his death. I attempted to bring this to you when you dismissed me that day at your office. After that, I continued to investigate it on my own, along with some other leads I had," Rex answered.

"Any other surprises that you held back from the police investigation," Jose Leon asked.

"Sir, I held back nothing, and you know it. I collected and maintained the chain-of-custody for the DNA and other evidence that was missed the first time around. I made sure samples that were collected, and not submitted, were processed, and I followed up on the witnesses and other leads that we uncovered. I did my job, Sir." Rex Lester answered.

Jose Leon realizing there was nothing to be gained by continuing to cross-examine this witness, stating, "I have no more questions."

The day had grown long, and several members of the spectators' gallery were seen stifling yawns. Lee leaned over to consult with Kisha before addressing the judge.

"We have just three more witnesses to call before finishing our defense, Your Honor. I am sure that we can complete all of the testimony tomorrow, and start closing arguments." Lee offered.

"What about your special witness? Judge Ward asked, taking the words out of Jose's mouth.

"Your Honor, to be honest, she's the reason I think we should stop for now. She just flew 22 hours to get to Memphis, before my team picked her up and brought her directly from the airport an hour ago. She's waiting in the hallway outside to testify, but she looks completely exhausted. I think it would be better if she could get a night's sleep, shower, and eat before I place her on the stand." Lee Filderman responded. Once the judge nodded his assent, Kisha went out into the hallway to speak to the wearied witness and the waiting driver. The woman looked almost gray in color in her fatigue. She gratefully took the arm of the driver as he led her out of the courtroom.

It was only 3:30 in the afternoon, but Judge Ward agreed, but instructed the jury, "Now, y'all remember if we are close to finishing tomorrow but it's 5:05, I need you all to stay until the end, alright?"

The jurors nodded their assent, then were dismissed for the day. A spring thunderstorm looked to be darkening the skies outside the courthouse, so it was with relief as spectators filed out and found their cars in the adjacent lots and headed home before the worst of the rush hour traffic. The defense team, along with Ember walked back to the office on Third Street. "I think today went well." Kisha said, starting the conversation.

"I do too. I almost feel like this nightmare might end." Ember answered. She looked at Kisha and Lee and asked, "Is there anything I need to prepare for tomorrow?"

"No, I don't think we will need you. I won't be calling you to the stand tomorrow. I don't think that there is anything that your testimony can add to the case. Just remember to keep your composure tomorrow. You have done an excellent job so far, but tomorrow will be difficult too." Lee said.

"Go home, sweetheart. Have a good meal. Think about something else." Kisha said. She had gotten to like the straightforward client and felt almost maternally protective towards her. They were the same age, but Ember seemed like such a lost young woman sometimes. She leaned over and gave Ember an embrace, which Ember welcomed wholeheartedly. Once she got into her car, Ember called her father.

"Daddy," she said, feeling like an eight-year-old girl again. "Thank you for coming today. It means a lot to me."

"Baby girl, you do know that you are always my baby girl. None of your sisters can ever replace you. I am sorry I haven't always been there when you needed me." Jack Prince answered.

"I'm sorry too." Ember answered.

"But I was there today." he answered, feeling the years of neglect suddenly and acutely.

"Yes, Daddy, you were." Ember said, "Thank you."

"I'll see you tomorrow!" Jack said before he hung up.

It wasn't a happy ending, and it didn't make up of the years of apathy, absence, or neglect, but it was something and right now, Ember needed that connection. She continued the drive home, feeling a little less alone. Then she followed Kisha's advice, making a simple but savory pasta with pesto and a small salad.

She scrolled thru the remote to find an old comedy to watch. She drifted off fairly quickly on the comfortable couch under a soft, fleecy blanket. She began to dream almost immediately, that she was on the witness stand, with her actual life on trial. Scenes from her life were being reviewed, with emphasis on her failures and losses. The prosecutor kept asking what she had to show for her life, and she couldn't answer. She opened her mouth to respond and realized, nothing. Nothing but a murder charge. She woke abruptly, to find that the movie had ended, and an episode of Law & Order had started. She untangled the blanket from around her torso, turned off the tv, and headed to the bathroom to brush her teeth before padding off to bed. She should be exhausted, but the dream still resonated in her brain. She slept poorly that night and felt as beige and washed out as the pantsuit she chose to wear the next day in court. She paired it with a pristine, ivory colored, lace trimmed blouse that any Victorian minister's wife would have found acceptable.

****

Kisha Mack was in her glory that morning in court. She wore a suit that would be the envy of every woman in the Sunday morning COGIC services east of the Mississippi River. It was a black suit with a snakeskin printed pattern. The lapels and cuffs were black leather along with a belt that cinched the jacket at her waist. Just to the side of the leather lapel, she wore a medium-sized pin with a black rose adorned with two small black feathers. If she'd had a matching hat, she could have led the runway for Memphis Black Fashion Week. As it was, her black shoes with gold heels clicked elegantly as she approached the bench. Her hair, a soft golden brown, framed her face with curls. Lucious lashes with understated gold shaded eye make-up called attention to large brown eyes. Several pieces of bright gold, chunky jewelry gave her a finished and polished look, and her chocolate cherry colored lipstick framed a welcoming smile.

"Good morning everyone. Good morning, Your Honor," she said as she addressed the court. While the prosecution often seemed to dispense with these formalities in their rush to present their case, Lee had taught Kisha to take a different tack. He relished these rituals, and enjoyed interacting with the jury, and they knew it. In turn, they responded to him, warmly, grateful to be acknowledged for more than just their civil duty. He acknowledged them as people, and this goodwill went a long way in building rapport with his client. Kisha had learned from the master, and now did the same. It didn't take much, a pleasant greeting, a genuine smile, some eye contact – and maybe, if the moment was right, a little humor. This last part didn't come as naturally to Kisha and came with some peril. Humor at the wrong moment during a trial such as this could come off as callous or uncaring. So, Kisha stuck with sweet smiles and kind greetings, like she did this morning. Next, she thanked the jury for their service before calling her first witness.

"Your Honor, I'd like to call Anna-Karina Raga to the witness stand." Kisha said with another of her glorious smiles. As she did, a petite brunette in her early fifties made her way to the front of the court. She was rather nondescript in appearance given all the anticipation of her testimony, with serviceable shoes, a plain white blouse, and a navy suit. She wore minimal make-up. What saved her from absolute anonymity and utter blandness was the large, ornate, jeweled collar she wore. It was made of large ropes of gold, and had a pendant that was hammered gold, adorned with semi-precious stones and iridescent fish scales in the shape of a large leaf.

"Bonjour y Bienvenidos, Senora Raga," Kisha said in a mix of Spanish and French.

"Thank you." Anna-Karina said in a soft voice.

"Would you please state your full name and occupation for the court?" Kisha requested.

"Anna Karina Raga. I am a fine jewelry maker with La Fabrique Nomade." Anna Karina answered.

"You have come a long way, haven't you?" Kisha asked.

"Yes, ma'am. I am working in Paris, France." Anna-Karina answered, in her accented English.

"I would like to thank you for coming such a long way to help us solve this murder." Kisha said.

"Objection! This witness is not a detective. She isn't solving a murder, she is testifying in a trial. Let's not have a repeat of yesterday's theatrics." Carrie Bryant called. She had been emboldened after a game day style speech from Jose Leon that morning.

"Overruled. Now Ms. Bryant, so far this morning, the only theatrics have been yours. Proceed cautiously." Judge Ward ruled.

"Ms. Raga, is France your country of origin?" Kisha asked.

"No, it is not. I am from Venezuela," Anna Karina answered.

"Were you a jewelry maker in Venezuela?" Kisha asked.

"I studied law in the 1980's, but was unable to finish, so I switched to an art school to study jewelry making. Then after graduating, when I was 22, I went to apprentice with a master jeweler at a well-known shop in Maracaibo. Soon he promoted me to staff jeweler, and then later, head jewelry designer. I have been making jewelry since then, though when the economy began to deteriorate, I had to take other jobs to make enough money to survive." Anna-Karina answered.

"Why and when did you leave Venezuela?" Kisha asked.

"The family that owned the jewelry store fell out of favor with President Hugo Chavez, due to some kind of problems with the president's son, Hugo Rafael. After that, their business started to go badly. The government seized a lot of their holdings, including the mines, and they had to leave the country." she said.

"I was able to continue working at the jewelry store even after they sold it and left Venezuela, but it wasn't the same. The new owners didn't know how to run a business, and the economy got much worse after the president died. Things were getting very bad, so I was working at a restaurant, giving tours, doing anything I could to make money to survive." Anna Karina said.

"Soon it became very difficult to find food and other necessities, no matter how many jobs I had. I left Venezuela in 2017." Anna Karina finished.

"Tell me about your work in France," Kisha asked.

"Once I came to France, I found a trade organization that specialized in assisting migrants to resume their craftwork. This allowed me to start making jewelry professionally again. I worked with another designer, Monica Trevisanut, for the first two years, making a name for myself in Paris." Anna-Karina answered.

"Were you working with the designer, Monica Trevisanut, when you created the earrings that Sergeant Lester contacted you about?" Kisha asked.

"Yes. We had just finished a large jewelry exhibition at the Instuit Nacional Metiers de Arte where we gave several lectures in addition to showing our work. I was contacted by a young woman after the lecture. We scheduled a private appointment to design a custom piece." Anna Karina answered.

"Did you recognize the young woman who contacted you?" Kisha asked.

"I didn't see her in person until she and her boyfriend came into the shop. That's when I realized I had seen her back in Venezuela." Anna Karina answered.

"How did you know her in Venezuela?" Kisha asked.

"She was the youngest daughter of the family I worked for in the jewelry store. She was just a little girl when I first met her. Over the years, she would come into the store to see her older brother, who would take her for ice creams, give her small pieces of jewelry, and such. Before the family sold the jewelry store, she had become a local beauty pageant contestant. She would borrow jewelry for various competitions, so I saw her quite a bit then." Anna Karina answered.

"Then you would recognize her pretty easily?" Kisha asked.

"Yes, because I watched her grow up. She looks the same as she did as a beauty contestant, after she had all the surgeries she needed to win. Maybe a little older, is all." Anna Karina answered.

"Would you tell me about the piece she commissioned?" Kisha asked.

"Yes. After the investigator came to see me with photographs of the earring, I went back and found my original drawings of the design." Anna Karina explained, "These are copies of my drawings."

"Your Honor, I would like to enter these two drawings as defense exhibit D," Kisha stated.

Bailiff Bronson rolled over a tall corkboard, as Kisha opened the first rolled drawing. "Oh my goodness, this is beautiful!" she said as she looked at the full color ink rendering.

The jury looked towards the cork board eagerly to see the poster sized drawing. There were soft murmurs from the gallery. Kisha then took an enlargement of one of the laboratory photos which showed the earring being held with tweezers and placed it on the corkboard. It was unmistakably the same piece of jewelry.

"This is a very unique design, Ms. Raga. A previous expert has testified that it is also a very expensive one due to the gemstones. Would you tell me more about how you ended up with this design and these materials?" Kisha asked.

"When Laura and her boyfriend came to see me, Laura picked out several of my finished pieces that she liked, but she wanted something more unique, one-of-the-kind. She didn't like the idea that someone else might buy the same piece. They commissioned me to make a custom piece using more expensive materials." Anna Karina answered.

"Have you made any other similar pieces before or after taking this commission?" Kisha asked.

"No, I had to promise not to make any similar designs," Anna Karina said.

"Is this a common request?" Kisha asked.

"I've been asked before, but it's not something that artists usually agree to. This is our livelihood. I can't let it be limited by someone else's vanity." Anna Karina said, displaying mild annoyance.

"But in this case, you made an exception. Why?" Kisha asked.

"They offered me a tremendous amount of money in addition to my usual fees for design and materials, for one." Anna Karina said.

"And there was another reason?" Kisha probed.

Anna Karina seemed uncomfortable as she glanced around the courtroom before answering, "The other reason was that her boyfriend made me really uncomfortable. He scared me! He seemed like one of those mafia, criminal types. I didn't want to see what would happen if he thought I went against his wishes." she answered, almost embarrassed.

"Tell me about this boyfriend, Anna Karina." Kisha asked.

"Objection! Relevance!" Carrie called out.

Kisha addressed the judge directly, "I think it's extremely relevant if the boyfriend is the reason that this is an exclusive jewelry design."

"Overruled. Ms. Mack makes sense." Judge Ward answered.

"I was never formally introduced to the man that accompanied her, but the way he touched and caressed her made it obvious that they were lovers. I didn't get his full name but she called him Alex. I knew immediately that he had a lot of money, even before he pulled the gemstones out of his pocket because he was a lot older than her, and not very attractive. I mean, he wasn't ugly, but he looked like someone's dad, and she wins beauty contests." Anna Karina answered.

"What did you find threatening about him?" Kisha asked.

"He wasn't mean or menacing, but they arrived with two huge bodyguards. I could see that they had weapons underneath their jackets and that terrified me. That's not a thing that you see in France." she said, almost shuddering with the memory.

"The other thing was that he seemed very… controlled. He didn't laugh, or smile or anything the whole time they were in the shop. He wasn't affectionate towards her, though he did seem to view her as a possession, with the way he kept his hands on her. It all seemed very.. transactional." Anna Karina said.

"Tell me about these gemstones that he pulled from his pocket." Kisha asked.

"They were incredible! I knew what they were immediately because of the sparkle and fire, but I couldn't believe it. I'd never seen Alexandrite in person before, and he just pulled a couple of loose stones out of his pocket." Anna Karina said, animatedly.

"I called over another jeweler to help me weigh and inventory the stones he gave me. He tried to give me three, but I knew the earrings wouldn't need that many, so I gave one of them back. I didn't even want it in the safe in my shop because I could never replace it if something happened to it. He seemed to enjoy my discomfort." Anna Karina remembered. "That was the only time I heard his chuckle, as he talked to his two bodyguards in Russian."

"How did you know it was Russian?" Kisha asked.

"There have been a lot of Russians in Paris for a long time, so it's still pretty common to hear it spoken on the streets. There's a Russian Orthodox Seminary a few streets away from my workshop. They teach the classes in French, but most of the students are Russian. They like to drink and smoke at the coffee shop across the street. I've even picked up a couple of phrases." Anna Karina explained.

"How would you have characterized the man in his relationship to your female client?" Kisha asked.

"There is an American term I learned one day that I think fits, He is 100% wealthy Russian Sugar Daddy." Anna Karina replied, smiling.

"Are you absolutely positive that this earring that you designed in Paris, France for a private customer is the same earring in the crime scene photo here?" Kisha asked.

"Yes. I designed and created that earring for Laura Triana Africano in December of 2019, and her boyfriend paid me 75,000 euros to do so." Anna Karina replied.

"Thank you, Ms. Raga." Kisha said, "I have no more questions."

Carrie Bryant was in charge of cross-examining Ms. Raga but it was only a formality. After the Alexandrite stones had been examined and detected in the earring, it was a given that it was a rare, rare piece. To challenge Ms. Raga's testimony would only make the prosecutor's office look weak and desperate.

"Ms. Raga, thank you for coming all this way!" Carrie said. The defense team's charm offensive hadn't gone unnoticed. "Is this your first time in the United States?" Carrie asked.

When the witness answered in the affirmative, Carrie smiled and said, "Well, welcome to the mid-south! I hope you get a chance to take in some of our native flavor before you return to Paris."

From the corner of her eye, she saw a couple of ladies in the spectator's gallery nodded encouragingly.

"Ms. Raga, were you forced to come here to testify?" she asked.

"No, ma'am. Mr. Lester made sure to tell me that it was entirely voluntary." Anna Karina Raga answered.

"What compelled you to come testify then?" Carrie asked.

"He said it was a murder trial – and that my jewelry was found at the scene. How could I stay home?" she answered.

"Well, Thank you Ms. Raga, I wish all of our citizens were so civic minded." Carrie answered.

"Were you paid anything to be here?" Carrie asked.

"No, and I had to close my workshop to be here. They did pay for my flight and my lodging. I am staying at a nice little house where the owners make me breakfast every day. It's very nice." Anna Karina answered.

"Well, it's been lovely meeting you Ms. Raga. You are a real artist." Carrie said in closing.

"Your Honor, I have no more questions for this witness,"

"Now, Ms. Raga, please stay another day in Memphis, until closing arguments, in case we need you back on the witness stand." Judge Ward said, kindly adding, "Be sure to check out the Lorraine Motel and Civil Rights Museum, and some of our fine restaurants. I find the Majestic Grille to be a lovely place for a nice dinner."

Ms. Raga gave a shy smile as she left the courtroom.

"Judge Ward, may I see you in chambers?" Lee asked. Judge Ward looked surprised but assented. He, Lee Filderman, Jose Leon all entered the judge's chambers.

As Judge Ward settled himself behind an enormous oak desk, he said, "Okay, now what's this about? And no legal game playing between you two." he scolded.

Jose Leon looked bewildered while Lee became annoyed though he did his damndest to hide it.

"Your Honor, my material witness, Veronica Triana Africano, who received a subpoena to appear today appears to have disappeared. My assistant has been calling and texting every half-hour with no answer."

"I became concerned, so I sent Rex Lester over to her apartment this morning. He called the deputies when he couldn't get an answer, and they broke down the door. It looks like she's cleared out. While there is still furniture in the apartment, it looks like there are clothes and personal items missing. Her personal laptop, and part of the files from a small file cabinet appear to be missing. Neighbors say that she left with another woman, with several suitcases late last night. It appears that she has willingly absconded." Lee finished.

"What was the nature of Ms. Triana's testimony?" Judge Ward asked.

"She could have potentially cleared my client. She is the significant other/ wife of the deceased and her sister was the owner of the earring that Ms. Raga just testified about. I was going to ask that you declare her as a hostile witness. As Sergeant Lester had previously testified, she had a lot of questions to answer to. It's why my team was keeping a close eye on her." Lee finished, looking extremely frustrated.

"I'll issue an arrest warrant for her for contempt of court. Have the deputies notify the Tennessee Bureau of Investigation as well as the Federal Bureau of Investigation." Judge Ward said.

"When you find her, you better turn her over to the police." Jose Leon cautioned.

"Speaking of which, why don't we swear out an arrest warrant on that sister too. We can sort it out once we have them both in a cell." Judge Ward declared.

"In the meantime, I want you both out there, to continue this trial." the Judge declared.

"Don't you think we should consider a motion to dismiss, Your Honor? If the prosecution is interested in pursuing the Triana sisters, as Jose Leon just mentioned." Lee Filderman asked.

"Nice try, Filderman. Get out there and argue your case. Unless you and Leon here can come to a plea agreement? I understand the prosecution previously had an offer on the table?" Judge Ward answered.

Lee Filderman knew he was risking contempt but he openly snorted! "A plea deal, when my client is clearly innocent. No thanks!" he said.

The Judge and attorneys exited chambers. Jose Leon could clearly see the questions on his associates' faces, while Kisha Mack, having attempted to contact the witness all morning knew exactly what was going on.

Judge Ward addressed the courtroom, "Before the defense calls their next witness, I want it noted for the record, that we have issued a bench warrant for the arrest of Veronica Triana Africano for contempt of court for her failure to appear today."

"So noted." Daniel Valderrama, the court reporter replied as keys clacked.

Unperterbed outwardly, Lee Filderman approached the jury box, saying, "The defense would like to call our next witness, Rod Barron to the stand."

A youthful looking man in his mid-forties entered the courtroom and walked to the witness stand. He had reddish brown hair with a sprinkling of grey, that was echoed in a fuzzy but well-barbered beard. He had a smattering of freckles over his sun-pinked cheeks. He was dressed in what looked like his Sunday best, finished off with a pair of worn, but clean cowboy boots. He looked like he would be at home on top of a tractor, which wasn't too far from the truth. He had been raised in rural Arkansas and had only recently moved to Southaven, a small Mississippi suburb of Memphis.

"Would you state your name for the record, Sir?" Lee Filderman asked.

"Rod Lynn Barron," the man answered, looking around a little bit nervously at the courtroom's surroundings.

"Was that always your name?" Lee asked gently.

"Um, no, Sir," the man said flushing a bit, "I mean, it's always been Rod, never Rodney or anything. But I changed my last name a few months ago." he finished. A few beads of sweat dotted his hairline, catching the light.

"Why did you do that?" Lee gently probed, allowing the witness to take his time, and to relax. Out of the corner of his eye, he saw the jurors lean forward to listen to the witnesses' response, as he approached the witness box.

"Um.. Well, last year, after some stuff happened, my mom finally told me about my real dad, and I wanted to carry his name. I never got to know him. He died before I was even born." he finished. He looked a little embarrassed and glanced over at a neatly dressed, attractive elderly white female in the spectator's section. Karen smiled reassuringly at her son, and Rod Barron, visibly relaxed.

"Now, Mr. Barron, could you please explain a little more precisely about what 'stuff' happened last year?" Lee coaxed.

"Last year, my momma sat me down and told me that Mr. Hunter Baron, the politician, was my dad. He loved my mom, but his nasty old ex-wife had threatened my momma if she ever said anything about it to me, or anyone else. So, my momma waited until Belle Baron died before she told me." Rod answered.

"And how did all of that make you feel?" Lee asked gently, almost kindly.

Rod took a deep breath and heaved a great sigh. He looked over at the jury and said, "As you can imagine, it made me feel all kinds of ways. I felt happy, because I'd never known anything about my daddy, except that he died before I was born. Now, I could see pictures of him, and see that we have the same eyes, and the same chin. I always wondered if maybe I had gotten my laugh from my dad, and I was able to find a speech on the internet and hear that I have his voice. He talks less country, of course." he answered.

The jurors laughed.

"What else did you feel, Rod?" Lee asked.

"Well, I felt sad, because I had spent so many years not knowing anything. I had kind of just made up all sorts of stories about what he was like, and what had happened to him. When I was a lot younger, I thought maybe he was a soldier, that died over in Viet-*nam*, but then I realized that the war ended several years before I was born. So, then I imagined that he was a secret agent, and that was why momma didn't have a lot of photos or stories to tell me." He answered with kind of an embarrassed shrug of his shoulders.

He looked over at the elderly woman again, and continued, "But mostly, I just felt mad. Mad at that old witch for threatening my momma, and mad because she made her feel ashamed. Mad that she had to keep the truth from me all these years. I also feel mad that my dad never knew I existed. That wasn't right. I deserved to know, and he deserved to know me. I had a right to know. He was my dad!"

The elderly woman in the spectators' section was crying silently now, with tears tracking down her cheeks.

"So, if Hunter Baron, II. was your father, that means that Hunter Baron III was legally your half-brother, correct?" Lee Filderman asked.

"Yes." Rod nodded as he answered.

"And did you meet the decedent, your alleged half-brother before his death?" Lee pressed.

Rod started to look uncomfortable. He looked over at a lovely brunette woman who was sitting with his mother. She looked up and smiled at him, to encourage him. He seemed to take strength from her gaze and straightened his shoulders.

"Yes." Rod said, closed lipped.

Lee Filderman approached the bench to speak directly to the judge, "Permission to treat as hostile, Your Honor?"

Both the judge and the lawyers at the prosecution's table looked startled at the request. The jury leaned forward, interested. Lee also noticed how several of the jurors seemed to look at his disapprovingly, so he abandoned his next few questions. He could come back around to those questions, without alienating the jurors.

He turned to address the jurors directly. "Do y'all know what that some of this legal talk is? I know many of you probably do, with all them lawyer shows and law-and-order programs on television." He smiled engagingly at the jurors, continuing in his friendly conversational style, as if he was addressing some friends asking for legal advice. "Well, that's just fancy talk to say that I am about to ask this witness some questions that he may not like. We have to do that when we interview someone who might not want to tell the truth – "

"Objection!" called Carrie Bryant, "Prejudicial."

"Sustained, now re-frame." called Judge Ward.

"Or maybe the witness might have a reason to say something that hurts my client that isn't true. Or maybe NOT say something, that would help my client. By declaring this person a hostile witness, I can ask my questions in a different way. So, for example, if the client only wants to answer yes or no, and I need to get some other information, it lets me ask a more detailed question. It doesn't mean that I don't like Mr. Barron or any of the other folks I've had to declare hostile over the years. He seems like a nice man, in a bad situation, to me, if you know what I mean?" Lee finished, gratified to see several jurors nod their heads in agreement to his assessment of the witness.

"Now, if that makes a little bit more sense to all of you." Lee said, as he returned to face the witness stand, "Then I have just a few more questions for Mr. Barron."

A visibly shaken Rod Barron looked at Lee almost fearfully now. Rod had almost a feral or instinctive look on his face, as he braced for another attack from the disarmingly affable lawyer. Lee was one part Matlock old-style Southern charm with at least one part F. Lee Bailey showmanship and legal genius. It had a somewhat predictable effect on jurors, particularly the middle-aged and older female ones, thought Jose Leon, disgustedly. So much for the judge's warnings earlier. Judge Ward certainly didn't look annoyed now. He looked downright entertained.

Jose looked at his assistant prosecutor, pointedly, as to say, "Now let's keep this weasel in check." Carrie understood his glance and prepared herself to launch a verbal assault of objections as soon as Lee presented the opportunity.

Of course, had Lee known about Jose Leon's mental comparison between F. Lee Bailey and himself, Lee would have been furious. Matlock was fine – Andy Griffith was a bit corny, but wholesome. Lee wasn't as impressed with F. Lee Bailey's reputation as some. He personally thought he had been a drunk, a crook and a manipulative bastard. They may have both been defense attorneys, but it was certainly nothing that Lee aspired to. Lee had detested it when legal pundits had compared him to the bumbling Robert Kardashian after he had been unexpectedly sidelined in the original Baron case last year. Greta Van Susteren and her wild supositions had put him on edge last time.

Of course, had Jose known all this – he would have made sure that Lee knew exactly what he was thinking. In fact, he probably would have made it into a tasty, crunchy, but salty little sound bite for the evening news. Lee just brought out that instinct in everyone in the prosecutor's office.

"Now, Mr. Barron, I am so sorry about asking all of these questions, but you know, part of my job is due diligence. So, I couldn't let a big red flag like this go without a few questions. I hope there are no hard feelings between us." Lee said in smooth, conciliatory tones. Despite himself, Rod was nodding in agreement.

"Now, Mr. Barron, I just have one last question – and it's really just a paperwork thing." Lee said off-handedly.

"Now, I noticed on all the court paperwork, depositions and such, that I had to submit when I made up the witness list, that you spell your last name as B – A – R – R – O – N. Now that struck me a little bit after finding out that you were related to Senator Baron, because he doesn't spell his name that way. In fact, none of the Barons around here do. Can you explain why you spell your name that way?"

"Objection! Relevance." Carrie called out.

The judge raised an eyebrow at Lee.

"It's relevant, I promise." Lee answered.

"Overruled." Judge Ward answered.

"Now, back to my question." Lee said.

"So, was it a clerical error, with that extra R, or was it something else?" Lee asked, seemingly ignorant of the answer. Of course, he knew the answer – it's one of the basic premises of being a interrogating attorney. Never ask questions if you don't know the answer. In cases like this, where he didn't want to tip his hand during depositions, well, that's where the private investigators came in. He settled his face in an expression of casual interest as he waited for Rod Barron to answer.

"Wasn't it because Hunter Baron threatened to sue you, if you attempted to capitalize on the family name?" Lee pressed when Rod hesitated.

"I wasn't trying to capita-" Rod started.

"Now answer the question, *Rod*," Lee said with inflection on Rod's name.

"Yes or no. Did Hunter Baron threaten to sue you if you took the Baron name?" Lee asked.

"Yes." Rod answered, his face red and flushed.

"Oh, wait. I almost forgot. I do have a few more questions." Lee said. He had to proceed carefully here with this witness.

"Didn't you recently file something else with the Shelby County Courts?" he said, gently.

Rod looked appalled but didn't answer. Lee used this to press his advantage.

"*Didn't you* file a claim against Hunter Baron for a portion of his inheritance?" Lee probed.

"*Didn't you* make the claim that as the only blood relative of Senator Baron that your claim trumped that of his namesake, who was adopted?" Lee pressed harder.

Objection! Witness was not given sufficient time to answer." Carrie called. She was on her feet as Lee barreled forward, to get the third question out and in front of the jury.

"*Isn't it true* that you told the filing clerk that you were more entitled to the estate than the deceased?" Lee asked pleasantly but insistently.

Now Lee stopped and waited for the answers. He needed Rod Barron to provide them because he couldn't present the court filing as an exhibit. If he did, he would have had to present it to the prosecution during discovery, and that would have tipped his hand.

"Now, Mr. Barron, the court is waiting for some explanations." Lee admonished.

Judge Ward addressed the witness box, "The witness is instructed to answer," before turning to the court reporter, saying, "Please read back the first question."

The court reporter looked over at the older woman in the spectator's section with a shrug, and said, emotionlessly, "Didn't you recently file something else with the Shelby County Courts?'

"Yes," Mr. Barron answered.

"Next question." the judge instructed.

"Didn't you file a claim against Hunter Baron for a portion of his inheritance?" the court reporter repeated.

"Yes, but – " Mr. Barron answered.

"Just yes or no, Mr. Barron." Lee instructed.

Judge Ward signaled for Daniel to read back the next question. Daniel felt sorry for the young man, and made his voice as inflectionless as possible as he read, "Didn't you make the claim that as the only blood relative of Senator Baron that your claim trumped that of his namesake, who was adopted?"

"Yes." Mr. Barron said miserably.

The judge signaled again, and the court reporter read back, ""Isn't it true that you told the filing clerk that you were more entitled to the estate than the deceased?"

"Yes." Mr. Barron answered.

"Now, if we are all caught up, Mr. Filderman, let's continue." Judge Ward admonished.

Lee's associate, Kisha Mack, took his place; as she approached the witness box, looking at some index cards. "Mr. Barron, is Jessica Saucedo Lynn related to you? I mean, she's your wife, isn't she?" she corrected quickly, so he couldn't capitalize on her error.

"Yes." he answered, the ebullient and talkative Rod Barron was long gone. This version of Rod Barron just wanted to finish his testimony and get far, far away from the courthouse and the miserable witness chair.

Kisha walked closer to the witness box, her navy blue heels clicking on the tile as she walked. The big floppy bow on her bright fuchsia blouse bobbed slightly as she moved forward. She perused her notes as she advanced forward to stand directly in front of the witness box. She turned and with a nod of her head and a smile, acknowledged the jury before turning back to Mr. Barron.

"Now your wife, she's that pretty brunette over there in the peach sweater, isn't she?" Kisha said with a disarming smile. Out of the corner of her eye, she saw several jurors' heads swivel to take in Rod's wife, who was sitting quietly in the second row.

Mr. Barron had a guarded look on his face as he mumbled, "Uh huh." He didn't know where this was going, but he didn't like it. Neither did the prosecutor.

"Objection! Relevance. Judge, what kind of fishing expedition is this!" Carrie Bryant said indignantly.

"Some leeway, Your Honor. It's relevant, I promise," Lee said, "scout's honor," with his right hand raised. Judge Ward didn't look amused, but several jurors smiled.

"I'll allow it." Judge Ward growled, "But get to the point!"

Kisha's voice changed, to one of steel, "Mr. Barron, doesn't your wife work for an industrial chemical company?"

"Yes." Rod Barron answered, his voice almost inaudible.

"That's Brenntag company, isn't it? I heard she's a might good salesperson over there. In line for all kinds of promotions, in fact." Lee said with an audible drawl.

Carrie was on her feet faster than a jack-in-the-box after the final twist of the handle. Her blond coif bobbed with the rapid movement. "Objection, Your Honor. Is there a question in there, or doesn't the defense just like to hear himself talk?"

Carrie scored a point that time, with both the judge and jury as Judge Ward laughed openly. Lee Filderman's reputation for rhetoric and courtroom style filibuster-like arguments was legendary.

"Sustained. The prosecution has a point – so Mr. Filderman, get to yours, or finish with your witness." Judge Ward said.

"Yes, Your Honor," Lee said seemingly chastened.

"Now, Mr. Barron, let me get to it then. Isn't it true that your wife was recently promoted as lead salesperson for the entire mid-south?"

Carrie bobbed up again, "Objection, Your Honor. Relevance!"

Judge Ward looked at Lee in exasperation and said, "Now, I've given you plenty of leeway, but I am glad to fashion that into a noose if you are wasting this court's time. This is my last warning, counselor."

Lee looked at the witness, and said, "Mr. Barron, please answer the question. I promise, there are just a few more."

"Yes." Rod Barron answered, guardedly.

"Now, and judge, I promise this is relevant." Lee said, winking at the jury, "I hear that your wife does such a good job with her customers, that sometimes she offers to deliver those big old containers of stinky chemicals herself. Do you remember any specific occasions where she has done that?"

"Well, yeah, sure." Rod answered.

"Now would it interest you that your wife hand delivered several large containers of chemicals, including industrial thallium salts, using your truck, to Jan-Pro cleaning services, in your very own Ford F150, with license plate Mississippi Mro-Krt?"

"No." Rod Barron answered sullenly.

"Well, I bet it would interest both the judge and the jury to know that the pathologist's report, which we will be introducing now as Exhibit E, showed that your adopted brother, the legal and acknowledged son and heir to the multi-million-dollar Baron estate had evidence of thallium poisoning. What would you say about that?" Lee ended with a small flourish.

Rod Barron looked up startled, and said, "What?"

Lee relished the moment. "I said, does it surprise you to know that the man who was adopted by your real father, the man who had inherited your father's money, was found to have been poisoned with thallium, the same chemical that your wife hand delivered to one of her clients, several months ago." He continued, raising his eyes, at the jury, "A client who later complained to Brenntag about being overcharged for that very same chemical, which appeared to have the seal missing." he finished.

"Rod, have you ever heard of something called Brandenburg Blue? Because I have a receipt right here with your name on it, for an internet order of Brandenburg Blue from Macsen Labs in Liberty Township, Ohio."

Rod stammered, "No. I don't know what you are talking about."

"Now just a bit more, Mr. Barron." Lee said going in for the kill, "Isn't it true that your wife is more than a salesperson at Brenntag? Isn't it true that she has a master's degree in chemistry and started in the Brenntag Laboratory, where she was actively involved in mixing chemicals? So, she would certainly know all about thallium salts and Brandenburg, or should I say, Prussian Blue?"

Rod appeared dumbfounded by the barrage of questions.

"Isn't it true that your wife has an advanced degree in chemistry?" Lee stated.

"Yes." Rod answered quietly.

"And isn't it true that before she became a successful salesperson, she worked as a lab chemist?"

"Yes." Rod answered in a strangled voice.

"I have no more questions for this witness." Lee declared.

The prosecutors' table was stunned by this turn of events. Carrie Bryant and Sabrina Price, were madly pawing through the box of documents at their table, to review their copy of the pathology report. The lead prosecutor's face was as red as a cherry tomato, as a large blood vessel appeared to stand out on his forehead. His jaw was clenched, and his neck was stiff, with the muscles straining against his necktie.

He quickly composed himself to address Judge Ward, "The people would like to request a recess, Your Honor before our cross-examination of this witness."

Judge Ward looked at his watch, and at the jury, who were squirming in their seats. "Let's take a 45-minute lunch break everyone. Bailiff, make sure the jurors proceed to their break room without interference." he said.

****

As soon as the jury filed out, the Kisha asked Lee Filderman, "So why didn't we depose that guy's wife instead?"

Carrie Bryant, overhearing the conversation, shot daggers at the defense team as she answered, "Because then she would have been on the witness list."

"Then the prosecutors would have asked themselves, why?" Lee said, with a laugh. "Maybe they need to swear out a couple more arrest warrants."

"I know that thallium salts are used as a poison, but what is the Brandenburg blue for?" Kisha asked, ignoring Carrie Bryant.

"Well, you tell me, Kisha. But if you are handling a tasteless, odorless, water-soluble poison, don't you think maybe you'd like to have some of the antidote nearby?" Lee answered.

****

As the prosecution's team moved to re-group, one of the secretaries brought in a plate of subs, while another came in with several bags of chips and some bottles of water. Several other junior staffers from the prosecutions' office were there, in the conference room, as they scurried to find the pathologist reports, as well as photographs of the crime scene.

They did their best on cross-examination and re-direct of Rod Barron, but the damage had been done.

"Now, Mr. Barron, I know it seems like you've had a pretty hard time here up on the stand, with people making all kinds of scurrilous accusations. But that's just a nasty defense tactic, you see. We aren't here to try and make you look bad – we just want to get at the truth, okay?" Jose asked as the newly composed Rod Barron returned to the stand.

"Yes, Sir." Rod answered.

"Now, tell me truthfully, since you are under oath, did you or your wife have anything to do with the death of Hunter Baron?"

"No Sir!" Rod Barron answered in a strong voice.

"Did you have any plans to harm or incapacitate Hunter Baron so that you could access any of his financial holdings or inheritance?" Jose Leon asked.

"No Sir," Rod answered.

"Then why, in God's name did you file that paperwork?" Jose asked.

Several jurors looked at the witness intently.

"I wanted to force him to answer me, legally. I thought maybe the courts could make him acknowledge me. I couldn't get him to sit down and have a coffee with me, on my own. But I thought he'd have to answer a lawsuit. Then maybe, he'd realize that all I really wanted was to get to know him, and to have a family relationship with him." he answered sadly.

"And what about now?" Jose asked.

"I don't think it would have changed anything, but I still wish we could have had that coffee together. Now, I will never get the chance." Rod Barron answered.

"No, I mean, what about the lawsuits and the claims of inheritance now, Mr. Barron? Are you still trying to collect part of the estate?" Jose asked.

"No, Sir. It was never about the money. Anything he had left, well, that should go to his boy. I wouldn't mind a photo album though, if it had pictures of his dad in it." Rod answered earnestly.

There were no more questions from either side for this witness. Rod Barron stepped down, a very different man than the man who had entered the courthouse that morning.

"Does the defense have any additional witnesses?" Judge Ward asked. It was 4:15 in the afternoon and he was cognizant of his agreement with the jury the day before.

"No, Your Honor, the defense rests." Lee Filderman answered.

Closing Arguments

Jose Leon offered the closing argument to Carrie Bryant, but even she wasn't green enough to think the case was going well. She wasn't ready to take center stage on another losing case. Sabrina Price didn't see it that way. She took whatever opportunities the district attorney's office sent her way. She wasn't a cute, little blonde, small-town girl that could wheedle her way up the career ladder. She was a mature, professional African-American woman, which made her a threat to many of the people in the office. They would have denied it if they were confronted by it, and would have declared their anti-racist beliefs, and been stung by the accusation. But it was true nonetheless, and it had never been any different. Sabrina had always had to work harder than everyone else, be smarter than everyone else, be better than everyone else, just to get the same or slightly lesser opportunity. Now as she prepared to give closing arguments, she reconsidered the previous offer she had received last year, from a defense attorney. At the time, she had turned down the offer, which had consisted of a significant pay increase, her own office and secretary but considerably more working hours to stay with the district attorney's office. But maybe that was no longer what was best for her. Over the course of this case, her feelings had become increasingly conflicted. What had initially been presented as a slam-dunk case now seemed like something else entirely.

She pushed these thoughts away as she rose to stand at the podium, dressed beautifully, tastefully in a royal blue skirted suit, with a black blouse with large yellow cabbage roses printed on it. Blue was her power color, and it gave her the confidence and courage to address the jury despite the now obvious holes in her case.

"Good afternoon, ladies and gentlemen. I want to say thank you to each and every one of you for serving on this jury. It's more than your civic duty, it's a noble and moral thing to do. Today you are law; and you will determine not only the guilt or innocence of the woman in beige over there, but whether she goes free or not. You determine whether the death of Hunter Baron will be punished or not. We know that the victim who was an imperfect person, who functioned within an imperfect society. We all remember that the victim himself was on trial last year. But this isn't that trial! The victim, Hunter Baron III can't speak for himself this time. That means the law has to speak for him, whether we like him or not. Sometimes we don't like the victim, sometimes they aren't good people, but that doesn't mean that we can ignore the law." she said confidently.

"There is another big elephant in the room too, it's one we have alluded to, skirted around, but never really directly tackled. That's the issue of privilege. Both our victim and the accused have it. Whether we like to acknowledge it or not, that changes things in the justice system. It shouldn't but it does. Let's imagine for a moment that our victim was a homeless person, and the defendant was just a regular citizen. Would this even be news? Would the front row of the court be filled with reporters and journalists? Would these seats be filled with spectators? You might not know the answer because you are only on one jury, this jury. But I do, I have argued before the court, in this very courtroom in such cases, and it's lonely in here. You can hear the walls echo, due to the emptiness. There isn't even a jury most of the time because it goes straight to a plea deal. But our victim wasn't a homeless guy. The defendant, this defendant, well she's certainly somebody. That gives her resources; the kind of resources that allow her to have a whole defense team, who are solely dedicated to her case. If she wasn't somebody important, a name, so to speak, she'd have another one of our overworked public defenders. I know, because I did that for my first few years after graduating from law school. And you know what, I'd push her, really push her to plea this thing out. And no one would care. That's the ugly truth that we don't talk about."

Sabrina continued, "But in a lot of ways, there is justice in anonymity too. Our justice system may not be blind, but it's sadly overworked. As I mentioned before, the likelihood that this case would have ever gone to trial if we had a different victim and a different defendant is very small. Maybe 2% of all cases go to trial, with 90% of defendants taking a plea offer. That means that in 90% of cases, someone pays for the crime. It might not be as long of a sentence as we, the prosecutor's office or the victim's family would have liked, but someone pays for the crime."

"A person was killed here, in a brutal and violent way, and fancy legal maneuvers by the defense team don't change that. Ember

Prince was being blackmailed by our victim. He was threatening to destroy her career and her budding election campaign. He was threatening to humiliate her in front of everyone she knew, every donor, every volunteer, and social acquaintance. He was planning to send clips to the news. Now, Action 5 news here in town might not have shown any of the film, but they would have talked about it. But what about Fox News? I think they would have salivated to have this footage, and leak clips of a democratic candidate. It would have served their audience and their narrative, which is more important to a television network that Ember Prince's right to privacy. Ember Prince knew this, and she couldn't let it happen."

"She had the motive, that is clear. But not only that, she had the means and the opportunity. How many other people do you know that have a security detail at their disposal? You don't think she'd ask her daddy to loan her his bodyguards for a little help? Don't you think that daddy's loyal henchmen might actually take pride and pleasure in helping the boss's daughter? That's why there were several sets of male DNA at the crime scene. There was lipstick on the wine glass. No DNA that we could get, but that proves that she was there – organizing, and directing the show while these men murdered for her."

Sabrina was hitting her stride as she continued, "You saw Jack Prince here in court yesterday. It's the first time I've seen him without his entourage. Maybe his band of killers didn't want to chance showing their faces here. It sure took him a while to show up, didn't it? Maybe that's because even a corrupt politician like Jack Prince couldn't stomach outright murder? Or maybe it's just because cameras were banned from the courtroom. I don't know, and I don't care. That doesn't really matter – but what matters is that money, wealth, privilege and power have stepped in time and time again to make this family immune to the consequences of their actions."

"Do you really think that they wouldn't murder to protect one of their own, from humiliation, from political failure? They didn't get to be Teflon by playing nice.

"Murder for hire, and conspiracy to murder still end the same, in the death of an individual. The defense may have muddied the waters a bit, but they never even offered a real alibi for their client. They just threw a whole bunch of guesses, random facts and wild theories out there hoping that one would stick. They tried to impress you by bringing witnesses from other countries, making wild conspiracy theories and conjecture. The maybe wife, the secret brother, the Russian mob. It's like a cheap Lifetime movie, isn't it? Isn't it convenient, that the so called real killer that they were going to serve right up to you today, failed to appear? Easy to blame a name without a face, isn't it? It would be a whole lot different if that same witness was here in front of us. But let's forget fantasy, and stick with reality. We have motive, we have means and we have opportunity. Ember Prince was going to lose everything and she just couldn't allow that!" Sabrina Price finished, feeling sweaty and suddenly tired after the surge of adrenaline. She stepped away from the podium and sat down.

Lee Filderman felt confident as he prepared to address the jury for closing arguments. He had spent much of the trial projecting a jovial, friendly personality, so as to not alienate the jury with his real feelings, which had been slowly building over the course of the case. From her initial arrest, pre-trial motions, arraignment and now the courtroom, he had felt the slow burn of injustice and indignation ignite in his belly. Over the last few days, when it became more and more apparent that the police hadn't bothered to pursue other suspects, and the prosecution had rubber stamped the charges, that slow flame had become a raging inferno. He internalized all of it, bottled it and saved it for now.

"At the beginning of this trial," he said, "we promised several things. We promised to prove that the prosecutors would be unable to prove that our client committed this heinous crime. We promised that they didn't have the evidence, and they don't. The prosecution hasn't presented one single fact or piece of evidence that clearly points at my client." He began.

"But we also told you that the people working to solve this crime had become single-minded in their pursuit of our client, even when it became clear that she was not involved – and we have shown that. We even presented a decorated career detective, Sergeant Rex Lester, that left the Memphis Police Department rather than continue, once it became clear to him that the police weren't really interested in fully investigating this crime.

"They never investigated the chronic arsenic poisoning – something that had to be done by someone in close proximity to the victim on a frequent, if not daily basis. Was this a lover, an ex-lover, a disgruntled neighbor or a disliked colleague? Is this an attempt by an estranged wife to claim an early inheritance? We do know that arsenic has long been known as an *"inheritance powder"* due to it's frequent use for such illicit reasons.

"But, we don't know because they never bothered to investigate. What about a half-brother, wrongfully deprived of both his heritage and his share of his father's legacy? Wouldn't he, and his wife, the chemist have both the motive and the means to commit this poisoning? Did the poisoner become frustrated at the time it was taking for the victim to die? Is that what led to the second poison and the violent act that finally ended this victim's life?

"Of course, you, the jury might not have even heard about the poisonings if it hadn't been for our own investigators and a private lab in Atlanta. The police couldn't even be bothered to send off any evidence that contradicted the cute and neat theory that they developed early on. No sign of a struggle? Unless you count the statue that they didn't bother to check. Or the wine glass? There was a plethora of evidence at this crime scene, that the police couldn't be bother to look at. That's convenient when it turns out that this evidence points at suspects other than my client. There were foreign fingerprints and foreign DNA found on the weapons. Now none of those fingerprints or DNA matched my client. You can bet that if it did – we would have heard about it, first thing. But the foreign DNA was male DNA – mostly likely of a Caucasian, Eastern European individual. Did the police even look for a suspect that matched that description?

"Did they pursue any other angle? Maybe it was a drug deal gone bad – I mean, the corpse was full of cocaine, and he was tortured and killed, which is standard procedure for drug dealers. With most drug dealers being men, that might have made sense. But did they even look into that scenario? I doubt it. They have never presented any evidence of any pursuit or elimination of any other suspect, because as we all know, they never looked. Detective Payne admitted as much. She doesn't believe my client – and she doesn't believe anyone who can alibi my client, because that doesn't fit her theory. But she also can't tell us much about the other three women that Hunter Baron was blackmailing?"

"What about the owner of the earring? We brought a witness, all the way from France, the actual designer of this custom piece of jewelry who is adamant that she didn't sell it to Ember Prince, or any other member of the Prince family. She stated that it uniquely designed for one client, a person that she knew from her native Venezuela. This wasn't some Walmart trinket. This was an expensive, one-of-kind piece that was sold to a Laura Triana Africano, accompanied by a, in her exact words, "wealthy Russian sugar daddy" who paid in cash. I suspect that some of us know exactly who this woman is, and most of the rest of us can make an educated guess. Do you want to wager on whether that wealthy Russian man's DNA might be found in Hunter Baron's apartment? We never promised that we, the defense would tell you who committed this crime, because that's not our job, and we don't have to. We don't even have to prove that our client didn't do it – but we have certainly shown that she didn't. Our only job here was to show that the prosecution failed to prove, beyond a reasonable doubt that our client committed this crime. They have utterly failed to do so. I wager that there is not one person in here, other than Detective Payne, who has her own motives, that reasonably believes that my client had anything to do with the death of Hunter Baron. And for that reason, you must acquit.

"We can not punish people unjustly for who they are, and the families they come from. There is no such thing as guilt by family tree. The prosecution has failed to prove their case, and that means that whoever is the accused, Prince family or not, they must go free. Thank you for your service and I know you will all do the right thing."

Lee's heart was pounding wildly as he finished. He looked over at the jury but couldn't read anything on their faces. It was in their hands now, all he could do was wait.

The Verdict

The closing arguments ended at 6:30 pm. The jury deliberated until 9 pm, when they returned to their homes to retire for the night. Despite multiple predictions that the jury would return their verdict rapidly, that failed to happen. The West Memphis sportsbook decided to start taking bets after the second full day of deliberations. Bets were running 3:1 for a hung jury. By the end of the third day of deliberations, nerves were frayed taut on both sides of the aisle. Notes were sent back and forth to the judge asking for clarification on different points of fact.

On the fifth day, just as spring was settling heavy thunderstorms all over the mid-south, the jury came back. All of the players; the prosecution, the defense, the press and the spectators gathered in the courtroom. Ember's stomach was doing somersaults. All her previous confidence was gone. She entered the courthouse with her father gripping her hand tightly on one side, with Kisha on the other. She felt faint, as if only their hold on her body kept her upright, but somehow her legs kept propelling her forward.

There was no glamour or demure ingenue today at the defense table. Both of the defense attorneys wore khaki style pants and oxford shirts. Ember wore her favorite summer dress, with a cardigan sweater for warmth and modesty. Her leather boots were spotted with water from navigating the rivers of rain on her way inside. Her face was scrubbed clean, of both makeup and emotion as she sat down at the defense table.

All too soon, it was time for her to rise as the jury made their way into the courthouse. No one looked at her, and she felt a sinking feeling in her stomach. The room started to swim.

"Has the jury reached a decision?" Judge Ward asked, formally.

"We have." the jury foreman, an impossibly slim and worn looking middle aged man said. His name was Michael Woods and he was a mechanic, Ember remembered suddenly.

The jury was seated, and she was made to rise again, with both attorneys flanking her. She felt grateful for their strength. The whoosh of blood thru her ears initially made it hard for her to hear and understand what the jury was saying.

"We the jury, find the defendant Ember Rain Prince, not guilty on all counts." the jury foreman delivered in a slow, precise voice tinged with a hint of a southern drawl. Then the foreman and the judge went thru the formality of reviewing each and every count, but Ember couldn't hear a word of it. It was drowned out by the continued deafening roar of blood in her ears.

It wasn't until Kisha Mack turned and hugged her that she calmed down as the news settled in. Then, like the aftermath of a close football game, people came crowding in, hugging and crying.

Judge Ward called for order, as he dismissed the jury and thanked them for their service. He made some statements to Ember but she was still in a state of shock and was unable to hear them.

She left the courtroom in the same haze. Her father drove her home, but the ride was wordless, as if they had nothing to say to each other. As she closed the car door after getting out, she thought, "What do I do now?"

****

Epilogue

East Memphis apartment during defense testimony

Veronica hadn't really been following the trial. In her mind, the less she thought about Hunter Baron, the better, and that included the trial of his accused killer. She had been surprised when Ember Prince had been identified as a person of interest, and then the main suspect in the case, but not enough to read the trial notes that were published in the *Commercial Appeal* or the dramatic and shmaltzy true crime stuff by that Marnie Gellhorn. It had been bad enough when the writer had tried to drag Vernonica into conversation at the funeral, and then again a week later. But Veronica had done a good job deflecting the persistent journalist so Marnie wouldn't have much to write about. She had heard rumors, of course about poison being found in Hunter's body, but since the police hadn't come back to talk to her after the first brief interview, she wasn't too worried.

She hadn't killed him, of course, but she'd been home alone, working, the night he died. If she had been worried that this might look suspicious, she didn't have time to. Her sister, Laura had been quick to provide her with an alibi – swearing that the two of them had stayed home and watched movies together. She even somehow provided a receipt for the pizza delivery. She also helped skirt over the whole relationship issues by stating that Vernonica had been busy entertaining Laura during her visit to Memphis, which is why she hadn't seen Hunter Baron in the days immediately before and after the murder. They had been too busy driving the Blues Trail, heading to the casinos, and taking a quick dash to Nashville. Laura had wanted to see everything, you know, before she returned to Paris.

The tall, older male cop seemed a bit skeptical of Laura during the interview, but the younger detective, the woman, acted like the information just confirmed what they already knew. Laura ended her visit abruptly after the police left, but that wasn't out of character for her erratic baby sister. The day after the police interview, Veronica came home to her bland apartment to find that all traces of Laura had disappeared. All of her clothes, shoes, the piles of lingerie and scattered jewelry, even the cosmetics that had been strewn across the bathroom, were packed in two small bags by the front door. There was a post-it note on the refrigerator that said, Dishwasher is clean, but that was it. Veronica found it strange that her sister, so chronically spoilt, even knew how to run the dishwasher. If there was an unfamiliar stainless steel cheese knife in the dishwasher, Veronica said nothing, and just ran it through the dishwasher again before putting it away in a kitchen drawer. It would have been smarter to throw it away, but she couldn't seem to part with it.

Once she started the dishwasher, out of habit, she supposed, Veronica went to the closet and started packing. When her sister returned to the apartment a few hours later, she was ready to go. She didn't even ask Laura where they were headed. On the way to the airport, she spoke to the attorneys for the woman accused of the crime, and again assured them that she was ready to testify. She made up some story about getting the day off work before turning off her phone and throwing the sim card out the window as they cruised along the highway.

They left her car in the Atlanta International Airport, unlocked with the keys inside in the long-term parking lot.

"Don't worry, Ronnie," Laura said once they were on the first leg of their journey, "you will love the condo! It's right on the beach. And Paphos is beautiful!" Laura giggled with glee and that's when Veronica truly realized that her gorgeous baby sister was broken.

Midtown Memphis, Following the verdict

"Well, I guess this means you are leaving us again to go back to sunny California," Rachel's daughter, Iris said. I was surprised to see her face crumple up as she said it. Rachel too, looked sad at the thought of Marnie leaving town again. The three of us were eating at one of Memphis' cute little midtown restaurants, The Beauty Shop. Brunching or lunching at the Beauty Shop had become a local tradition over the last several years. I always prefer BBQ, of course, since I can never seem to get it out of my blood, but I was happy enough to meet Rachel at The Beauty Shop, Stacks, or any of the other cute but trendy places that always seemed to pop up and last a few years before fading away to make room for the newest incarnations. Besides, I had news I wanted to share with my friend, now that the Prince case was over.

Well, that's actually the reason I wanted to meet you both for lunch," I demurred, being uncharacteristically and intentionally vague. I enjoyed seeing the excited look that came into Iris' eyes as she tried to interpret my words. As usual, the combination of Rachel and her teen daughter, Iris, brought out my own playful nature. I burst into a gigantic smile, and the words came rushing out. Gone was the cool, professional journalist. I could have been another member of a teen slumber party with my high-pitched squeal, that brought several heads swinging about.

"Oh my, oh my, oh my. It's been killing me not to tell you! Court TV has offered me my own show as part of their returning network! I'm the new host, and lead investigator of "Southern Murders, Mysteries and Scandals! I get to be based here, when I'm not off somewhere filming stories in Georgia, Mississippi or whatever!" I said before laughing excitedly and reaching out to hug Rachel.

"Murder, huh?" called out a middle-aged woman with a country western hairdo, who seemed mildly intoxicated on the complimentary mimosas. She'd been none too subtly eavesdropping since I had arrived. "Well, if it's murder you want, you've never have to leave Memphis ever again," she finished.

Rachel and I looked at her, then each other and laughed. "Can't argue with the truth, tho," Rachel said as she lifted her iced tea in a toast.

"Here goes!" I answered.

****

Just a few streets away, at the same time

Now that she had her passport back, Ember Prince was packing. She had one-way tickets, a small digital camera, a couple notebooks and pens. She added this to several pairs of plain khaki pants, loose woven shirts and an extra pair of shoes.

It was a long way – first to Newark Liberty International, then Gnassingbé Eyadéma International Airport, before a layover in Accra, and finally her destination of Roberts International Airport. Thanks to the wonders of the internet, she was able to contact her cousin, Emmanuel and he agreed to meet her there. She knew it might be dangerous, but she also knew it was something she had to do.

Olive Branch, Mississippi – 2 days later

Henri and I were staying with the Lesters again for a few days before heading back to Sonoma. We didn't have to, of course, but we'd checked out of the cute little rental a few days early after the trial ended to spend some time with Rex and Sandra. So much had happened during the course of the trial that I felt like we all needed a week just to mentally unpack it all.

As we were doing just that, sitting on the back patio, nursing a couple of Mexican beers, Robin and the other dogs laying at our feet. The sun was going down and the crickets were starting to sing. It was the most relaxed I'd felt since coming back to Memphis. I took a big sip of the beer before I asked Rex, "so, back to the homicide division, now that it's all over?"

Rex and Sandra exchanged a glance before answering. "Actually no," Rex answered. "I am taking a sabbatical of sorts, and using up some of my vacation time, that I never got to use. We are closing up the house and renting a little place right outside Clarksdale, where I grew up. I need some time to think about all of this. I gave over two decades to the department, and when I told them that they were on the wrong track with the Hunter Baron murder, I suddenly became the problem."

"The Clarksdale Police Department has already offered Rex a job, but I told him to take some time off before making any big decisions. He's earned it. Besides, I'd like him to think about retiring," Sandra said.

"I already looked up my childhood mentor! He's alive and well. I can't believe I let us get out of touch over the last decade. We are renting a house right down the street from him," Rex said, with almost childish excitement.

Rex's phone rang, and he looked at it and frowned. "It's the Memphis Police Department," he mouthed just before he answered.

Sandra and I looked at each other. "I bet he has to do some more paperwork," Sandra assured me while Rex made noncommittal sounds into the phone.

Finally, he said, "10-19 Rosewood, got it, yes sir," before hanging up.

Sandra said, "no, no, wait a minute, I know what that means! Rex!"

"I know, but it was Police Chief Davis herself. There's been a high profile murder at 1019 Rosewood Avenue, and they think I've proved my impartiality. I couldn't say no, Hobbit," Rex answered.

Looking at me, Rex said, "No, no, Marnie.. I am not telling you anything! Go work on your book on the Ember Prince trial. This has nothing to do with you."

It looked like they could use some privacy, so I gathered Henri up and made my way to the back bedroom. It killed me to walk away, but I made myself do it.

****

Several thousands of miles away – and a world away from the seedier side of Memphis, murder and politics….

Dykstra Hall, UCLA – Los Angeles

The young film student took a deep breath and looked in the mirror. The smoldering hazel eyed young woman quickly swabbed her cheek and then placed the swab into a small container. The swab and the container went into a larger pre-addressed brown envelope. She quickly closed the envelope and pressed closed the adhesive flap before she changed her mind. Then she strode purposefully from the bathroom down to the lobby of the building to the mail room. She stopped for a moment, closed her eyes, took another deep breath and centered herself before dropping the envelope into the mailbox. Without slowing her stride, she headed out of the building towards the Powell library.

****

The End..

Acknowledgements and Thank yous

I would like to acknowledge the many wonderful people that helped me during the writing and (especially!) the editing process. Writing a historical fiction series like Murder in the Mississippi Delta requires an extensive amount of research. While the characters and their actions are fictitious, the settings they live in are based on established facts. It would be impossible to craft these stories without numerous deep dives into Memphis and the Mississippi Delta, with the help of the Benjamin Hooks branch of the Memphis library, the Mississippi Department of Archives and History and the Olive Branch local library.

I have unending gratitude for the invaluable assistance of Ms. Eileen Fields, librarian at the Hernando library as a fact-checker, grammar authoritarian and general editor. She, along with Susan Eckland and Rahmah Grant helped polish this story from 400 pages of general chaos of misplaced commas and fractured run-on sentences into the (somewhat) coherent story you just read. I couldn't have done anything without Eileen's unwavering and endless assistance. I am sure she lost hope at several points along the way, as several personal tragedies threatened to overwhelm me and my work. But, with a lot of help and support from Eileen and many, many others, I was finally about to finish.

Finally, I would like to thank all of my friends and family who listened to me chatter away as I worked on the plot to this sequel. I would particularly like to recognize Mr. Vicente Ochoa, who spent a frantic two weeks with me as I finished up the last half of the novel, and listened endlessly as I discussed, debated and revised storylines, plot twists, crucial case evidence and character descriptions. His good-natured patience may have been assisted by his limited knowledge of the English language, but he was patient and kind all the same.

about the author

Marnie Gellhorn is a former overseas correspondent. She has covered stories from all over the world, but most often in areas of conflict, like Syria, Iraq and Afghanistan. She has dedicated her career to putting a human face of the geopolitics of our international policies.

As a frequent contributor to AP outlets, often the only byline you will have seen is Associated Press. But if you've read enough of her work, you can almost hear her soft gravelly voice in the stories.

The Princes of Shelby County is the sequel to the first book in the series, Murder in the Mississippi Delta. The first book, *The Barons of Memphis* introduced readers to the family of Hunter Baron III, a dissolute playboy. Hunter is accused of murdering his elderly socialite mother, who is a staple of the Memphis social scene. This book, the Princes of Shelby County introduces another Memphis political dynasty, one that has been at the forefront of Memphis politics for generations.

Marnie and her constant companion, Henri Arthur George split their time between Memphis and Sonoma as she continues to work as a travel writer. She is a frequent contributor to Wine & Cheese magazine.

Interested readers can follow Marnie on social media and her personal website, www.therealmarniegellhorn.com

Instagram: the_marnie_gellhorn

Marnie also has a serialized podcast, *"Murder in the Mississippi Delta: the Barons of Memphis and other stories."*

Made in the USA
Monee, IL
17 February 2025